TWISTED *Family* VALUES

Also by V. C. Chickering

Nookietown

TWISTED
Family
VALUES

V. C. Chickering

St. Martin's Griffin
New York

www.stmartins.com

Library of Congress Cataloging-in-Publication Data

Names: Chickering, V. C., author.
Title: Twisted family values / V.C. Chickering.
Description: First edition. | New York : St. Martin's Griffin, 2019.
Identifiers: LCCN 2018055441| ISBN 9781250065292
  (trade paperback) | ISBN 9781466871939 (ebook)
Classification: LCC PS3603.H5453 T88 2019 | DDC 813/.6—dc23
LC record available at https://lccn.loc.gov/2018055441

Our books may be purchased in bulk for promotional, educational, or business use. Please contact your local bookseller or the Macmillan Corporate and Premium Sales Department at 1-800-221-7945, extension 5442, or by e-mail at MacmillanSpecialMarkets@macmillan.com.

First Edition: June 2019

10 9 8 7 6 5 4 3 2 1

Acknowledgments

I heartily thank: my family; Beth Davey at Davey Literary & Media for your boundless enthusiasm and eternally sharp mind; Eileen Rothschild for the fab title and giving it new life; Philip Pascuzzo for nailing the cover art; Tiffany Shelton, Meghan Harrington, Marissa Sangiacomo, Elizabeth Catalano, Donna Noetzel, DJ DeSmyter, and India Cooper for your stellar skills at SMP; Lucy Sykes for your fantastic blurb; Jen Weiner for your sage advice; Abby Sher & The Collective; Brendan Deneen; Emmy Laybourne, Elly Lonon, and The GONK for writerly advice; Suzanne Githens, Lisa Haarmann, Rob Larson, Linda Powers, and Kay McClellan for generously offering to read early drafts; Laura Booker for being my go-to-gay; Wendy Shanker for being my wrock; my muses: Sarah Beach, Marcelle Karp, Amy Baily, Betsy Hawkings, and Amanda Strand; Trish O'Gorman, Jude Webster, and Jason Neff for mental health maintenance; Liz Dubleman at Digital Daughter for your calm tech savvy; David M. Tenzer for your kind counsel; Julie Pauly at Able Baker for letting me poke around; Kim Hammer at the Fringe Salon for all the great hair days; The Village, Pack, BHBG, Montys, and heavens; and Rebecca Rounsavill for getting the ball rolling; the Facebook Copy Edits Crew for your hilarious input down to the wire; my indispensable "tour manager" Jessica Ganjon; and all past-present-future book tour event hosts, including but not limited to: Carrie Harmon, Jenny Clark, Lydia Butcher, Nancy Dougherty, Virginia Sigety, Betsy Vreeland, Bill Johnson, Katherine Birch, Lisa Haarmann, Molly Fubel, Abby Chickering, Carla Carpenter, Kip Prather, Jenny Kellogg, Becky Baeurle, Marissa Rothkopf, Chrissy Adams, Nancy Lochtefeld, Sarah Reilly, Lynne Mercein, Jane Ridolfi, Gail H. Kellogg, Kim Kiss, Maie Webb, Lara Richardson, and Amy Demas—all of your fabulous hospitality and support has made the ride so much fun. And to anyone who's ever said, "How's your book coming along?" Thanks for asking.

TWISTED *Family* VALUES

1968

A sumptuous nursery in an upscale commuter suburb,
Firth, New Jersey

"Don't you just love the smell of diaper cream?" Cat Babcock
said, inhaling Desitin. "I loathe it," said her sister, Claire. "It's
like exhaust from a New York City bus." They were checking
on their napping children. Their mother had agreed to take the
grandkids for the day. The two stay-at-home moms slash die-
hard volunteers were headed to their garden club meeting. Only
Cat said "Aww," peaking over the wood railing of the Thornden family crib. Claire Chadwick merely glanced in as she lit
another Marlboro. *They're sleeping. We've checked. Let's go.*
Their toddlers, Bizzy and Choo, dozed soundly together, arms
and legs unconsciously entwined. Dark wisps were matted to
the little girl's forehead. The boy's diaper pin had unfastened.

As Cat repinned her son's cloth diaper, Claire yanked her
daughter's pinky from his mouth. "Why did you do that?"
whispered Cat. "They'll wake up. Are you nuts?"

Claire scoffed. "Choo has his own thumb to suck."

"What does it matter? They're sound asleep."

"I find it unbecoming."

"Bizzy's a *ba*-by. They're *cousins*, for crying out loud."

Cat shook her head. Claire exhaled a stream of smoke over the slumbering children, setting the mobile's wooden zoo animals in slight motion. "Well, then, it's unnecessary."

"Oh, for heaven's sake," said Cat, gently sweeping her niece's moist tendrils off her face. Claire was too busy in the mirror to notice her daughter's discomfort. A tall, raven-haired beauty with cobalt eyes and a dimple, she towered over her younger, boxier sister. Claire was told—ad nauseam as a teen in the fifties—she was the spitting image of Elizabeth Taylor. Deciding her looks to be the sum total of her value, she set a laser focus on them without distraction. Cat—nicknamed Cat-in-the-Hat as an impish child—was the shorter, curvier version of the Thornden sisters. She shared the same raven hair and dimpled right cheek but had a playful spark her icy sister lacked. Claire found no humor in Cat's pointless antics and dismissed her subpar beauty. Cat rebelled by becoming a real free spirit, cultivating an audacious, risk-taking personality; whereas, Claire remained immersed in lipsticks and creams, allocating her energy to social positioning.

"We're going to be late," Claire said, snubbing her cigarette out in the ashtray. She left the nursery in a snit. Cat stayed behind and whispered to her slumbering cherub, "You, my darlings, are perfection. Bizzy, your mother's a piece of work, and I will do *everything I can* to be your ally." Choo rolled over; his eyes fluttered as he burrowed deeply into his cousin's armpit. "And you, my sweet son, are doing wonderfully. Keep a low profile and we'll all be fine. Just, whatever you do, don't turn into your father. And Bizzy, don't you become your mom."

Before leaving, Cat clicked on the large box fan wedged in the window since mid-May. The rubber diaper cover Claire insisted Bizzy wear was clearly the reason she had been overheating. *Appearances have always mattered more to her than people,* Cat thought, deftly removing the diaper cover. Then she returned Bizzy's pinky to Choo's searching mouth. "You both have my blessing to behave as unbecoming as you want occasionally. Ignore her and have some harmless fun."

1977

A well-appointed suburban kitchen,
Larkspur, New Jersey

Drapes and patios, families and slacks—the citizens of tony
Larkspur were cut from a prescribed cloth. Major appliances
were endlessly updated and swimming pools de rigueur. Cat's
turn-of-the-century Colonial had splendid white shingles,
dormers, and black shutters. Her front door sported a worn
brass knocker in the shape of a mallard duck. The knocker
on Claire's house next door was a fox. The two stately beau-
ties were separated by a tall, privet hedge, flanked by award-
winning gardens that erupted every spring. Their combined
eight-acre backyard, however, was open and continuous. It
boasted a massive lawn, in-ground pool, hoops, and a trampoline. The homes' interiors strictly adhered to the mandatory
design code of the day; among the approved colors were sage
green, cranberry, orange, and shocking pink. More ducks and
foxes repeated themselves madly on chintz upholstery and
wallpaper, with the occasional smattering of crossed tennis
racquets and geese.

"Do you think our children are weird?" Claire asked Cat

while looking out the kitchen window. She bristled as she said it; the thought horrified her to no end.

Cat craned her neck to see all five Thornden cousins playing touch football in the sprawling backyard. Everyone was dressed in wool sweaters and hats for the annual New Year's Day game, with the exception of twelve-year-olds Bizzy and Choo, who were wearing Charlie's Angels wigs—Farrah and Jaclyn, respectively. Twenty or so assorted family friends' kids joined them, their laughter visible in the brittle, late-afternoon air.

"Which ones?" Cat teased, knowing full well. She didn't think she'd ever heard her sister use the word "weird" and almost asked if she knew what it meant. "Are we talking about Bizzy and Choo?"

"Yes. Obviously," snapped Claire.

"And what kind of weird are we talking? Adorable weird or depraved weird?" Claire nearly said, "Oh, for heaven's sake, they're only twelve, how depraved could they already be?" but didn't. Realizing she was being baited, she reached for her drink and another pinch of paprika. Her burgundy, high-waisted slacks set off her narrow, lithe figure, and Final Net kept her hot-rollered hair just so. Cat sipped her Tab as she watched her sister's thin outstretched arm. "You're not the queen of England, you know. You can stop anointing the eggs." Claire dragged on her Marlboro with the other hand as they worked in Cat's new avocado-and-orange kitchen. The appliances were also new—top-of-the-line Amana—and naturally preordered to match. The sisters readied the crushed nut–covered cheese ball and sprinkled paprika over six dozen deviled eggs. They'd been arranged magazine-perfect on porcelain platters as if this had been their aesthetic destiny all along.

Cat looked out the window just in time to see her son, Choo, pass the ball to Bizzy, who shoved it under her fisherman-knit sweater and dashed to the goal line made of plaid scarves in the snow. Their victory celebration was a spontaneous polka—something they'd certainly not learned in ballroom dance class.

"Adorable weird and I'm through talking about it," Claire said and drained her Mount Gay and tonic.

"How many have you had?" said Cat, nodding toward her sister's glass.

"Don't become one of those people who turns into a pill just because you can't drink anymore." Cat couldn't believe her sister would say such a thing. Then she thought, *No, of course she would.* Yes, she was annoyed Claire continued to drink in front of her after she'd entered AA a few years back. "Not my problem," Claire had initially said to Cat with all the sensitivity of an alcoholic herself. But Cat knew deep down Claire was right—it wasn't her problem to manage.

"Takes one to know one," said Cat, sorry she'd said anything in the first place.

Claire knew she'd gotten to her sister. *Touché,* she thought. *We're even.* "Relax, Friend of Bill W," said Claire. "Grab the clam dip and let's get these eggs out. They're not going to pass themselves. You've done a good job, Cat. Everything looks delicious. Oh, I added sherry to the fondue."

Claire helped Cat untie her apron, and Cat forgave her for being a judgmental harpy. Then Cat called in the troops while Claire put a cup of plastic sword toothpicks with the sausage balls. She reminded herself of what laid the bedrock for their long, productive relationship—their simpatico devotion to family and friends, an appreciation for art and culture. There was also the desire to create a storybook childhood and give their children a lasting legacy. It's why they'd bought houses next door to each other and created a communal Shangri-La. It's why they herded the cousins as siblings and forgave each other again and again. Yes, sometimes Cat grew annoyed by Claire's relentless party onslaught and occasionally tossed a few deviled eggs into the hydrangea for sport. But she went along with her sister's largesse so her kids would know the right people. She'd made a mess of things in her past and didn't want retribution visited upon the innocent. Nor could she risk any fallout from her secret. That, above all, was key.

The sliding glass kitchen door opened to a brood of loud, steamy children with opened coats and sweaty brows. "Rumpus room! Keep moving!" shouted Claire like a stage manager shuttling filthy extras toward the basement door. "Except for you two," she said, stopping Bizzy and Choo in their tracks. "I need you to pass these hors d'oeuvres to the grown-ups. Take off the wigs and fix your hair, both of you."

"What wigs?" said Bizzy.

"Where are your hats?" said Claire.

"We couldn't find them," Choo lied on the spot without remorse. They loved to needle Claire—all the cousins did. Bizzy added, "These wigs are wicked warm, Mom. You should try it! They're *better* than hats!"

"I'll do no such thing. And stop saying 'wicked.'"

Choo said, "Aunt Claire, if you want us to *really* sell the eggs, you should totally let us wear the wigs." He flipped his tresses over a shoulder and clasped two fingers to his ear, pointing skyward. "They're integral to our mission. Should we decide to accept it."

"Please stop saying 'totally.'"

"Oh, you're accepting it, all right," said Cat. "Take the eggs and find the microfiche. Go."

"Got it, Boz," said Choo, and reached for a platter. Claire grimaced, knowing majority had ruled. Cat shooed them toward the living room. "Good luck, Kate and Farrah. And don't come back 'til they're empty."

"I'm *Jaclyn*, Mom," called Choo with mock indignation.

"Sor-ry!" sang Cat with a chuckle.

Once the kids were gone, Cat said to Claire, "Okay, yes, Bizzy and Choo are slightly weird. How can they not be? They're *our* kids. *We're* weird, you know."

"Speak for yourself," said Claire, redirecting a curl already in place.

"And yes, they're joined at the hip, but that was our goal, remember?"

"They're a little too close if you ask me. They have no other close friends except that little bully Piper."

"You wanted this, Claire. They're best friends, so mission accomplished. And if you think that's weird, well then, that's sad."

Cat knew Claire wouldn't like hearing her darling Bizzy was weird in any way, but she said it, partly because she wanted to pull her sister off her high horse and partly because it was true and she wanted Claire to hear it. "Bizzy and Choo are the grandchildren of Marjorie and Dunsfield Thornden, for chrissake, keepers of the flame for all things precious and antiquated, drenched in tradition—for better or worse—wearers of pocket squares and daytime lipstick—raised by us, the Tweedledee and Tweedledum of Larkspur. How can they not be a little odd?"

Claire did her typical job of not showing the comment stung. "Please don't call us that," she said. "It's unbecoming." Cat felt sorry for her. Nothing had ever been able to make her content, not even her daughter's blithe spirit in the face of an unavailable dad and a critical, social-climbing mother. "Everything's going to work out," Cat consoled. "They'll grow up and go off to college and make lots of new friends. Even high school will be different, just wait. Life is short and life is long, like Mom always taught us. Let them be each other's best friends now. They have their entire lives ahead of them to grow apart. It'll happen naturally; let's not insert ourselves. And please don't be concerned with what other people think."

But Claire *was* concerned with what people thought. It was why she'd stayed married to Les for so long even though he was a morose, cranky drunk. He had a sterling pedigree and the money seemed bottomless, so Claire "hung in there," following her father's stern advice. Claire and Les had a son, E.J., who carried on not only his father's name—Ellister Junior—but also his insufferable cynicism and disposition. It was as if his "terrible twos" became the "terrible interminables." Local mothers whispered the apple didn't fall very far, etc. No one surmised Les was clinically depressed. *There's no reason for this behavior,* Claire thought—*he could snap out of it if he wanted to, he's just not trying hard enough*. Then, three years later, in 1965, though they'd barely exchanged a word, Elizabeth Thornden Chadwick was unexpectedly born. They called her Bizzy for her boundless curiosity. Choo was short for Choo Choo Charlie. Their nicknames implied a wink they knew their privileged lifestyle would tolerate. When one summered and skied with the right people, seriousness of purpose was incidental. A Benjamin could introduce himself as Benster with a straight face in a job interview for Lehman Brothers. And Lord knows how many debutantes named Cricket were revealed as Catherines on their wedding invitations. Bizzy and Choo were fine names and never disputed for a moment.

Claire folded linen napkins and placed them in a perfect tower of crisp white triangles. Cat thought about the original question. "Depraved" was a pretty strong word, conjuring scenes of illicit goings-on. Sexual deviance? Witchcraft? Nothing came to mind. As toddlers they slobbered in each other's spit, poked, bit, and grabbed daily. But the drama didn't deter them—each morning the previous day's infractions were readily wiped clean. In kindergarten their penchant for arguing resulted in seats on either side of the room. Their teacher likened the experience to directing an all-five-year-old cast of *Who's Afraid of Virginia Woolf?* But by third grade their flair for drama mellowed, and they morphed into a secret society of two. Their private made-up language began about then. *Sure, they could be secretive, and a big pain in the neck,* thought Cat, *but depraved isn't in the ballpark—not them.*

Bizzy and Choo passed the deviled eggs to the hungry crowd of inebriated adults. Shocking pink and frog-spit green was the favored color combo of their social set, as pervasive as tasseled loafers, grosgrain belts, and endless scotch and sodas. Many of the men sported bushy mustaches and aviator frames, while the women used headbands to hold back their hot-rollered curls. Everyone contributed to the smoke, and ashtrays overflowed as abundantly as booze. The sound of rattling ice cubes underscored the laughter, which nearly drowned out the Bee Gees' *Saturday Night Fever* disco soundtrack album. No one danced because WASPs didn't dare until after dinner was cleared and everyone was good and plastered.

Cat and Claire's raucous holiday parties sealed their hostess status year-round. They were co-matriarchs of a genetic jackpot and inseparable as a social force. At private schools and clubs, their circle of friends and hangers-on emulated Claire, tolerated her husband, Les, and treasured quirky Cat. They were relieved when Cat divorced Dick and married sweet Ned, whom she met in an AA meeting after she first got sober. Everyone liked Ned right away and quickly forgave their infidelities. It was obvious they made a better couple, and not drinking only added to their quirkiness. It was rare new families were folded in, but occasionally, when it happened, it was understood the sisters' pull was indisputable. After initial introductions, the assessment was "Cat's the fun one and Claire's tough." Though it usually took years to see past the assumption. They were complicated women with a talent for making their lives look easy. No one thought to think otherwise, when they themselves were busy keeping up.

Bizzy and Choo's wigs barely got a reaction as they squeezed themselves between the well-heeled bodies of their parents' friends holding a small stack of cocktail napkins in their left hands, platters balanced on their right. Between gracious smiles, they conversed with each other over their shoulders.

Bizzy said, "Jeeze. Look at these kooks. I can't wait until I'm a grown-up and get to throw parties and get wasted all the time."

"Pretty sure there's more to adulthood than that." At least Choo hoped there was.

"Is there? You should tell them."

Bizzy noticed one of the moms' pregnant bellies being used to rest an ashtray and her bourbon, drained—drinking for two. "You know how I want to be a famous costume designer like Bob Mackie, right? And go on Johnny Carson and make millions?"

"And hang out with Cher. I remember."

"I also want to be a mom. Look how much fun they're having. After dinner they'll move the coffee table again and dance like crazy. Everyone's always laughing all the time."

"Our moms aren't," said Choo.

"These moms are. And your mom's fun. Aunt Cat can take a joke. Only mine can't."

"I guess. But I think my mom had more fun when she was drinking."

As they wove their way through the house, there wasn't a single woman looking at her wristwatch. None of them asked to borrow the phone to check on their kids. None were worried about getting home early to relieve the sitter. They threw their heads back to cackle when they weren't leaning in to whisper—their tinkling 24k gold charm bracelets adding to the din. Long chain necklaces dangled fist-sized owl pendants against ribbed turtlenecks showcasing perky, braless chests. Many of them still wore sexy hoop earrings even into their late thirties. And some had mastered black liquid eyeliner like Audrey Hepburn or Aretha. Bizzy was enthralled. These moms had it good, and she would have it good, too. Much better than *her* mom—crabby Claire the Bear.

At one point Mrs. Burrbridge leaned in close to Choo's face and waved a tiny red plastic sword, which held a gin martini olive. Bizzy swung by to see if Choo needed saving as he assisted Mrs. Burrbridge in her quest to choose the right deviled egg. Bizzy spoke to him in their secret language they'd made up when they were little, saying, "os knurd," instead of "so drunk." They'd named their language Terces, for "secret" spelled backward, and were so well versed by now that to the uninitiated they sounded like Swedish Chefs. Over time their fluency grew from halting words to entire sentences strung together like casual pearls. When questioned by strangers they politely explained their Klingon roots. Their family first found it adorable, but later complained it was rude.

Bizzy said, "Trilf," to remind Choo Mrs. Burrbridge was

only flirting. In the voice of Scooby-Doo, he answered, "Rikes."
"Aren't you divine," slurred Mrs. Burrbridge, tapping Choo's
broadened chest. *"Je suis,"* he joked, knowing she wouldn't
remember. He was used to being hit on by his parents' drunken
friends. Though his mom and dad's divorce had been typically
loud and messy, Choo emerged with the grounded confidence of
a handsome, intelligent kid. He was tall now with a deep voice
recently changed. Choo—née Charles, as his jackass father still
insisted on calling him—was the Adonis of the cousins and
Bizzy the obvious Venus. Her hair was long and raven-hued,
her eyes piercing green like her mom's. Choo's were hazel with
dark rims that appeared to warm when hit by the sun. His hair
was lighter than the others', dirty blond and shaggy. But they
both had their grandfather's height and Nana's dimple.

Bizzy redirected Mrs. Burrbridge so that Choo could sneak
away. Then they consolidated the remaining eggs for the basement feeding frenzy.

The rumpus room, as it was referred to, resembled an illegal
betting-parlor scene from *Bugsy Malone,* the mob movie with
an all-child cast. Ten- and eleven-year-olds shared cigarettes and
twelve-year-olds sipped beer while older teens smoked joints
and made out in the shadows behind the furnace. Thankfully,
the debauchery had its codified limitations: the elementary
school crowd was in the master bedroom asleep on the mink
coat pile, and any child younger was home in bed with a sitter,
as any reasonable parent would insist.

Nearly all the kids grabbed a deviled egg off the platter, even
Piper, who claimed she hated food. Someone picked up the needle
from the Eagles' *Greatest Hits* album and started "Take It Easy"
again from the beginning—no one minded because everyone
knew the whole album by heart. The song's strumming guitar

open galvanized the crowd once again and they sang aloud in a chorus with gusto. "Well, I been runnin' down the road tryin' to loosen my load, I got seven women on my mind . . . ," they shouted and air-guitared. It had been the only record played on the stereo for months. Choo caught his little sister, Rah, inhaling a menthol cigarette while playing Atari Pong. "What the hell," he lashed out, "you're only ten!" The butt hung out of her mouth like a pro. Rah ignored him and played on—bee-boop, bee-boop. Controller in hand, staring at the screen, she said, "You told me *you* were ten when you tried your first cig, and I'm almost *eleven*."

"Yeah, but I'm a *boy*," said Choo, and blocked her view.

"*So what! Move!*" Rah shouted, and tried to sweep her big brother out of the way. He remained immoble. "Just because you're a boy and I'm a girl—" Choo made a swipe for her cigarette, but Rah scrambled over the back of the nubby plaid couch and fled under the pool table, knocking over the Hot Wheels loop-de-loop track the younger kids had been building. Cries of "Hey, cut it out!" were roundly ignored except for Bizzy, who crouched down to help rejoin the lengths of bright orange plastic track where they'd been kicked apart. Choo's older stepsister, Georgia, looked over from making out and said, "Calm down, you're not in charge, Kristy McNichol."

"I'm Jaclyn Smith, you twat," said Choo in a huff.

"Nice mouth," Georgia said, and went back to deep-tonguing a neighbor boy from down the street who was home on break from one of those boarding schools for rich kids who struggled in school. Georgia was thirteen and a half and only recently their big sister. Choo was initially Cat's oldest child, soon followed by a little sister named Rah, short for Sarah. Then when Dick left and she married Ned, he brought his daughter, Georgia, to live with them. The move invited unwelcome comparisons to the Brady Bunch as she became Choo's big sister overnight, and there was more drama behind closed doors than anticipated. But over time the children worked out their new adjusted birth order, and the first Thornden blended family was formed.

"Slut," said Choo as a matter of course.

"Dickwad," responded Georgia as familial greeting.

Bizzy's older brother, E.J., yanked her Farrah wig off her head. "Cut it out, assjerk," she said, too late to snatch it back. "It'll look better on her," said E.J., and tossed it to Piper, their neighbor from three houses down. There was no need for Piper to cover up her glorious shrimp-hued mane of curls, but E.J. needed a reason to talk to her. "Try it on," he said. "No thanks," she said on an exhale, then pushed it off her lap and onto the sticky wall-to-wall carpeting. Piper made smoking look the raddest of everyone. At thirteen, she was the closest thing Bizzy had to a girlfriend and the best at inhaling. She also had the biggest boobs—almost as big as Georgia's—and a bossy nature that everyone endured. Piper was mean to Choo, too, but Bizzy thought she liked him because she always stuck her chest out as if it didn't already have a neon blinking sign that read BIG BOOBS. E.J., on the other hand, annoyed Piper, and everyone knew it. But E.J. annoyed everyone. At fifteen he still grabbed stuff out of people's hands.

Piper told everyone sitting around the coffee table it was time to start a new round of Spin the Bottle, so they did as they were told. She had Bizzy hold her cigarette while she grabbed the broken flashlight that had rolled under the couch. E.J. said he wasn't playing; instead, he played Simon to show off his "genius memory skills" but, of course, wouldn't move over to let people in. The rule was that if you spun and the bottle landed on someone who'd just landed on you, you had to spend seven minutes in the furnace room, or "seven minutes in heaven." Everyone else had to drink and keep playing while someone timed by counting "one one-thousand, two one-thousand." The grandkids mostly played games like this with their friends in the summer, because Grandpa Dun and Nana Miggs only let them watch TV on Sunday mornings—cartoons on their 28-inch color set. "Use your nimble minds, children," Grandpa Dun said on balmy days. "Go outside and make a fort." Nana Miggs added, "You never know when you're going to be taken prisoner of war and need to know how to pass the time."

The kids had also made up sibling rules, because so many of the neighborhood kids were from big families. If you spun and got a sibling, you had to spin again and drink. If it landed on a cousin you kissed cheeks, even if you thought it was gross. If you refused to kiss someone you had to go directly to the furnace room as a punishment for missing the game, which is what happened when Bizzy landed on Choo after he'd landed on her. He'd gotten away with kissing Bizzy on the cheek for his first turn, but not this time. Davie and Robbie were pounding their knees, chanting, "French, French, French!" to which Bizzy rolled her eyes and said, "As if, you imbeciles, we're cousins." Piper said, "You know the rules, seven minutes in heaven." So off they went, slightly buzzed on warm Rheingold.

"You're not the boss of me," Bizzy said to Piper, without looking directly at her.

"Yeah, she is," said Choo with a chuckle, and stood. "Of all of us."

"I think cousins should just spin again. Stupid rule," she said to the crowd.

"You're stupid" was the gist of the apathetic reply. It didn't cross their minds they had made up the rules and so could change them at any time.

In the furnace room Bizzy and Choo leaned against the thin door made of scrap pieces of 1940s beadboard. Choo sipped the beer he'd stolen, wondering when he would feel drunk, and not having the wherewithal to realize he already was. *God, beer tastes gross,* he thought, then squinched his face. *How do parents drink this shit?*

"Why does beer have to taste so bogus?"

"This is so totally boring," Bizzy said. "How long do we have to be here?"

"What do you think?"

"Oh, right. Duh."

"Yeah, no duh," said Choo, laughing. Bizzy cracked up at her own idiocy and took his cigarette. She dragged on it as if she'd been smoking for years when in fact she'd only just started on her birthday. Claire had said she could smoke as long as she waited until she was thirteen. She cheated and started a year early.

"Okay, let's practice," said Bizzy.

"Practice what?"

"Kissing. C'mon. You're probably sucky at it, and I haven't really had any practice yet, so we may as well."

"We're *cousins*!"

"No shit, Sherlock. That's why it doesn't count. Jeeze. C'mon. Show me your best try."

"You're a dipwad," said Choo, but he straightened up and faced Bizzy, then took another long, warm sip. She was right that he was unsure of his abilities and could probably use the practice. He hadn't kissed anyone outside of Spin the Bottle.

Bizzy said, "I know you are, but what am I. C'mon, kiss me

and I'll tell you what you're doing wrong, and then we'll switch.
That way we'll be wicked good for when we get real boyfriends
and girlfriends."

"Ha. Like that's ever gonna happen," said Choo.

"You're like the hottest guy in seventh grade. Why don't you
ask someone out? Like Piper."

"Echh, I'm not attracted to her. They're all like annoying
sisters, and I already have that."

Bizzy laughed. "You're a dork. Okay, let's do this, but remember, we don't count for each other."

"A-doi," Choo said but thought, *You count for me.* Bizzy
was far and away the most fun person in his whole dumb life.
Her smile always calmed him down when he felt himself winding tight. And even though he saw her every day he never tired
of her belly laugh or sense of unpredictable adventure. *Just
because I like to be around her doesn't mean I have a crush,*
Choo thought. But he felt the stir of tingles when she was close.
For Bizzy, kissing in general was like an after-school sport—
something she could practice and improve upon. It wasn't personal; she just wanted to become really good at the thing she
and her girlfriends talked and thought about ad nauseam. Like
Choo, she also felt stuck with boring people she'd known since
kindergarten—lame-os she had no interest in kissing. Choo was
the only boy she wanted to hang out with. *Why not practice on
him?* she thought. *Plus he's cute, but who cares? I mean, what's
the big deal?*

"You start. This is so dumb," Choo said, cupping the last
inch of his warm beer.

"Don't be a dweeb. Put down the beer."

Bizzy leaned in to get close and brushed her recently de-
veloping breasts up against his chest by accident. She wasn't

entirely used to having them yet; she'd just had a growth spurt and before that had been flat as a board. She watched Choo watching her—her seafoam eyes wide open—then stopped and said, "I think we're supposed to close our eyes." Choo said, "Fine," and shut his tight, but Bizzy kept hers open a little, wanting to make sure their mouths connected at the right spot. They were careful to keep their bodies from touching. She moved in slowly and placed her lips on his, then pulled back, remembering to lick them first. "Lick your lips, both of them," she directed, and he did. The next time she let her lips sink into his, she reminded herself to pucker. Then she rested her hands on his shoulders and briefly wondered where his were.

At the brush of her lips, Charlie flinched slightly but remained, tilting his head so their noses wouldn't bonk. He planted his lips squarely on hers and lingered—*soft, wettish, warm,* he thought—then returned her pucker two or three times and was quickly bored. He liked the way her mouth felt on his but was distracted because his pants felt full. He balled his hands into fists and put them safely in his pockets. Bizzy couldn't think of anything wrong with his kiss, which led her to wonder if he'd had practice, outside of Spin the Bottle, Spin the Flashlight, or Spin the Flip-Flop or Shoe. Bizzy had only known the pressure of kissing in front of a circle of friends and relatives, sometimes under the duress of teasing and chanting. Kissing had been a spectator sport up until now, but here, alone and with Glenn Frey's pleading lyrics to coerce her, Bizzy felt excited. Their privacy emboldened her. Bizzy parted her lips the width of a penny and let the tiniest flick of her tongue reach Choo's mouth. He pulled back, annoyed. "What are you *doing?* We didn't say *tongues.*"

"We didn't say *no tongues.* Shh. Don't have a cow. This is

just Frenching. It's no big deal, doesn't even count as a base. *Chill.*" Choo felt more confused than annoyed. The pressure in his pants was becoming distracting and his head felt hot and tingly, but he stayed where he was, riveted to the cement floor. "Don't tell me to chill. I hate that," he said, "and no one can hear us, it's like Ringling Brothers out there." On the next try, Bizzy allowed her mouth to open the width of an almond. Though it felt slimy and weird to be touching tongues with her best friend, she persevered, her goal in sight. The inside of Choo's mouth was warmer than the outside. And slimier. *Eww,* she wanted to say. This was something she'd have to get used to, so she tried not to think of the wriggling tadpoles she'd held in Miss Githens's classroom.

Choo closed his eyes again and licked his tongue against Bizzy's. It was an odd feeling but okay, he guessed. He remembered watching people kiss on *Love Boat* and how they broke it up into segments: lips touch, then tongue, then hands moving through the hair. He was definitely not putting his hands in Bizzy's sweaty touch-football hair, but he was starting to get the hang of it. Bizzy was, too. Weak knees and warm thighs—this was starting to feel like an amusement park ride. And definite tingles they'd not felt previously, in unfamiliar places.

Bizzy pulled away to take a quick break. She decided she liked the way her head felt light and her legs soft and buzzy. She felt relaxed and noodle-y. Choo did, too. Sort of. He wiped his mouth with the sleeve of his Brooks Brothers button-down and took another sip of backwash. He hoped she wouldn't notice the prominent object pressing against his jeans and dangled the empty beer can in front of his fly. This hard-on felt bigger than any he'd had before. What the hell was he going to do to make it go away? He couldn't even think straight. Bizzy noticed his fidgeting and looked down. She wondered if she was looking at a hard-on, though she couldn't be certain. She'd heard an eighth-grade boy whisper to his friend about one in the lunch line, but she was afraid to ask Piper. It had been years since she'd seen her brother's actual penis, or Choo's when they were little. She'd begun speculating about what they looked like up close lately. People knew what boobs looked like—they were in movies all the time—but dicks were mysterious. Not that she ever planned to touch one—ew. But still, she didn't think it was fair.

"Your pants look weird."

"Don't worry about it," said Choo, and tried to think about algebra.

"Hey, what does your dick look like?" Bizzy asked matter-of-factly. "Is it the same color skin as your regular skin or lighter or darker? Is it smooth like a hot dog or more like celery?"

"It's blue and hairy like Cookie Monster," Choo said straight-faced. "It shoots cookies when I pee."

"Very funny. I was serious, but forget it. It's probably gnarly with moles."

"Like yours down there."

"Yeah, right. Like *you* know."

"I know Grandpa Dun's *Playboys*."

"How come you get to see pictures of boobs and private parts and I have no idea what a dick looks like? We should be able to sneak naked men magazines. But there aren't any."

"I think there are. I think Burt Reynolds was in one."

"He *was*?! No way. Okay. Just show me what it looks like. Or, fine, don't show me. Draw me a picture. Just make it look real. I want to be prepared when I see one."

Choo laughed. "Prepared for what?"

Bizzy was exasperated. "I *don't know*. That's what I'm *saying*!"

Choo's hard-on was officially gone as he recalled his favorite car chase from *Baretta*. Robert Blake was always up for adventure. Choo thought he should be more like Baretta. *I'm up for adventure,* he thought. "Fine, I'll show you. Jeeze," he said with a smile, and unbuckled his belt. "I can't believe I'm doing this."

"Who cares, let's go," Bizzy said, excited about the prospect of seeing a real live penis and not just some dumb photo from *National Geographic*. "It's gonna be soooo ugly. I can't wait."

Choo ignored her and unzipped his fly, saying, "This is so lame."

Bizzy's eyes were glued to Choo's pants. "C'mon, it's no big deal. It's for research. Is it gonna be gross? I don't want to be grossed out."

"Then cover your eyes. It's *not gross*. It's my dick. Don't tell anyone, okay?"

"Obviously. Cross-my-heart-hope-to-die," Bizzy said as if it were all one word.

Choo reached into the flap on his plaid boxers and pulled out the weirdest, wrinkliest, hot dog-looking thing Bizzy had ever seen.

"Is that it?"

"That's it."

"Totally gnarly."

"Hey, be nice. It's my dick. Don't touch it."

"Gross." She crouched down a little to examine the flaccid penis and noticed the tiny slit in the center of its smooth dome top.

"Isn't it magnificent?" said Choo with bravado. He, too, found it comically unimpressive.

"Is that where the pee comes out?" said Bizzy.

"Among other things."

"Ew! Gag me. Don't be gross!" she said, and thwacked him on the thigh.

"You wanted to learn about it, Miss Body Science Professor."

"It seems wiggly. And not very big."

"It gets bigger."

"Oh. You mean it *will* get bigger. When you get older?" Bizzy was studying the penis as intently as she might a pet turtle in a cardboard box.

"No, I mean it gets bigger, um, sometimes. It was just . . ."

"Oh," Bizzy said, but didn't understand what he meant. Then she put it all together and decided to ask him point-blank. "Was that a *hard-on before*?"

"Yup."

"I *thought* so. Is it distracting to have that thing always dangling in your pants?"

"I'm pretty used to it," Choo said, and turned it this way and that as if he, too, were looking at it clinically for the first time.

"It's *gotta* feel majorly strange," she said to herself, convinced she knew the truth of its strangeness. "Just *hanging* there, in the way, like, *all* the time."

"It doesn't," Choo said, perfectly at ease with his penis in hand. "And it's not in the way. I've had it my whole life."

"Do you ever wish you could unhook it and keep it in a shoe box until you need it?"

"I do not."

Candid questions and deadpan answers continued downstairs while upstairs Choo's father, Dick, arrived two hours early.

Richard Muir insisted on being called Dick. However, behind his back he was also known as Dickhead, Dickweed, or Douchedad by his erstwhile family, even before divorce was imminent. To his face, his children had eventually refused to call him Dad and only used Dick, with an emphatic *D*, launching the word into the air with multiple earned innuendos. It irked him, and he corrected them every time.

Tonight he was taking Choo and Rah back across town to his apartment for the remainder of the weekend and had showed up early. He often did, or late, so as to keep the family constantly off balance. It was his way of lording it over his children, wielding the power he still needed to feel. He would claim, "I'm just teaching them how the world really works," but they hated him for it. Cat did, too.

Not wanting to talk to Dick unless she had to, Cat wordlessly pointed to the basement door. "What a dick," she said once he was gone, as she had time and again.

Dick blustered his way downstairs in his tan Burberry overcoat and paused when he reached the bottom landing, just long enough to survey the depravity. "Where's Charles?" he groused. Georgia looked up from the melee to say, "I don't know," but Piper overlapped, "In there," and gestured toward the furnace room door.

What followed was a scene that could have been contained had Dick been a better or bigger man. Unfortunately, empathy had always eluded him—that and the ability to identify his emotions and control his hair-trigger temper. It was one of the main reasons Cat kicked him out and his children loathed spending time with him. But they had no choice; the grown-ups made the rules. Dick had forgotten what it was like to be a child full of innocent wonder. He was also a product of the fifties, coming of age at a time when good girls didn't let certain thoughts cross their minds, much less ask questions or explore their urges. And here was Claire's daughter—his ex-wife's niece—in such a vile and unladylike position, kneeling in front of his son. Or the child thrust upon him as such.

Dick's temperature spiked and all reason left his grasp. It didn't make a difference in his mind that Bizzy appeared to be simply looking. He called Bizzy disgusting and yanked Choo away by the upper arm—his belt partly unbuckled, lips trembling—then slammed his son against the flimsy wood paneling and dragged him out of the room with his privates exposed. The commotion drew Claire to the basement first, with Cat and Ned following on her heels. Cat tried to defend Bizzy, not clear on what had happened but certain her niece's misdeed couldn't possibly have invited such public shaming. "I was just looking! Like in health class!" was all Bizzy could think to shout, her arms outstretched, flapping the sentiment as if it would help win her case. *"Don't you get it?! It was dumb! Nothing happened! Nothing, nothing!"* As the sisters and Dick pitched simultaneous fits, Ned tried to calmly intervene, but it was no use. Choo implored Ned as he was dragged up the stairs in his father's unforgiving grip, "Tell Bizzy I'm so sorry," to which Ned answered kindly, "I'm sure you did nothing wrong." Then Choo could be heard letting loose a string of invectives against his father with a fiery vitriol he'd learned from the man himself.

Downstairs, in front of the roomful of stunned children, Bizzy felt weak and fell to her knees. Tears streamed down her face and she choked on the words as she looked up at her mother, pleading, "Please believe me," over and over again. Claire stood erect in the basement rumpus room she rarely visited, surveying the wreckage—the underage smoking and drinking—and calculating the loss to her social standing in town. Only the last of these was any real issue to her. She watched, quietly and steely, as her daughter's entreaties devolved into hiccupping sobs. Her husband, Les, was nowhere to be found. Some of the younger kids were scared and whimpering, oblivious to what they'd witnessed but still quaking in the wake of Dick's ire. The older kids stared at Bizzy. They'd known her forever as full of curiosity and blithe-spirited fun and wondered what happened and what pieces they'd missed. And though most of what they saw and heard wouldn't fit snugly into a rational—if morally questionable—explanation for many years, they were pretty sure it was bad.

Claire marched a crying and gasping Bizzy upstairs to the master bedroom, hissing that her behavior was "deplorable, loose," and "depraved." She grilled Bizzy with an icy composure that frightened as much as it condemned her. "What did you and Choo do in those blanket forts you made in the back hall linen closet when you were little?" Incredulous, Bizzy answered, "*Nothing!* We were *playing*! We were *little kids, Jesus!*" Claire glared for a moment, then said, "Don't say the Lord's name in vain, young lady," and left without shutting the door. Bizzy sucked in what she hoped was all the air that existed in the world, or at least in the upstairs of her Aunt Cat's house, and screamed, "We're *not. Even. Catholic!*" But no one heard her above the party's din. The drunken revelers were too busy singing along to "Love Will Keep Us Together" by the Captain and his doting Tennille. Except for Les—he heard her. Across the hall, Bizzy noticed her dad sitting on the edge of the bed in the guestroom, a scotch in hand, the ice having long since melted. He sat still as if sitting for a figure drawing class, not looking toward Bizzy but staring forward at God knows what.

Claire went back down to the basement and lifted the needle off the stereo. "Desperado, why don't y—" The older kids cringed; they feared permanent damage to their favorite cowboy sad song. "Children, there's no need to bother over what went on tonight. It doesn't concern you. And rumors are of little use to anyone, so no need to discuss what you don't understand. Bizzy and Choo were just playing a little made-up game that got out of hand, that's all. Do you understand?" Her apparent question was met with blank stares. "Do. You. Understand?" she repeated, this time enunciating the beginning of each word. The children mumbled, "Yes, Mrs. Chadwick," in varying layers of volume and fear. Claire glared for punctuation, then left.

Upstairs, Bizzy waited until she was able to catch her breath before looking out the doorway across the hall again to her father. "Hey, Dad?" she called thinly. Perhaps he didn't hear her; maybe she hadn't been loud enough. "Daddy, do you believe me?" she called this time with more effort. He turned and looked into her watery eyes, but his were just as hollow as before. "Why did you marry her?" Bizzy asked quietly, without condemnation but with honest wonder. It had never made sense to her. They had never seemed to like each other very much. She'd never seen them laugh. Les turned away from his only daughter and resumed his drunken stare. *He probably can't hear me,* she decided.

Cat was shaken. She spoke to Claire in a tone she hoped concealed her panic. "Claire, I think you should go easy on—"

"We'll handle it tomorrow," Claire snapped. "It's time to pull the lasagnas out of the oven." And with that she redirected their focus back to the party.

Cat thanked God she was no longer drinking while wanting, more than anything, to drink. She calmed herself by pouring

French dressing onto iceberg lettuce for the oblivious masses and intoned the Serenity Prayer away from her sister's view. To steady her hand she took deep breaths—she loathed seeing her ex.

Cat regretted her impetuous nature at age twenty-two and how she was overcome by Dick Muir's charm in three short weeks. He was handsome with a forthright confidence, and red flags she ignored. When she couldn't get pregnant after two years of trying—heartbreaking failure, an eternity back then—Dick's mother, Agnes, summoned them with her edict. She shamed Dick for not being able to impregnate his wife, then ushered forth his younger sister as a convenient solution. Peggy had become unintentionally pregnant with a married sculptor's child while a junior abroad in England. Too late to take control of the matter, Agnes decided Dick and Cat would raise the child as their own. In return for their long-term discretion, Dick would be given a salaried position he'd not earned at Barclays in London. Cat would be the wife of a prosperous financier and have her motherhood wish fulfilled. Peggy would carry on with her reputation befitting a Philadelphia debutante intact, and the child would escape the shadow of being a bastard.

Cat and Dick hopped the *QE2* the minute everything was decided. The family was told Dick's job offer couldn't wait. Cat spent the months readying their London flat as Dick settled into his new job. No photos were expected; pregnancy images were distasteful. A visit from Claire was out of the question since she had little E.J. to chase after and Cat told her parents not to make the trip. The instant Cat cradled her new infant, Charles, she felt an overwhelming mother's love. "Sent from heaven," she cabled her friends. They moved back home within the year. Dick, however, couldn't square himself with "raising another

man's son." He was unkind to Choo and ignored him, prefer-
ring to read the paper or play golf. When Rah was conceived
two years later, Cat was shocked and thrilled beyond belief.
Dick muttered, "What good's a girl?" So Cat wrote him off and
raised them together with Claire, without his involvement, permission, or support. She parented pickled, alternating between
sherry, black coffee, and bourbon, but never told a soul, not
even her mother or Claire. Even after she met Ned in Alcoholics
Anonymous, Cat wore Choo's secret like a second skin. It was
the 1960s and people could be cruel, even some in her town, in
her own family. Keeping Choo's secret meant securing his place
as a Thornden—regardless of Agnes's bribery, threats, or social
condemnation. Cat would rather die than have Choo grow up
questioning his worth. She vowed to take to the grave that he
wasn't a blood relative.

Claire called a meeting the next morning in her kitchen between Bizzy and Choo, Les, Cat, and Ned. She reiterated in a
tribunal-style manner that "nothing happened." Choo retorted,
"That's because nothing *did* happen. Jesus, Aunt Claire."

Cat said, "Watch your tone, young man."

To which Bizzy added, "Oh, I forgot to tell you, Choo, we're
super religious now."

Cat said, "Let's just not discuss it, okay?"

"There's *nothing* to *discuss. Everyone just stop having a
hairy conniption over this, okay?*" Bizzy said, exasperated; then,
bored with all adults and their idiot ways, she put her forehead
on the table and spoke into the cherrywood. "Plus I have homework."

"So do I," said Choo. And with that Claire dismissed

everyone, and, true to WASPy form, the matter was closed, to Cat's great relief. But that evening as Bizzy was falling asleep she became stuck in a disparaging spiral. Was there something wrong with her? It was just a penis. *If it was his elbow no one would have freaked.* It was pretty dang ugly for everyone to flip out over. *Just because he pees out of it, who cares? It's not like I broke it. Jesus.* It took her hours to fall asleep.

The rumpus room episode appeared swept under the table, though Claire still sent E.J. or Rah to check on them occasionally, even if they were only playing rummy in the next room. Claire felt it her job to be vigilant. Bizzy and Choo saw through her mistrust and egged E.J. on to mess with her. Delighted, he reported back to his mom they were playing "strip backgammon." Then they giggled together as Claire lost her mind. Of all the folks caught up in the tumult, Bizzy and Choo moved on the quickest. Piper did her best to stoke the rumors at school in order to improve her social worth, but wasn't sure what exactly had happened, so the stories eventually fell flat. She spread that Bizzy and Choo had been caught making out, but the idea was so gross it didn't stick. Local parents shot down such outlandish notions—*not the Thornden kids, I highly doubt it.* Choo's anger over the event occasionally wound him up like a spring, his hands and shoulders tight, wanting to punch something. But as he and Bizzy walked home from school she counseled him, speaking calmly. "It's all going to work out. Just ignore them." His breath always steadied and his shoulders lowered as if a gentle tide had passed through him. He could experience calm again as if he'd been gently unwound. Only Bizzy had such a soothing effect. Not even his mother could make Choo feel this depth of belonging. Not even Cat could make him feel this much at home.

Time healed Choo's wounds and faded the community's lingering doubts. By the end of the school year it was in the past. The cousins graduated from junior high and transitioned to the upper school. Choo channeled any residual anger by penning dark comics. Bizzy had plenty of guy friends in high school, but no one ever made a move. She figured it was because they'd all known each other since kindergarten. Having no boyfriends at Larkspur Academy freed her up to make out with visiting shy boys at games. She became a connoisseur of French kissing under the bleachers but never bugged Choo to practice. She knew he had his hands full with Sissy Bickers. Sissy was Choo's four-year, on-again/off-again girlfriend, who was too adorable, apparently, to let herself sleep with him. He, in turn, was too nice to pressure her and so became Olympic at patience and masturbation. All the while Bizzy became a champion at drinking.

On weekends they entertained—their moms taught them well—having friends over for pool parties and Quarters. Bizzy's self-appointed job was to get everyone dancing, and Choo's job was to keep everyone alive—especially those who were pushed into the pool in all their sherbet-colored, stonewashed clothing. There was always Lipton's onion soup and sour cream dip, and mini-eggrolls to soak up the alcohol, plus port wine cheese spread and peach schnapps stashed behind hedges for late-night retrieval. Bizzy was terrible at Quarters and lost often, so had to drink more than most, which made her horny and want to dance more, especially if someone put on *Rumours*. Choo held her long hair back when she upchucked, then stealthily put her to bed, placing her Dr. Scholl's on the floor and drawing the covers up to her chin. Then he set the kitchen mixing bowl on the floor next to her bed in case she needed it in the morning.

By senior year Bizzy excelled in English, history, and art and spent long hours after school on the home-ec room sewing machines. She made hats and elaborate Halloween costumes at fifteen dollars a commission, excelling at bathmat Chewbaccas and bedsheet Princess Leias. Piper continued to bully Bizzy, making her feel lousy about herself, and Sissy Bickers made Choo feel unwanted. So the cousins watched old black-and-white movies Nana Miggs recorded off the TV and played endless games of Ping-Pong in the shed. Choo had had a successful run, doing well in chemistry, soccer, and DOS computing. But his real passion was directing like his idol, John Cassavetes. He shot scenes he'd written after school with Ned's Betamax camcorder and bribed Piper, Georgia, and E.J. to act naturally. E.J. insisted he play the lead, which was fine with Choo, and Piper played Gena Rowlands with her cigarette held high. The island counter in his kitchen stood in for a bar, and the *Charlie's Angels* wigs always managed to make cameos. Bizzy cheered on Choo's ideas for new script concepts while he cheered her sketches for hats that looked like desserts. *Blues Brothers* meets *Blade Runner*? "Yes," she'd tell him, "go for it! I dare you!" *Eraserhead* meets *Eating Raoul*? "Why not?" A wide slice of chocolate mousse cake worn at a rakish angle? "Totally," Choo told her, "knock your socks off."

Just don't get too close to me, and I'll keep my distance from you, and everyone will leave us alone.

1984

Two fairly decent, liberal arts college campuses, Boston, Massachusetts

Bizzy and Choo did well enough on their SATs to get into the kinds of Boston liberal arts colleges that people of their caliber pretended were excellent though they were academically lesser robust institutions. Bizzy was off to Seldon University for art history, and Choo was headed across town to Finley College to study economics—at his father's insistence—with a minor in French New Wave cinema. Both Claire and Cat separately sat their kids down and gave them the lecture about starting a new chapter. They went on about turning over leaves and how this was their chance to make new friends up in Boston—"friends you'll have for the rest of your life." "Uh-huh," the cousins murmured, listening dutifully. *Whatever,* they thought independently. *I already have a best friend.* There was so much emphasis on starting fresh and reinventing oneself that they decided to pick new names. Bizzy shortened to Biz, and Choo became Charlie. And for fun they decided not to tell their family about the change or let the world know they were cousins.

Choo was slightly homesick, and Bizzy chided him gently, but being away from the family did them both a world of good.

They aligned their class schedules so they could check out ska bands at night and art galleries and movie houses during the day.

Biz would have minored in fashion if Claire had allowed her, but devoured Seldon's art history curriculum regardless. She was jealous of Charlie, who knew he wanted to be a film-maker, and clung to the conviction her ideal career would appear. She knew she loved making crazy costumes, and sewing, and glue guns. She knew she loved absurdity and tequila. But there was one thing she could never divulge to the other art buffs in her classes. What Biz really wanted was to become a mom. They would have deemed it uninspired, too bourgeois and uncreative, so she never told them. Nor did she tell Charlie.

Claire and Cat drove up to Boston together for Parents' Weekend, leaving the men and younger kids at home. They shared one car, having no interest in learning the T, and stopped at Biz's dorm room first. Tindy Weldon answered the door in peach wide-wale pants, painted barrettes, and a lemon Izod shirt. She had excellent posture and spoke with the anxious-to-please lilt of a Disneyland tour guide. Claire assessed Tindy and was immediately relieved. Biz's mom had approved her college roommate.

"Hi! One of you must be Biz's mom. I can totally see the family resemblance. Neat-o. Here's our room. And this is my bed. And this is Biz's bed, and . . ." Though her voice was cloying, she clearly came from the right background—PLU, or People Like Us, as Claire always said. Tindy continued her prattling. "Biz isn't here. Probably with Charlie. Did she know you were coming?"

Claire said, "She knows. I'm her mother, Claire. I left a message this morning."

Tindy looked up as if delighted by a cartoon hummingbird hovering just out of reach. "Ohhh, that's what that meant," she said as if putting two and two together were something novel. Cat extended her hand. "Hi, I'm Bizzy's Aunt Cat. Did she say when she would be back?"

"Who's Charlie?" asked Claire. Cat glared at her sister.

"Oh, her best friend, supposedly, but everyone thinks they're dating," said Tindy, pleased with her role as ace communicator.

Claire ignored her sister's look. "What do you mean by 'supposedly'?"

"Oh, they say they're not dating, but everyone assumes they are. They're partially inseparable. I mean practically."

"Neat-o," said Cat facetiously.

Just then the door flew open. It was Biz, flushed and panting. "Oh, my goodness, I'm so sorry I'm late!" she said, and gave her mother a perfunctory hug. Her aunt's hug included a kiss on the cheek.

"It's fine, sweetheart," said Cat. "We're so happy to see you! What a terrific room. Isn't it, Claire?" Claire followed her sister's enthusiastic lead with a forced smile. "Tindy was just telling us about your new best friend, Charlie. Does he want to join us for lunch?"

Biz looked as if she'd been prodded with something small and sharp. "Um, nope, that's okay. He's at a tournament. All weekend. He's a tight, uh, guard. It's an away game."

Cat rescued her niece. "You don't have to tell us any more about him if you don't want to, sweetheart. You're entitled to your privacy now that you're a coed. Isn't that right, Claire? Our Bizzy is a young woman, all grown up."

Claire put on a thin smile as if trying on an ugly handmade sweater in front of its maker. "I'll handle Bizzy, thank you very much."

"It's Biz now, Mom. People are calling me Biz. Let's eat!" she said, and ushered them out the door before they could invite Tindy to join them. *What a total spaz,* Biz thought. *Of all the people I could have been assigned to. Christ. I can't believe she told them about Charlie.*

Claire insisted they lunch at L'Espalier, which seemed a little much to Biz, but anything to placate her mother—she could be impossible at restaurants. Before ordering, Claire went to the restroom, leaving Cat and Biz alone. Cat lifted her butter knife and with assuredness, said, "Please pass the rolls, my dear. Also, your friend Charlie is Choo, yes? You're better off telling me now, because we only have a few minutes to devise a game plan, and it would be a shame to waste even one second on you trying to deny the truth."

Biz's eyes grew wide as she looked at her aunt, who was on the money as usual. Why should she feel guilty about hanging out with her cousin? Biz wanted to wring Tindy's neck.

Cat said, "I thought so."

Biz took a moment, then inhaled. "It's not. *Dammit.* We're not—" Biz was ramping up for an overblown defense. Cat cut in, "I'm not suggesting you are. You've been best friends your whole lives. I'm not suggesting you stop now. If your mother prods, tell her your relationship with this young mystery man is new and you don't want to jinx it by talking about it. There are a million Charlies out there. Say that if it becomes something worthy of announcing, she'll be the first to know."

"Thanks, Aunt Cat."

"Why didn't you tell people you were cousins? It's going to bite you in the ass, young lady."

"I know. I know. It was dumb. But everyone had such a freak-out that night in the basement, and I feel like Mom's looked at us cross-eyed ever since."

Cat did not disagree with her. She was glad to feel some measure of control over their clandestine relationship, which conveniently assuaged her guilt. "It's fine with me, but if anyone calls Choo Charlie in front of your mom, you're sunk. You two are dingbats, you know that?" said Cat, no nonsense.

"I know, I know. Please take her to see Charlie's dorm, I mean Choo's, as soon as our lunch is over. You don't need to come back here. I'm having a great time at school, promise. Passing grades, no drugs, clean sheets—all that. She just needs to see I'm alive, right? Then she can go back home, or visit E.J. or whatever." Biz hadn't thought about Charlie in a boy-friend-y way. *I mean, sure he's objectively hot,* she thought. There were plenty of hot guys at school. *You make one mistake when you're twelve and the world crucifies you forever.*

"And if you can assure me you and Choo aren't . . . You're cousins, remember?"

"Aunt Cat." Biz looked her straight in the eyes. "There is nothing kinky going on between me and Choo. And of course I remember we're cousins—what a weird thing to say. Plus I'm still a virgin, for crying out loud. Didn't you see the neon sign on my forehead?"

Cat answered wryly, "Oh, is that what that was." She realized in hindsight it *was* a weird thing to say. She needed to watch her step now that her niece was older and sharper. She couldn't slip up and spill the beans—had to stay on her game.

"I've been trying to get rid of my virginity, but I've only met boorish douchebags or preppy jackasses. I thought, *finally!* I'm at college and no one knows that stupid story about me and Choo. But I'm trying to lose it, I really am. I have to kiss a lot of frogs and all that, I know."

"Oh, dear. You sound serious. Would you like me to get you on the pill? Unless your mom has already offered . . ."

Biz's eyes popped. "Ha! No way, José. You would do that for me? Yes, *please!* But we can't tell Mom."

"I would have to agree."

Biz had loved her Aunt Cat more than her own mother for years. She discovered this in junior high when asking her mom for advice. Claire would inevitably blame Biz for whatever incident was causing her to second-guess her own behavior. Biz finally defaulted to Aunt Cat for guidance. She was met with compassion and level-headed advice. Even Uncle Ned listened with patient counsel.

Cat said, "Okay, I'll see what I can do. I don't want you to be reckless."

"Like you?" Biz smirked.

"I beg your pardon, missy, but yes. Like me." Cat smirked back. She had an inkling Larkspur felt provincial to Biz and she might want to sow her oats once she moved on. Cat had had impulses, too, back in her day, and wanted to make certain Biz was protected from any slip-ups that might hamper her academic career. Or, unintentionally, the rest of her life.

Claire was winding her way back to their table.

"How about the waiter?" asked Biz.

Cat looked at Biz wide-eyed. "Sweetie, I get that you're ready, and I don't mean to be unkind, but I think you can do better than a waiter for your first time."

Biz cracked up. "So we *can order,* Aunt Cat. But thanks for being my pimp." They chuckled, then, "Shhh."

The moment Biz said her good-byes she hurriedly ran to a corner pay phone and called Charlie's dorm to ask the front desk to ring the fourth-floor hall phone. No one answered; she panicked. Biz had to come up with a message that could be written quickly and would explain everything Charlie needed to know in a condensed, unambiguous fashion. Plus it couldn't be long because Randy Rude the Front Desk Dude would cut people off if he had to write too much down. Biz said, "This is as short as I can make it. Please don't have a cow." "Fine," Randy snapped. Biz dictated, "Don't be Charlie. Be Choo. Your mom knows!" She added, "And please make sure you put an exclamation point." "Oh, brother," Randy said, and hung up on her. Charlie picked up the note from his box just in time, and his dinner with his mom and aunt went smoothly. Whatever crisis loomed was avoided for now.

After the visit, Biz knew she should branch out. They both did.

Once Aunt Cat got her on the pill, she went a little nuts at Seldon and in the surrounding Boston metro area. Growing up, she'd never read, seen, or heard of a woman masturbating. There were no scenes in movies or discussions with her friends from home. So Biz pleasured herself with a string of quick and mostly satisfying guys. European, Jew, black, or Californian, Biz was an equal opportunity lay. She was less interested in the cumbersome bother of a relationship. This was the eighties, and she was *not* going to be in a desperate rush to find a husband—even if she did secretly long to be a mom. The most important thing to Biz was that she be able to dance at bars, shoot some pool, share a laugh, and climax. She was usually, but not always, sauced—tequila shots her downfall—and her clothes slipped off easily, with little regret. AIDS awareness campaigns made condoms an obvious part of the plan, but drunk, they were easy to dismiss. Most of the girls she knew were too shy to carry or insist on them and defaulted to assessing potential partners by their outward cleanliness. Biz, at least, carried one in her wallet with the best of intentions, but often blew it off in the rabid heat of the moment. Later, she'd scold herself, then get tested at the free clinic, but eventually resume the invincibility of a nineteen-year-old. She made a rule that if a guy couldn't bring her to orgasm by the second date, she moved on to someone better worth the risk. She knew her behavior would be deemed "slutty" or "risky" back in Larkspur, but in Boston she could enjoy her hedonistic foray. Sex would be one of Biz's vices, she decided. *Everyone's entitled to two or three.*

Charlie had one vice—cold, Canadian beer. His dorm's pay phones ran a close second. He spent long hours and many quarters sitting in broken chairs, talking Sissy Bickers out of being convinced he was cheating on her—which he wasn't. The rest of the time he did his homework, played his crappy keyboard, and wrote screenplays about hapless misanthropes who felt trapped.

By Thanksgiving, a blustering storm early in the season left branches naked and gave the air a frigid bite. But there was comfort in the weather's turn, as well as the Thornden holiday routine, which was a surprise to absolutely no one. The entire family was summoned to Firth—a village ten minutes from Larkspur—to Grandpa Dun (né Dunsfield) and Nana Miggs's large, rambling manse. Every detail from who brought which sides to who opened the champagne was practically etched in heavy stone tablets. Nana Miggs (née Marjorie) had carried on the traditions of her mother and grandmother before her. Then, once she discovered painting oil landscapes in her late fifties, she suddenly and irreversibly backed off from her role as head nurturer. It was too trying to juggle the family holiday goings-on with mixing colors to match the upholstery in her homes. After one particularly stressful Thanksgiving, she announced, "I'm over it," and placed the turkey onto the table with a slight thud. "Take over, girls," she said. And take over they did. Cat and Claire were finally in charge. They'd been angling to get control of the event planning for years, conferring in corners of barbecues and luncheons. In hushed tones they discussed what they would have done differently—the invitations, lighting, music, and menu (too stuffy, bright, slow, and too 1950s). Finally, it was their turn to shine.

Cat and Claire were in peak pre-meal frenzy when a life-sized, homemade papier-mâché and fur-fabric horse bumbled into the kitchen. Neither sister broke their rhythm; they knew exactly who was inside.

"Naaayyyy," said Charlie, muffled from somewhere near Biz's butt.

"Amscray, you two," said Claire, "and take that thing off."

Charlie said, "Take what off?" in the approximate voice of Mr. Ed.

Claire was not amused. "Right now. We need your help. Choo, please go play the piano. You know what your grandparents like." Charlie rolled his eyes, which no one saw, and did as he was told. He stepped out of the horse pants and trekked to the living room. Biz stayed behind to help out in the kitchen.

Cat said, "It's still one of my favorite costumes you've ever made, dear."

"Thanks, Aunt Cat," Biz muttered from inside the sweaty head. "Me, too."

Ice cube trays were refilled and cream-cheese-based dips passed around. Cocktail hour lasted exactly that. Charlie dutifully played the music his grandparents adored, and cousins and siblings teased him for knowing. He reveled in the escape from meal-prep tension and lost himself in the beloved standards. Coaxing the baby grand's worn pedals and keys, he hummed, ". . . just the way you look tonight." It was an uncomplicated playlist from the forties and fifties, which included, "The Very Thought of You"—his grandparents' wedding song. He relished the gentle unfolding of so many precious poems, attending to their chords without interruption. Entranced by his own fingers floating effortlessly below, he lost himself in "S'Wonderful" and "Easy to Love." He sang softly, noting the rhyming schemes of past authors' lyrical genius, which had soothed heartaches and set desire aflame for decades. He believed his own heart thawed in deference to their magic. He felt at ease and hopeful when he played.

Georgia snuck into the dining room sipping a Heineken and looking like Pat Benatar lost at the Ritz. She wore a leather miniskirt, fishnets, and a teal waffle-weave acrylic V-neck sweater—braless and backward, to show off her buoyant tits. She switched her place card with Rah's so she could sit next to Charlie at the long rectangular dining room table. The pumpkin-hued damask tablecloth set off four tall white tapers in sterling candlesticks down the middle. A sumptuous arrangement of mango calla lilies, fall hydrangea, and hypericum berries crowned the center in a tarnished Tiffany golf trophy bowl.

Moments later Biz swung through and swapped the place cards back. Biz and Charlie—still Bizzy and Choo to their family—always sat across from each other and she didn't want Georgia interfering. Nana Miggs and Grandpa Dun sat at either end, their children and teenage grandchildren between them. The dress was semiformal, except for Grandpa Dun who sported a bow tie with a silk pocket square in his blazer. The women wore wool skirts and pearls; the boys, collared shirts and scuffed loafers. Helen Forrest sang, "Long Ago and Far Away" softly on the record player, and everyone sat up straight.

At grace, all hands clasped and heads bowed with closed eyes, except for Biz and Charlie. When they were younger, they peeked, sticking their tongues out at each other. As they became older, they smirked without giggles. More recently, they'd devised a game where they raced to hang spoons from their noses. Georgia peeked once when she first joined the family—she envied Bizzy's connection with Choo. After that she always fake-coughed during the prayer so she could watch their silent hijinks. The fact that he was technically her stepbrother was just that to Georgia, a formality. She minced around him and leaned in close. Charlie found her attentions absurd. Biz knew it was hypocritical to be annoyed by Georgia, but in the grand taxonomy of inappropriateness, she found stepsiblings way worse than cousins. For them, such rules were malleable.

Grandpa Dun, a man for whom tweed was apparently created, issued the post-grace topic, as was the custom. "Marjorie"—he nodded toward his wife of forty-two years—"and daughters, this looks exquisite." Everyone raised a crystal glass in joyful praise, chiming, "Here, here," as clinking rang out in the air. Cat and Claire, who'd worked their butts off to make the meal appear effortless, smiled demurely like the martyrs they were.

E.J. farted and blamed it on Rah. Rah squealed, "Ew, grody! That *was not me*," to which Nana Miggs said, "Children," with the gentle firmness of Mrs. Ingalls, then lifted her fork, and everyone dug in. Seemingly indifferent to the flatulence indiscretion, Grandpa Dun began his routine questioning, circling around the table for updates. "Four out of five of my exceedingly impressive grandchildren are returned from university for this familial *bon repas*. And one will be heading thence next year, my dearest young Sarah. What say ye all about your continuing education?" This vacillation between Olde English and French was Grandpa Dun's idea of jocularity and tolerated by all who knew him. "Ellister Junior, let's begin with you." E.J.—gangly, bespectacled, born a wiseass—knew this was coming. Grandpa Dun always started with the oldest.

"You'll be pleased to hear, Grandfather, that the brainiacs at Hillsbury College will be cordially inviting me back to dazzle them further in business and law."

"Was there any question, young man, as to your return?" Grandpa Dun raised an eyebrow at Claire, who shook her head, eyes to the heavens.

"Never," said E.J. "The faculty is as delighted by me as you are, Grandfather." E.J. called him Grandfather as an overt ploy of flattery. Intended to charm and disarm, it was laced with sarcasm, which everyone but Grandpa Dun was privy to.

Claire admonished, "Watch it, smart aleck. Be respectful to your elders."

"Yeah, show some respect," said Rah.

Cat said, "'It's 'yes,' not 'yeah.'"

"It ain't?" said Rah. Nana Miggs laughed. She knew Rah was teasing.

"No, it's not, young lady," said Cat with a smirk.

"She said 'snot,'" said E.J.

Generally thought of as the brainiest of the bunch, Rah had already been accepted early decision at Pembshire. She'd been recruited for a highly competitive spot in an exclusive acceler- ated mathematics program with an eye toward civil engineering. This made it something of a study in digression to see her be- have with juvenile flair. The truth was she was the only one still at home and missed the others, especially her cousin E.J. E.J. shoved the corner of his napkin deep into his right nostril, then looked at Nana Miggs with a straight face and a white shock of fabric spilling forth from his nose. Rah yanked the napkin out of E.J.'s nose and rolled her eyes. Nana Miggs barely contained her delight—she loved anything and anyone who ruffled her husband's feathers. E.J. knew it and played every gag to her.

"That's enough. Grow up," hissed Claire. "Grandpa Dun, please continue."

"Georgia? What pearls of wisdom did you glean this first half of your second *année*?"

Georgia said, "I learned that if one is contrarian enough to a slovenly roommate who also pries and snores, the roommate will request a change of venue on a phony premise, thus solving the conundrum."

"Major?"

"Psychology."

Grandpa Dun nodded his approval like a judge hearing rea- son. "Cunning use of the word 'conundrum,' Georgia. Keep up your studies," he said warmly.

"Thank you, Grandpa Dun," said Georgia, and returned his smile in earnest. She appreciated how fully her stepfamily had embraced her as one of their own. Even though her dad broke up Cat's marriage, she never heard the family lay blame.

It was a brutal transition: a new household at a miserable time—middle school—and right when Georgia's mom's alcoholism was ramping up to a dish-breaking pitch. Their Thornden customs and asinine nicknames needed some getting used to, but her father seemed much happier now, relaxed and less on edge. After all those years of her mom's childish shrieking, who could blame him for leaving her? And knowing he and Cat had both betrayed their spouses gave Georgia comfort in their fallibility. Now she'd never have to aim for perfection, and could permit herself to angle for Choo.

"Charles? What do you report?" asked Grandpa Dun.

Charlie straightened to attention. "I still haven't met my roommate due to a rousing case of mono."

"You basically have a single?" Georgia asked with a sideways glance.

"Your studies, young man?" Grandpa Dun continued.

"I'm at Finley College, also in Boston. Economics with a minor in film studies." Nana Miggs beamed at her Choo. She loved the closeted artists in her family and rooted for them to drop the charade of whatever banking or law career was expected of them. She'd had many artist friends in her day who'd ended up in finance—and eventual soul-sucking emotional depravity.

"Capital, young man," said Grandpa Dun. "And should that not work out for you?"

"Finance," said Charlie with a measure of vacancy in his eyes.

There it was, thought Nana Miggs, his inevitable fallback and road to existential ruin. Aloud she said, "I hope you'll show us whatever films you make, young man."

"Of course, Nana Miggs. I always do."

"Atta boy." Charlie was warmed by his grandmother's remark. He'd always felt that besides Biz, Nana Miggs was the only one who supported him without a trace of judgment. Grandpa Dun cleared his throat to resume control of the proceedings. "And have you been a source of support and familial comfort for your sister, Georgia, and cousin, Elizabeth, embedded with you there in Boston?" He often referred to Biz as Elizabeth. He was the only one.

"I have," said Charlie. Georgia had a curious expression of doubt on her face, which both Charlie and Biz picked up on. "Well, Georgia's at Garrick, which is about forty-five minutes outside of Boston." He wasn't about to let the guilt of not visiting Georgia yet take hold. "More like thirty," Georgia cut in, but Charlie plowed through. "And Biz is at Seldon, Grandpa Dun, about six stops from Finley on the T. I've helped her settle in a bit. We've been to the movies, and I've escorted her to mixers." Charlie knew his grandfather would like hearing the term "mixer" again. He also felt it was his job to prove to his grandfather—and the rest of his family—that he wasn't the heartless jackass his father was. E.J. mouthed "suck-up" to Charlie as Grandpa Dun beamed approvingly. "Now, Elizabeth, are you comporting yourself appropriately at these mixers?"

"I am indeed, Grandpa," said Biz with a corny thumbs-up.

"And you're studying . . ."

"Art history."

"Fine choice for a young lady." The women's revolution hadn't made it to Firth, nor had it made a dent in Grandpa Dun's psyche.

Nana Miggs interjected, "No fashion design courses for you? What about all those wonderful costumes you create?"

Biz said, "Oh, those are just for fun, Nana Miggs. Mom decided I should focus on something more practical. She said my life goal should be more than getting on *Letterman*."

"Yes," said Claire, "she can't possibly make a career out of such nonsense." Biz rolled her eyes. Only Charlie caught it. He mouthed "awesome nonsense" to her. Claire peered down to the middle of the table and said to her daughter and nephew, "I thought I gathered from Parents' Weekend you two weren't seeing much of each other." Cat wondered where this was going. "We aren't," Biz jumped in a little too quickly, then caught Charlie's eye and realized she would need to nimbly dig herself out of the hole she'd just tripped herself into. Grandpa Dun looked confused. Biz continued, "Except for when we do. Which is rare, but often enough." E.J. coughed, but it was no ordinary cough. He had perfected the "bullshit" cough from *Animal House* with such nuanced subtlety only his cousins heard it. Biz ignored him. Claire bristled. Cat listened, fully alert. Claire said, "So are you or are you not spending time with each other up in Boston? Why don't you see if you can give me a more definitive answer, Choo."

Charlie began, "Sure, Aunt Claire. I'd be happy to. Biz and I—" Biz interrupted again, saving Charlie from having to lie. "Of course we hang out. We have other friends, too, Mom. My roommate is totally bitchin'. I hang with her a lot."

Claire balked. "I beg your pardon, young lady, but don't try to tell me for one minute that you spend an ounce of time with that nitwit Taffy."

"Tindy."

"Taffy's better," said Charlie under his breath.

Biz looked to the end of the table for support. "Nana Miggs, you've always said life is short and we should surround ourselves with the people who appreciate us and make us feel good about ourselves when we're with them."

Nana Miggs nodded. "I have. It's imperative you stay true to who you are. It's the only way you'll attract real friends and honest love. I also say that life is long, so take your time."

Biz said, "Charlie and I just—" then stopped herself. "I mean, Choo and I do normal things." She hesitated. "In groups. With other friends. Outside."

"Quit while you're behind," said E.J.

"Museums and art openings, that sort of thing."

"Sounds tedious," Georgia said under her breath.

"Sounds dubious," chimed E.J.

"Back up," said Claire. Something clicked in her mind, and both Cat and Biz knew the conversation was about to turn. "Did you just call him Charlie?" Claire glared at Biz. "Taffy told us you were seeing someone named Charlie." No one in the family had perfected the art of diffusing one of Claire's laser-like glares, though many had tried. Cat tried to quell the rising tide of accusation, but Claire brushed her off and repeated the question.

"Uh-oh," said E.J., who was focused on this new twist with wide eyes and rapt attention. "This is getting interesting."

Rah came back from the bathroom. "I feel like I'm missing something."

"You should tune in," said E.J. dryly, "it's better than *Dallas*."

"I—" Biz said, then stopped abruptly. Her mind was a dusty blank. She'd always been a lousy liar but wanted to be better— smooth like a Bond girl—which is why she kept going. But she was a fumbler. She could feel perspiration gathering beneath the underwire of her bra. Charlie was better at squirreling his way around the truth. He'd had ample chances evading his father's wrath. Biz looked over to him with a trace of pleading. Charlie took over with casual confidence. "She *is* dating someone named Charlie. I've met him. He's a decent guy. But she made me keep it a secret because she doesn't want to jinx it. So leave it alone. Let her do her thing." Charlie looked over at Biz as she drew an imaginary zipper across her mouth. Georgia said, "Sounds fun. You'll have to tell us if it develops into something more."

Biz said, "Don't worry, I won't," and smiled broadly at her family.

Charlie added, "Coincidentally, I decided to start introducing myself around school as Charlie. I felt Choo was too *Mister Rogers,* so I'm trying Charlie on for size. I didn't tell you all because I didn't want to have to put up with the hazing."

E.J. said, "Things are tough enough at the chocolate factory, are they?"

"Case in point," said Charlie. "And yes, there are lots of Charlies at school. I've already met two others. I was even thinking for simplicity's sake that perhaps I should switch to Chet or Chaz, but Charlie's already stuck."

"What about Charo?" said E.J.

"Or Cheesey," said Georgia. "People like cheese."

Charlie ignored them both but Rah knew the way to her big brother's heart. "How about Chewie?" she said.

"I'd contemplated that," said Charlie, "but then I'd have to wear Biz's Chewbacca costume, and it gets wicked hot."

"Plus the shedding—" said Biz.

"And pesky stormtroopers," added E.J.

"Exactly," said Charlie.

Biz knew her moment of possible discovery had passed and felt emboldened. "And *I've* decided to be Biz. I thought Betsy might be fun, but I kept forgetting to use it when I met *all my new friends, Mom.*" She said it emphatically, with champagne bravery, turning her head toward Claire. "And by October I realized it was too late to change it again. So I'm Biz now." She punctuated her declaration with a raised glass and wide smile in hopes that this new tidbit would deflect from the original insinuation.

E.J. said, "I hear there's no biz like show biz."

"Honestly, will you please go die?" said Biz.

"Mo-om," E.J. said with mock affront.

"Enough," said Claire, unamused.

"Well done, everyone," said Grandpa Dun. "I couldn't be more proud of every last one of you. Let us raise a glass to doing your Thornden best." And with that he raised a glass to his handsome brood, and they responded enthusiastically, "To doing our Thornden best." Some rolled their eyes, some smirked at the mantra, but regardless, it was ingrained since childhood. Claire looked over at the only empty chair at the table. Les had slipped out of the room ten minutes before and had yet to return.

After the toast, Cat covered for her sister's embarrassment. "What about us, Father? Don't you want to hear how Claire and I moved the garden club's spring flower show venue? Or how Ned's latest textbook edit is coming along?"

Claire joined in. "We cleaned out your garage."

E.J. said, "You and Dad? Where is Dad?"

"No, me and Cat. I'm sure your father will return soon."

Everyone looked around. A few said, "Where's Les?" E.J. stage-whispered to his cousins, "We should do a shot every time someone says, 'Where's Les?'" They nodded and chuckled. Rah said, "Yeah, totally," to which all of her cousins chanted in unison, "'Yes,' not 'yeah'!" Rah blew the table a rousing raspberry, and any mounting tension floated into the ether.

Cat visibly relaxed now that Claire's third-degree session had passed. She knew Biz and Charlie were lying and probably spending loads of time together. But how much legitimate trouble could they honestly get into? Nothing would ever change the fact they weren't blood related. *Let Claire think what she wants,* she thought, *as long as my Choo feels like family.* That would always be Cat's chief priority.

"Fuck them," Biz said to Charlie as they hurled their duffel bags onto Amtrak's overhead luggage rack. "I fucking hate the scrutiny. How can they not trust us. We were twelve, for godssake." "Hey, pipe down," Charlie admonished. "There's no one here," Biz spat back. They'd made up a bullshit excuse about having to train back early in order to miss the dreaded carpool up to Boston with lecherous Georgia and her nattering friend. The Saturday-night-of-Thanksgiving train was pretty dead. Charlie stepped aside so Biz could have the window seat of the very last row of the last train car. Once settled, Charlie said, "Look, your mom is always going to be suspicious, probably because of that night. And my mom will be suspicious because she cheated on my dad, so she's predisposed to see it in others. Ignore them all." He lit a cigarette he knew they would share. Wordlessly, Biz took it from him and let a slipstream of smoke hover, trapped, over their heads like a forest mist.

Rah had sent them off with turkey sandwiches, Nutter Butters, and deviled eggs, of course, and two Sunkist sodas. Biz set out their late-night picnic, then pulled out a flask. "What's that?" asked Charlie.

"Tequila and OJ," Biz answered, and took a long swig, appearing relieved.

"Ugh," he said, and took the flask from her. "What are you, still fourteen?" His swig was shorter. He made a face. "You couldn't have pilfered the Macallan?"

"Who said I didn't?" she said with a wink, and took it back from him. "Trust me." Her lengthy pull took him aback.

"Whoa, Nellie," he said. Biz was determined to get drunk.

"What else are we going to do on this godforsaken five-hour ride?" Biz looked out the window. Her left leg jostled at the knee. She had a truckload of pent-up energy after being with her family for the weekend and wanted to cut loose a little. She was pissed at them and needed to remind herself she was in charge of her life and they could no longer tell her what to do. *I'm in college, for chrissake,* she thought. *I'm going to do what I want, live dangerously. Screw Mom's expectations.* Biz pressed PLAY on her Sony Walkman and turned it up so that "My Sharona" leaked from the headphones. She took another swig. "You know, I've never much liked the name Sharona, but I love this song. Should we dance? We're practically alone in here." She bopped her head and shimmied her shoulders—her hips jerked rhythmically as she closed her eyes, succumbing to the Knack's take-no-prisoners percussive engine. Charlie was concerned where her drinking might lead. She was a fun drunk, for sure, but sometimes her uninhibited streak led in dubious directions. "I brought cards," he said. "Let's play Rummy 500."

"Yay," she said, "deal," and cleaned up the waxed paper wrappers from their sandwiches.

"You're not really hanging out with Tindy, are you?" he asked.

"What do you think?"

"I didn't think so. And you're not really dating anyone, either." He shuffled the deck.

"Who says I'm not?"

"I say you're not. I can tell." He was pretty sure, but he was also bluffing. He couldn't really tell and wondered if he was losing her to the world, her independence, and herself.

"Can you?" Biz said, and stretched as she arched her back, then took another sip. She whipped her head back and forth in time to the music. *God, this song is sexy,* she thought. Ever since Biz had started to notice the attention her body was getting, she'd worked on honing its power for good. She was aware she turned heads—stunning in a healthy all-American way like the teens in a Sears catalogue or *Seventeen* magazine. She was tall, fit, and lean but not skinny or hungry-looking, with a shapely ass and legs like a Nordic athlete's. Her modest breasts looked fetching in a boy's Brooks Brothers oxford, where the middle button fastened at the beckoning of her cleavage. She was enjoying the new sexiness she transmitted to the world—that loose, powerful energy that made strangers bend to her will. Ornery waiters, DMV employees, and even humorless cops—no one was immune to her dimpled wiles. Charlie had always been like a brother or best friend to her; she wondered what he was to her now.

The overhead lights dimmed for the few deep sleeping passengers up front, and their train car took on a film noir vibe. Biz became drunker—and hornier—by the minute. The alcohol warmed her face as she arranged her cards. Three sixes and a short run of spades made her grin with promise. Annie Lennox sang to Biz, daring her with the lyrics, "Sweet dreams are made of this . . ." Biz adjusted the headphones so the music could overtake her, not caring that it was rude to Charlie. She let the song swallow her whole and her body became slippery. She misjudged her head's distance to the headrest. *Thwomp.* Charlie said, "You okay?" and she giggled, so he commandeered her flask. No way was he going to hold her hair back in that tiny stall bathroom—not on his watch, no way, not tonight. Charlie drained the flask so Biz couldn't have any more. *No matter,* she thought, and routed Grandpa Dun's Macallan out of her duffel. "Jesus!" he said, and took that from her, too. A longer string of giggles followed. "Let's focus on the game," he said, balancing a run of diamonds on his knee. Then, changing the subject, "Feels like some skittish guy in a trench coat will board next. Very Hitchcock. Or *High Anxiety.*"

"Whose cock?" Biz said, then placed her hand on Charlie's thigh. She ran it slowly up his inseam with a come-hither look. The tilt of her head told him she wasn't making a joke. He casually moved her hand onto her own thigh. "Very funny," he said. "Look, I'm not dumb. I've seen *Risky Business* like four times. But let's not be lazy. There are plenty of people out there in the world we're not related to—"

"But they aren't on this train," Biz said, discarding. Charlie was tall and gorgeous, irresistibly hot, his lower lip plump like a cherry. His jaw had grown to be square and strong like a man's, and the angled shape of his eyes hinted at Paul Newman's. Of course, she knew there were handsome guys roving around out there, but the ones she met weren't funny *and* smart. They didn't know how to play Gershwin *and* which fork to use. They didn't look out for her the way he always had. And they weren't sitting in front of her on a dark, sexy train. *Amtrak sexy?* She wanted to find out.

"There are at least six or seven other people in the world, besides me," Charlie mocked. "Including India and China adds another forty-seven." He was trying to keep her at a distance, but she'd tripped a wire in his body and set him on a dangerous trajectory. He tried desperately to refocus. "You should get out in the world, take a semester somewhere fun overseas."

"You don't mean that, do you?" Biz said, slightly hurt. She'd never been apart from Charlie and couldn't imagine a day without him near. "No, I don't," he replied, feeling similarly and weak. Panicking, he reached for the Macallan. He was powerless around her and becoming confused, sauced, and horny. A little exploratory play wouldn't be the end of the world. Biz put her cards facedown on her lap and pulled her Fair Isle sweater off over her head. Her button-down rode up on her torso, exposing her bare stomach and a trace of shiny, snow-white cotton-blend bra. Charlie reached forward and held down her shirttails. "What are you doing?" he said, conflicted as hell.

"I'm hot. Besides, no one can see us back here. Relax." Biz rolled the sweater into a ball and shoved it under her elbow.

"I'm relaxed," Charlie said with a trace of defensiveness.

"Are you?" Biz said, and locked in on his eyes for the first time since they'd taken their seats. Without breaking her grin, she reached for his thigh again, this time letting her fingers graze over his swelling bulge.

"What are you doing?" Charlie said, "People will think we're gross."

"People are uptight," said Biz. "Besides, no one is near us and no one else has to know. Freakin' Puritans trying to ruin

all our fun. It's none of their business and it doesn't count."
She allowed her middle finger to find the center seam on his
jeans. "Stop," said Charlie, but it was hardly a command. He
closed his eyes and leaned his dizzy head against the headrest.
"Stop," he repeated with hardly an audible breath. Biz took his
cards and the cigarette, enjoyed one last drag before snubbing it
out in the ashtray. The opening bass line of "Every Breath You
Take" could be heard strumming, small and tinny, from her
Walkman's headphones—one of Biz's make-out faves. "Blame it
on Sting," she said, sliding her hand over Charlie's. "Close your
eyes." And she raised his fingers and led them under her shirt.
She felt a bolt of electricity awaken her very depths. "Mmm,"
she uttered then, "remember, none of this counts." She whispered it again with a flick of her tongue on his ear and hot
breath that caused Charlie to softly groan. He felt his rational
mind slip away like a helium balloon—too late to grab the thin
string.

"Let's go for it," she whispered, and bit his lobe. "It'll be
fun. We can be somebody else."

"Who?" he uttered.

"Anybody. Anybody but us."

Charlie's rummy sets slipped off his legs and onto the floor
as they slouched down the Naugahyde banquette. His hands
glided over Biz's miraculous body as she undid his worn belt—
the leather slipping easily through the buckle. She wanted more
of him, all of him, and for him to find her below. Charlie understood this and reached up to grab his pea coat from the luggage
rack and drape it over them. Biz kissed him deeply, her head
floating above, their tongues dancing in dips and swirls. She
guided his hand to the elastic rim of her panties, then arched
her back and grazed her chest against his. He ran a finger over

the tiny bow, then ventured beneath, meeting her downy, dampening tide amongst her warm depths. The folds of her flower felt swollen and inviting. He felt at once welcome and wrong.

Charlie rested his head on her chest and tightened his already shut eyes to focus as he felt his universe pitch and build with the movement of her busy hand. He boiled under the woolen pea coat, tuning out the train's screech and rumble, all of them moving forward. Any brain matter still in his command he used to silence his own screams and keep his hand moving under her as she writhed. Sliding her jeans off her hips, Biz grabbed him as she came, moving her mouth into his neck to muffle her cries.

She bucked and the pea coat slipped off them onto the floor.

"I'm close," she whispered from heights unimaginable.

"Me, too," he said, and a bright chemical flood overtook them as they reached climax—Charlie cresting a high wave as it crashed and Biz gently tipped over a cliff. Tingles echoed as if fairies sprinkled pixie dust near her ears. She emitted a tiny squeak, like the wheel of a suitcase needing attention. She writhed slightly as Charlie released stiffly into her hand, and then she convulsed, aftershocks slackening her body, robbing her of her bones. "You're glistening," said Charlie, sitting up, slumped, legs akimbo. He was already trying to put out of his mind the electric glint in Biz's eye, trying to push aside the smell of her hair, perspiring skin, and wet depths. He aimed to banish the memory of her undulating hips and was grappling with the fact of their relation. But she was the most beautiful woman in the world at that moment, so the forgetting would have to wait.

"How did you get so skilled?" she panted.

"How did *you*?" Charlie asked, and Biz declined to answer. She looked at him in his sweaty disarray. "You look like you fell in a river." He cracked up and unearthed her sweater. He ran it behind his neck and forehead, then used it to clean himself off. "Yuck," she said, "you're definitely carrying it now."

"Then who's going to carry you?" he said. Biz broke into a grin. "Just give me an hour to regain consciousness."

He said, "Be my guest, take your time."

Biz and Charlie slipped into sleep, his was deeper than hers. Then after a while they stretched, moaned, and salvaged what was left of Gin Rummy. The train finally slowed to its jogging pace, and the PA speaker cracked with information. Charlie took down their duffel bags as Biz pulled the rest of her ponytail out of its holder. The last sun-kissed wisps freed themselves from the elastic's bondage, slipping out to dance and play around her flushed cheeks. There were no raccoon circles of mascara to wipe away, no errant crusts of lip liner to dab. Her pale seafoam eyes were vivid and awake, barely containing their spark. She was a natural beauty, a study in offhanded dishevelment—a mess and ablaze all at once. She looked like a European model on her day off, or a woman who'd recently achieved orgasm.

Biz and Charlie suppressed their chuckling until after thanking the platform conductor. The postmidnight air was crisp and shocked them out of their haze. Even so, they shared the exhausted smug laugh of movie cowboy bandits. *Butch and Sundance ain't got nothin' on us.* Biz was already plotting their next time and summed things up, "That was fun!" *What a bitchin' way to pass the time.* She wobbled as she walked. Charlie, however, was far less drunk and, without a doubt, much more confused.

In the morning, he woke from a dream they'd poured themselves into a cab and wound their way back to his dorm room. There, they had fantastic sex until the sky lightened through broken blinds. A fuzz-coated tongue, however, ruined it. The sensation of an ice pick jiggling its way into his skull put a damper on his reminiscing. But there was something else disconcerting about this preconscious landscape. "Hello?" Charlie attempted tentatively to the empty room. His voice was groggy as he groped for the bottle of Tylenol he kept on the floor. While feeling around he came across a girl's barrette. *Had it been there the whole time? Was it Biz's?* She could have dropped it weeks ago. He wished he could think.

As his head cleared, Charlie noticed foreign items dotting the landscape—stacks of books and VHS tapes, deodorant on the other dresser. A bespectacled mop of hair in a grubby bathrobe holding a towel, spoke in a round voice at odds with his lanky body. "I introduced myself last night, but I highly doubt you remember. I'm Foster Barnstock," he said eloquently, extending his hand. "And you're Charlie Muir."

With effort, Charlie reached out. "I am," he rasped as if he'd been chain-smoking filterless Camels since early childhood.

"I'm your new roommate. Please forgive the cramp I'll be putting in your style. Thought I'd settle in early."

"Oh, right. You have mono."

"I did. Past tense. I'm fit as a fiddle now. Your sister dropped off your dopp kit earlier this morning."

"My sister?" Charlie livened up. Had Biz slept over? Ow, his head hurt. "What time is it?"

"One P.M. The blonde."

"Georgia? She must have taken an early train. She's my evil stepsister."

"Evidence to the contrary," Foster stated as if in a courtroom. "She was charming. She also ran her fingers through your hair while you were sleeping." Charlie thought, *Jesus, Georgia. What the hell?* He also thought, *Who says "charming"?*

Foster sat down at the wobbly alcove desk, booting up what looked to be a cube-shaped, school library computer. Charlie managed to prop himself onto his elbows, but that was all the height he'd be able to muster. The room started to spin. Foster said, "She told me you're a weirdo."

"Yeah, well. Consider the source."

"Noted," Foster called over his shoulder. Charlie remained in bed, trying to piece together the end of the night, the part after the train. They finished all the booze. Did they buy more on the corner? One of them might have thrown up on a shrub outside. Foster spoke again without turning around in his chair. "Your other friend, Liz, called and said to call her when you woke up." There was a long pause that hung in the air. Charlie forgot to say "Okay" out loud. At last Foster spoke again. "Welcome home."

"Uh, yeah," Charlie said, and thought he sensed Foster smirking.

Back at her dorm room, Biz's body jerked awake to Charlie's imagined touch. *What a night!* she thought and jumped up, thankful she didn't get hangovers. She was psyched they'd messed around and knew he wouldn't want to discuss it, which made her feel weightless and invincible—like a lady ninja. It was as if her body had been reset and now her brain was ready to hit the books. Heading to the showers, Biz searched for songs with "train" in the lyrics. "Just a small town girl, living in a lonely wor-orld . . ." had her written all over it. "Last Train to Clarksville," "Crazy Train," and "Midnight Train to Georgia" worked, too. Once her songs ran out, she was left with the realization; *We should definitely try harder to meet other people.* But where were the interesting guys? The ones who had an actual sense of humor? The ones who were independent thinkers? The punk dudes Biz met were good in bed but hadn't grown up with table manners. The baseball cap dudes would fit in in Larkspur but were mostly bone-headed jocks. It seemed like everyone relied on sarcasm in lieu of intelligence and wit. *That's not a sense of humor, it's just lazy and mean.* "Kiss a lot of frogs, kiddos," instructed Nana Miggs. Biz would kiss frogs for as long as she had to. In the meantime, she had Charlie.

Charlie tried to focus on school, but he was distracted by Sissy Bickers. She promised if they were still seeing each other in the summer she would finally "give herself to him." He tried not to think of the train episode as cheating—*it didn't count*, he repeated like a mantra. Then he suffered through a string of winter road-trip weekends by rounding second base with Sissy over and over. Biz said, "Gag me with a spoon," when he told her. The other women he met in Boston wore so much makeup and teased their bangs so high that he worried they would ignite if he lit a cigarette. The rubber-bracelets-and-ripped-fishnets-like-Madonna thing wasn't doing much for him. The preppy girls, the ones dedicated to embodying the "good girl" ethos left over from the fifties, were so repressed he rarely bothered trying to seduce them. What was the point? If they were that self-conscious about making out, he reasoned, it was unlikely they'd be fun in bed.

By mid-May all the grandkids were cleared out of their dorms and headed back to Larkspur. Soon they would be scattered, working the summer jobs they'd acquired by way of familial connections. Charlie would head to the Jersey Shore to work as a sail-racing instructor at Plover Point Yacht Club's competitive sports day camp. Biz would move into a four-way, two-bedroom share on the Upper East Side and intern at Sotheby's. But for two weeks before their jobs began they were all together in Larkspur, planning Rah's big graduation party combined with the annual Thornden Memorial Day Weekend family barbecue.

The cousins crisscrossed each other with wheelbarrows in the backyard like sweaty Smurfs in a Smurf village. Biz carried hoses to spray down the screens while Rah repaired broken garden lattice. Charlie spread mulch under the peonies and roses while E.J. was on pool cover duty—they all had their jobs, knew what to do. Billy Joel's *Piano Man* album blasted from the outdoor speakers, and one of Rah's jobs was to move the needle back to the beginning of the record each time it ended.

Claire stepped outside onto the patio and surveyed the activity. "It's coming along, kids," she said, then sent Georgia and Charlie out to the shed to get the trampoline mats. "Grilled cheese sandwiches in ten minutes, everyone," she hollered as she headed back inside. Georgia and Charlie walked toward the shed, which housed all the yard equipment in addition to the Ping-Pong table. Georgia said, "Would it kill your mom to say 'thank you,' like, ever?"

Charlie said, "Yes, actually. Her doctor told her she needed to cut down on gratitude because it was compromising her health. I think she's down to one 'thank you' per year."

"You must be relieved."

"We are. It was touch and go for a while." Charlie smirked, but Georgia was still miffed. He continued, "Look, I'm with you. I rarely hear either Mom or Aunt Claire say 'thank you' or 'I'm sorry,' but they're liberal with the 'love yous,' so that's something."

Georgia offered a limp grin. "I guess one out of three ain't bad."

"That's the spirit," Charlie said, and set a ladder in place just below the shed's rafters. "I'll hand them down to you. Watch for crap falling in your eyes." Georgia watched her stepbrother's strong, well-defined arms reach out above her, and Charlie could feel her eyes on him—he always had, ever since she moved in.

Charlie was ten when his mom first married Ned, who brought his eleven-year-old daughter, Georgia, to live with them. Button-nosed with a blond ponytail, Georgia never said much when she wasn't crying. Charlie remembered collecting Wacky Packs and water pistols while Georgia read Judy Blume and slammed doors. His mom told him and Rah to be friendly, yet keep a respectful distance—she was "going through a lot" and needed "space." They even gave Georgia her own room. But though Charlie was in his world at school and Georgia was in hers, and long before he was aware of the attention he was getting for his good looks, he was aware of Georgia's eyes on him.

"Seeing anyone up in Boston?" she asked. Strands from her ponytail had fallen around her face and attached themselves, sticky, to her long neck.

"Nope," said Charlie, and handed her down another trampoline mat.

"Is that code for 'None of your beeswax'?"

"Yup."

"I've been meaning to ask: Are you gay? Someone who saw you in a family photo in my dorm room wanted to know. I said I was pretty sure you weren't." Charlie exhaled to end the line of questioning. He was pissed that just because he didn't talk about women the way E.J. did, or treat them like the jackasses at school did, people thought he must be gay. Georgia said, "Okay, fine. Seeing a lot of Bizzy? Or Biz, as we're supposed to call her now." Charlie shook his head. He wanted to abandon this chore; he could see she wasn't going to let up. Charlie said, "Yeah, we hang. Don't know if you'd call it a lot, but sure."

"How come you and I don't hang?"

"Get the wheelbarrow over there and stack them up. Uh, I don't know. Because you're a pain in the ass? Because your school is way the hell outside of town? Are you ever in the city?"

"Sometimes," Georgia said.

"Well, look me up. Okay, that's all of them." Charlie climbed down off the ladder and carried it over to where it lived in the darker recesses of the shed near the snow shovels. When he turned back, Georgia was standing behind him. "Uh," he said. He hadn't heard her creep up. She grabbed onto the rake to one side of him and the shovel on the other. "Hi," she said.

"What?" he replied. It didn't occur to him what she was trying to do, until it did.

"You know we're not really related," Georgia said. She tried to sound matter-of-fact. He looked down at her with a mix of incredulity and annoyance. He was hoping his overt disinterest would exempt him from having to speak the words he resented having to say aloud. But Georgia didn't budge, nor did it appear she was going to anytime soon. "I'm aware," he said. "*What the hell* are you *doing?*"

"Well, I thought that if you and Biz are no longer, you know, we could—"

"Are you fucking *kidding me*?!" Charlie pushed past her with unleashed anger. "Unbelievable. I'm outta here." He picked up the wheelbarrow and marched out the door. Someone yelled, "Grilled cheese!" in the distance.

.   .   .

As soon as the Thornden grandkids were old enough to carry a bag of ice they were expected to work the parties. Cat and Claire brought them up to understand that a party wasn't for the hosts to enjoy per se, but a present one gives to friends. There were usually three or four staff hired from the local golf club to serve food and clean up, but the grandchildren knew they needed to be working all day through dessert and coffee, then could punch out until cleanup time. The cousins didn't exactly dread it—it was fun to see all their friends—but they didn't exactly get to partake wholeheartedly, either. It was exhausting work, and they had to wait to join the drunken trampoline jumping until very late in the evening when they made up for lost time with a vengeance.

There were incidents of late-night cousins misbehavior, some publicly witnessed, some not. Loud splashes indicated falls or pushes fully clothed into the pool. They'd been left unattended for hours near open bars and leftover beers, which they began stealing and drinking around age ten or eleven. Georgia was prone to rounding the bases in dark recesses with blond boys and Rah could usually be found passed out in the shed. Charlie was susceptible to bursts of temper and fights with E.J. were common, but Biz could usually defuse them before she, too, threw up. Then Charlie would take care of Biz by fishing her out of the shallow end, finding her some dry clothes, and tossing her wet ones into the dryer.

Eventually, the stereo was switched off and the porch floodlights on. Anyone who didn't live under one of the two roofs was shooed home. It was about this time that Charlie caught Biz's eye and wandered over to where she was sitting on the edge of the deep end with Rah, dangling her bare feet in the aqua water lit luminescent from below. "Klat ot deen," Charlie said to Biz, who quietly responded, "Gnop-gnip." She drew her wrinkled toes up out of the water and headed toward the Ping-Pong shed. "You guys are so weird," said Rah, then rolled onto the cement and looked up at the stars, nearing sleep.

They were both pretty drunk—Biz more so than Charlie—but neither of them was approaching wasted yet. They nested the empty plastic cups and found two sandpaper paddles wedged between the duct-taped cushions of the retired rickety wicker couch. "There's some shit going down I have to tell you," said Charlie without levity. He sent a ball over the net to Biz, who returned it.

"Okay, then, spill the down-going shit," Biz said, serving.

"Georgie . . ."

"Yeeessss . . . ," Biz responded, already exasperated. Georgia was known to pull all sorts of stunts, few of which interested her.

"She, uh."

"She what?"

"She, um. She sort of cornered me," Charlie said, then made a pained, squinty-eyed grimace. Biz caught the ball and put the tip of her paddle down on the table. She put her other hand on her hip. "In what way . . ."

"In *that* way."

"Oh, brother," Biz said, letting go a hearty laugh. "Are you fucking kidding me?"

"It's not funny!" pleaded Charlie. "She said we weren't *really* related!"

"Is she *crazy*?" Biz served again, half chuckling but also irked.

"Uh, no more than we are."

"Oh, come on. You can't compare that to us. *We're not serious!*"

"Maybe she's not, either," Charlie countered, playing devil's advocate.

Biz said, "How far did she get with you?"

"Are you *joking*? I shot her down. Jesus."

"She can be persistent. I've seen her in action."

"So have I. Thank God I'm taller than she is." Charlie shook off the thought, and served. Biz waited until the end of the next volley, then asked casually, "Did you want to?" She was nervous about the answer and embarrassed by feeling threatened.

"*No!* Christ. Do you even *know me*?"

Biz aced her serve. "Yeah, I do," she said with a raised brow.

They hit back and forth with the ease and grace of people born to a community of roomy basements and garages—grand old homes with former studies and libraries that now housed foosball, pool tables, and Ping-Pong. Charlie and Biz continued this way, both lost in their own take on the situation, not wanting to keep score, but not wanting to lose their connection. The sound of the ball was mesmerizing enough that neither noticed E.J. in the doorway carrying an armload of tiki torches.

"Jesus, you two, why don't you get a room."

"Fuck off," they responded in unplanned unison.

"Oh my God, listen to you two, you're like *Children of the Corn,* thinking each other's thoughts."

Biz said, "Can you tell what we're thinking now?"

"That you're disgusting?" said E.J. as he turned to leave.

Charlie called after him, "That you're a *tedious blowhard*!" But he was gone.

Biz and Charlie resumed play. Finally Biz said, "We need to meet other people for real. We need to date."

"Sounds like a pain in the ass."

"Doesn't have to be. I'm not suggesting we marry the first people we date, we just need to get some distance. And it'll shut them all up and get them off our backs." Charlie took his time answering. Biz knew better than to fill the silence with verbal drivel and let him say what he needed to say. "It's just that it probably won't work," Charlie said. "There's no one like you." They'd been saying this to each other since they first watched *The Wizard of Oz* when they were small. Bizzy had mangled Dorothy's famous line, saying, "There's no one like home," then Charlie mangled it further, "There's no one like you." He'd intoned it a few times absentmindedly as they grasped hands and spun in circles, falling dizzy on the rug in a fit of squeals. "There's no place like home" meant the same thing to them because, they were each other's home.

Biz smiled, knowing it took a lot for Charlie to say that out loud. "I know, my friend. There's no one like you, too." She suggested Sissy Bickers for his date, but he vetoed her for obvious reasons. "What about Piper? I think she's going to be a live-in mother's helper down in Plover Point for the Huntingtons this summer."

"Seriously? She's a nightmare."

"With a killer bod. Give her a chance. And I'll give the douchebags on the Upper East Side a chance." Biz aced Charlie again and raised her arms in a V-for-victory à la Nadia Comaneci, repeating the stance to each corner of the shed. He cracked up. "God help the douchebags," he said, hoping Biz wouldn't fall in love with one of them and possibly and quietly break his heart. The thought of handing her over to some random dude who might not appreciate her made him uneasy and he ached with dread. The ball bounced under the table and they both chased it down in a mad scramble, ending in wincing laughter. Charlie tried to wrench it from Biz's formidable grip. Their heads were close and they could smell one another's sweat from the long day. Charlie leaned in and kissed her. She was surprised, but pleasantly so. Biz leaned in, too, and parted her lips, beckoning his tongue to mingle. Charlie opened his mouth, unable to resist her. They were just losing themselves when Ned's voice boomed from the doorway.

"*Georgia!*" he called out. His voice seemed agitated.

Biz answered, "It's us, Uncle Ned! Biz and Charlie, we're in a tie-breaker!" They emerged from under the table wishing they hadn't at the same time. Biz thrust the ball into the air. "We found it!"

Ned hesitated. "What's going . . . on? You two were told to . . . uh, not . . ."

Charlie interrupted his stepdad. "We were just looking for—"

"Of course, kids. I'm sorry," said Ned, pretending he didn't mean what he'd clearly implied. "Have either of you seen Georgia?"

"Check the rec room," said Biz. "They were watching *Stripes.*"

"Okay, kids, two minutes to wrap it up. Your mom's trying to put this day to bed."

"Okay, thanks, Ned. We will," said Charlie, but his stepdad was already gone. None of them believed for a second Georgia was watching *Stripes.*

Biz looked forward to her summer internship and hoped to learn a thing or two at Sotheby's. She'd *really* wanted to intern for a famous theater costumer or infamous designer for drag queens, but fine art was what fell into place because fine art is what Claire wanted. Sadly, Claire had no Thornden connections to drag queens. Charlie planned to immerse himself in his sailing job during the day and do puzzles with his grandparents and edit his screenplay at night. He'd live with Grandpa Dun and Nana Miggs in their rambling weatherworn beach house in Plover Point, the charming Jersey Shore town on the edge of quiet Tern Bay.

Charlie had a routine. After ensuring all his campers had safely sailed in and unrigged their boats, he would amble up to the beach to bodysurf and read. Piper was usually there, overseeing the Huntington kids about thirty feet away. Each time he spied her squeezing lemon juice into her big loopy curls, or rubbing Bain de Soleil on her tan, flat tummy, he tried to dismiss the possibility that she had a sweet side. But then she would apply zinc oxide to the little ones' sunburned noses or lift the youngest by his wrists over the waves, and a softness was revealed as if it had been there all along. Charlie told himself to ignore her. He used to squirm every time Piper teased Biz when they were little. He wanted to stick up for Biz and kick Piper in the shins, but she seemed so powerful and cruel. Now that they were older, Biz was able to hold her own, and Charlie was taller and no longer afraid. Piper could still be intimidating, but Charlie could spin it as confidence. He liked strong women and was fascinated by her vulnerability. It reminded him of a movie—actually, every movie ever made.

One sunny postcard afternoon, a Frisbee clipped Charlie's shoulder, and Piper jogged over to retrieve it. "Filthy beasts," she said to Charlie with a demure smile. She felt he'd recently become an undeniable fox. He looked up to see her freckled face crowned by a mane of salty hair. Each mustered a "Hi," which was the only nudge they needed. Charlie's grand plan of puzzles and biographies fizzled; he decided to heed Biz's advice. Piper used to mother's-helper alongside Biz and missed having a friend to boss around. So, the two formed an unlikely alliance as new partners in crime and filled the vacant space Biz left in both their summers. Before long they were gliding around town at night on their bikes, barefoot and no-handed, avoiding cops and looking for trouble.

One moonless Saturday evening at the beach, Piper and Charlie sat up against snow fencing, long after the others had gone to forage for loose beers. The gentle breeze picked up a slight chill off the ocean. Piper rubbed her arms, and Charlie lent her his college sweatshirt. "I see chivalry isn't dead," she said, pulling it over her head. "Not dead yet," Charlie said in the sing-song reply from the "bring out your dead" scene in *Monty Python and the Holy Grail*. Piper looked flummoxed, a gentle reminder she was no replacement for Biz. As thanks, Piper leaned in slightly with a pucker. Charlie hesitated; he hoped she wasn't messing with him, but Piper cocked her head slightly and met him head-on. She softened her lips and kissed him, pulling back slowly. He waited, but no snarky commentary followed, then she remained, still willing. He thought of Biz, who'd told him to explore his options, Piper chief among them. He moved in for another kiss. This time when their lips met, she pressed into him and he into her. Charlie's cock woke up, desire flooded his brain, and all thoughts of Biz dispersed. Then his head whirled and body ignited—everyone else ceased to matter.

At midnight, ankle-high waves crept in. Their friends never returned, nor did any distractions. They made out for hours until the sky lightened and their jeans became damp with dew. Over the next two weeks, Charlie and Piper moved through the bases, sneaking up to the beach and under porches where broken bikes went to die. During the day, Piper treated him with teasing and detachment. Charlie tried his banter but it fell flat. At night, however, she locked in on him once again with the heat of the day's sunburn radiating off their skin, and hormones stirring the salty air between them. They necked and grinded in tucked-away places until Piper's chin was pink and rough from Charlie's stubble. Eventually they would both come, leaving them weak-kneed and dizzy—and Charlie with a dark wet mark on the front of his jeans, which he covered while pedaling home.

One night at high tide, Charlie and Piper lay on a towel under an overturned lifeguard boat near the dunes. She took his hand and moved it under her skirt, parting her legs slightly, beckoning him to explore. As he discovered her downy wetness, she cooed a low moan. Nothing in her body language suggested he stop. Charlie's head nearly spun off his spine and his brain began the task of shutting down. *Is this going to happen? Here and now—with Piper?!* Before he could wonder further, she told him to enter. Fumbling, he slipped inside her, almost climaxing too soon. "Shhhh," Piper calmed him, emitting a longer, louder "mmm." It occurred to Charlie she gave directions with ease and seemed well rehearsed, but he decided not to care. He was ready for whatever experience came next. He liked that she was willing to take the reins. And Piper liked that her hunch about Charlie Muir's anatomy was more than she'd even imagined.

Their sounds were absorbed by the boat's wooden hull as the waves crashed loudly nearby. Charlie had no earthly idea what to expect, though he'd dreamed about this moment for years. In the darkness, he closed his eyes without needing to, moved his hips without rational thought. He hoped his erection was enough for Piper as she wrapped herself around him tighter. In under a minute he was overtaken by a blast, like a rocket exploding from the inside. Then there were tremors and panting, exhaustion and sweat. Charlie had come and it was over.

His virginity was jettisoned in a swift minute of ecstasy, and now Charlie was extremely tired. Slowly returning to consciousness, he noticed Piper's hand. It was still circling under her skirt as she undulated. He offered to help in any way he could for her middling finale but she said, "It's fine, thanks" and carried on without him. Charlie was shocked and excited to see a real woman masturbating—she looked confident and relaxed in her approach. It also kept his mind off his poor performance. Mercifully, her words interrupted his ego's spiral. "It'll get better," Piper panted once she'd finished herself off. "Usually does," he heard her say as he fought sleep. Their heavy breathing created a cramped sauna under the boat, and Piper's quaking helped Charlie feel accomplished. Next time, he knew, he should try to last longer; he'd call a friend or ask his roommate. Piper used Charlie's boxers to wipe herself, then untwisted her underpants and skirt. She'd trained at least one boyfriend before. Charlie Muir was totally worth the effort.

Charlie was a willing student—improving slowly but surely—and wished the summer to last forever. Piper was pleased with his progress and ability to take direction, but "forever" turned out to be three more weeks. Then she dumped him for Robbie Dodd, her regular summer fling, just back from eight weeks at Outward Bound. Charlie was blindsided, felled by rejection and shame; his shoulders slumped and eyes dimmed. He spent his lunch breaks at a pay phone calling Biz, who nursed him through his heartbreak from Manhattan. She suggested he write Sissy Bickers to distract him, but he'd been ruined by Piper's voracity. Her willingness to screw any time, anywhere had ruined him, so instead, he chose to wallow. From here on out, he decided just before Labor Day, it would be only girls who didn't need convincing. He'd only ask out girls who wanted *that* feeling—girls who actually liked sex.

Biz spent her days at Sotheby's outside picking up lunch orders and dropping off catalogues. It wasn't intellectually taxing or creatively rewarding but looked impressive on her résumé, according to Claire. She'd sketch her absurd costume ideas during breaks and hobnob with the other interns after work—well-connected sorority types partial to button-down bars like J. G. Melon's and P. J. Clarke's. It was there she met a steady stream of Wall Street clones from J. P Morgan and Bear Stearns—predictably attractive and well-groomed young men boasting athlete's bodies and toothy smiles. They were full of themselves to distraction like some fraternal scrum of mutual admiration. For every three guys who bought her a drink, only one asked, "Where do you work?" And only seldom might he follow up with the uninspired "Where do you go to school?" This was usually the point at which his curiosity peaked. Any forthcoming original thoughts were cauterized by beer. They were too invested in their pecking order to get to know her. With three roommates living in her share, any guy had to be worthy of introductions in the morning over buttered toast. And he had to be good in bed, which meant generous and creative, and none of these guys seemed either. So Biz started slipping out before the second round of shots and stopping off at the corner bar near her building.

Mongey's was an Irish pub dwarfed in shadows as the city built up around it over decades. There were yellowing laminated team plaques nailed to the wall and paper shamrock decorations left up year-round. Biz ordered a Macallan's whisky from atop a worn varnished stool. It was Grandpa Dun's drink, and she thought she'd try it on the rocks with a twist. It smarted as a prickly flame briefly engulfed her chest, so she shook the ice, hoping it would become smoother. The bartender was a short Irish lad in a black collared shirt with piercing summer-sky-blue eyes. As she licked her finger, she caught him looking. He quickly glanced away. He had the unattended teeth of Ireland's middle class, a thick brogue, and jet-black hair. He joked easily with the regulars and made them feel less grizzled. She wondered if he was smart and/or single.

Biz sat quietly, sketching her oddball designs—a three-piece suit made of Astroturf, a strapless chenille gown—and was intrigued that he left her alone. She drank half her scotch, left a dollar before she left. They did this dance for a full week.

The bartender knew from years at the job that this dimpled beauty was trouble. He knew he represented a way to get back at her parents, a dalliance, which never ended well. She was exciting, persistent, and subtly intoxicating—the easy confluence of privileged America. He was witty and street smart but sorely undereducated—too sweet, and his heart too vulnerable.

Biz sat opposite the glass-washing sink, on the eighth night trapping him in front of her. "You're going to make me guess your name, aren't you?" she asked.

"I'm not going to make you do anything," he said without smiling. But she'd seen his eyes gleam when he threw his head back to laugh.

"I'm Biz. Short for Elizabeth," she said, and waited. "Now, I know your mother taught you better manners."

"Hello, Elizabeth," he said meeting her eyes for a half second.

"Biz is fine," she countered, but he said nothing.

"And your name is . . . Paddy." He rolled his eyes.

"Danny." He shook his head.

"Juan Carlos? Mohit? Kareem? It's Kareem." He exhaled, exasperated.

"This is painful," he said, looking away, trying not to grin.

"Oh, I can do this all night."

"Why is that? Don't you have to get up in the morning?"

"I have relaxed hours. My boss is the daughter of my grand-father's college roommate."

"Of course she is."

"Francis, Finnbar, John-Patrick, Sean-Patrick, Patrick Michael McPatrick O'Finnigan."

"You're hilarious. Now go home. It's past your bedtime."

"I'll leave when you tell me your name." Biz looked right at him with her seafoam eyes. His brogue was killing her, but she tried to hide it. She'd removed two barrettes from either side of her hair earlier, and it fell thick and dark, cascading around her shoulders. She tucked a healthy chunk behind her ear and grinned.

He said, "How about I tell you my name and you pick an-other bar to write in your diary and nurse your half-empty glass of whisky."

Biz slid sideways onto one elbow, anchoring herself to the bar. "It's not a diary. It's a sketchbook."

"What do you sketch?"

"Crazy clothes and bespoke costumes. I call it my Outlandish Couture line."

"Fine," he said. "It's Finn. I've got to keep moving."

Biz got up off her elbow and smiled. "Fine. And it's half full. G'night, Finn," was all she said as she grabbed her purse. This time she left him two dollars.

It didn't take Biz long to win Finn over, though longer than she expected. She would utter wry commentary under her breath when he had a particularly challenging exchange with a customer. She stayed until closing one Friday night and asked him to walk her home. He acquiesced, knowing there was no point refusing. "You're the kind of girl who doesn't hear 'no' a lot, aren't ya?"

Biz looked over her shoulder and said, "Who, me?"

"You've got nerve."

"I've got pluck."

"Is that what they're calling it these days?" Finn grabbed his keys, hit the lights, and gave in. Her dimple carried him to the door.

Biz and Finn circled her neighborhood, chatting for forty-five minutes before arriving across the street from her apartment— three doors down from Mongey's. When he realized what she'd done, he said, "Are you daft, woman? You must be joking!" Biz looked him straight in the eye, the streetlight adding to her glimmer. "Do I look like I'm joking?" she whispered, then gazed at his sky-blue eyes.

Finn O'Donoghue looked into Biz Thornden Chadwick's sage-green eyes for a very long time and sighed. He was weighing the pros and cons of his next move. His final thought was *For fuck's sake, it's summer*; then he kissed her. Biz backed away slowly and took him by the collar. She tugged him into the dark alley and pulled him in so their hips aligned, hungry for the connection she'd been craving since Charlie. Shock waves warmed her nethers as she felt a firmness at her thigh. Finn answered her with his own wordless appetite. He'd been in the States for a year and a half and had yet to meet anyone fun. Up until now he'd only met "ninnies" or divorcées, sloshed and slurring. His focus was to earn money and stay under the immigration radar; everything else was a calculable distraction. "Elizabeth, maybe we shouldn't . . ." but Biz didn't let him finish. She liked the way he called her Elizabeth, and the way he kissed. She liked his starkly pale skin. Where she came from everyone was tan.

Finn moved his hands onto and over her, tracing the body he'd wondered about for weeks. She let him discover her, then lifted up her skirt. They had an incredibly hot four minutes, Biz leaning against a brick wall. Finn filled her up and her mind flooded with chemicals. *Things can only go up from here—especially on a bed*, she thought. "Was that meant to happen?" he asked. "Oh, yes," she answered, adjusting. If he was the kind to kiss and tell, his divulgences would have no bearing. Their social paths would never cross, and his stories would never reach Charlie. Finn O'Rourke O'Malley was Biz's calculable distraction. He would be her summer fling—*this will do nicely.*

Three times a week they met at her apartment during her lunch break and before his shift started. It was a heavenly way to pass the summer, and her roommates never caught on. But over time he became clingy, broodish, and less adventurous. He left too many messages on her answering machine. She could tell he was dreaming of a green card and chubby babies like his friends had back in Ireland. Biz wanted kids, but no time soon, and definitely not with Finn. When Labor Day came, she was relieved and gave him a fake university name. She knew he'd never look it up at the library. She wished him well and told him she'd be in Florence all fall on an art history expedition.

"Don't try to write," she told him.

"Because Italians have no postal service?"

"Not with all the religious holidays, and strikes."

Then she kissed him sweetly, leaving him bereft in her wake. She didn't mean to be cruel, but he wouldn't accept it would have never worked out. She wouldn't be having babies until her thirties, she reasoned. And marriage was a long way off, and wasn't summer all about fun? She knew Finn would hold a torch for her for weeks.

On Labor Day weekend Charlie and Biz stood next to each other, scraping layers of charred seafood off the grill. It was time for their end-of-the-summer intimate family beach house barbecue—twenty expected for a sit-down dinner. They hadn't seen each other since Memorial Day Weekend; this was the longest they'd ever been apart. Biz nudged Charlie. "I've been dying to ask, but I wanted to wait until I saw you in person. How was the sex?" Her eyes flashed, curious. "Piper any fun in bed?" Charlie remained silent, still nursing his wounds. "Was it quick? Is she on the pill? Did she orgasm?"

"I'm not answering you," Charlie cut her off. He'd been dreading this line of questioning, anxious to know if he'd feel differently about Biz, now that he'd been with Piper. He'd hoped the distance would make him not want her. Just the opposite, he wanted her more. And probably loved her, but didn't dare say it.

Biz spoke in a low voice out of the side of her mouth. "Those long legs must be good for something. I heard from Putty Gringham that last week Piper and Robbie—"

"Knock it off," he said, the wound still fresh.

"Ooooh. You in luuuv?" She drew out the word "love" like an obnoxious schoolyard kid. Charlie hated himself for feeling used and wanted to gently throttle Biz. But the sky was a bright expanse of blue that day and lit Biz's green eyes from within. Her golden skin made her teeth all the brighter, and her dimple just made him angry.

"What about *you*?" Charlie shot back. "Sleeping your way through all the douchebags on the Upper East Side couldn't have been easy." His eyes crackled with vengeance; the outburst surprised her.

"It was only one douchebag, and he was actually nice. You'd have liked him."

"I'd rather not meet him, thanks."

"You won't. Past tense. He's not our kind, dear." Biz allowed for a measure of quiet. "Hey, I'll stop. I was only kidding. It's Piper's loss," she said sweetly, and bumped his shoulder. "There's still no one like you," she whispered. Charlie tried to shove his feelings for Biz in a box.

E.J. walked toward them with a stack of folding chairs. "Hey, Jan and Peter, why the long faces?"

"Toidi," Biz said to Charlie in their secret language. "None of your beeswax. We're fine," she told E.J., but he called them out on their bullshit. "No, you're not. I sense a rift." He slowed to examine them. "You're not your usual Captain and Tennille selves."

"Get lost," said Charlie, and shot E.J. a look. E.J. went after his sister. "You jealous of Piper? Lovers' spat? Has he heard about the losers you screwed?"

"Fuck off," said Biz.

"Yeah, really. Fuck off," added Charlie.

Cat wandered up and sensed tension. "Everything ducky here, kids?" E.J. exhaled a loose puff of air and walked away. Over his shoulder he called back, "Hey, geniuses, it's 'yes,' not 'yeah.' You've got four hours to get it straight before Grandpa Dun annihilates you."

Cat zeroed in on her son, Charlie; she remembered her idea that might brighten his mood. "Hey, you two, if there's someone either of you are dating, why don't you invite them home for Fall Festival? There will be plenty of room, and it would be fun to see a few new faces—give Grandpa Dun some fresh meat to interrogate." It would also afford herself, she was well aware, some welcome peace of mind about those two.

The Firth Fall Festival was a big deal in their community, and the Thornden clan had been going for generations. Family activities sprang up all over town, creating a magical, olde-timey Brigadoon. Carnival games, petting zoo, pie baking contest—it was *Little House on the Prairie* without the bonnets. After the Twilight Dance, everyone always slept over at Nana Miggs and Grandpa Dun's. In the morning they enjoyed pancakes in their pajamas. "Sounds great, Mom, thanks," said Charlie. "We'll try." Cat waited a brief moment for her son to make eye contact, but when he didn't she thought better of pushing him and went on her way.

Charlie turned to Biz once his mom had gone. "I'm so done being treated like some creepy V. C. Andrews duo. It's like they're looking for it now, or pretending not to. Who the hell are we going to invite out for the weekend just to prove we're not screwing? Piper is still with Robbie—no fucking surprise. Are you going to invite your Morgan Stanley guy from the summer?"

"He wasn't that kind of . . . No, I'm not. Listen, let's do what we talked about. This'll be fun. It'll be like *The Dating*

Game but with a finish line. We can help each other find someone." She knew Charlie better than anyone and would have a keen sense of who he'd click with. She also knew he had her best interests at heart.

Charlie exhaled. "I hate games."

"Please don't be cranky. You're less handsome when you're cranky."

"Oh, God."

"You love to play Othello and backgammon. This'll be like a totally bitchin' elaborate game of backgammon."

"Will it?" He looked unconvinced.

"No. Not really." Biz beamed. Charlie broke into a grin. "Yeah, I didn't think so." His Crest toothpaste smile dazzled Biz even when he wasn't trying. His bangs were thick and slightly shaggy in a movie-actorly way. She fought the urge to reach out and tuck a loose brown wave behind his ear. She still found him achingly attractive.

"There ya go, cowboy. At least you're handsome again."

"Thank goodness," he kidded. "That's all that matters."

Back at school for their sophomore year, Biz met Charlie at his dorm before heading over to the Wreck Room, the official unofficial campus bar.

"Hey, Foster," she said, plopping onto Charlie's bed. "How'd you end up with Charlie again?" Foster deadpanned, "Just lucky, I guess." He was on his square beige personal computer, the kind that Biz had only seen in her college library. He never looked away from the screen when they had these short exchanges. Biz wondered absentmindedly if he had a face.

"What is that, a Macintosh Apple?" she asked.

"You mean a Mac? No, it's an Amiga 1000. But I have a Mac, too."

"Of course you do. C'mon, Charlie, you ready?" Biz said to Foster, "We're heading to Wreck's if you want to join us."

"Thanks, but I'd rather stick forks in my eyes."

Charlie said, "Atta boy. Way to be a joiner."

The Wreck was sweaty, packed, and humming for a Thursday night. College students crammed shoulder to shoulder, crowding the foosball and pool tables. The jukebox and dartboard were just as popular. There were dim hanging lamps over each high-backed booth and cheap beer-logo mirrors screwed to the walls. The names of bands and lovers were carved into every inch of dark, tacky pine—barely legible and filled in with grime. The chipped linoleum floor was perpetually sticky as were the tabletops and most of the silverware.

"I'll have a vodka tonic, please," Biz said to the bartender, who took her order ahead of the guys already waving ten-dollar bills in the air. "And a Molson," added Charlie. He turned to Biz. "Really? Vodka? Don't you want to start with beer?" "It's vodka o'clock somewhere," she said in a jaunty mood. She was looking forward to their hunt like a game show contestant. Charlie was dreading it and wanted to leave. Biz bopped on her stool to the new Simple Minds tune that had played all over MTV and the radio since it debuted over the summer. The raucous bar crowd took a collective break in conversational slurring to sing the chorus in unison at the top of their lungs. "Don't you . . . forget about me. Don't, don't, don't, don't!" Charlie waited to speak until the shouting was over and the crowd had settled back into its base-level cacophony. "I didn't come here to listen to a room full of wasted lame-os sing."

Biz spread her arms out in a wide, sweeping arc like a queen addressing her kingdom. "These lame-os are our people. Among these lame-os lies the key to our salvation."

"I think that's stretching it."

"Okay. How about, we have a job to do. This is your mission, should you decide to accept it . . ."

"Fine."

"What about her?" Biz said, pointing down the bar. "She's got big boobs."

"So?"

"Okay, not a boob man. Noted." Biz mimed taking notes. "Not . . . a boob . . . man."

Charlie said, "Boobs are fine."

"*Fine?!* Boobs are excellent! Get in the game, dude! You're wasting precious time. You could have any woman in this gin joint."

Charlie rolled his eyes and looked around. "And that's a good thing?"

All the guys—mostly white—had shaggy-ish hair and barely distinguishable features. They wore primary-colored Izod or rugby shirts and faded Gap jeans. If aliens had arrived at this bar they would have thought that male Boston earthlings were only Caucasian and had a mandated uniform.

"Ok," Biz said eagerly, "me, now."

Charlie gestured with his thumb toward the fire exit to a guy wearing piano suspenders and leaning against a pay phone, doing what looked like an impression of a theater kid smoking.

"What about Mork over there? You seem to be into faces. He's got a face. And very snappy suspenders."

"You're terrible at this."

"That's because you're asking me to pick out some random guy for you to sleep with. Of course I'm terrible at it."

"We're only going to act like we're sleeping with them, remember?"

Charlie looked at Biz. He was silently pleading with her to end the game, but she didn't get the message, or pretended not to. She was busy looking over Charlie's shoulder at the lithe blonde. "That girl reminds me of Tindy. Hey, what about Tindy?"

"No."

"Why not?"

"You have to ask?" Charlie paid the bartender seven bucks for the two drinks and left two singles on the bar.

"She'd be adequate. Or are you still pining for Piper? Too soon?"

"Too dumb. And too soon," Charlie said. "If this is going to work, we need to split up. No one can see us together or we'll end up cock-blocking each other."

"A double cock-block. Would that be 'cocks-block' or 'cock-blocks'?"

Charlie ignored her and began to survey his options in earnest. "I'm ignoring you starting now. Let's meet back at this stool in forty-five minutes."

Biz gestured to the douchebag sitting on the stool next to her. "Did you say this tool?" Charlie rolled his eyes and walked away.

Biz downed her drink, then headed in the direction of the dudes at the pool table.

Charlie meandered to the dartboard, where three different groups of women stood in clusters. Their pretty, tanned elbows rubbed against one another, leaving no discernable space for any man to make an in. Girls were such dingbats, he thought. They got all dressed up, then shuffled around in packs like chained prisoners in *Take the Money and Run.* How was any guy supposed to penetrate that? He bumped into one of them and asked if there was a sign-up for darts. "I don't know," was all she could think to say. Charlie smiled, said thanks, then scanned the crowd for Biz. He caught her eye, flashed a zero, then pointed to her and mouthed "You?" Biz was watching a game of pool. She, too, had asked if there was a sign-up to play next but had gone about it in a different way.

"Which one of you jackasses has the winner?" she said straight-faced, then waited for an answer. A funny guy would have taken the bait, would have made a snappy retort like "That would be me" or "Isn't it obvious?" These guys simply looked at her confused. One guy said, "Who you calling a jackass?" Biz said, "It depends, are you playing the winner?" and let loose her dimples on the room. No one bit. When she caught sight of Charlie, she flashed him a zero in return. She was turning to leave when one of the players said, "What if I win? What does that make me?" He looked over at Biz with cool detachment, warm brown eyes, and a nice jawline.

"A champion," she said, "and the king of all you survey."

He didn't look at her; instead he lined up a shot and with a slow steady stroke banked it before kissing the cue ball into the nine and sinking it in the corner. He said, "So, all this could be mine?" "Wot, the curtains?" she asked in a thick British accent. It was a *Holy Grail* reference. She and Charlie had seen it a hundred and forty seven times. The guy looked impressed, then continued his turn, running the table, sinking the eight ball last. Nana Miggs had beaten "Always take off your hat indoors" into them since birth—but Biz might make a concession for this guy. One of his minions moved in to take over the pool cue, but Mr. Winner spoke up. "Let's let her play."

"Really? Jesus, Mike," said his friend, and skulked off with the others.

"Tough crowd," Biz said. "Your name is Jesus Mike?"

"No, but I make them call me that."

Biz cracked up. She'd caught herself a live one.

"I'm Mike Van der Berg. Want to play me?"

"Sure. I'm Biz Chadwick. Don't let me win."

He smiled an orthodondically preeminent smile. Biz wished he'd ditch the baseball hat as she racked. Then she slowly bent down—aware of her ass in Guess jeans and her cute new pale pink Esprit sweatshirt. Stretching out against the bright expanse of shamrock felt, she drew the cue back on her inhale and broke confidently, scattering the balls. Their firm clicking told Mike she knew what she was doing and it would be a decent game. She sank the seven and nine.

Across the bar, Charlie met two more duds before discovering a gem. She was waiting in a long line for the ladies' bathroom while he waited in the shorter line opposite for the men's. She was tiny with tight dark brown curls that she partially tamed with a headband, and blackish-brown eyes set off by thick lashes, the kind that didn't need mascara. "Really, ladies? Let's step it up, beauty queens," she said in a thick Long Island accent. Or she might have been from South Jersey or a Boston native; the accents were so close Charlie couldn't differentiate. "It's like they're all in there prepping for some pageant," she continued to no one. Then she hollered toward the door, "It's a filthy bar full of miscreants!" Charlie snickered. He was standing opposite her in the same cramped narrow hallway lit by a single dim bare bulb. He knew she wasn't his type, but she was funny and he liked her shtick. She was bawdy like a character actress who always plays the best friend. "Who you calling a miscreant?" he deadpanned.

"You're telling me you're not? You're here, aren't you?"

"Maybe I'm just here to count them. Maybe I'm the miscreant census taker."

"Trust me, the numbers don't go that high."

"Are you from here?" Charlie asked, chuckling.

"Is that your best work? What are you, a Borscht Belt comic? You can do better."

"No," Charlie stammered, amused. She'd totally caught him off guard. "Please hold," he said, heading into the men's room. "Holding," said the little spitfire. Charlie shook his head, amused as hell by her. When he returned he paused in front of her, resuming where they left off. "I just thought with the accent, maybe you're a local."

"First of all, what accent?" She pronounced "all" *awuhl*. They both had to laugh. She reached the front of the line.

"Well, this is my stop."

"I'm Charlie Muir. Can I get you a beer?"

"I'm Becky Rosenfeld. And no, thanks. I've had my limit, hence this line. But thank you for the ride. What a nice goy." Charlie thought she said "boy." Becky disappeared into the women's room. Charlie waited for her to come out even though he was late for his debrief with Biz. When Becky emerged she was surprised to see him waiting. As TV handsome as he was, she knew he was way out of her comfort zone. And no way in hell was he Jewish.

Charlie said, "Hey, I've had a really nice time meeting you."

"Nice? Shoot me."

Charlie laughed. "Can I get your number?"

"Why?" Becky said, not joking.

Charlie cracked up. "I don't know, so I can call you?"

"What, to invite me to a cotillion? Trust me, I'm too short. The long white gloves would reach my armpits and get me all schvitzy."

Charlie didn't know what that meant but was sure it was funny as hell. He smiled. "No. I was thinking to grab a beer sometime?"

"Yeah, right."

"I mean it."

"Sure ya do."

"I do. But not if you don't want."

"Sure, what the hell. Stranger things have happened, right?"

Charlie hadn't really thought this through. He didn't think she'd be right for the Fall Festival mission; he just knew he liked being around her. Flustered, he said, "I guess so."

Becky said, "Trust me, they have. You got a pen? Or should I scratch my number on your forehead with my car key?"

"Shit, no, hold on," he said, patting his empty front pockets. "Wait here." He took off.

Becky said to no one, "Famous last words."

Biz handed him a pen from her purse. "What are you, a rookie?"

Charlie said, "No, but I play one on TV," as he raced back to Becky, forgetting to grab something to write on.

Biz and Charlie debriefed. They decided Mike Van der Berg was right for the job and Charlie should totally call Becky. A fairly sharp cookie, Mike kept up with Biz for the most part, but there were some cultural references she had to explain and tedious sports talk she had to withstand. She found it lazy how quickly he stopped wanting to get to know her. *Some guys are convinced just showing up is enough.* But when Mike kissed her good night Biz's juices began to flow, so she went forth with the master plan. They went out a few more times as the festival weekend approached, though he was vapid and vaguely disinterested. She felt interchangeable to him. *And what's sexier than that? Just about everything.*

When Charlie called Becky, she agreed to meet him "anywhere but the Wreck," as she put it. So they went to the Pour House, a quieter place with renowned chowder and draft beer. They discussed the political ramifications of Duran Duran's hair—if any—and the dystopian message in *Mad Max*. Becky was impressed Charlie had seen *Brazil*.

"You *have*?" she said.

"Yes, why do you seem so surprised?"

"You seem more like a Rambo guy to me."

Charlie laughed. "You wouldn't be here if you really thought that."

"You're absolutely right." Becky's eyes glimmered as she sipped her beer. He felt as if he'd known her for years. She asked if he was dating someone. A friend from her dorm knew someone who heard he had a girlfriend named Liz. Charlie felt his head tighten and his hands reflexively clench. "No, she's just a—I don't have a girlfriend." He looked at his beer, then remembered he should be looking at Becky. And probably should have thought this through. "Uh-huh," she said skeptically. Then Charlie flashed to the Fall Festival plan to when they'd all be staying in the same house together—the jig would most obviously be up. He and Biz would make lousy secret agents. They'd never discussed the part where they reveal they were cousins. They didn't have the brilliant criminal minds he thought they had. *Idiots.* Was this an issue? He didn't think it was. He didn't remember denying outright they were related; he simply never disclosed they were. Charlie looked at Becky. "The Liz your friend mentioned is my cousin, Biz. We hang out a lot. We're best friends."

"Oh." Becky didn't see that coming. "Why didn't you say so before?"

"I don't know. Our mothers are sisters, and we grew up next door to each other. We've basically been close since we were born. Her brother, E.J., calls us 'Damien' and 'Omen II.'"

"Nice. Why don't you tell people?" Becky was still confused.

"I don't know. Because it's embarrassing? Because we don't want people thinking we don't know how to make friends?"

Becky said, "So, be best friends. You can be cousins and best friends."

"If you're Italian, maybe."

"Ha. Well, true. I'm guessing your family isn't Italian."

"No." Charlie laughed. "Are you Italian?"

Becky looked at him like the dummy he was. "No, I'm Jewish."

Charlie could count the Jewish kids he knew growing up on one hand.

"Is Becky a Jewish name?" he asked. He didn't know much about Jewish people, but from all the movies he'd seen, it didn't strike him as sounding Jewish. "It sounds more to me like a character from *Oklahoma.* Not that there aren't Jews in Oklahoma." He paused slightly. "Are there Jewish people in Oklahoma?"

Becky cracked up. "Not happy ones. My guess is the gefilte fish is subpar. But then there are unhappy Jews everywhere."

Charlie chuckled, too, without knowing why. Becky continued, "My real name is Rebekah. I'm Bekah at home, and at camp and temple. I'm Rivka at my grandparents' house, but that's a whole other world I don't think you could handle, trust me. Them either. And I'm Becky in Boston. What about you?"

"My full name's Charles Thornden Muir."

Becky said, "Oh, a nice Jewish boy."

Charlie's face fell. He said, "Uh, no," in earnest, feeling he was letting her down.

"Yeah, no kidding," she laughed. "I was joking. God, you were funny the night I met you. What happened?"

Charlie realized he would have to stay sharp to keep up. "Sorry. I'll lighten up. I promise. I could slip on a banana peel . . ."

"If you think it would help." They both smiled.

Charlie leaned back in his chair. "My nickname was Choo growing up, and now I'm Charlie." Becky choked slightly on her beer. Charlie was pretty sure she did it for comic effect, but he'd also never told anyone outside his family that he'd still be introduced as Choo with a straight face if he hadn't changed it himself.

"Excuse me?" said Becky, incredulous.

"Yes, like the train," Charlie said. "My family is a little nickname obsessed. My sister, Sarah, got stuck with Rah-Rah. But we call her Rah now."

"Is she a cheerleader?"

"No, she's into physics."

"And she can pull off 'Rah'? Wow. You guys are *really* not Jewish."

"I have no idea what that means."

Becky said, "Case in point."

They talked and laughed for hours that night. And again the next time, and the next. At the end of their third date, on a darkened stoop a few doors from the entrance to her dorm, Charlie bent way down and kissed Becky on the cheek. She said, "C'mere, pal," grabbed his rugby shirt collar with both hands, and drew him back down to her soft, full lips. He felt warmed by her mouth and stayed in her kiss, at ease with the way she tasted. She moved her short, Rubenesque body into his so he would feel her ample bosom. He wondered what it would be like to hold someone naked who wasn't tall and thin. The sudden feeling he had below the belt told him he was excited to find out. He liked having so much woman pressed up against him like a heated cushion. He flashed forward to the possibility of exploring her rich curves. So he stayed in her kiss for as long as she'd let him, which was longer than Becky Rosenfeld thought possible. *What the heck,* she thought. *I'm rolling with it. Who knew?*

The few times Biz called Charlie's dorm to check in on how he and Becky were progressing, he wasn't there to pick up the hall phone. Randy Rude the Front Desk Dude announced the phone call over the fourth-floor PA, but no one picked up, so he took a message and stuck it in Charlie's mailbox. Biz felt a twinge of jealousy but reminded herself this was their plan. The Firth Fall Festival—or fethtival, as they'd thay—was the first weekend in November. They needed to log as much time with their dates as quickly as possible beforehand. Their relationships needed to appear relaxed and legit.

The more time Biz spent with Mike Van der Berg the more she missed Finn, and the more she thought about Finn the more she tried not to think of Charlie. But Mike fit the profile and was definitely the right guy for the mission. What neither of them was able to foresee was that Mike would get pneumonia. And forget to tell Biz and she wouldn't find out until just before they were meant to leave. She immediately called Charlie's dorm from a pay phone—no luck—then hopped into a cab and raced over to tell him they had to abort their plan. She knocked this time before barging into his dorm room. Charlie's bed was smoothed over in a halfhearted attempt, and his toiletry bag was missing from his dresser. Foster was in the alcove, typing away. "Did he leave?" Biz said breathlessly to Foster's back.

"He did," Foster replied, typing.

"Shit, shit, *shit*!" said Biz, then plopped onto Charlie's bed. *"Dammit!"* She cupped her hands to her face. "Dammit, dammit, *dammit*."

Foster didn't say anything right away; he had a line of code to finish. Finally he asked, "Anything I can do to help?" He spun around, adding, "Help, help, help?"

"I doubt it," Biz said, and flopped back onto the bed. Her head was spinning with probable outcomes, none of which were life threatening but all of which were an enormous nuisance.

"Try me," said Foster.

"Charlie and I had a plan to bring dates home this weekend."

"Aren't you two dating each other?"

"No, duh, we're cousins. People spaz so we don't tell them."

"But you *have* had sex," said Foster. Biz raised herself up to look at him.

"*No*. We're *cousins*. We're *best friends*."

"Uh-huh. Right," Foster said, and spun back around to his computer.

"Don't be a dickwad. Our family thinks we're socially

maladjusted because we're not dating dumbasses like you, so our plan was to each bring a date up to introduce to the family so they'll back off and stop thinking we're weirdos."

"But you are weirdos."

"Takes one to know one."

"What are you, seven? Let me get this straight: you two are cousins and best friends who aren't screwing, and everyone else in the world is a dumbass."

"Correctamundo."

"What about Charlie's new friend, Becky—is she an idiot, too? Because he seems to be spending a lot of time with her."

"I haven't met her. I sort of saw her but not really. She looked short. But nice."

"One can be both?"

Biz ignored him. "Have you met her?"

"Yes."

"Is she a dumbass?"

Foster spun his chair back around, slowly. "No. Not even in the ballpark. She's very bright, and funny. And since you've made the argument that you're cousins, I'll assume jealousy's an impossibility."

Foster followed his comment with a raised eyebrow. Biz slid back onto the bed so he wouldn't be able to read her face. He seemed to have a handle on her somehow, which she found simultaneously unsettling and intriguing. She weighed calling Finn but knew he had to work the weekend shift; plus it wouldn't be fair to him after all this time. She was resigning herself to the idea that she'd have to be the third wheel to Charlie and Becky palling around together all weekend when Foster spoke up. "I'll go."

Biz laughed. "Ha."

"I've got no weekend plans. Is the food at your house better than the student union's?"

"It's not my house, it's my grandparents', and yes, my mom and aunt are great cooks."

"Do I get my own room with a door that closes?"

"Uh, yes. Probably."

"So then *I'll* be your fake date. Can I wear a false mustache? Do I get to call you 'hon'?"

"No and no," Biz said.

Foster flipped the switches that powered down his computer and started to pack a bag. "Do I need to dress for dinner?"

"No, and what do you know about dressing for dinner?"

"I'm from Glendon."

"Connecticut?"

"No, Alabama."

"Hardy-har. So you *do* know a thing or two about dressing for dinner. How's your grammar? Your table manners up to snuff? My grandfather still uses phrases like 'up to snuff.'"

"Napkin in lap. Elbows off the table. Twenty-three skidoo."

"Good Lord. Grandpa Dun will love you."

"And your grandmother?"

"If you look her in the eye, you'll have her eating out of your hand. Can you do that?"

"You tell me." Foster looked Biz steadily and confidently in the eye. Then he walked over to her without breaking his gaze, and offered his hand to help her up from the bed as if he were a prince helping a duchess out of a carriage. She took it, and he bore her weight with ease, then stood still, waiting for her to speak. In a rarity, she was at a loss for words; they'd never been this close. His neck was clean-shaven and he smelled like Old Spice. She wanted to touch his shoulders.

"I can't believe I'm doing this," Biz said, and was the first to avert her eyes. "I'm pretty sure Charlie's going to kill you."

"Or you."

"Ha, true," she said, worried in earnest. But this was better for her.

Foster grabbed his coat and threw a few things into a worn canvas L.L.Bean bag with Kelly-green straps. He mumbled something on the way to the elevator and Biz said, "What?"

"Charlie would never kill you because he's in love with you."

Biz stopped short and shot him a glance. "Hey, that's got to stop or else I'm calling this off."

Foster said, "Okay, sorry. Just joking."

"Well, don't. It's not funny." She clearly meant business. Foster pantomimed turning a key in front of his mouth. They stepped into the elevator, and Biz said, "You're a dork." Foster knew that. He also knew he was going to enjoy this little adventure immensely.

Charlie offered to carry Becky's hard plastic suitcase through Back Bay Station, and she let him. They stood where they could watch the giant board with all the times and destinations— close enough to hear the letters and numbers flipping over each other, fluttering as the trains were called. *Flap-ap-ap-ap-ap-ap* the board purred in the background. Their easy banter passed the time.

"What's in this thing?" Charlie said.

"My rock collection," said Becky. "I thought you said to bring rocks." She looked at him with a straight face, but her eyes gave her away. Charlie laughed. "I said *socks*. Bring warm socks!"

"Oooohh." She pretended to catch on. They snickered at their vaudeville routine. The air around them crackled with anticipation. Her curly hair was brushed fluffy like Jennifer Beals's and the deep magenta cardigan that stretched the buttons taut at her chest brought out her ruby lips and the pink in her cheeks.

"You look nice," Charlie said in earnest.

Becky said, "Are you sure they're not going to give me a hard time for being Jewish?"

"I don't think they'll even know. They'll probably think you're Italian like I did, or Greek. But my cousin E.J. will cut into you for being short. See if you can do something about that before tonight." Becky chuckled at his comment but also to herself. WASPs were so utterly self-isolating, living in tiny slivers of their separate worlds. They rarely sought out opportunities to observe differentiated nuances. Jewish, Italian, Greek—to them other cultures didn't exist, and the ones that did were interchangeable variations. But the Jews Becky knew were narrow-minded, too. "Their people," she'd heard her extended family say a million times growing up. Everyone was an "other"—it always boiled down to "us" and "them." At least Charlie had seen a lot of documentaries and was taking Ethnology and Film. He seemed pretty open-minded for a gentile.

"I'll see what I can do about my height," Becky said. "And how are you going to explain us?" She said it casually, trying to toss off the question, but waited for his answer with a small pit in her stomach. It had never crossed Charlie's mind their relationship needed defining. She was so easygoing, and they'd been having so much fun. As Charlie gave the question a thoughtful moment's deliberation, her pit grew and split open, leaking self-doubt. Charlie said, "How about we tell them we're having fun getting to know one another?" Becky did her best to hide she was crestfallen. She'd been counseled by her friends not to ask this very question because she'd have to be okay with his answer. Or act like it.

Charlie waited for her reaction, pretty sure he'd said the wrong thing. Becky struggled to stop her throat from tightening and her eyes from welling with tears. They let their attention divert back to the flipping letters on the board. Becky found comfort in the soothing voice of the confident woman who called the departing trains over the loudspeaker for all to hear. *I bet she doesn't let men define her relationships, or her self worth, or her future.* Becky decided the all-knowing wise woman must surely be the voice of God. "This is the final call for the southbound North Corridor Amtrak train four-oh-six departing at gate two. All aboard." Charlie leaned down and kissed Becky on the mouth, pointedly and sweetly. He felt he'd said something wrong, but wasn't sure what. Further destinations flipped and skittered their way up the board as the 406 disappeared entirely, presumably to join its travelers on the grand rail journey from Boston down to New Jersey.

Biz and Foster caught the next train home. They passed the journey to Penn Station swilling apricot brandy and getting their stories straight. Foster was quick-witted but talked slowly and deliberately. No one rushed him, least of all Biz. Every time she came up with a wild lie—"Let's say we met at a football game"—Foster put the kybosh on it. "Let's not and say we met through Charlie. It's easier to remember the truth." They chatted easily as the train rumbled along, with plenty of silences between them. He looked out the window or read the thick biography of Robert Moses he was toting. Biz sketched, answering his questions about her inevitable success as an entrepreneur, and liked that he showed interest in her ideas. She was glad he wasn't Mike, and by the time they boarded the local to Firth, she'd convinced herself Charlie would be pleased. Foster was an adequate sub, whom he knew and liked, or at least didn't detest.

They dropped their bags in Nana Miggs's garage and made a beeline for the festival games. "Oh, I almost forgot, my family might call me Bizzy. And Charlie, possibly Choo."

"You can't be serious."

"Yes. Get used to it. And my brother, E.J., might say some shit about Charlie and me being an item." Foster tossed a ring and missed, but stayed cool as a cucumber. "Noted."

"My given name is Elizabeth. They didn't go with Betsy; don't ask me why."

"Do *all* the adults in your house have nicknames fit for children's programming?"

"Bring it up and I'll put you on the next train back and you'll eat ramen for the next six meals." Foster mimed the lock and key again, and Biz slapped his arm. "Quit that. Let's get a beer."

Both couples made the most out of the carnival games and rides, eventually meeting up as they'd planned before the Twilight Dance began. Charlie noticed Biz first through the thick mob surrounding the gazebo. She looked great, as always, though a little drunk, as always, but he was relieved to find her in the madness. He was also nervous to meet Mike and craned his neck to see his face. What didn't compute was seeing his roommate, Foster, walking next to Biz.

Charlie shook Foster's hand. "Hey, man. How's it going? What are you doing here?" Foster turned to Biz. "Do you want to tell him or shall I?" Biz elbowed Foster in a chummy way, much to Charlie's horror, and said, "Mike got pneumonia at the last minute, and I raced over to tell you but you'd already left. Foster's my date, for lack of a better word, but he just came for the home-cooked meals. Turns out he has a face and a mouth that speaks in full sentences. And can be totally civil if the mood strikes."

Charlie was confused. How did that happen? Biz had told him how it happened. But *how*? He thought they had no secrets, wanted to believe her story. Why on earth would she lie? Distracted, he failed to introduce Becky, who was feeling shorter than usual, and ignored. If he didn't introduce her soon, she'd head over to the Ferris wheel and throw herself off. Biz said, "Xaler, Oohc," to which Charlie answered, "Retsof? Tahw eth lleh?" What looped in Becky's head was *This is a mistake.* "So, you must be Becky," Biz said with genuine warmth, then drew her in for a hug.

"Uh, yes I am. Becky Rosenfeld. Pleased to meet you both."

"I'm Biz. I've heard so much about you, but not too much, I promise."

"Only the appropriate amount, let's hope," said Becky feeling awkward. She also felt dowdy next to Biz, who exuded wholesomeness with maddening ease.

Foster cut in. "I haven't heard a damn thing about you, Becky, so lie to me all you want. I'm Foster, Charlie's roommate. And Biz's—"

"Trial friend and travel companion," Biz interrupted. Charlie couldn't help but grin. It was fun to watch her torture someone else for a change. He decided not to be jealous, but it was odd nonetheless, and would probably test his patience and generosity. Biz said, "Think you can handle it, Charlie? Or is this too weird for your delicate constitution?"

"It'll be my pleasure," Charlie said. He turned to Foster. "Welcome, moocher."

Just then a man parted the crowd, arms outstretched. "Fuck you!" he railed, flipping the bird to everyone in his path. He looked older than his forty plus years and had a stained trench coat, rumpled like Detective Columbo's. He perched two sets of eyeglasses on his forehead—neither of which he needed— and marched as he walked, as if late for a meeting. Charlie and Biz glanced at the man and said, "Hey, fuck you, Carl," in a friendly manner. "No," he said, stopping at their little huddle. "Fuck *youuu*!" Then he repeated it, this time with more pizzazz, and flipped the bird with a rough growl. This exchange was enough to appease FU Carl, and he nodded before continuing on his way.

Charlie said to Becky and Foster, "That was Fuck You Carl."

Becky said, "We gathered."

Foster said, "Why do they call him Fuck You Carl?"

Biz rolled her eyes and said to Charlie, "Ignore him." She bumped Foster a little as she said it, which set Charlie's neck hairs on end. Biz said to the group, "We could hang around here and watch the old farts dance or we could sneak home before the grown-ups and play some games . . ." Charlie knew Biz meant drinking games. Becky and Foster did not.

"Well, I'm up for anything," said Becky. "Anything but clogging and bagpipes. And Renaissance fairs. Which this scene is eerily reminiscent of." Charlie took her hand. "You would dazzle at a Renaissance fair." Becky lit up, Biz was unfazed, and Foster found the whole scene curious. "Follow me," chirped Biz as she plowed through the crowd. She liked Becky and wasn't intimidated in the least. Charlie put his hand on the small of Becky's back. "After you," he said, and she warmed to his touch. She felt lucky, but also anxious, as if diving into a public swimming pool wearing an ill-fitting suit complete with noticeable wedgie.

They let themselves into the dark, quiet house and carried their bags up to their rooms. Foster and Becky were quietly in awe of the grand staircase. Fading watercolor landscapes and stuffy oil portraits lined halls wallpapered in busy flocked prints. The hallways tilted and floors creaked, leaving the impression of either a very solidly built two-hundred-year-old house or one about to crumble at any minute. Biz led them to Grandpa Dun's bar cart, and Foster pointed to the Macallan 18. "I'll take some of that," he said, controlling his excitement. Becky tugged at Charlie's shirt. He leaned down and she whispered, "I'm not much of a drinker."

"Oh, that's okay," he said. "You can sip it."

"It might put me right to sleep."

"Nothing wrong with that," said Charlie, patting her on the shoulder like an old friend. Becky wondered what he meant but was too out of her element to ask. Biz grabbed bottles of rum and tequila and headed for the kitchen. The first floor of the house was typically cavernous and cold—the heat rarely set above sixty-seven—but the kitchen felt snug, a portal to 1950. The floor was flecked black-and-white check vinyl, and there were aqua and yellow overlapping quasars on the Formica table with aluminum trim. The slightly oddball, somewhat inebriated foursome slid into the L-shaped breakfast nook. An empty rocks glass was placed in the center and filled to half with Labatt's Blue.

They played Thumper, and Quarters, which Becky had to learn but joined tentatively. She knew there was some rhyme warning of drinking beer before wine or liquor but couldn't remember how it went. She'd heard WASPs made drinking the center of every social occasion but had never experienced the peer pressure firsthand. Biz tuned the transistor to WPLJ and turned up the volume so it echoed tinny throughout the house. Charlie and Biz sang "boner of a lonely fart" to "Owner of a Lonely Heart" and encouraged everyone to get up and dance. Becky shook her head no, and Foster stayed seated, whistling the "Autumn" movement of Vivaldi's *Four Seasons*, just to be a noodge.

Charlie excused himself from the revelry to pee. Weaving his way back, he was drawn to the "good" living room. Unbroken vacuum tracks were visible on the peachy orange carpet, and tasseled throw pillows were pouffed to perfection. Occasionally he and Biz snuck in to gaze at sterling silver frames crowded with well-heeled people cradling infants in long christening gowns. And though the room was verboten except for holidays and sanctioned special occasions, Charlie *was* allowed to play the grand piano as long as he asked permission.

The upright in his dorm's common room was so discordant he hadn't used it except to play "Crocodile Rock" for drunken students. But now he felt emboldened and wasn't so inebriated that he didn't recognize the part of him that wanted to make Foster jealous. Feeling rogue, Charlie played "Christmas Time Is Here"—the dreamy, spellbinding waltz. *Who cares if the Christmas season doesn't start until December first.* It could come early to impress Biz.

The Charlie Brown classic wound its way into a delicate variation of "Moonglow," so exquisitely wrought that Vince Guaraldi himself—Charlie's favorite pianist—might have closed his eyes and leaned back in his chair to listen. On its heels he played the wistful, "Embraceable You," which he'd been dragooned to learn to make his grandparents happy. The raucous kitchen sing-a-long to Prince's apocalyptic "1999" underscored the song's declaration of love as he played. He relished the layered incongruity of distant voices against his chords and laughed as he merged the two tempos. At the end of the songs he was resting his hands on the warm ivory keys, waiting for his muse to tell him what to play next, when an actual voice at the far end of the dark room spoke in the studied tone of an aging tenured professor.

"Very good, young man. Your diligence has paid off," said Grandpa Dun. Charlie bolted upright from the piano bench like a guilty six-year-old. "Sit, sit," Dunny said, then to Marjorie, "What's the song, dearest heart, the one Ruby Keeler sang in that—"

"'I Only Have Eyes for You,'" she said.

Nana Miggs interrupted, her voice rich and patient with the institutional knowledge of a lifetime finishing the sentences of one man.

"Would you like to hear the verse?" asked Charlie.

Nana Miggs stage-whispered, "Dunny, our handsome, talented grandson knows the verse. Yes, dear, we would love to hear the whole megilla."

Charlie could see his grandparents smile as he played: hers encircled by deep crevices that held her signature cranberry lipstick, and his in his eyes, hooded by the white bushy eyebrows befitting a former titan of industry. The revelers emerged from the kitchen to find the silver-haired couple swaying sweetly and lip-syncing with precision and grace. Introductions followed. "I'm Marjorie Thornden, and this is my other half, Dunsfield. Please call me Nana Miggs. Everyone else on God's green earth does, and call this one Dunny. He won't answer to anything else."

"Notice she didn't say 'better half,'" said Grandpa Dun, extending his vein-striped hand for firm shaking. "Thank you for having us, Mr. and Mrs. Thornden," said Foster. He and Becky were loose from the booze and passed muster with flying colors. He also knew full well they would prefer to be called by their surnames and that first impressions mattered greatly, so he straightened up, and Becky followed suit. Charlie was instructed to pick up just where he'd left off and noticed the knees on his grandmother's slacks swaying slightly out of the corner of his eye. At the top of the chorus she sang quietly under her breath, "Are the stars out tonight, I don't know if it's cloudy or bright . . ." Grandpa Dun joined her, his slacks swaying as well. "'Cause I only have eyes . . . for youuu, dearrr . . ." Charlie finished with gentle command, slowing at the end to milk the delicate promise of the lyric.

Foster said, "I had no idea."

"I did," said Biz with delight. Something swelled in her watching him play. "He's been playing since we were kids." Biz had learned at a young age that if her calming voice or jokes didn't work to hoist him out of a mood, walking him over to the piano could work wonders.

Charlie held the room with an understated and irrefutable power. It was impressive. And sexy. Foster felt it, too. Feeling intimidated and sauced, he stood closer to Biz, letting his shoulder rub against hers. Charlie noticed.

Becky said, "Nice work. How am I supposed to top that?"

"No need, young lady," said Grandpa Dun, and winked at Becky. They were all still standing in the dim light of the tiny piano lamp when Claire and Les, and Cat and Ned, arrived for the second round of introductions. The cousins would be along much later—ending up at someone's garage after pilfering beers from their houses during the day and hiding them in bushes for later retrieval. Grandpa Dun was predictably jovial, all pomp and circumstance introducing the two newbies to the others, referring to them as paramours. Biz corrected, "They're not paramours, Grandpa. Please, it's awkward enough."

"Do you feel awkward, Becky?" he bellowed. He, too, had been drinking expensive scotch.

"Not in the slightest, Mr. Thornden," she replied in equal volume, rosy cheeks and shored-up bravery.

"And you?" Grandpa Dun said to Foster.

"It takes a lot to make me feel awkward, Mr. Thornden."

"And to what do you attribute such a feat, young man?"

"It tends to already be my waking conscious mode, sir."

"I see. Very good. Well, *bon chance, mes amis*. I trust everyone to behave appropriately. Children, do your Thornden best."

Becky and Foster looked at Biz as if to say, *What on earth is that?* And Biz shook her head as if answering, *Ignore him*. Charlie played the Looney Tunes riff as if wrapping a comedy bit, but his grandfather was already turning toward the staircase. Nana Miggs looked the newcomers in the eye one at a time and said, "It's very nice to meet you both. Please make yourself at home. *Mi casa, su casa*. Don't be shy. Heaven knows we're not."

Charlie gave a gentle kiss to her powdered cheek. "Goodnight, Nana. Sleep well."

"Sweet dreams, my dear." She reached up to pat him on the shoulder. "Be good."

"Always," he said. And to Biz, Nana Miggs said, "And you . . ."

"Never," Biz said with a wry smile.

"Atta girl," said Nana Miggs under her breath, and headed off after Grandpa Dun. They watched as she laced her arm through his and tenderly steadied him up the staircase. Claire and Les, and Cat and Ned, followed suit reiterating niceties steeped in Emily Post. Becky and Foster played their parts of affable pals along for the ride—like travelers met at a hostel and brought home to see firsthand how the locals in this region live.

On their way back to the kitchen, Charlie pulled Biz aside, whispering under the transistor's bitchin' Chaka Khan single "I Feel for You." He thought their plan was going smoothly and they should meet later to debrief. He suggested the linen closet—a narrow upstairs back hallway where they'd logged hours as little kids, making blanket forts and hatching secret plans. "How much later?" Biz asked. Charlie replied with a twinkle, "Four A.M.?" She twinkled back, "Okay, but we're *not* going to fool around." Booze always made her horny. "No, we are *not*," said Charlie while grinning and slowly nodding yes. They were well versed in the coy opposite-speak of a generation brought up on black-and-white movies, where "no" meant "maybe" or "probably" or often "yes."

"There's no point. You're probably lousy in bed, anyway," Biz teased.

"*You* are," said Charlie.

"No, *you.*"

Charlie told her to stop drinking so she wouldn't pass out, but Biz blithely waved him off. Becky, he knew, would sleep soundly through the night, but he worried Biz would foil his plan. He wanted to make sure they had a chance to rendezvous, to reconnect—*us against the world*. He was threatened by Foster who was maddeningly charming and chummy with Biz. He knew the plan was to let her go, but not this weekend, and not to his roommate.

Cat and Claire paused on their way to bed to debrief at the top of the landing.

Claire asked, "What do you think of Foster?"

Cat said, "I think he's perfectly darling."

"You know what I mean. Do you really think he's dating Bizzy?"

"No."

"Neither do I."

Cat said, "What about Becky?"

"I don't know what to think. She *is* darling. And clearly gaga for Charlie."

"I actually think there could be something between them." Cat was impressed Claire appeared to be loosening up. "Welcome to the eighties," she almost said out loud. Cat had dated a Jewish boy in high school, on the sly. She'd dated an Italian boy, too. Marjorie had known but had to keep it from Dunny. They didn't tell Claire, either, as she wouldn't have approved.

Claire said, "It'll never last."

Cat thought, *So much for loosening up*. "It doesn't have to last. These days they experiment. Kids barely even go steady anymore."

"We didn't experiment or date around," said Claire.

"Yes, and we ended up divorced and miserable."

"I'm not miserable," said Claire. Cat shot her an accusatory look. Claire added, "Per se."

Cat said, "Please," and tilted her head as if to say, *I don't buy it.* Cat continued, "This is 1985, not '55. These kids can date whomever they please. And now we know they aren't gay. I know you were thinking it."

Claire said, "*They?* You actually thought my Bizzy might be *a lesbian?*" She said the word as if she were describing someone from an underrepresented, obscure nation.

"There are lesbians in the world among us," chided Cat.

"Yes, but not very many. And no one *we* know."

Cat looked at Claire, then accounted for the time of night. This was not the hour to educate her sister on the prevalence of gays and lesbians in the world. *Lord, how she lives a narrow life.* The only gay person Claire recognized as such was Paul Lynde from *Hollywood Squares*—and even then, it wasn't discussed. Cat said, "Dear Claire, there are as many lesbians as there are gay men in the world today, most of whom are living secret lives. And yes, we probably know plenty of them, we just don't know we know. But that's another conversation for another time."

Claire was already turning away from her sister. "Well, I don't know what to think. I'm going to bed. The kids know to sleep in separate rooms, I hope."

Cat said, "God, yes. You told them to, right?"

Claire stopped in her tracks and whipped around. "No. I didn't. I thought you did."

Cat said, "Okay, let's relax. Certainly Biz and Charlie aren't that dumb. I'm sure they know better." Claire looked unconvinced. "They're good kids," Cat defended, always giving the benefit of the doubt.

"We were good kids," Claire said, glossing over the truth, which was that she caved to her impulses nearly as often as Cat; she just didn't get caught.

Cat smiled thinly in the dimly lit hallway. "For the most part."

"And the other part?"

"I'll check the rooms."

Charlie and Biz were in agreement that they, too, should retire before E.J., Rah, or Georgia returned home and stirred things up. Biz said, "Let's head up, I'm pooped." Becky snorted at the comment, which sealed the deal that it was time for bed. As the shuffle and bustle of settling in and locating bathrooms took over the upstairs hallway, Biz passed Charlie, who said, "Eb ereht ro eb erauqs." She would be bunking with Becky in one of the spare bedrooms, and Foster would have his own room on the third floor. Charlie said, "'Night," to everyone in the hallway, then closed his bedroom door. The thought of meeting up with Biz made it difficult for him to fall asleep, so he thought about Valerie Bertinelli and masturbated into a sock. It did the trick just as it had in high school.

Becky was focused on getting into bed without knocking anything over, and Biz put two Tylenol into her right palm and a tall glass of water on her bedside table. "Thanks," Becky said, too embarrassed to look her hostess in the eye. "Stick with me, kid, we've all been there," Biz said, then left Becky to her bedspins.

Once under the covers, Biz attempted to picture Foster in pajamas. *What an odd bird,* she thought without feeling at all tired. She wanted to muss his hair a bit, tell him to grow it out so that the sides would fall over his ears. She thought he had potential.

Then she thought about sleeping with Foster and wondered if he'd be any good. She was drawn to his I-don't-give-a-crap-what-you-think attitude. She was also drunk. And horny. She wondered if he could kiss. Her rice-paper wall of defense was undoubtedly weakening. *Did anyone remember to get Foster a towel and extra blankets?* she thought. *The attic can get cold. I'd better check.* If her mother had taught her anything, it was how to make guests feel comfortable during their stay. Biz headed up the back stairs to the third floor as quietly as possible, stepping only on the very outsides of the creaky wooden steps. She checked under his door for light before gently tapping her knuckles. The door opened wide, and Foster was still fully clothed.

"Welcome," he said in his regular day voice.

"Shhh," said Biz, whispering loudly, "are you crazy? You'll wake the whole house."

"So then stop talking to me."

"God. *Stop!* Being such a spaz," Biz said, then took a small step into his room and moved over so he could close the door. He remained in front of her now, not backing up, and made no effort to fill the silence. *So formal,* she thought. *Or maybe that's just how nerds are.* She hadn't grown up with many. Charlie had loved comic books and the *Batman* TV show in high school, but that didn't count as nerdy.

Biz said, "I just wanted to make sure you have everything you need."

"Well, let's see," Foster said slowly, looking behind him. He appeared to be in no rush to end this conversation. In fact, he was luxuriating in it, having drunk just enough alcohol, but not as much as Biz. "There are two beds. One for me and one for a wayward roommate."

Biz rolled her eyes. "You'll be in here by yourself tonight."

Foster continued, "Um, a table lamp for light bedside reading—always pleasant and very thoughtful, thank you. A window for climbing out of for when I have to escape you all when you turn into zombies in the dead of night." Biz grinned. "Yes, I would say it's all here. Everything I could possible need."

She stalled. "How about an extra blanket? The attic can get cold at night."

"Can it?" was all Foster said. He looked at her long Lanz nightgown, her hair free of its ponytail holder, cheeks flushed from tequila. Most guys hated those damn flannel tents for obscuring a woman's entire body from the neck down, but he found them intriguing. They reminded him of Mary Ingalls from *Little House on the Prairie*, whom he'd always fantasized about because she was hot *and* blind. He had a pretty good idea of what Biz was hiding under there; he'd seen her stretched out on Charlie's dorm bed.

Biz decided one kiss wouldn't be the end of the world. At least then she would know if Foster sucked at it and could stop thinking about him that way. His hair was slightly greasy and stylistically ignored, though it framed his long, interesting nose, reminding her of Robby Benson. *Maybe without his glasses he'd be handsome,* she thought. Aviator frames did not suit everyone. One kiss and she would go. But only if he made the first move. Otherwise she'd leave.

Except Biz was impatient. And didn't really want to leave. *Life is short and life is long*—the first half was more apropos in this instance. So she took the tiniest step forward and placed her lips exactly on his as if winning Pin the Tail on the Donkey. *I started it,* she thought. Would he have had the nerve? *I guess we'll never know now.* She figured if something were to happen, she'd have to take the lead. But then Foster Barnstock took over.

Biz dismissed her paltry willpower and gave in to his beckoning lips. She wanted to unleash his controlled countenance, show him the wild abandon she'd grown to enjoy. Like all the women before her, she assumed she'd have to teach him to let go. She removed and folded his glasses. He said, "You've done that before." She demurred and dove back into their kiss, giving in to the swish of their tongues. Then she leaned up against him and said, "Lucky me, a face *and* a woody." He shushed her and moved his hands down her back to cup her exquisite ass. His hesitation belied his discovery: Miss Chadwick wasn't wearing underwear.

Foster pulled her into him more fully, and Biz moaned slightly. She felt weak-kneed, tingly, and aflame. A swirl of electricity went off like a flare. "Oh, my," she said. *So much for Charlie.* Foster slid the brass lock across the door, then walked her backward in foxtrot steps. They fell onto the bed, groping arms and bent knees. Biz thought, *I should really stop about now. But it's not like there's any reason to. Who knows if Charlie will even wake up? This guy's a great kisser, and I'm horny, and so what.* "Wait, wait, wait," she said, then jumped up from the bed and untwisted her nightgown from around her waist. She nudged his legs open, nestling herself between them, then hesitated, embarrassed to speak.

"Do you have a, um . . ."

He answered her, chiding, "A whisk? Golf ball? Shoehorn?"

"No, dummy. You know."

"I do not have a condom," said Foster, and leaned back on his elbows. "Do you?"

"*I'm a girl!* That's *your* department, mister."

"Are you on the, uh . . ."

"Pill? Sometimes."

"I thought that was an all-or-nothing kind of thing."

Biz had swallowed the little pink pills almost daily while sleeping with Finn but had blown it off when summer ended because of the menacing extra five pounds. Lately, she took them when she remembered, though, Aunt Cat had made her promise to keep up. *No biggie. It's not like I could get pregnant anytime.* At least that's not what she learned in sixth-grade gym, when they showed the boys and girls different filmstrips in separate rooms. "'Sometimes' only works in horseshoes and hand grenades," said Foster. "I can pull out."

"You could, but I'm also due any day now."

"So, you're saying . . ."

Biz didn't really know what she was saying. She'd never bothered to go to the library and look up the details, and her friends weren't much help. No one ever discussed how her reproductive system worked because no one knew—except for doctors. Her gynecologist, Dr. Harry Sims, never explained its nuances, and her mother sure as hell never enlightened her. Sure, she'd read the instructional cartoon insert inside the Kotex box, but it was pretty vague and only explained so much. All Biz knew was that sperm made babies and the pill killed the sperm—or something—and she probably couldn't get pregnant when her period was due, which was probably tomorrow or the day after. And maybe there was enough pill in her system to carry over until Tuesday. And she would totally use a condom if he had brought one and would put it on himself, but he didn't. And he said he would pull out. *So that's all there is to it.*

Biz didn't give it another thought.

She dipped her tongue lightly into Foster's ear and whispered, "Go for it," then crossed her arms and pulled her nightgown off over her head. "Tah-dah!" She giggled and threw her hands up with a flourish as if ending a family trapeze act. Wide-eyed and slack jawed, Foster looked shocked and delighted. She knew he wouldn't expect such a stunt. Biz was excited for her little adventure—*one last carnival ride*. "C'mon, you, under the covers," she said. "I don't have all night." Foster was taken aback. "You have another appointment later?" he asked as they nestled under the chenille bedspread. Biz said, "As if," but didn't meet his gaze. Instead she closed her eyes and reached for him, jaunty and erect. And he found her slippery with the clear, mysterious goo the filmstrips never bothered to explain.

The two delinquents fumbled their way through awkward, abrupt sex—Biz coming quickly with muffled squeals, and Foster following suit with stifled grunts. He pulled out about halfway through and came onto her smooth, flat stomach. She drew a spiral in the puddle as he felt along the floor for a sock. Biz grinned mischievously and said, "Hope you brought an extra pair." Foster mopped up the mess with care, then crashed next to her on the twin bed. He muttered, "Apparently low in calories," before falling fast asleep. She scootched an inch away so she could revel in her own separate space, trying to remember where her nightgown was, too lazy to hunt it down. She'd get up in a sec and go back to her room. For now she was going to rest. Just for a minute or two. *A short nap. Only a second.*

A few hours later, Charlie opened the linen closet door as quietly as humanly possible. He'd overslept by about fifteen minutes and hoped Biz wouldn't be too upset. *She's not here yet,* he thought when he entered the tiny alcove. *She must have overslept, too.* Then he got to work grabbing blankets and pillows off the shelves and padding the narrow length of floor. There was just enough room for them to fit lying on their sides, next to the shelves, heads near the back stairs. He wanted his little nest to appear cozy and hospitable. *When the hell is she getting here?* he thought. He'd left his Swatch back in his room.

Charlie lay on the floor looking out the tiny octagonal window, high above the cedar wardrobe, and craned his neck to see the moon. He tucked the foil-wrapped condom under an empty suitcase next to him and waited, sleepy but nervous. Making love to Biz would end a years-long saga of patience, yearning, and desire. He wanted her with a one-sided longing Jim Jarmusch had made achingly clear. Now destiny was finally alighting in a shimmering bubble—like Glinda the Good Witch. He understood he adored her more than she loved him and didn't resent her for it; he couldn't. He knew this was little more than another adventure for her, like stealing street signs or trespassing for fun.

Must not fall asleep, Charlie thought before dozing off, certain Biz would wake him when she arrived.

Biz liked the feeling of being spooned as the dawn sunlight coaxed her awake. Tiny beads of perspiration formed on her neck from being warmly enveloped. Then she became aware of her dry, wooden mouth and the throb of a blossoming headache—the reckoning of last night before even opening her eyes. No sense in reaching out for a glass of water; she hadn't brought one into the linen closet. She didn't think Charlie had that much hair on his chest.

Oh, no, no, no, no, no.

Biz opened her eyes to an undisturbed twin bed just out of reach. "Dammit," she said, and launched herself upward, then hit the pillow hard, shooting pains from ear to ear. Her tongue wore a dense, burlap sweater. "Ow," she said in awe of her discomfort.

"What?" a male voice said, but it was *not* Charlie's. She knew damn well whose it was.

"Goddammit," she said, and lifted her head as if balancing a goldfish in a bowl.

"Overslept" was all Foster said, flatly. He had nothing to feel guilty about, so continued to doze. Biz, however, was up, in a swivet, and reversing the sleeves of her nightgown. *"Foster!"* she stage-whispered when her hand reached the doorknob.

"What? Shh."

"Don't tell anyone any of this, do you understand? I mean it."

"Yes, sir."

"Shhh, Jesus, can't you whisper? Say, 'I promise.'"

Foster took in Biz's mussed hair, pleading eyes, and the lips that encased the tongue he'd been grazing three hours ago. Under that goofy tent of a nightgown was the most spectacular body he'd ever known and—he felt certain, with all the conviction of youth—would ever know. He wished he'd been slower to discover it, was irate at the dawn's new day. Foster also sensed from her obvious guilt that he'd never be alone in a room with her again. He watched Biz Chadwick waiting for his response, her eyebrows furrowed and tense. Then at last he murmured his answer, regretting, "I promise," and she was gone.

Biz flew down the stairs with her head throbbing in time to hear bedroom and bathroom doors opening and closing. She was desperate to check the linen closet and hoped to God Charlie had given up and returned to his room. *Or maybe he overslept!* These thoughts berated her as she waited for the hallway coast to clear. Charlie was rising to consciousness at that moment and felt a hard wall against his knees. He wondered for a split second if he was in a train couchette like the one in his dream—that Hitchcock film with Eva Marie Saint. Then he heard footsteps and a hand on the knob. "Hello," his mom said, "is there someone in here?" Charlie froze, his breath seized in his throat.

He leaped to stand as Cat opened the door. There was Charlie, in boxers and a Police/Synchronicity concert T-shirt, blocking what appeared to be a pile of linens on the floor. "Hi, Mom," Charlie said, rubbing his eyes and yawning. He made a snap decision to play the dazed-and-confused card, the still-woozy kid who must have blacked out. *Though it might present its own set of problems since Mom's in AA, but better than the alternative.* "Are you looking for something, dear?" Cat glanced at the ransacked shelves. Only hair dryers, hot water bottles, and electric heating pads remained. "Is this where you slept?" she asked, trying to get a better look behind him. Charlie rubbed his eyes again. "Look at me, please," she demanded. "Were you here alone?"

Charlie looked up at his mom and saw Biz behind her over her shoulder, looking beautiful and remorseful as hell. "No," he mumbled, and glanced at Biz to assess her reaction. Her face fell. Charlie continued, "I had my dignity to keep me warm. Oh, wait. No I didn't."

Cat was impatient. "Charlie, tell me what—"

"Mom, it's no big deal. I got up to pee and then I was cold and remembered the extra blankets and must have . . ." He trailed off.

Cat said, "Did you forget where you were sleeping?" but didn't wait for an answer. Her fingers poked the air as she rattled. "You kids had better watch your drinking. This is how alcoholics are born, blacking out like this with no idea where you're supposed to be sleeping. It runs in our family, you know. They're now saying it's hereditary. Do I have to hide the booze? Drag you to my meetings? Scare you straight?"

"No, Mom. I'm sorry. I'll be careful."

"Don't you remember that CBS movie? *The Boy Who Drank Too Much*?"

"Not really. You told us about it, but it was on too late for me to—"

"Kids can be alcoholics, too, you know."

"Mom, I'm not Scott Baio, and I promise not to play hockey."

"Famous last words," said Cat. She was livid, her hands clenched. Biz mouthed, "Sorry" behind her back and Cat spun around to see who Charlie was looking at. Biz rubbed her eyes and fake-yawned, too. They were both such hack actors. Cat shook her head. "Downstairs in two minutes to help with breakfast. And the kitchen had better be clean."

On her way downstairs, Cat caught sight of E.J. sleeping next to Charlie's empty bed. His Walkman headphones askew around his neck, he looked like an angel, flushed with pink cheeks. Cat knew she should count her lucky stars, but felt uneasy all the same. She was trying to keep the big picture in mind: how lucky that they were all healthy and basically got along. Even E.J., who was a jerk to everyone. He'd done nothing to deserve his cousins' endless forgiveness, yet they still included him in their reindeer games. They could drive her crazy and worry her to pieces, but she loved falling asleep to their laughter and the sound of a quarter bouncing off the table. But too much drinking, she thought. *Not enough moderation.* They were growing up in a culture of the almighty cocktail—the keg party, to-go cup, and roadie. Hell, she'd learned to make martinis for her parents when she was *nine.*

Biz took a step toward Charlie to explain, but he recoiled, shooting daggers with his eyes. More bedroom doors opened, and she thought better of drawing attention to the muddle on the floor. She also needed more time to work out what she would tell Charlie and whether or not the truth would be involved. And Charlie needed to decide if he would ever speak to his best friend again. Grandpa Dun passed by and held out his arm for Biz, saying, "Good morning, young lady. Help me down the stairs, will you?" "Of course, Grandpa Dun," she said, and steadied him as he took the railing.

Aunt Cat had returned to the bustling kitchen at peak chaos. Family members inched past one another sideways, carrying platters and bowls back and forth to the table. "Where are the houseguests? And where's Choo?" asked Rah as she carried a hot bacon-onion-egg-and-cheese soufflé to the sideboard. Biz didn't answer; she was still in emotional triage mode. How would she behave around Foster? Plus there was her hangover to nurse. *Where* is *Choo? And where is* Foster? *Crap,* she thought for the first time. *This might not be as cut and dry as I thought, if I'd given it any thought, which I didn't because I was drunk on tequila, the bane of my existence . . .*

Foster entered the kitchen fully dressed. "Hello," he said with calm composure. No one had reminded Becky and Foster to stay in their pajamas for breakfast. "Someone didn't get the memo," Rah said as she passed him by. "What's the other one's name?"

Foster nodded hello to Becky. "That's you."

"Becky," she said, also fully dressed, standing in the doorway next to Foster. "Good morning, everyone. I'm the other one who also didn't get the memo. Should we change back?"

"Heavens no," said Claire.

"We're very open-minded here. You're perfect just as you are," said Grandpa Dun.

"*Who's* open-minded?" said Georgia in disbelief, traipsing into the kitchen in a short, loosely-tied satin kimono over a shorter cotton nightie. Her hair was tousled effortlessly; she looked undeniably sexy. Foster raised a slight eyebrow at Biz, then reintroduced himself to Georgia.

"You're the roommate," she said with a grin.

"And you're the sister," Foster replied.

"So they say," Georgia said, aware of her bare legs.

Claire asked, "Georgia, dear, won't you be cold?"

Cat and Georgia both answered, "No." Cat shook her head minutely at Georgia as if to say, *Ignore your Aunt Claire, dear.*

"Where am I sitting?" said Georgia.

"Next to me," said Claire, Cat, and Biz simultaneously.

"Let's have Georgia next to me," said Nana Miggs, her eyes bright with innuendo.

"Bizzy, where's Choo?" said Cat.

"Don't look at me," said Biz. Her headache was pounding.

"Who are Bizzy and Choo?" whispered Becky to Foster.

"Biz and Charlie," he replied.

"Oy," said Becky. "I'm going to need coffee."

Claire pointed. "Coffee's on the stove. Grab a plate and serve yourself. Becky, you're sitting there between Grandpa Dun and Charlie, wherever he is, and Foster, you're sitting between Biz and Nana Miggs." E.J., Rah, and Ned filled in boy-girl-boy-girl, modeling various versions of Scottish plaid flannel pajama sets. Cat and Claire wore Lanz nightgowns with fuzzy functional bathrobes, monogrammed and knotted at the waist. The table was set with sterling silver, white-wine glasses filled with chilled juice. Decorative gourds, nuts, and autumn leaves were scattered down the center as if brought in on the tiny backs of woodland creatures. The Thornden clan did its best to make

Becky and Foster feel welcome at the fringes of their forced family ritual. And as usual, Les was nowhere to be found.

"I've got Choo!" said Rah, bounding back into the kitchen. "I mean Charlie."

"Thank heavens," said Claire. "We were about to say grace."

"He wouldn't stay in his pajamas. I tried."

Charlie walked into the kitchen without pausing to say hello and headed straight to the aluminum drip coffeepot warming on the stove. "Good morning, sweetheart," said Cat to Charlie's fully clothed back as he poured himself a cup without answering his mother. "Please hurry, dear," she said, "everything's getting cold." Cat said it to mask his insolence; it was unlike her son to be rude.

"Start without me," Charlie muttered.

"Sit down, young man," boomed Grandpa Dun, "and liven up. If you can't soar with the eagles *dans le matin,* do not attempt to hoot with the owls at night."

"Sounds like I missed a winner," said Georgia. Charlie sat, making no eye contact.

"Where were *you* last night?" E.J. said to Georgia.

"I'll never tell," she demurred coyly.

"That's a departure," said Rah. "Hey, can I invite my roommate, Susan, next year?"

"May I," corrected Grandpa Dun.

"Of course, darling," said Nana Miggs.

Grandpa Dun began, "Let us bow our heads," to which Becky said to no one in particular, "Is Jesus going to factor into this? Because if so . . ."

"Don't worry, dear," said Nana Miggs, "we're lapsed Episcopals. You may enjoy the table decor if you prefer. Or say a silent prayer from your people."

Foster mouthed "*your* people" to Becky, who giggled and whispered back, "They're all mine." Biz elbowed Foster with a stern look; Cat noticed the electric energy between them. "Thanks, Mrs. Thornden," Becky said to Nana Miggs. She was doing a commendable job of ignoring Charlie's douche-y behavior and found the rest of his family affably entertaining. Biz looked over to Charlie at prayer time, but he still wouldn't look back. *Uh-oh*, she thought. She waited to see if he was just slow in remembering the little ritual they'd been sharing their whole lives, but he remained stalwart, head bowed.

However, Charlie wasn't praying, he was fuming.

The glint in Biz's eye fell away and a shadow crossed her face as she realized she must have hurt him, perhaps deeply. She wouldn't have minded if Charlie had ended up with Becky last night, though if she'd waited in the linen closet and fallen asleep on the floor she'd be pissed, too. *Look at me,* she thought desperately, *look up so you can see how deeply sorry I am with my big sad eyes. I was just having fun. Please look,* she implored Charlie with defective ESP, but he wouldn't look up, and Grandpa Dun's prayer was concluding with a nod to those "less fortunate than we." At the last moment she glanced at Foster, and to her shock he was sitting bolt upright among all the other rounded shoulders, looking directly at her, eyes wide open. He'd witnessed the entire Russian novel play out across her face. And there was that grin again—infuriating and cocksure. Georgia caught the tail end of the exchange between them, and Foster grinned over at her, too.

"Nice work, Dad," said Cat, and patted Grandpa Dun's arm.

"I do my best to show gratitude for our abundance."

E.J. jumped in, "Speaking of abundance, we must have had

a full house last night. Where did everyone sleep, if I may ask?" He looked at his little sister. Biz replied, "You may not ask." She said it to cover for Charlie, but realized she'd only implicated herself. Charlie looked at Biz for the first time all morning. He might have given himself the hangover but blamed her for his humiliation. He cupped his coffee with both hands and tucked in all but his middle finger. Biz noticed and hoped to catch a smirk on his face, but none followed. *Fuck you*, he was telling her. And he meant it.

Claire said, "Here's a little story. I got up in the night, which I never do, but I heard a peculiar noise. I thought perhaps a clock radio alarm had gone off, stuck between stations. So I did a bit of sleuthing and, lo and behold, it was one of our guests, sleeping soundly." Claire winked at Becky, who sighed good-naturedly. "Guilty as charged," she said raising a hand. "I should have mentioned my somnambulistic ways. Please accept my apology, Mrs. Chadwick. I hope you were able to fall back to sleep."

Grandpa Dun piped up. "Excellent word, my dear. 'Somnambulistic' is a real *beauté*."

Claire said, "I was, my dear, without delay. Biz, your bed was empty when I checked in on you two. Were you in the bathroom or did you end up on a couch?"

E.J. said, "Good question, Mom," then swiveled toward Biz, who wished she could hog-tie her brother and shoot a poison dart into his neck. Foster, too, was enjoying Biz's torture and his time with the Thornden bunch immensely.

Biz took a very long sip of coffee. "Yes, I slept on the living room couch for a while but then wished I had more blankets, so I headed back upstairs. Alone."

E.J. said, "I thought we had *plenty* of extra blankets," with mock surprise.

"So did I," said Claire, suspicious of her answer. Biz stared at the streaks of syrup on her plate. *Don't react,* she instructed herself.

"I'm sorry if I caused any trouble," said Becky.

"I don't think you had anything to do with the trouble," said Rah.

Cat launched into Biz. "Later I'm going to give you the same lecture I gave Charlie about your drinking, young lady."

E.J. said, "I'll wait for the movie version. Foster, were *you* warm enough?"

Foster glanced at Biz, then let loose a small chuckle, "Um, yes." Biz shot him a look—*don't you dare*—but it was too late. He didn't have to say anything; his eyes were gleaming with the postcoital zing of their recent screw. Charlie caught their exchange and Foster's smug smile—a smile he'd never seen on his roommate in all the time he'd known him. A smile so wide and laced with unrepentant delight it could have belonged to a conquering hero. It explained why Biz hadn't shown up. She was too busy fucking his roommate.

A well of fiery outrage ignited in Charlie's gut. His ears grew hot and numb; his stomach tightened. It was all he could do not to sweep everything off the table. He wanted to yell and scream and smash his chair to bits. He realized he had to get distance from Biz as soon as humanly possible—transfer schools, study abroad, get away.

Abruptly, he pushed back from the table, stood up but didn't move. He froze for a few odd seconds, just staring. When no pronouncement was forthcoming, his family searched one another, exchanging shrugs. Except for Biz, who watched Charlie, aching to hold him. There were times as children when they watched TV—something with true pathos like *M*A*S*H*—when Charlie needed her close to endure the intensity. She'd place her hand on his heart and snuggle in to give him mettle. She wanted to steady him now but could feel his ire. A mixture of damnation and defeat, it cut her to the bone without mercy. She realized in that moment she'd been cruel.

Grandpa Dun said, "You look a little lost, son." Charlie snapped to. He wanted to point a finger at Biz—call her a bitch and a dirty slut—but knew he was to blame for caring too much. He'd been wrong from the beginning to want her for himself.

"I have to go," Charlie said, then turned and left the room.

Rah scooted her chair back and said, "I'll deal." Nana Miggs asked, "Does anyone know what's upsetting him?" The table waited for Biz to answer. "I don't know," she finally replied, which was unexpected. Claire said, "You *don't?*"

"I can't read his mind," said Biz, and took another bite of soggy pancake.

Georgia said, "You *can't?*"

E.J. said, "That's not what you've been telling all of us since you both were five. I thought you shared the same brain. What happened to 'God broke one brain in two pieces and gave us each half,' remember?" Biz ignored E.J. and then did the oddest thing that Cat or anyone would notice all day—nothing. She glanced at Foster, wishing she hadn't. Her mom caught the exchange; so did Aunt Cat. *Something isn't quite right between the three of them,* she thought, *but why wouldn't Choo spill it? And what on earth was there to spill?*

"Um," said Becky tentatively, "is he coming back?" She was unsure of her next move and felt abandoned. In truth, Becky was not so much confused by Charlie's behavior—he was obviously honestly upset by something—as she was by his family's reaction. At her grandparents' house in Westchester, her mother would have insisted he sit back down and finish his meal, then have seconds. Failing that, every member of her family—aunts, cousins, and Bubbe—would have tromped up the stairs, banged on his door, and demanded to know what just happened. It was fascinating to see WASPs in action—avoiding conflict at all costs. It's a wonder they ever got anything sorted out.

Cat didn't approve of her son's behavior but kept it to herself. He was reminding her of her first husband and behaving like a dick. But she was too afraid of his temper to put him in check. And she didn't want to ruin the family meal. Claire said, "Keep eating, everyone. What shall we talk about?" Then she pasted on a smile, which did little to camouflage the disappointment that her yearly tradition had been marred by a childish snit.

E.J. said to Becky, "Is our special brand of awkward family denial anything like yours?" Becky was not charmed. She said, "You're a real piece of work, you know that?" Then to the table, "Where'd you get this guy?" Nana Miggs said, "Woolworth's Five and Dime."

Rah entered the kitchen breathless. "He's leaving." The front door closed with a thud.

"Elvis has left the building," E.J. said.

"Shut *up*!" said Biz.

"*Elizabeth*, we don't use that phrase in this family," said Claire.

Cat offered, "Ned can give him a—"

"He says he wants to walk to the station," said Rah. "And he'll see everyone in a few weeks for Thanksgiving." Georgia looked over at Becky and said dryly, "More forced family fun. Want to come back?" Becky lifted her eyebrows and said only, "Um."

Later on, Cat found her sister in the linen closet, refolding and stacking the bedding, which had been stuffed back onto the shelves willy-nilly. The unspoken goal was perfection, like one would find at Bamberger's or B. Altman's. Cat reflexively grabbed a blanket and anchored the middle edge under her chin. The sisters spoke as they worked—the way women of their generation did—rarely allowing themselves the luxury of a chat without multitasking.

"What on earth do you think happened in here?" Claire sighed as she bent down again to the floor.

"I don't know," said Cat, "but I want to ask you something. What do you think went on at the table this morning?"

"I can't be bothered with the two of them. They're either bickering like on *The Honeymooners* or thick as thieves like in *Harold and Maude*. It's hardly worth trying to keep up. They always come around."

"You didn't actually see *Harold and Maude,* did you?"

"No, but you get my point."

Cat refocused the conversation. "You're not answering my question." Claire paused for a moment and said, "I don't buy that Choo's sweet on Becky. To me, he seemed upset that Bizzy and Foster were so chummy."

"I agree, but why?" Cat pried.

"I don't know," Claire said, avoiding her eyes. She had a hunch she refused to follow.

"And why are we cleaning up bedding off the floor in here?"

"I don't know."

"Foster had his own room. If he wanted to sneak someone in, he could have." Claire was following her sister's reasoning but pretended not to. "What are you saying?"

Cat said, "I'm saying I think Bizzy and Choo met up here. But then something happened and they got in a fight. Or something went wrong—"

"To do *what*?" said Claire, the *t* at the end of the word slicing the air between them.

"*I don't know! That's what I'm asking you!*" Cat hissed. She'd come into the linen closet to get her sister's take on a theory she'd had, but she also wanted to stick it to her for ignoring the unsettling truth in her midst, for only opening her eyes to what was pleasing—for ignoring their kids' other connection. If Charlie was jealous of Foster, Cat could save him the hidden heartbreak and tell him he was free to follow his impulse. But their world would never condone it, having been raised as first cousins, *and her dad wouldn't forgive the scandal. Agnes would revoke the trust fund and E.J. would have a field day. Nope, the truth would have to stay knotted.* But Claire had to be made aware so they could address it.

"There is another option, you know," said Cat. She stopped folding. "That something happened between Biz and Foster to upset Charlie, and *not* because he has a crush on Foster . . . Because Charlie has a thing for Biz." Claire froze. *Bingo,* thought Cat; *she knows I'm right.* She continued, "I think, possibly, Biz and Charlie have been romantic with each other. I don't mean romantic exactly, more like sexual. Or maybe I do mean romantic. I don't know. Remember when you caught them in the furnace room when they were young? What were they doing? You never told me. You just said they were 'depraved.'"

"I didn't witness anything," said Claire. She deployed white lies as rationalizations with little effort or remorse.

Cat went on, "We left them alone a lot when they were little. It's possible they explored over the years. And you know how kids experiment. Something about the way they were behaving this morning made me think of jealous lovers, and I was wondering if you picked up on it or if—"

"I did not." Claire thought back to that moment in the basement. She didn't actually *see* anything untoward but had merely jumped to what she assumed was a legitimate conclusion when she saw Choo dragged from the room unbuckled.

Cat prodded, "And all this bedding all over the floor—"

"Stop. Stop it right now," Claire fumed. She paused, trying to cobble together the sentence that would bundle everything, neat and tidy, but it eluded her. "*You're* depraved!" was all she could think to say.

"I'm *serious*!" Cat snapped back. "Remember how we used to have a crush on Cousin Matthew? How he looked so much like Rock Hudson we couldn't help ourselves from mincing around him at holidays? Poor man, now he's dying and it turns out he was always gay—"

"Stop it!" Claire raised her sharpened voice to a level that surprised Cat. Though it didn't shock her; she'd been navigating her sister's temper for years.

"No. I won't stop it," said Cat. "I'm telling you it might be something we have to consider. We may have to be supportive, plus things could get bumpy. I had a friend in college who married her first cousin, and the whole family—"

"*Enough!* Bizzy and Choo are *not* having a secret love affair."

"No, but Biz and Charlie might be. They're in college now, practically adults. We have to give them space to—"

"No, *we don't*. And don't pretend this is all right with you. You're just taking this moronic tack to get at me for drinking in front of you—"

"*What* are you *talking* about?" Cat was incredulous. "I don't give a shit that you drink in front of me. I'm taking this tack because it's the path of least resistance, because if this is the life they choose, they're going to need our support. Especially in Larkspur, New Jersey!"

"I'm not listening to any more of this!" Claire said, leaning into Cat's face. She'd been shutting down fights this way since they were kids. Her precious daughter would meet someone at the beach club or in the city at a mixer. She would stop making those inane homemade costumes, settle into a legitimate career, then quit to have a nice family of her own with a handsome financier. Claire thought, *Cat's insufferable,* then hissed, "Leave me out of it." She wedged a blanket onto the shelf and stormed out, not bothering to slam the door.

Cat remained, furious. She hated her sister for being so closed-minded and unwilling to evolve with the world around her. *If Claire doesn't think about it, it doesn't exist.* She'd always been big on revisionist history. *She would have made a great mob boss or dictator's wife,* Cat thought as she studied the closet's hardwood floor. She imagined how Bizzy and Choo might have fit together side by side, noses and thighs touching, arms intertwined. *It is a cozy spot,* she thought, *like a hidden faraway fort.* She imagined them there in their pajamas, warming each other in the early-morning chill, finding one another, stifling giggles.

Cat remembered dancing with Cousin Matthew on New Year's Eve when she was fourteen or fifteen. As he shuffled her around the living room carpet her palms grew sweaty. They were half drunk on pilfered champagne. To calm her nerves she sang along to Nat King Cole, mumbling the lyrics of "Unforgettable" she knew so well. When she looked up at Matthew he was smiling in the most peculiar way. Their eyes locked, and the smell of his bay rum cologne made her want to kiss him, then run away. But she couldn't escape. Though he held her lightly, she felt soldered to his arms. At last, she broke from his gaze before she could blush. "I have to pass hors d'oeuvres— probably some stupid deviled eggs." Cat didn't look directly at Matthew again for years, until he was married off and her desire had thoroughly subsided.

Eventually, Claire will have to consider it, Cat thought. *And if it lasts, I will have to spill the truth. But if I tell him and he doesn't truly love Biz, I'll have lost him his inheritance for nothing. They're both too young. It'll have to wait. Let's see how things play out.*

Before leaving she was straightening the row of beat-up Louis Vuitton suitcases, when a corner of silver foil revealed itself under faded leather. Cat knew before bending down that she had found a condom. *Could be anyone's.* But who was she kidding. She tucked it in her pocket, then weighed her options: dispose of it, or keep it as proof.

Cat cornered Biz alone later on when they were packing. Biz panicked she might have to lie. She'd learned long ago to withhold pieces of truth from her mother but didn't want to do that with Aunt Cat. "May I speak with you for a moment?" Cat said, and sat down on the edge of the bed without waiting for an answer.

"Sure," said Biz.

"I'm here because I love you and Choo, excuse me, Charlie. And I'm worried about you both." Cat grabbed a blouse and helped Biz fold.

"Okay," said Biz warily, and continued packing, looking down, busy as a bee.

Cat tried to meet her eyes. "What's going on with Charlie?"

"I don't know."

"Please be honest with me. And don't say 'Becky' because I don't buy it. He didn't even notice she was in the room."

"I like her," said Biz brightly, and meant it.

"Don't change the subject, young lady." Cat continued, "I think Charlie's rude departure had something to do with you and his roommate, Foster. I think something happened—"

"Nothing happened between me and Foster," Biz was too quick to say.

"No. Between you and Charlie," Cat said and Biz faltered. "I'm wondering if perhaps you and Charlie have grown too close. Some would say inappropriately close . . ." She studied Biz's reaction. "Be honest, please."

Biz's eyes grew large, and her eyebrows arched with worry. "I can't miss this train. We have class in the—"

"Look at me," said Cat. It was a stern but pleading request that hung in the air with desperation, reminding Biz they both cared for Charlie more than anyone else in the world.

Biz finally met her aunt's gaze but said nothing.

Cat spoke slowly. "Biz, sweetheart, I think you understand more than you'll say. So I want you to consider this: it's now extremely important you make an effort to allow yourselves to grow toward other people, as hard as that might be. You need to give him space."

"We're trying to—" Biz began, then realized she shouldn't have spoken and froze.

Cat took in her niece's beauty. So many hours left to their own devices while the adults made daiquiris, played backgammon, and danced. Biz's statuesque figure—all those summers in bikinis—had to have been difficult to ignore, even camouflaged by flat-front chinos and boy's rugby shirts. Cat spoke gently, attempting not to sound accusatory. "I know you're both trying. And I like Foster and Becky. But Charlie needs a clear message. You may have to insist." Cat thought again of the condom. "You're stronger than he is . . . you have more, um, control."

Biz thought of how easily she weakened when faced with her growing sexual desire. "Trust me, he has more control—"

"The world isn't ready for . . . could never handle . . . just, please, be his *friend*."

Biz, used to seeing a confidante in her aunt, was now seeing a mother's concern. But not having children herself, she was unable to imagine the depths of its cost. She had no idea of the social expectations laid on Thornden wives and mothers. She and Charlie were instructed to play together and did as they were told. And, yes, Marco Polo in the shallow end had become cigarettes, booze, and sex—the inevitable developmental deep end. *A game's a game,* she reasoned with herself. *Learn the rules, play, and have fun.* They trusted each other implicitly, and that had to have value. They leaned on each other when their parents were awful, which had always been worth the world.

"I *am* his friend" was her only response. Aunt Cat backed down and left.

Biz clicked her suitcase shut, pushing the brass latches down with her thumbs. She liked the sound and feeling of making them lock at the same time. It punctuated the relief that came with surviving an emotional showdown with Aunt Cat—the grown-up in the whole world she loved most. Besides, Aunt Cat was wrong—Charlie wasn't as weak as she suggested. Biz found him self-assured, intuitive, and a very skilled partner. And now he was a gorgeous man with a body few women could ignore. Biz would like to think she had that much power over him but knew she didn't. They were in this thing together—equal partners, same goals. He knew she'd slept with other guys and had to have known Foster wasn't special. He was simply new and close by and she was drunk, no surprise. Biz decided that when she returned home to Boston, she'd give Charlie a night or two to simmer down. Then she'd head to his dorm, ignore Foster, and take Charlie out for a burger. She'd apologize, tell him Foster meant nothing; then they could get on with their stupid lives. And he and Becky might need a fresh start.

On Charlie's train ride back to Boston he came up with his own solution to their mess. In fact, Biz would probably thank him one day if he ever decided to talk to her again, which he had no immediate plans to.

On Monday morning he went straight to the Office of Overseas Student Study. He asked the tough-looking, sixty-ish broad behind the desk if it was too late in the semester to go to Paris. "If you don't mind making up the work you've missed in the first three weeks of classes," she responded flatly, barely looking up over her glasses. Charlie replied he didn't mind. "Swell, because the cutoff for add/drop is next week. How soon can you leave?" Her Boston accent was thick and tinged with the faint whiff of perpetual annoyance. "Tomorrow," said Charlie. He had money in the bank from his summer job and could afford a last-minute three-hundred-dollar one-way ticket. She removed her readers and let them drop onto her bosom, held by a cheap plastic chain. Then she leaned her chin on her clasped hands, noting the eyelashes on the Adonis before her.

Charlie figured her name, with the mood to match, was very likely Doris.

"What will you study?" she said, wanting to not like him.

"What've ya got?" He flashed his winningest dimpled smile.

"How's your French?" she asked. They both knew the answer didn't matter.

"*C'est super,*" Charlie said, sounding like an arrogant French bastard. She shook her head and grinned as she handed him her pen.

"Here's your stylo, kid. Better get started."

He took the pen, loosened his coat, and sat down to fill out the forms.

Biz arrived at Charlie's dorm late Tuesday morning. She was about to knock when she thought she heard music. It was classical, but not Bach—not the majestic sweeping sound Grandpa Dun blared all summer, windows open for the whole block to hear. It was a quiet, languid piano, less anxious and more pained. Perhaps Chopin, but she couldn't be sure, though it had the richness of honest, aching beauty.

Biz turned the knob and snuck in undetected.

There was no sign of Foster, but over in the alcove, Charlie played piano with his back to the world. The volume was loud enough to blanket a low squeak as Biz sat on the edge of his bed. She listened, slowly tearing as Charlie played, moved to see him ripped raw to his core. He was trying to master the transition after the first section of "Clair de Lune." It was that or punch a hole in the wall. For the first time he was tapping into the exquisite pain of the song he'd been made to learn as a child. He knew it was pedestrian but didn't give a fuck. *It's a goddamn classic for a reason.*

When the song reached its end, Biz's heart broke. She worried she'd hurt him inexorably. His shoulders were so hunched he looked shattered and torn. He paused, then outstretched his left hand, and began the bass chords for "Rikki, Don't Lose That Number"—one of their absolute jazz fusion faves. They slipped into the cool current of Steely Dan's world, where nothing else mattered except their tangle of yearning. Then Charlie stopped playing and abruptly switched off his keyboard.

Shame there'd be no piano in Paris.

Biz stood, the mattress springs giving her away. He whipped around, his eyes flashing with caged contempt. It was an unfamiliar feeling and rendered her mute. When he finally spoke his voice was robotic, devoid of warmth. And for that matter, friendship. And love.

"How long have you been here?" Charlie asked.

Anxious, she said, "Hi. I'm sorry."

"Why didn't you knock?"

"I just. You play beautifully. Like Billy Joel or Chico Marx when he gets serious." She was fumbling to mask the words she knew she shouldn't say to describe the feelings that had welled up inside her.

"Fuck you," said Charlie.

"I know," she said, "and the horse I rode in on. I agree. I suck. And you have a right to be pissed. But I tried to—" Biz unfolded the whole saga, even the parts she'd already told him, beginning with trying to reach him at his dorm before he left.

Charlie stopped listening and fully drank her in, knowing he wouldn't see her for a while. She was the most confident girl he'd ever met though her beauty unintentionally preceded her. Charlie had grown up listening to strangers pay her compliments out of the blue, and each time she demurred, pretending it was the first time. She lied to make them feel special, but if everyone felt special—Charlie reasoned—then no one truly was.

Biz concluded her speech and scanned the room. It was more chaotic than usual. A sky-blue hard-shell Samsonite suitcase sat open and full of clothes on Charlie's bed. She assumed he was unpacking from the weekend, but a travel alarm clock and power converter lay next to an electric shaver. Something just wasn't right. She said, "That's my story, now it's your turn. You behaved abysmally, too, you know, not only toward me but your family, and Becky, your roommate—"

"He," Charlie cut her off midsentence, "is dead to me."

"Uh, okay, Michael Corleone."

Usually Biz could make him crack, but not this time. Charlie remained stone-faced. On Sunday night Foster had made it clear he'd be writing his term paper over at the main library. "That's where the learning happens," he said before heading out the door. He and Foster had not discussed the weekend, nor did Charlie tell his roommate of his transatlantic plans: that he would be on a flight by Tuesday dinnertime. Then, hopefully, once surrounded by Frenchwomen and crêpe stands, Biz would finally recede from his mind.

"So be it," said Biz. "May Foster rest in peace." She'd knowingly teased Charlie's limits in the past, but seemed to have pushed buttons beyond humor's salvation.

Biz took off her coat and sat on the edge of Foster's bed as she spoke, hoping the gesture would transmit a familiarity that would return their relationship to normal. "Bottom line is, I slept with your roommate, big deal, who cares. Neither Foster nor I do. I came here to tell you I'm truly sorry for oversleeping—"

"You mean overfucking."

"And for your having to spend the night on the cold floor."

"You forgot hard."

"I beg your pardon?"

"It was hard, Biz. The floor. Among other things—unless he couldn't . . ."

"Very funny. Look, is this how it's going to be now? Do you need a week's break?"

"We'll get longer than a week," Charlie said, and filled an empty duffel bag with a Super 8 camera and a tall orange stack of square two-minute film reels.

Biz zeroed in on the European power converter. "I don't understand. Are you packing or unpacking? What's happening? Where are you going?"

"Paris," Charlie said with the same offhanded tone he'd use if he were heading to the dining hall. This was the moment he'd been looking forward to, and it was just as delicious as he'd hoped. He began to whistle "La Vie en Rose."

Biz was nonplussed. "What, like tomorrow?" She was kidding.

"*Mais non,*" Charlie chirped. "Six P.M. tonight." He'd felt a freedom since signing the documents for his semester abroad and was smug with the promise of adventure. Biz, meanwhile, felt hit in the gut. The rushing pulse in her head became distracting. "Does Aunt Cat know?" she asked, still processing the information.

"Yes. I told all the people who matter to me."

"Isn't it going to be a pain for them to reassign a new

roommate?" She didn't give a crap about dorm room administration; she was groping for an excuse that might keep him here. Grabbing at straws, she said, "Does Foster know?"

Charlie lost it. All composure went right out the window. "What the *fuck* does Foster have to do with *any of this*?"

"Don't shout at me!" shouted Biz.

"Don't *fuck with me*!" boomed Charlie. His father's predilection for alcoholic rage surfaced immediately as if prodded with a sharp stick. "I'm sick of you *fucking with my head*!" he yelled.

"Well, I'm sick of you fucking with mine!"

Charlie lunged toward Biz with burning eyes and put both hands on her shoulders. He could feel her thin clavicle bones through her sweater and squeezed her as if she were clay. He growled, "Hey, I know. Let's pretend I'm Foster," and plunged his hand down her jeans. Biz winced and let out a shocked *"Charlie!"* but he ignored her and kept shoving his way down. "Stop it, fuck, *stop*!" He reached her pubis; his fist was between her thighs. Biz pulled up on his arm as hard as she could but was unable to dislodge him. *"Cut it out!"* she cried, clamping her thighs together. She was pissed for not being as strong. His groping hurt and she began to feel frightened, but no voice in her head said to scream. *This is Charlie,* she thought, *I can handle this.* She leaned in and bit him hard on the shoulder. "Hey!" he yelped, and pushed her back. She tried to control her shaking, but he reached for her fly and unzipped it. She slapped him, urging *"Stop!"* through clenched teeth. She was kicking his shins wildly. He shoved her onto the bed. Her head hit the mattress and bounced back up abruptly. They were both stunned by the slam of her forehead. "Ow," Charlie said, and she tried to lock her elbows against his chest, but he was stronger and they gave way. Charlie used his full body weight to pin her while she lay squirming on Foster's bed. Fear overtook anger as he unbuckled his belt with one hand and kept her pinned. Yet, she was still afraid to scream for help because she didn't want to get him in trouble. So she spoke to him pointedly in a deep register, as if giving crucial, life-saving instruction. *"Choo, what the hell are you doing?* Knock it off, or I swear, Choo, I am *going to scream."* She hoped hearing his childhood nickname would snap him out of it and let her escape.

But Charlie stayed focused and spoke with eerie calm. "You weren't a screamer with Foster. Why don't you show me how quiet you were." He felt mean but chose not to care. Biz urged, *"Stop, Choo, or I'll scream,"* repeating it like a manic mantra. Yet of all the options her mind raced after, she was unable to raise her voice for help. Charlie felt entitled to ignore Biz's pleas as he felt he'd been ignored. They'd been grabbing things from each other their entire lives. Besides, she wanted it, too, he told himself. They'd talked about it for years. *Why not fuck her, then get on the plane.*

Charlie fumbled with his zipper while prodding her legs apart with a knee. He wasn't hard yet, but was sure he'd be in a minute. Biz wrenched a forearm free and reached out to the bedside shelf. Feeling for anything hard or heavy, she couldn't believe she'd ever wanted him. She grabbed a plastic VHS tape of *Repo Man* and smacked Charlie's head with purpose and fury. "Ow," he said, and shook it off, as if his task had been briefly interrupted. *"Choo, stop!"* Biz screamed in one short burst, then hit him again, this time harder. *"Ow!"* Charlie said in anger, and pulled back to look in her eyes. He was confused by what he saw; she was terrified and crying. He hadn't seen her look this scared since a clown took her hand when they were little. He was only handing her a circus balloon, but she'd screamed with bloodcurdling fright. Charlie had yelled at the clown to leave her alone, then hugged Biz as she cried. He'd protected her in that moment as she'd always protected him. Now, seeing her face masked in terror, he snapped out of his horrendous haze, dumbfounded he could be the reason. *Who am I?*

Biz wedged her knees between their chests and wriggled a foothold on his stomach, the way she did when they played airplane as kids. She kicked him away with her remaining strength, hissing, "You *fucking maniac*!" Charlie tumbled back off the bed, then checked his nose in the mirror. A trickle of blood made its way down his face. "What the hell," he murmured to himself. "*What the hell?!*" shrieked Biz. "Have you *lost your mind*?" She'd finally found her voice. Charlie was in the weird middle place of returning to himself. He felt confused like maybe that clown from the circus.

Biz scrambled off the bed and zipped her jeans. Her hands shook as she tucked in her ripped shirt. She buttoned her coat, then lunged at Charlie and pummeled him with as much force as she could summon. Biz had never wanted to inflict pain the way she wanted to hurt Charlie—profoundly, with marks he'd shamefully have to explain. "You *asshole*!" she screamed, and started to cry, her tightly balled fists losing speed and strength. Charlie deflected her swings, surprised by the attack, still unaware he'd been a monster. "Whoa, whoa," was all he said, as if wrangling a tantrumming child. He seemed genuinely flummoxed by her actions. Biz was too consumed with retribution to notice Charlie's wrath was no longer in control, and the person she'd always loved and trusted remained, though diminished. She grabbed his shirt in twists of cotton and brought her face close to his, tears streaming down her cheeks, jaw clenched. She spoke one word at a time, barely eking out the sounds. Her throat was swollen; she tasted salt on her lips as her nose ran loose and clear. "You. Will. *Never. Ever.* Touch me. Again," she said with fiery eyes. "*Never. Ever.* Again. Do you hear me? *Never.*"

Charlie said nothing and let her finish, having been taught it was disrespectful to interrupt. "I hate you," Biz said, then unhanded his shirt. She used her sleeve to wipe the small dot of blood on her forehead and the snot from her chin. "I'm sorry," he whispered. He couldn't believe he'd been the source of her terror. "I'm so, so sorry." Charlie remembered his father making him feel that way, small and unsafe. The fear was utterly and horrifically unspeakable. He'd never suspected he would become his father and put the thought out of his mind. Charlie's eyes grew large and round, his forehead wrinkled. *Oh my God, I did that to her.* "I love you so much," he whispered, and moved toward her, wanting to wipe her shiny, wet cheeks. She flinched and, cowering, backed toward the door. "Get away from me, you fuck, or I'll scream, this time for real." He froze where he was. "Bizzy, I'm so, so sorry." And he was, in fact, ashamed. He was angry at himself—and his father, but mostly himself. Then, in a cascade, he realized the devastation he'd wrought. "I didn't mean to hurt you. I'd never do anything . . . I'm so sorry. That was *totally wrong* and I don't know why . . . I was stupid and jealous. Forgive me. Bizzy, *I love you so, so much,* and *I'm sorry.* Please believe me. *I swear, there's no one like you.*"

Biz lowered her voice and said in a calm, steady stream of command, "Fuck off. I don't care. And back up or I'll scream."

"Okay, okay, I'm sorry, I'm stepping back now, I promise." Charlie backed away, hands up as if surrendering.

Biz's arms were folded across her chest, her hair in messy loops, her eyes and lips still puffy from salted tears. "I'm going to splash my face. Don't come near me."

"I won't, I promise. And I—"

"And don't talk to me," Biz said. She moved around him as if he were a snake.

At the sink next to the hot plate, she let cool water fill her cupped hands before smoothing it over her face, giving her fortitude.

It was then that Foster walked in.

"Hey," he said to Charlie without looking directly at him. The door had been unlocked, so there was no need to knock. Charlie looked down and said, "Hey." Biz noticed Foster enter and filled her hands again to drink, reclaiming strength with each sip. She grabbed a clean T-shirt from Charlie's bed and used it to pat her face. Then she tossed it on the floor.

As she left, Foster said, "Hey," to Biz, but she ignored them both.

"Bye," said Charlie, being careful not to move toward her.

"Bye," Foster added, but she was already down the hall.

Biz took the fire stairs directly to the outside alley. Her teeth were chattering, though she wasn't cold. She crossed to walk on the side of the street where she could feel the sun shining and closed her eyes a few seconds at a time, once oncoming pedestrians had passed by. She meant to walk fast, but a voice inside told her not to run. Also not to tell a soul what had happened. *Maybe it was a little my fault because I slept with Foster. And left Charlie alone in the linen closet, embarrassed.* She never meant to hurt his feelings and understood he was mad, but fuck him. *I did nothing wrong. Fuck. Him.*

Foster said to Charlie, "Hey, man—" and Charlie cut him

off. "Don't talk to me," he said and left without his coat. He headed in the direction he hoped Biz wasn't. He felt she should have her space. He leaned into the wind and was blasted by unseasonably frigid air that stung like shards of glass. Realizing his behavior had been unspeakably egregious, he wished someone would punch him in the face. He knew he deserved the pain and slammed his knuckles into a brick building as he waited with other pedestrians for the signal to cross. The light turned green, but Charlie turned around. He needed to get back and finish packing.

Biz spent the next few days in a torrent of anger, unreasonable short temper, and guilt. *Why the hell didn't I scream for help?* It seemed so obvious to her now but not at the time. Zombielike, she spent hours in her dorm shower, weeping. Though rife with indignation, she questioned her reaction. She hadn't been raped, she told herself, but the consolation did little to soothe. Were these extreme emotional aftershocks valid? Hadn't she been *almost* raped? Did that even *count*? Should she even be using that word at all? Biz had never felt so incensed, helpless, and hurt. She wanted vehemently to get back at Charlie but not get him in trouble. *The fucker is gone. I guess I'll eventually get over it.*

Biz felt unable to bring herself to exact retribution but vacillated about whether or not to tell someone what had happened. It never occurred to her to go to the campus clinic. What could anyone possibly do for her now? And what if she decided to tell her parents? Would she make up a fake name to protect Charlie? Then what was the point? Aunt Cat had taught her to listen to her gut about guys who made her uneasy. In high school she was told she could always call home for a ride. "Walk away, make something up, just get out of there," Aunt Cat had said.

But no one had ever discussed "almost rape." And certainly no one ever mentioned the possibility she might *know* the person. When she heard stories it was always a stranger and never a family relation. At times Biz vibrated with anger when recalling being pinned to the bed. She loathed hearing his voice and was still livid for being weaker. *You colossal prick, you're not supposed to scare me like that. You're supposed to protect me from assholes—not* be *the asshole.*

And now Charlie was living in fucking Paris. *Fucker. Fuck-face. Fuck.*

The fact that Charlie wasn't around at Thanksgiving for Biz to seethe and scowl at made it more difficult for her to resolve her hatred. Some of her anger was replaced by the conflict of missing her best friend. But how good a friend could he be if he tried to hurt her? She was able to slow herself from obsessing during the day, but in the evening had no control over her dreams. Night after night, alternate endings played out in a darkened dreamscape, more harrowing than her fading memory—endings that woke her out of sound sleep. Then she'd be wide awake for hours, her heart beating out of her chest as if overcaffeinated, no one chasing her but her mind. She'd try to calm herself by admonishing that she should be over it—time heals all wounds and all that. Then she'd think about how much she missed Charlie and what he might say to calm her . . . then she'd grow pissed at her own betrayal, and the cycle would begin again.

Biz's turmoil diminished as time passed and Christmas loomed. Did it even happen the way she remembered? Was it not as extreme or worse? Her emotions were muddled, and she kicked herself for not having made other close friends. Charlie had been her number one for so long, she'd never cultivated a second string. Maybe Piper had some advice; she certainly always had opinions. She was tough and probably knew how to move on. Biz picked out some monogrammed stationery, sat down and wrote her a letter—said she was asking for a friend. But once she learned Piper was studying in London for the semester, she crumpled it up and threw it away. By the time she might get a response—ten days in the mail each way—her drama would probably be over.

Two weeks before Christmas break, Biz developed a low-grade stomachache. She assumed it was a virus that wouldn't go away. She told Tindy her cat at home died—though she didn't have one—in order to explain her excessive sleeping and mood swings. Then she fainted in the shower, slithered down just like in *Psycho*. Her period was late. She bought a test. Biz was pregnant. Not knowing what else to do, she called her Aunt Cat from a pay phone, eight blocks west of her dorm in a student-less neighborhood.

"Oh, dear," said Aunt Cat.

"*I know!*" Biz sobbed.

"Honey, you're going to be fine. We'll figure it out. How far along are you?"

"Um." Biz counted the weeks since Fall Festival—since Foster. "Six? Seven?"

Aunt Cat didn't hesitate. "Is it Charlie's?"

"*Oh my God, no! Jesus!*" Biz said, heaving, "*I can't believe you would—*"

Aunt Cat cut in. "Do not raise your voice at me, young lady. I am trying to help you. I only asked because I found a condom in the linen closet, during Fall Festival, at the spot where

Charlie slept. And I am not an idiot, though I am continually surprised. So let's calm down and not bite the hand that's trying to save your ass."

"Okay, Aunt Cat. I'm sorry. I'll be nice."

"You don't have to be nice, just don't be Veruca Salt. Let's try this again, shall we? Whose is it?"

Biz lost her last shred of composure and resumed her sobs. "It's *mi-i-i-ine*!"

"Yes, that is correct, but who *else's*? Is it someone you love? Someone you're planning on marrying . . . You know what? Doesn't matter. It's the eighties, modern times. Do you want to keep it? Does the father know yet?"

Biz felt she was being hammered with questions, though in reality her aunt was quite calm. She settled down to consider her answers but forgot where to start. "I thought calling you would be easier than calling Mom," she whimpered.

"I know, my dear, but these questions are important, I'm afraid. I'll need the answers before we take the next step. Take a deep breath. Let's start at the beginning: I love you and I'm here for you. It's wonderful that you're fertile. Plenty of women can't get pregnant, so that's a plus. What do you think you'd like to do, dear?"

Biz stared at the pay phone's coin return, tapping the door so it swung in and out, catching it on the tip of her finger. "I don't know," she said, winding down, slowing her breath. But she did know. She knew no way in hell was she keeping a baby, and thank God she wasn't Catholic, because she wouldn't be pressured to keep it by her lapsed Episcopal mother. Biz was in college now, and when she graduated she wanted a career. She wanted to travel and fall in love. She wanted an abortion.

She just didn't know if she could say the words.

Aunt Cat piped up after giving Biz enough time with her thoughts. "This is a big decision, and I'm here to help in any—"

Biz interrupted. "I want an abortion." The moment she heard herself say the words she knew it was the right choice.

"Righty-o. I will take you," said Aunt Cat, also clearly relieved.

"I'm so sorry to make you do this, Aunt Cat. You have no idea."

"I *do* have an idea, and we've all been there in some form or another. You know what Nana Miggs taught us: it'll all work out fine. Besides, no one's perfect."

"Mom is."

"Including your mom." Aunt Cat wanted to add, "Especially your mom," but decided against it.

Biz cried jogging back to her dorm room, this time tears of relief. Life was short but life was also long; she was making the right decision. She splashed her face when she got home, as she'd been taught by her mother, then slept better that night than she had in weeks. She expected to feel conflicted or wrestle with her conscience, for her dreams to haunt her, but they never did. She felt unapologetic about terminating a pregnancy with a man she didn't love, for a baby she was ill equipped to take care of and not religiously compelled to keep. Aunt Cat would drive up to pack Charlie's stuff—he'd decided to stay in Paris until summer. She would chaperone Biz, who was grateful as hell—and wicked glad Charlie was gone.

The day of the appointment Biz awoke with angst and embarrassment—regretting her one-night folly, kicking her dumb self once again. The clinic was clean and well lit, and Aunt Cat was prepared for the wait. She brought an unfinished bargello needlepoint, a Snickers, and a cardigan sweater. Biz cried when they took her away to get changed—part apprehension and part self-scolding. When they asked, "Are you doing this of your own free will?" she answered, "Of course I am. I mean, who else?" Then, "Oh. I get it." She found the staff patient and friendly, though she was reticent to look anyone in the eye. In fact, she closed hers tightly during the vacuumlike extrication, which was louder than she'd imagined. Tears streaked her cheeks, and the stirrups were unbearably cold; she wished more than anything to be unconscious. Recovery felt endless with no wristwatch and bad cramps. Swaddled in the long row of La-Z-Boys, Biz stared at the ficus. She learned no one's stories and made no new girlfriends. She just wanted it to be over.

Afterward, Biz and Aunt Cat lunched at Daisy Buchanan's on Newbury. When her soup came with two spoons, Biz said to the waiter, "Thanks. I'm eating only for one, now." Neither of them laughed and the waiter walked away, confused. Then, Biz said, "I knew I'd find a joke today somewhere." During the meal Cat impressed upon her, in no uncertain terms, why taking a pill a day was nonnegotiable. She also gave a brief lecture on the pitfalls of pulling out, then rounded it off by marching Biz into a drugstore and making her buy condoms to carry in her purse.

"What if it falls out of my wallet?"

"Bat your eyes and make a joke."

"A dick joke? But I'm a girl."

"Women's lib. You'll think of something."

They went back to Cat's hotel and snuggled into the queen-sized bed and watched *The Cosby Show, Family Ties*, and *Cheers*. Biz took extra Tylenol to loosen the painful squeezing in her abdomen, then fell sound asleep and didn't stir.

.   .   .

Charlie had written Biz every few days from his tiny Latin Quarter atelier, stopping at the post office even before unpacking. She tossed the feathery powder-blue airmail letters unopened into a Chuck Taylor shoebox. They accumulated under her bed, and the ritual became trite.

Biz decided to open them, finally, on the night of her last fall exam. She laid them out in chronological order, then poured some tequila from her stash. They were genuine apologies, elaborate declarations of remorse. He begged to rekindle their friendship, once they "took some space." He wrote entire paragraphs in Terces and evoked games they'd made up as kids. He included a brief update on his current script. Sometimes he sent a little something he knew she'd love like a photo of Deyrolle's taxidermy shop, or the wrapper from oddly named candy. Each time he apologized for letting his anger take over, and for hating her that day and loving her too much.

By the last of the letters and the third shot of tequila, she couldn't decide if the pit in her stomach was from residual anger, missing Charlie, or a drunken agitation of both. She decided not to write him back—to punish him for his cruelty and entitlement, but also because the incident was finally fading in her mind. She didn't want to dredge it up and knew he felt terrible; that much he'd succeeded in making clear. Always he closed with "There's no one like you." She wanted to forgive him but wasn't convinced she should. Though Nana Miggs always said, "Resentment has little usefulness." Biz had thought she understood what that meant. Now was her chance to find out.

Charlie's exile of self-torture lasted many long weeks while waiting for Biz to answer his letters. He felt he would never be able to forgive himself and couldn't blame her for not responding. He'd been a monster, he saw that now, and made a mistake by running away. He missed his family and America, and should have faced his punishment in the States. He should have apologized in person and done whatever it took to make amends. But she wasn't writing him back, so he assumed it was better he stay away. The Sorbonne proved a welcome refuge from his guilt, so he immersed himself in his film studies.

A few days into December, in his Cinéma Pratique et Esthétique class, Charlie felt a peculiar presence. When he pivoted in his chair, there, a row behind him, under a mop of strawberry curls, was Piper. *In Paris?! I don't understand.* They anxiously partnered on a project to shoot a four-minute 16 mm film. While the other students brainstormed, Charlie and Piper excitedly debriefed.

Charlie said, "What are you *doing* here?"

Piper grinned like the Cheshire cat. "What are *you* doing here? I've been here since August. Actually, I've been in London since August, but the program was eh, and the food sucked, so I switched to Paris. At least the food is better," said Piper, unimpressed by the coincidence. "Where's Biz?"

"Very funny. She's in Boston."

"Wow, cut the cord, eh?"

"I can't believe you're here," Charlie said, nonplussed, though he knew he really shouldn't be *that* shocked. Plenty of eastern seaboard universities had programs abroad with the Sorbonne.

"Yeah, well, get over it," said Piper.

"Do you even know French?"

"Do you?"

"Touché," he said unintentionally, then realized. "There's one word we don't have to learn." Piper laughed, and Charlie felt a little less homesick.

Once at work on their project, he was impressed by the endless stream of shot ideas that sprang to Piper's mind. She rarely wrestled with story arc or second-guessed the way he did, and plausible solutions for shooting snags seemed always within her reach. Charlie kept a respectful distance during pre-production and on location. But hours at work late at night, shoulders touching and hunched over a Steenbeck, proved an aphrodisiac in their cramped, windowless edit bay. Piper snickered at his corny jokes as they replayed cuts on the seven-inch monitor, and he marveled at her timing and instincts. Snappy banter wasn't her strong suit, but he liked that she had drive. The French had a different sense of humor than Americans— lacking an awareness of the whimsically absurd. Piper was kind of French in that way, but otherwise reminded Charlie of home.

Once their parallel action project was turned in, Piper dragged Charlie to all the tourist destinations. They enjoyed museums and picnic lunches at Père Lachaise and Versailles. They strolled on the edge of the quay watching *bateaux mouches* rumble by. They sipped red wine and ate *moules-frites* at tiny round café tables where they discussed the works of indie filmmakers and the imperative they remain friends, but it didn't stick for very long. One late night at 2 A.M. after the Métro had shut down and there were no cabs, they hurried home in the rain. They scampered down the misty cobblestone streets of the Left Bank and up five flights to Charlie's and into bed. In the morning they made slow, sleepy love to each other; then Charlie reenacted *Rocky* in a heavy French accent. "You're quite good," she told him with a devilish grin.

"My accent?"

"No. In bed. Your accent's terrible."

"Thank you," he replied knowingly. "I don't suppose you're

leaving me again for Robbie. Let me guess, he's just getting back from Mount Everest and boy, are his arms tired. Is he waiting downstairs to sweep you off your feet again?"

"No, but he is checking off the Seven Wonders. I read it in the alumni magazine."

"And you're his eighth?"

"Ha, no. He's already engaged to be engaged. And besides, I like you. Always did."

"You had a funny way of showing it."

"You got over it," She grinned and pulled him back on top of her.

"You should see the scars," he mumbled, and they made love again. Charlie gave himself permission to feel joy again.

After that day, there would be no turning back. Charlie and Piper were a definite thing.

Charlie and his mom had communicated via postcards to devise a time for the long-awaited Christmas Day phone chat. They hadn't spoken since he left except for his initial call home to tell Cat and Ned he'd made it safely and would not be returning for the holidays. Charlie knew the drill: the traditional family tree trimming would take place at his mother's, as 1985 was an odd year—Aunt Claire hosted on the evens. He would use a *telephone card* to call from a pay phone at cocktail hour, East Coast time, on Christmas Eve—there would be less chaos at night. The next morning the families would open presents separately, then meet up again at Nana Miggs and Grandpa Dun's for beef Wellington and carols around the unopened piano. But Cat wanted to hear her son's voice before Christmas morning— and, more importantly, wanted him to hear hers.

Biz headed next door to Aunt Cat's in the dark at 4:30 P.M. on Christmas Eve, carrying a dimpled tray of deviled eggs.

Everyone had received word that Charlie would be calling at five, and they should all have a drink in hand for the annual champagne toast family photo. Cat had planned it down to a T. She'd hold up the phone for the self-timed picture—to represent Choo on the other end—then have the roll developed when the camera shop reopened, first thing after New Year's Day. Then she'd send a framed five-by-seven photo of Charlie's loving family to arrive in Paris by Valentine's Day. That way Charlie would know his family loved him.

Biz kicked off E.J.'s old snow boots at the back door and slipped into black heels without having to put down the tray. She felt an odd mix of excited and anxious to hear Charlie's voice—unclear how she might react; things could go either way. The women were all in the kitchen, the men at the bar getting them drinks. Biz was doling out hellos and air-kisses to all the ladies, when she heard an atypical man's voice in the crowd mixed in with her relatives'. "What on earth?" said Biz under her breath. E.J. was standing at the bar, filling cocktail orders. He nodded in Foster's direction and said, "Oh yeah, him. Surprise."

Biz made a beeline for Foster. "What the hell are you *doing* here?"

"And a very Merry Christmas to you, too. Georgia invited me. I'm in charge of the record player in Charlie's absence. I thought, considering the homogeneity of the crowd, I would begin my set with 'White Christmas.'"

"*Georgia?!* Don't you have a family of your own?" Biz was livid.

"I do. They're in Gstaad," he said, and picked up a sterling-silver-framed photo of the Thornden grandchildren in a pyramid on the beach when they were little. "So, you've always been touched by the gods and not just recently?" he teased.

"You could have told Georgia, 'No, thank you.'"

"That would have been rude. Plus I have a lab due. My team is working over the break, and this was a welcome distraction. Don't worry. I'm only here for the hot food. And maybe your hot cousin."

Biz leaned in and whispered, "Well, you're a dickwad."

Foster beamed a smile, wide and beguiling. "Takes one to know one."

Biz caught sight of Georgia in the doorway wearing a tight red tube miniskirt and low-slung studded belt; a matching tomato-red top, off the shoulder; and leather work boots like the ones Madonna wore in her "Like a Virgin" video—your basic Christmas whore. Biz looked like a crazy cat lady next to Georgia. She was wearing a crisp white blouse with a gold-star belt buckle topping a long emerald felt skirt decorated with actual ornaments and real silver garland as if it were a Christmas tree. "Nice skirt," said Foster.

"I made it," said Biz.

"No kidding."

Biz wished she didn't look like a goober next to Georgia. "It's a prototype. I'm planning to sell them to Christmas enthusiasts."

"There's a word for those types."

"What?"

"Christians."

"You know what? Don't talk to me," she sneered and walked away. Biz couldn't believe he was back. The guy who would have been the father of her . . . She damn well needed another drink. Georgia slunk her way over to Biz at the bar, the lace on her black bra highlighting her cleavage. Biz said, "Hey, Flashdance. You're looking chaste."

"It's just family," said Georgia.

"My point exactly."

"I'm one of Santa's elves." Georgia gave a slight shimmy, which made her jingle bell earrings tinkle.

Biz said, "Uh-huh. If Santa were a pimp."

Georgia laughed, unruffled. Foster sidled up to her and she placed a bourbon in his palm. "Here's your alcohol, dear."

Biz rolled her eyes. "'Dear'? Really? What an adorable surprise."

"I thought so," Georgia said, grinning.

"It's a Christmas miracle," said Foster, already sauced. It was weird he'd impregnated her and still didn't know it. Biz couldn't tell if he really liked Georgia or was caught up in the thrill of penetrating the Thornden inner sanctum. Though Georgia was more akin to an adjunct family member, having been dragooned into their ranks as a pre-teen. Biz figured he probably liked that she held outsider status, was able to move among them without becoming one of them. For all of these reasons, in addition to the fact that she was probably dynamite in bed, Biz had to admit she could see his attraction to Georgia. She figured, *how long can it last?* Thankfully Foster's presence to her was little more than a nuisance.

Biz turned to Foster. "You told me your family loved you."

"Oh, they do, just not until tomorrow. My flight's at nine A.M."

Georgia added, "I'll give you a ride."

"I'm sure you will," said Biz, and turned back to the bar to make herself a double.

At 11 P.M. in a corner phone booth, on a cobblestone street in Neuilly, Charlie was pressed up against Piper with his prepaid phone card ready to go. Piper gave Charlie a long, slow kiss, her lips lingering to brush his lightly before pulling away. He scanned her freckles and looked into her bright cinnamon eyes. He felt incredibly lucky to hold this familiar, sweet-smelling woman—someone he didn't have to explain his family or Americans to—and wondered what she would think if she ever knew how he'd behaved toward Biz. He was pretty sure he would never tell her.

Charlie was grateful for a second chance, and Piper was it. And he would never take her for granted.

He dialed, saying, "You're welcome to stay. You can say hi to everyone and help keep me warm." They kissed again—not the hungry kiss of new lovers but of two people beginning to deeply appreciate one another's company.

"It's a fifteen-minute *card*. You'll survive. It'll fly by," Piper said, and groped for the inside door handle. "I'll wait in the café across the street," she said. "I'll even order you a beer." She slid the phone booth door closed, then briefly opened it a crack. "And some *frites*."

"*Piper!*" Charlie called after her, but she was already trotting away. The peep in his ear began to count down the minutes.

"Hello? Charlie, is that you?" he heard through the tiny black holes in the receiver. The warmth of his mother's voice thawed his nervous chill.

"It's me, Mom!"

"You sound so close!" Cat cupped her hand over the mouthpiece and reported to the crowd sitting on the cushion and armrest of every chair and couch. "He sounds next door," then, back to Charlie, "How are you liking gay Paree?"

"It's wicked amazing, Mom. I'm having the best time. Learning a lot."

Cat cupped her hand again. "He said he's learning a lot and it's wicked amazing."

"He did not say wicked," said E.J. "What, is he in the Staten Island section of Paris?"

Rah said, "Mom, you don't have to relay everything in real time, you can paraphrase at the end. He's probably on a phone card with a limited amount of time."

"Oh, my dear. Okay, I'll hurry. Well, everyone wants to say hi."

Nana Miggs offered, "You can tell him Merry Christmas from his grandfather and me."

"Ditto," said E.J.

"Typical," said Rah.

Claire said, "Maybe we should do the toast now in case we run out of time."

Cat said, "Yes, of course," then, to Charlie, "We're raising a glass to you, darling. Everyone's here in the living room—"

E.J. shouted, "Even Foster!"

"Shut up!" hissed Biz. Georgia patted Foster's knee as he chuckled and sipped his whisky.

Charlie leaned closer into the pay phone as his far-off family shouted "Merry Christmas" as if doing so might transport him to his mother's living room in New Jersey. "What was that about Foster?" Charlie said. He couldn't have heard that right. Cat spoke hurriedly, no space between thoughts. "Nothing, dear. Did you ever look up Piper? Her mother said she was in London last time we chatted. We're raising our glasses to you at this very moment. We miss you so much and wish . . ." Her voice cracked with a mother's love—she treasured him so very desperately. "We wish you were here." Cat placed her hand over her heart; Charlie heard the tinkling of his mother's gold charm bracelet. Claire jumped up and commandeered the phone from her sappy sister. "It's Aunt Claire, dear. Your mother thought it would be nice if we passed the phone around so everyone could say a quick hello."

"Okay, but—" Charlie was okay just speaking with his mom.

The phone cord was stretched—nearly flattening the spiral—and passed around the room so that every voice might be heard saying "Hello, Charlie" or "Hey, Choo!" Each one tugged him a little closer to home, lodging a hitch in his throat that grew more pronounced with each turn. No one felt the need to say who was speaking, so sure were they of their vocal imprints. He could picture them—the drinks they'd made, the ties they'd chosen—and he missed them all, even Rah's display of indignant exasperation and E.J.'s acerbic sarcasm. Charlie's eyes began to water. Outside the booth it dusted snow.

Biz was the last to be handed the phone. She kept saying, "You go ahead, you go ahead," in an outward show of largesse, but really she was avoiding the inevitable. Finally, she could put off Charlie no longer—too many people were watching. "Merry Christmas," she chirped with forced cheer, trickier to do than she thought. It was a challenge to transmit holiday greetings with so many not knowing their story. *"Mele Kaliki-maka,"* Charlie said on the other end. His voice was meek and cracking with melancholy, but he sounded as clear as if he were next door. *Get it together,* they both thought to themselves. The Hawaiian phrase was an olive branch, an inside joke harkening back to the Christmas when they were fourteen and got hammered on the grown-up's eggnog. They'd giggled inanely to the Andrew Sisters' holiday album hit, betting each other they couldn't drop the needle back at the beginning without anyone noticing. Finally, Les got wise to the song's gnawing repetition and hid it. After that, *Mele Kalikimaka* was the only phrase they used at Christmas time. So when Charlie said it and Biz didn't echo the sentiment, it stung.

Charlie whimpered, "Are you still there?"

"I am," Biz said, composed.

"I will be sorry until the day I die. Long after you forgive me I will still—"

"Don't worry, I won't," said Biz with faux delight. She felt her jaw tighten. It was hard to hear his pain. But she carried on with her punishment because she could still remember his entitlement, and feel her own powerlessness and rage.

"Do you still think I'm a monster?" he asked in a very small voice.

"You know I always will," she said, smiling.

"I never meant to hurt you. Were there any bruises? Did you get my letters? I hope you—"

"Uh-huh," Biz interrupted, rubbing the tiny raised scar on her forehead.

The beeps from the phone card grew closer together—time was running out. He made one last attempt. "I love you so much and miss you like crazy. There's no one like you."

"Uh-huh," Biz repeated, dronelike. Her eyes were starting to well. There was another part—the other half of her heart. She loved him and missed him like crazy.

Just then the phone booth door squeaked open and a female American voice said, "Choo, sweetie, are you okay? Are you crying?" Thousands of miles away, Biz's face fell as a bolt of recognition shot up her spine. She whipped around so her family couldn't see her reaction, then heard Charlie's muffled

instructions. "Honey, you head back. Give me two minutes."
Honey?! Biz knew that voice. She'd grown up with that voice—
ingenuous and unkind. The voice of a bully. Biz's blood ran
cold; she felt sick to her stomach. She turned back to the
crowd, smiling, "Everyone say '*Bon soir*'!"

"But I still have time!" cried Charlie, his voice high and
pleading. "I want to keep talking! I miss you so much! Please,
don't—"

"Uoy welb ti," Biz said succinctly into the receiver, then
shouted gaily, *"Un, deux, trois!"* She held out the phone, and
they all chimed in, *"Bon soir!"* with additional choruses of layered "Merry Christmas!" *"Don't hang up!"* Charlie pleaded as
Biz walked the handset over to its cradle, but he was drowned
out by the peppy chorus of "Jingle Bell Rock" muddled with
sounds of people getting up out of their seats to refresh drinks
and check the oven. "Out of time," Biz said to no one in particular, and hung up without care.

Charlie had eighteen seconds remaining on his card.

Only Foster was still paying attention. He raised his glass
with a slight nod to Biz before jiggling the ice over his last sip.
As he walked by her on his way to the bar, he muttered, "Nice
performance."

She glared back. "Stop noticing so much. And stop this bullshit with Georgia. You're pandering to my family. It's pedestrian and obvious."

"I like Georgie. And I like your family and they like me."

"Well, I don't like you."

"Duly noted."

Biz countered, "Why don't you make yourself useful and
put on a record."

"Why don't I," said Foster, and pulled Vince Guaraldi's

Charlie Brown Christmas out of its album sleeve. He put on the song he knew would remind her of him. Biz beat him to the bar and poured herself a shot of tequila. She downed it in one pull, then poured herself another. Then took a breather.

Charlie Muir hung up the phone and wiped away a few errant tears. "Have a good cry, then splash your face and move on," he could hear his mother saying. "Buck up, kid, everything's going to work out fine." It was one of the Thornden family mottos, for godsake. Charlie emitted a long, growling sigh, then shook his head back and forth quickly, intending to flick away the conversation and rebound like a champ. He knew his cousin well enough to know she wouldn't hate him forever. He felt fairly certain she would eventually thaw and come around. Nana Miggs's saying sprung to his mind: "Life is short and life is long." He'd never thought the words useful. But now they bolstered Charlie as he walked briskly across the street and pulled open the heavy glass door of the crowded café. He had the rest of his life to make it up to Biz, and he would. A blast of steamy warm air hit his face. As he walked toward Piper, he pointedly tucked all thoughts of Biz away as if placing them in his coat pocket before draping it over a stool. He picked up his beer, kissed his bright-eyed girlfriend on the lips, and forced the sunny, dimpled smile that had always seen him through.

Upstairs, sitting at Cat's hallway telephone table, Claire sat in a daze, the handset held loosely in her lap. Footsteps snapped her out of it, and she hung up the telephone extension as quietly as possible, forgetting that it no longer mattered—there was no one on the other end to hear the click. She'd barely taken her hand off the receiver when her sister appeared on the landing. Cat had needed a quiet minute in her room to let down her guard, maybe have a brief cry. She knew one day she might lose her son to his future wife's family, but never expected he would choose to miss out before he had to. She saw Claire sitting stiffly with a look of incredulity on her face; Cat was worried someone had died. It wasn't a look she saw often, but showed unmistakable concern. Something made her glance down at the telephone table. There, on its side, was a single emerald clip-on earring in the shape of a holly leaf.

"You were listening," said Cat. "What was he saying on the other end?"

"I wasn't. It was nothing." Claire wouldn't look her in the eye. She ran the edge of her pinky under her lower eyelid in case her mascara had run and primped her hair.

Cat said, "You heard something between them, something Charlie said on his end of the line, and now you know. You can't pretend anymore."

"I can do whatever I like," Claire said, and reached out for the earring she'd removed in order to listen in on the conversation she shouldn't have.

"It will *eat you up*," Cat argued, "and it's *not* fair to them."

"It's over between them anyway. He's with Piper now."

"*Piper?!* You don't know that."

"I do," Claire said with unruffled authority, and clipped the earring back onto her ear.

Cat paused slightly before speaking. She was exasperated with her big sister and had been for most of her life. With the confident authority that comes with age, when a younger sibling finally finds an equal voice, Cat said, "It's not over until they're married to other people. And even then we both know not until they end it."

Claire chided, "Model parent," tossed her sister a dismissive glance, and headed down the back stairs without further comment. Her insolence pushed Cat's buttons more than she'd anticipated so she followed with a raised voice, tired of not feeling heard. "Don't you *dare*!" hissed Cat. "This has *nothing* to do with us!"

Claire stopped at the bottom of the narrow staircase and whipped around. "It has *everything* to do with us. We *live* in this town."

"*You're* the shitty parent, always worrying about what other people might say, putting your precious reputation before the welfare of your family."

Claire wasn't about to be lectured. She continued down the back stairs which led into the kitchen and stopped in the middle of the bustling crowd, thinking that would end it. But Cat followed her, irate, without regard for holiday decorum.

"If *you* paid more attention to *your* kids, maybe they wouldn't have to come to *me* with their *problems*!"

"What *problems*?" Claire spat. The kitchen hubbub slowed to a murmur; their family froze, watching and listening.

Cat caught Biz's eye and stopped short. "Nothing." *Thank God,* Biz thought. She was drunk, but aware enough to be on guard. Claire was incensed. "*What* problems?" She fumed, "Is there more than the fact that your son attacked my daughter?" Biz piped up; she wasn't quite slurring, but the alcohol dulled her acuity. "He didn't—who told you that?"

E.J. said, "Told her *what*?"

Nana Miggs said to Rah, "Who are we talking about, dear?" Rah ignored her grandmother, riveted to the argument.

Claire announced to Cat, "They can never see each other again."

"That's not for you to say."

"*Your* inattentive parenting got them into this mess. You're not supposed to be his *friend,* you're his *mother,* for godssake. *Parent him.*"

"Ha," said Cat. "Biz isn't so innocent, she's equally accountable. It takes two to tango, you know." Biz blurted out a snort, then covered her mouth.

E.J. whispered, but everyone heard him, "Is 'tango' code for what I think it is?"

Cat said, "It's no wonder she's a mess. She can't trust her own mother. Her father is out to lunch. Biz, you told me it wasn't Charlie's. Is that what this is about? Did you lie to me, too? *Was it Charlie's?*"

Biz was swaying and confused. She held an empty glass in each hand and her shirttails were untucked. "I beg your bardon?"

"You're drunk," said E.J.

"And you're short," said Biz, aware she was drunk.

Claire snapped at Biz. "Was *what* Charlie's?! *What's going on?*"

Biz screamed, "Stop it! *Stop talking*!" She held the rocks glasses up to the side of her head like earmuffs. "*None* of you were there. *None* of you know anything. Charlie didn't mean it, and he's already apologized."

Rah implored, "Apologized for *what*?"

Claire repeated herself. "Was *what* Charlie's?" She glared at her sister who glared back.

Biz addressed the room with finality. She was shaking and quite possibly slurring. "*You guys* wanted us to be friends. It's all *your* fault!"

"But you're *cousins,*" admonished Claire. Cat's mind raced: *This is the moment I set everyone straight. The moment I stop lying for Charlie's sake. But then we'll have to start covering up. And Charlie will suffer. And it'll never work, there are too many people. And it would break Daddy's heart. And ruin Choo's chances. I can't. I just can't.*

Biz broke the silence. "It doesn't matter when you aren't cousins and it doesn't matter if you are. None of it matters. *It was just experimenting! It's what kids do!* We were little and we didn't know."

Claire said, "You're not little anymore. You can't use that excuse. It's unacceptable and *you should know better.*"

Biz's eyes welled. She looked over at her Aunt Cat, who was tearing up with the crushing conflict of her secret. She had to stay the course. Even if it meant betraying Biz. The alternative was clearly worse. And as much as she loved her niece, she loved her son a tiny bit more. Cat said solemnly, "She's right," and Biz was devastated. How could her Aunt Cat sell her up the river? She shook her head as if writing her off before speaking with unusual calm. Biz said, "You know what? You're *all* shitty parents, and it's none of your business. Charlie's the way he is because of Uncle Dick, which is your fault, Aunt Cat, for marrying him, and I'm the way I am because of you, Mom. And Dad. And that's your fault, for being horrible people."

Under his breath, Foster said, "Where's your uncle?" to Georgia, who whispered, "The eternal mystery."

Biz continued, "I blame both of you for leaving us alone so you could go to all your stupid meetings and plan your precious parties. Did you get enough thank-you notes? I hope it was worth it." Biz stopped talking, but no one filled the void. She said, "It's too late to start paying attention now. We're grown-ups and it's none of your goddamn beeswax. And speaking of invitations, I invite you all to go to hell. Merry Christmas, everyone." She looked over and saw Nana Miggs and Rah looking at her with big, worried eyes. "Okay, well, not all of you. You know who you are. Half of you can go to hell, and the other half can have a dumb dinner." And with that Biz swung open the sliding door and marched in the deep snow over to her mother's house next door without a coat.

Her heels snagged bits of dirt and grass from the wet lawn as freezing slush rushed the spaces between her toes. Sitting in his vacant living room amid the twinkling lights of their tree was Les, staring at the TV, watching Lawrence Welk. Biz screamed, "Why are you even here?" as sobs finally overtook her. She ran past him up to her childhood room, threw herself onto the twin bed, and screamed into her pillow. How dramatic the world could be about such inconsequential things, she thought, then emitted a drunken chortle realizing *her drama*. Biz assessed how much she hated her mother for listening in on her conversation and generally being a raving bitch. And she was furious at Aunt Cat for doubting her, which she knew wasn't fair considering how supportive she'd always been. Normally, Charlie would have consoled her and said something funny, but not anymore. She was now profoundly alone.

Catching her breath, Biz forced herself to think of the bright side: at least dating would be easier now that Charlie was with Piper. All she'd need was to find the right guy, rent a little storefront for her costume business, and become a smash success—maybe in California. She'd pop out some kids and fly home twice a year to visit. It was an easy plan, practically a foregone conclusion. Nothing was going to stop her from following her dreams and being happy—especially not her bogus family. *Charlie and I will be friends again, someday.* She hadn't known her life to transpire without him.

"No one can know," said Claire to the stunned room.

"Know what?" said Georgia. Foster squeezed her hand to quiet her.

Rah added, "If you don't tell us what happened, we're only going to think the worst."

E.J. said in an aside, "Our Thornden worst."

Cat railed at Claire. "You're just going to behave as if everything's normal? You have *no idea* what I know!"

"And *you* have no idea what *I* know," Claire challenged. "Everything *is* normal. And if any one of you ever says otherwise, I'll deny it." She said it with a veneer of merriment that disgusted Cat. Foster raised an eyebrow at Georgia. Rah and E.J. exchanged looks. And Grandpa Dun could be heard shuffling about the living room like a bewildered, off-duty Santa. He called out, "There seems to have been a mass exodus of elves! Who's going to refill my bourbon?" Claire remained steely and gave orders. "Everyone refresh your drinks. E.J., please tend to your grandfather. Someone put on Bing Crosby. We're eating in fifteen minutes." Foster headed for the record player. Rah grabbed the crystal water pitcher, and Claire stirred the creamed onions like the seasoned pro she was.

After the meal, as plates were being cleared, Aunt Cat snuck next door before dessert was to be served. She felt partially responsible Biz had missed Christmas dinner and knew Claire would do nothing about it. She also needed a break. Cat walked into her niece's old childhood bedroom and found her asleep, fully clothed, under the covers. A *Teen Beat* pullout of the Hardy Boys was still on the wall next to framed posters of Cher, Prince, and the Police. Cat woke her gently, smoothing the hair off her forehead, and told her to come back over, that they'd saved her a plate. Biz roused herself slowly; her eyes were moist. She'd been dreaming Shirley MacLaine was her mother. Shirley had just been pounding on the counter to get nurses to give Biz her shot. It was dark in her room and she felt hungry. She also felt without shame. *I have to eat, what the hell,* she thought. Biz swung her legs onto the floor and ran a brush through her hair. Cat said, "I do accept responsibility, you know. You're partially right in blaming us. We should have been paying closer attention. We didn't realize—"

Biz said, "I know, Aunt Cat. It was no big deal to us. Kids are supposed to run around and get into trouble. I mean, imagine what our childhoods would have been like if you'd been in our faces all the time. We never could have sneaked the car out to go to the diner."

Cat held out Biz's sneakers. "Imagine wanting to spend that much time with your children. *Heavens!*" she laughed. "When did you sneak the car out?"

"Oh, my god. All the time when you guys were passed out."

"When did you start doing that?"

"Like fourteen. We wanted fries."

"Criminy. I wasn't even drinking then. I had no excuse."

"We rolled it down the driveway with the lights off. We were super stealth and you were all very sound sleepers."

"Apparently."

Biz was glad to see her aunt's sense of humor returning. She hated being mad at everyone. She put down the hairbrush and laced her shoes. Aunt Cat asked, "How are you two now, you and Charlie? Your mother was listening in on—"

"I know. She's horrid. I guess poisoning her is out of the question."

"It is."

Biz thought about how she would distill her relationship with Charlie into a bite-sized morsel. "We're too close, which is why we had that fight—which was unimportant, and not worth going into, trust me."

"Did he . . . hurt you?"

"Not really. It's okay."

"Did it have anything to do with—"

"He doesn't know I was pregnant."

"But did he actually, literally hurt you? Claire used the word 'attack.'"

"Mom's crazy. She doesn't know what she's talking about. Charlie and I got into a massive blowup and he left. I know you miss him, but he needed to get away. From me. And Uncle Dick, and the rest of the family. I guess we kind of all do, eventually. But don't worry, Piper will take good care of him. He's getting everything he deserves."

Aunt Cat lifted a dirty T-shirt off the floor and blotted where she was certain her mascara was running. She was grateful for whatever happened to drive him away to Paris, though she could tell there was more to the story than Biz was letting on. This way she felt less responsible for pushing them apart. Time would pass, he would find someone else, and her conflict would magically resolve. Or maybe he would end up with Piper. She didn't think Biz liked Piper very much, but maybe she'd changed. *We all change, over time. Don't we?*

Biz wanted a cigarette more than life itself. She said, "We're going to be fine. It's all going to work out. Haven't you drilled that into us since we were little?"

Aunt Cat grinned warmly. "It's what Nana Miggs drilled into me."

"And has it held true?"

"Ha," Aunt Cat blurted out. Had everything worked out for her? Not exactly, but for the most part, so far, sort of. Cat chose to ignore her lousy first marriage and alcohol addiction, and refocused the conversation on gratitude. "Yes. I love Ned, and you kids are all healthy. It's all working out just fine. But there's no way E.J., Rah, and Georgia aren't going to talk about what just happened. Your mother thinks she can control everyone and everything all the time."

"Of course she does. She's like Bea Arthur but without the rapier wit. I'll just deny everything. Pretend nothing happened. They know Mom is crazy."

"That's what she told us to do."

"The old apple, eh?"

Yes, and a little scary, thought Cat, how unaccountable they'd all become. "So let's not worry. Fuck 'em," she said brightly. Oh, the thrill Cat got from saying the F-word at her age—a suburban housewife in her forties. *Can you imagine?* "Just promise me you won't ever . . . you know, you and Choo," she said, taking in Biz's face. There were traces of the blithe innocence her niece radiated as a child, before her mother began harping and her father drifted away. She'd been like a little wood sprite—so different from her own logical Rah. Cat loved her so, though she worried about her drinking. "I promse," Biz slurred, and at the time she meant it.

Cat was relieved to be soldiering on as she followed Biz back out into the snow. *It's all going to work out, and I am doing the right thing,* Cat convinced herself. *Lord, I certainly hope so.*

1990

The cousins' childhood neighbor's tree house,
Larkspur, New Jersey

"You never really told me about your road trip," said Biz, standing barefoot on the cool evening grass. She'd chosen not to wear panty hose to the engagement party, though her mother had instructed her to. It was warm for early May, and she didn't want to be bothered; plus they were super lame, and no one her age wore them anymore. Claire had sent Biz to buy more ice, but someone had blocked her in, so Charlie offered to take her in his car, which was a manual shift. He also didn't think Biz should be driving.

"Our trip was Ameri-tastic," said Charlie, missing the first rung as he climbed the ladder of their neighbors, the Roundsavilles' tree house. "Heart of Glass" could be heard in the near distance. He'd already had a boatload of margaritas. This time he grasped the rungs carefully and kept a close eye on his feet. "We live in the United States of Awesome." He had just switched to Miller Lite and probably shouldn't have been driving.

Biz called up after him, "Very funny. Seriously."

"I'm being serious. Every U.S. citizen should have to, by law, drive across country at some point in their lives. It's an incredible place, varied and vast—a cornucopia of flora, fauna, architecture, and fried food—"

"No one says 'cornucopia.'"

"—tattoos, and sideburns. Americans are a bizarre and hilarious breed. I took a ton of photos. Piper's making an album."

"She's a doer."

"Hey, be nice."

After Piper and Charlie's year in Paris, his dream of moving to L.A. withered—Piper refused to live there—but their relationship grew regardless. Post-graduation, they rented a one-bedroom apartment on Manhattan's Upper West Side. He shot second-unit footage for corporate promos, while she became a commercial production manager. A few years later, when they were both between jobs, they decided to take a trip across country. The plan was for Charlie to write a feature screenplay with Piper at the helm. Nana Miggs said, "If you can drive across country with someone and still like them by the end, you should marry them." Then she winked.

Piper was skilled at reading maps and finding the best family-owned diners and cheap motels. And Charlie was afforded long stretches of intellectual space to write longhand while she drove. Things went smoothly with Piper in charge, which embedded a dynamic of least resistance. If she was so competent navigating this unplanned journey, it stood to reason she would make a good mother. And since Piper had been in the basement at that party when they were twelve, Charlie felt assured of her acceptance and forgiveness, which made her an excellent bet. So at the end of the road trip, after unloading their bags, he got down on one knee and proposed.

Biz was waitressing at Exterminator Chili at night and making outlandish couture during the day when she heard the news of Charlie and Piper's engagement. She decided to be happy for them—after all, Biz was also living her dream. Since graduation she'd been living on the Lower East Side, crafting the zany creations she hoped the world would thrill to. She handed out business cards at galleries and gigs—at every event she crashed. She took out ads in *The Village Voice* and taped flyers to pay-phone booths. She also drank too much, and slept around, but that didn't get in her way.

Biz's plan was to buy a little storefront in Alphabet City and hang up a sign that read OUTLANDISH COUTURE—but it wasn't that easy. She sewed and glue-gunned her madcap heart out, hoping someone would discover her, knowing it was just a matter of time. Getting the word out proved challenging, though. She knew a few local performance artists who occasionally needed offbeat stuff, but they often made their own. She tried to break into the drag queen circuit, but it was a closed loop with its own savage talent. And though some got a kick out of her clever paper-clip-fringed miniskirt, or faux-peanut-butter-and-fluff-sandwich bustier, they lacked either the vision, chutzpah, or money to invest.

Biz hiked up her floral, tea-length/V-waist dress with the big puffy sleeves and lace collar, and scurried up the tree house's ladder like she'd done a thousand times before, but in less fabric. "Not bad for a twenty-four-year-old broad, eh? I wish you hadn't made me pour out my Zima."

Charlie smiled, watching from above to ensure she made it up safely. "I'll get you another when we get back to the party. And twenty-four is hardly old," he said. He thought she looked terrific in spite of her dress. They were still strikingly attractive—both Thorndens at peak gorgeousness, dewy and dazzling with health and youth. "Watch your dress," he cautioned. "It wasn't built for derring-do."

"Oh my God, this horrid thing? I hope it dies a slow death at the dry cleaner."

"Your mom picked it out?"

"How'd you guess?"

"You look like a frothy botanical nun en route to her junior prom."

"No kidding. She thinks the 'right man' will be drawn to me in this thing. She keeps bugging me to wear longer skirts. So, sounds like you won't be moving to France."

"No. Who said we were?"

"E.J. said he heard it from Piper."

"Ignore him. Now and forever—like the musical, *Cats*."

At the top Charlie held out his hand and Biz took it while claiming she wasn't tipsy. She said she took it to show their relationship had matured—hatchets buried. Charlie sat on the filthy futon, unaware pollen was dusting his best blazer. He'd lost weight and appeared slighter but was still dashingly handsome, Biz thought. She was elated they weren't moving to Europe. She leaned on the doorframe to steady herself. "So, why do we have to be in the Roundsavilles' tree house for you to tell me this supposedly big thing? We're missing your engagement party, you know, and the ice is totally melting. Plus they're playing 'Funky Cold Medina,' which I had to lobby Mom hard to let the DJ play."

"We can hear it from here, and no one needs more ice. They're already totally smashed."

Biz put her hands on her hips. "What do you need to tell me? You're already getting married next month, what else could—" Then it hit Biz hard; her face fell. "Let me guess. Piper's pregnant."

Charlie laughed. "Jesus, I hope not. Let me get through this wedding first." He said it with a mix of black humor and exasperation.

Biz asked, "So then, what?"

"Come sit down," Charlie said, and patted the seat next to him. Biz rolled her eyes and stumbled a little as she sat. She hoped cobwebs weren't getting in her bangs—it had taken her ages to blow-dry them poufed like in *Heathers*. Charlie said, "I don't know if I'll ever be allowed to see you again, alone, after I'm married."

"Yeah, Piper's quite the—"

"Please don't say anything negative about her. I know we did when we were kids, but she's going to be my wife. And there's a side to Piper . . . I want you to like her."

Biz looked at him with mock wide-eyed innocence. "Who, *moi*?"

"Yeah, *toi*."

"Don't say 'yeah.' If Grandpa Dun hears you . . ."

Biz brushed specks of yellow pollen off his collar. Charlie tried to stay on topic, but was drunk as well. "Piper's resourceful and supportive. She's unfloppable. Flippable. Strong as a bubble. Ugh, she's strong. And if our marriage is going to work, I have to take her side from now on. So if you have anything mean to say about her, tell Georgia or Rah, not me."

"Fine. Can we go? 'What I Like About You' is on. The best dance song of all time!"

"No, please, just listen." Charlie took a deep breath and watched a daddy longlegs traverse a torn curtain. Biz's eyes anchored on his, waiting for him to speak. "I want to tell you how sorry I am about what I did to you in my dorm room. It was horrible, and I—"

"It wasn't that bad—"

"Biz," Charlie put his hands on her shoulders, then realized he shouldn't and placed them in his lap. "It was absolutely *that bad*. I almost . . ." He paused. "I forced myself on you. I attacked you. It was the worst thing I've ever done in my life. Nothing about it was okay or excusable. And I want to tell you I'm sorry again, in person, and I'm hoping you accept my apology. And I hope to God I didn't alter your, um, mess you up in any way . . ." What he wanted to say was that he hoped he hadn't broken her beyond repair.

Biz smiled. "Thanks. I'm a woman of the nineties. I'm tougher than I look."

She'd had to fight off plenty of groping, slurring guys in bars since the incident. However, she was more careful now to get to know a guy before inviting him back to her apartment. She'd go out with him a few times first and walk away if his temper raged. Biz had had a few steady boyfriends, but nothing serious—she was in no hurry. If anything, she felt sorry for Charlie, rushing into marriage, playing it safe. She felt he'd let his ambition be ground to a halt, believed he was making a huge mistake. Charlie worried that Biz's spark had diminished, that she was losing her drive and enthusiasm. Each assumed the other's fire was being extinguished by the daunting specter of adulthood. And each buried the desire to help the other reignite it.

"I'm fine," Biz said to Charlie, "and I forgive you. And I love you. And honestly, you didn't mess me up any more than I already was. Ha." She took his hands in hers and raised them up above their hearts so they hung in the air between them in an awkward tangled nest.

"Do you believe me?" Biz asked.

Charlie said, "I do."

Biz announced, "You may now kiss the cousin."

Charlie gave a small sweet grin and stayed right where he was; however, Biz leaned in with her whole body. She wanted to prove her trust and forgiveness, that he was a good man; they could pick up where they left off on Amtrak. She also knew their window of opportunity was closing unbelievably fast if she was ever going to drag them back to normal. So, instead of turning to give him her cheek, she gave him her tender mouth, slow and full, directly on his lips without apology. She let herself sink into him, moving her hand onto his lap, hoping for a last chance with her very best friend. He was getting married, but he wasn't quite married yet. *Then things will change with us forever. This is it,* she thought, *let's seal the deal.* Biz decided to make her desire transparently obvious, and expected Charlie's total retreat, but he didn't pull away and remained locked in her kiss. Their lips parted, tongues lurched, and bolts shot through their bodies as they tasted boozy wetness and cigarettes. Biz inched closer to Charlie and he placed his palm hesitantly on her waist. She decided right then and there that if he was game, she was, too. The whole world was elsewhere; all that mattered was in this tree house. They could finally give in to their desire. So she whispered, "Let's have a quickie," and they both went weak.

"No, no, no, bad idea," Charlie said, pulling away.

"Wait!" Biz said, her eyes mischievous and crackling. "Think of it as our last hurrah to finally get us out of our systems! Or I could get you something off your registry. Your choice: clean-slate sex or a salad spinner."

"I don't think—"

"Don't think! Just *c'mon!* Till death do you part! Please?" Biz unfurled the word coyly and placed her hand on his fly. "Hey, looks like the party's already in your pants." She gave his hardness a squeeze. "Atta boy," Biz urged Charlie, not ready to say good-bye. She also felt sex could seal her fate as his number one, with secrets still to keep perhaps forever. "This shouldn't happen," Charlie said, his hands trying to rub the thought from his face. But he had something to prove, too, that he could be kind. Giving her this would conveniently absolve him of his monstrous guilt, and he could return to Mr. Nice Guy—clean slate. Plus it would be the last decision he'd get to make all by himself, before he'd have to run everything he did—every choice he wanted to make—by Piper, his wedded wife.

With both having so much to prove, they should have kept the world in their way.

Biz said, "Let's do it super fast, then you can carry on with your life, and I can get on with whatever it is I'm doing, and everybody wins." Biz kissed Charlie with everything she had, even scratched her fingers through his hair; he slithered onto his knees on the dirty floor. It was his lame last-ditch attempt at trying to get away, but his brain flooded with a wash of chemicals and he was sunk.

"Are you sure this is what you want?" he asked.

"Fo-shizzle. It'll be fun! We just need to chillax." Biz leaned back on her elbows and inched her skirt up to her waist. Charlie placed his hands on her smooth thighs, feeling her radiant heat. He'd been dreaming about this moment since he could remember. He moved his head toward her, acquainting himself with her soft folds and wet depths, as Biz squirmed and winced in ecstasy. She basked in the chemical rush and quickly felt close to climax. "Quick," she said, and motioned him upward, leading him inside her. But he hadn't stayed fully erect, so needed a little more time. She started to lose her edge, and he cursed—they'd both done too much drinking. But then he was ready and filled her up. "Oh my God," he said, astonished. "Amazing," she moaned, from an odd position, reaching for something to hold. It was proving tricky to find the right angle, and Biz swiveled to fit lengthwise, but then Charlie had no room for both knees. So one of his feet remained on the ground, his khakis pooled around his ankle in a small pile of dust and dead leaves.

They took up their mission again, but things still weren't quite right. Both of them shifted and groped, preoccupied with finding ways to brace. The time for kissing had long since passed. Neither felt connected. "Deeper, please," Biz whispered, and Charlie answered, "I don't want to hurt you."

"You can't," she said. But they both knew it wasn't true.

"I'm close," he said, and thrusted.

"I'm not," answered Biz, frustrated she could feel so close—on the maddening edge—then so infuriatingly far away the next moment. "Love Shack" started its groove, and a cheer went up in the distance. Biz was slightly annoyed she was missing another dance fave, and even more so knowing she wasn't going to climax. She thought they should get back. *Maybe this was a dumb idea.*

"Go for it," she said to Charlie, followed up quickly with, "But pull out."

"What?" he said, and within seconds let loose an urgent moaning growl, accompanied by four underwhelming thrusts, each one less crucial than the last.

"I'm sorry," he said, "I didn't hear you."

"It's fine. It just ended the other day."

"And I'm sorry I couldn't get you to—"

"Also fine," said Biz. "We need to get back. I left my pashmina in your car. Do we have anything to . . . ?"

"I can give you my boxers . . . I'm really sorry you didn't . . ."

"It's okay, not a big deal. Not worth worrying about. Let's pretend it never happened and get you back to your party."

Biz froze, waiting for Charlie to take off his boxers, not wanting to spill. She had the creeping sensation that what they'd done was pointless and hadn't served her purpose. It wasn't the ceremonial portal to the closeness she'd envisioned. It wasn't special and not that much fun—a mediocre bang with an unremarkable finish. As Biz mopped herself off, she remembered another Nana Miggs–ism: "Regret has little usefulness." Or was it "resentment"? She returned his boxers. Charlie felt immediate and crushing remorse as he shoved them under the mattress. *I should* never *have done that. I feel like shit.* Neither spoke as they briskly clambered down the ladder, desperate to put this in the past. The answer was to forget it ever happened and get wasted. Piper would be waiting for him near the bar.

The guitar strains of "When Doves Cry" rose through the canopy of oaks as Biz and Charlie returned, carrying dripping bags of ice. Piper was not the suspicious kind; she knew exactly who she was marrying. She and Charlie had shared the same cast of characters their entire lives. She was tolerant of his world, which was why she didn't bristle when he and Biz returned together after being gone a while. She figured laziness and comfort were why they ended up together. And only once all evening did Piper apply the same rationale to herself—

perhaps that was also why Charlie was marrying her. Then she rejected the thought out of self-preservation.

Biz's night had not gone as planned, but so what else was new—neither had her life thus far. But not one to dwell, she devised a plan: first, she would tear up the dance floor, then have some carrot cake and a shot, then maybe jump off the diving board in her dumb dress she hoped to ruin. Charlie's plan was to wash his face and dick in the bathroom sink, then do Goldschläger shots with E.J. and his best man in the shed. He felt so much self-loathing for having had sex with Biz—whom he cherished—while engaged to Piper—whom he loved—that he decided blacking out was the only way to go. He was well on his way when Piper found him and, taking him by the hand, dragged him onto the dance floor to save him. Georgia, Rah, E.J., and Biz were dancing to "We Are Family," and Piper felt Charlie should be in attendance. She noticed his discomfort, but chalked it up to too much booze, and felt it served him right—he was being an idiot.

Charlie danced with Piper to Gloria Gaynor's hit, "I Will Survive," his eyes riveted to those of his fiancée. He was desperate not to lose the one woman in this world who knew his deepest flaws and wanted him anyway. They would build a fresh life for themselves, Charlie thought, as he spun Piper out and in—separate from his family, and away from Biz and this town. They would strike out on their own and start over quietly, no longer tethered to his privilege or burdened by his muddied Thornden past. Charlie would finally—without regret—carve out a permanent life without Biz. Then he made a wish his cousin would do the same.

2002

**Georgia's lush green front lawn,
Firth, New Jersey**

"Ever since 9/11 I've wanted to do this. Life's too damn short!"
Georgia shouted out the window.

Biz shouted up, "Well, then, you married the right man!"

"Or the wrong man, as the case may be!"

Georgia disappeared for another trip. She had a short blunt
cut, now—was a bottle blonde with dark roots—and wore
baggy shorts and a 5k Fun Run oversized T-shirt, the typical
androgynous uniform of American motherhood. Biz was down
below watching her throw armloads of men's Dockers onto
the growing pile of clothes amassing on her thick front lawn.
The cherry trees had just exploded in all their pink-and-white
glory—the forsythia in swaths of bright yellow. It was a gorgeous spring day, perfect for a marital showdown. Thank goodness the kids were at school.

Biz was reclining in a broken folding chair, a few feet from
the pile's outer edge. She was enjoying the fresh air and domestic spectacle. "I wouldn't know!" she shouted then thought, *So
many golf shirts with tournament insignias. It must be lonely
having a husband who golfs. Maybe it's lonely having a hus-*

band, period. Though the thought didn't stop her from wanting one. However, Georgia's predicament gave her pause; she suspected marriage was harder than it looked.

Biz was smoking and reading an article in *People* about J.Lo and Ben Affleck. *Bennifer,* she thought to herself. *Match made in heaven.* Moments later Georgia returned to the window with another armload of men's shirts. Biz imagined what the pile would look like to passersby once Georgia cleaned out her cheating husband's stuff, or made her point, whichever came first. She took another drag and turned the page. Apparently, Ted Williams's head was severed from his body to be cryogenically frozen for future reattachment. "Now that's planning ahead," she said to no one, then, *"Get it?"*

Charlie crossed the yard, approaching Biz. "Are you seriously laughing at your own jokes?"

"You don't know what it's like to be single."

"Let me guess. You're your own best audience?"

"Close. I'm my *only* audience." Biz gestured to another beach chair in the pile nearly obscured by *Golf* magazines. "Pull up a seat. Which will last longer, Jennifer Aniston and Brad Pitt or Ted Williams's frozen head?"

"Head," said Charlie, unfolding the chair and plopping down beside her.

"You missed my Ted Williams pun."

"Let me guess . . . something, something, planning ahead?"

"Killjoy."

"Nah, I can read your mind, that's all." Charlie still enjoyed making Biz smile.

It was the Thursday before Memorial Day weekend, and he'd stopped by to borrow Georgia's hedge trimmer. It still felt odd for him not to be getting ready for their big annual Thornden family shindig. He'd assumed they'd be hosting those parties with canes and walkers forever. But something had driven a wedge between his mom and Aunt Claire; their closeness had shifted to a façade. His mom had refused to cohost again the summer he returned from Europe. Aunt Claire threw a fit, worrying it would look suspicious, which made no sense to anyone. When Charlie asked his mom why the parties were ending, she snapped, "Nothing gold can stay."

"But what will all the families do on holidays?"

"They'll figure something out. The world doesn't revolve around us." It was the first time he'd ever considered the notion and life, shockingly, went on. Then when news of Cat's breast cancer got around it became clear why the Thorndens weren't attending parties, either. The chemo had been brutal, and there were complications. By the time his mom's mastectomy had healed, new traditions had been carved out by younger families who'd never heard of the Thorndens. Unfazed, Nana Miggs counseled, "Resentment isn't useful. Just think of all the money we'll save on deviled eggs." Cat nodded solemnly, feeling responsible for their snubbing. Claire scoffed. She, too, blamed her sister. But Charlie knew he couldn't blame his mom.

Twelve years prior, Piper had become pregnant right after their wedding—some suspected slightly before. Two years later she was pregnant with their second when Cat's biopsy came back positive for invasive ductal carcinoma. Charlie put his film career on hold to help with the treatments, but not for purely altruistic reasons. He suspected deep down he'd never make it in Hollywood—unless you knew someone in the biz, the biz didn't know you and Charlie had no connections. He felt he should have tried harder to convince Piper to move there on their trip out west, before she got pregnant. Instead they agreed to raise their kids in Larkspur and Charlie would renovate the neglected Art Deco movie theater in Firth. That way they could both be there for his mother while Ned worked to protect his health benefits. Cat loaned Charlie the money from his secret trust. On completion he renamed it The Wonder. He showed film classics like *West Side Story* and *Young Frankenstein* in the evenings, and Marx Brothers fare for children's birthday parties in the mornings. It was also used as a center for film classes during the day and rented out for soirees at night. And though Charlie was providing for his family and community, he still felt he'd failed at his filmmaking dream—a fact Piper was well aware of behind closed doors.

Georgia tossed a drawer full of men's bathroom products out the window; they scattered like candy from a piñata when they hit the ground. Charlie said, "The Student Shorts Film Fest went well."

"I'm sorry I missed it," Biz said, looking him in the eye. "I was at the bakery until late finishing up a friggin' *Sopranos* birthday cake. How did it go?"

"That's funny. I'd like to meet the—"

"No, you wouldn't."

"The kids did a great job."

"And *you* did a great job. You're teaching them how to channel their creative energy, craft a story, create tension . . ." An iPod, MP3 player, and Palm Pilot rained down onto the pile. Biz and Charlie scootched their chairs back another three feet. "Speaking of tension . . . ," Charlie said, and they shared a chuckle as rolls of socks bounced all over the lawn.

Georgia emerged from the garage and tossed a bag of golf clubs onto the pile.

"Happy birthday, Georgie!" Charlie shouted gaily. "Forty! Wow! Any big plans?"

Georgia rolled her eyes. "Come up and help me with the TV."

Biz laughed. Charlie said, "Nope. Sorry. Not taking sides. No aiding or abetting."

Georgia tried her erstwhile charm. "It can be your birthday present to me."

"Too late. I already have something for you."

"You do not."

"I named a star after you."

"Liar."

"I got you concert tickets to Nickelback."

"Bullshit. You're useless. I'll use his desk chair. It's on rollers."

Georgia disappeared again.

Charlie turned to Biz. "That could have been us, you know." Biz smirked. "I'd thought of that." She watched Charlie as he grabbed a club and putted balls of socks toward her feet. She was savoring being alone with him—a rare delight ever since he married, especially once they both had kids. He'd aged well, the bastard, distinguished gray at his temples. He was a slightly older version of his young Adonis self. "Lucky for us, you got Piper knocked up."

"Yes. Lucky us," Charlie said with casual sarcasm. But he felt fortunate to have two healthy kids and a wife who was a good mother. He was also glad to be friends with Biz, though they tried not to be alone together, for his family's benefit—and to be safe. Charlie tried to sound off-the-cuff. "Remind me again who knocked you up?"

Biz gave Charlie the same world-weary look she'd given him

for the last thirteen years. "Please. Your attempts are getting lazy. You used to be more creative."

"C'mon, everyone and their uncle thinks Ruby's mine. You may as well just tell me. You know I can keep a secret." People in town had their suspicions. Only Biz and Charlie were twisted enough to joke about it when they were alone. Everyone else in the family ignored the chatter and maintained denial.

"Immaculate conception," said Biz.

"Ha, you liked sex too much for that."

"*Liked?* Past tense?"

"Forgive me. Present tense."

"I'm not dead yet. Jeeze, I'm in my prime. And if I haven't told anyone up to this point, what on earth makes you think I would tell you now?"

"Because I'm not anyone. I'm me." Charlie smiled.

"Nice try. Your dimple doesn't work here. Besides, you became 'anyone' when you married Piper." Biz meant it to sting a little. "Carry on with your life and don't mind mine, thank you very much. We're all doing just fine."

"Ruby has a dimple," he baited her. Charlie had always wanted to know, though he agreed with Biz that the truth was superfluous.

Biz said, "We all have dimples, and she looks just like me."

"She laughs like me."

"Oh, please—"

"Doesn't she ever ask—"

"Stop," Biz said with no intention of divulging what she herself didn't know for certain. Let Charlie think she knew and wasn't telling. "Please, let's not rock any boats."

"You mean other than the boat being rocked before our very

eyes? Does he know about the pile?" Charlie was referring to Georgia's husband, who was also his dear old friend.

"I have no idea. He's at work, and I'm staying out of it. I was merely asked to stand guard to make sure random passersby didn't steal his crap. That includes you. Put the putter back."

"You're the Switzerland of domestic disputes."

"*Je suis,*" said Biz.

"So then you don't blame him?"

"I don't blame anyone. That's not my role. You can never know what goes on in a marriage. At least that's what I'm told by everyone who's ever been married, ad nauseam."

"It's true," Charlie said. "So the bakery isn't crumbling without you there? Get it? Crumbling?"

"Hardy-har, I get it. They barely know I'm gone. It's a well-oiled machine. Are you going to call Piper?"

"Nah, she's carpooling now and doesn't want a cellular phone—she thinks they're unnecessary and showy. I might tell her at dinner."

"I thought husbands told their wives everything."

Charlie spoke with remnants of guilt. "You of all people should know that's not true. I'm noticing Georgia threw the clothes out first to make a cushion for the electronics. Did she do that last time? Do you think that means there's a part of her that still loves him?"

"Nope," said Biz. "I think this one's gonna stick."

Charlie mused, "It's almost as if she planned it."

"Are you kidding?" Biz looked up from her magazine. "None of us could have possibly planned any of this."

At that moment, a faded diesel Mercedes pulled up the driveway. It was butter yellow with a distinctive engine's rumble. Foster Barnstock emerged in a Tommy Bahama Hawaiian

shirt, blasting "Don't Stop Believing" at top volume. Georgia
had been begging him to upgrade his car for years, but he was
stalwart and stubbornly refused. Once he decided to like something he dug in his heels. It was that mind-set that made his
online start-up millions in the tech sector—and helped him woo
the glamorous and sexy Georgia. But it was also the mind-set
that had brought them all to this histrionic scene in front of
Grandpa Dun and Nana Miggs's old house. "Great highway
torque," Foster repeated in his car's defense, but it was the diesel rumble that gave away his third affair.

Foster watched, without flinching, as his Bose Wave speakers took flight. A police officer slowed and parked, presumably
to take in the show. With that, Foster briskly strode past Biz
and Charlie, saying, "'Morning." They echoed his sentiment
brightly as if passing a gardening neighbor and not witnessing
the dramatic midlife conclusion of someone's faltering vows.
"Just a minute, sir," the three of them heard the officer say. Foster yelled up to his wife, "Georgia, knock it off!" "I'll be right
down, dear!" she sang after tipping a boxy Bondi Blue iMac
off the sill onto the debris below. The desktop computer landed
precariously at the top of the sloped mountain like a climber
reaching the harrowing summit. Simultaneously, Charlie and
Biz stood up. "Let's amscray," said Biz. Foster said, "Where
you going? It's about to get fun."

The policeman asked Foster, "Sir, would you like to press
charges? This is destruction of property."

Foster said, "Uh, no, thank you, officer. This is how we
pack. We're going on vacation."

Biz started to giggle and couldn't stop. She knew this was a
painful day for them but couldn't disengage from the absurdity.
After all, there was no clear winner; Georgia had cheated, too.

"I'll help them pack" was all Biz could think to say, then knelt down and began folding Foster's clothes.

Seconds later, the electric garage door rose, revealing Georgia holding a giant sledgehammer over her head. "Um, Georgia" was as far as Foster got before the officer spoke.

"Ma'am, please put the sledgehammer down."

Georgia paused, stunned by the sight of the blue uniform, then said, "What sledgehammer?"

Charlie said, "He can arrest you."

There was another pause as everyone watched Georgia's wheels turning. "Officer, I'm glad you're here, I have a question." She smiled thinly for punctuation.

"Hypothetically," Foster interjected.

"Yes, thank you, dear. Hypothetically, if we own everything fifty-fifty in the eyes of the law, can't I wreck my own property on my own land? Do I have the constitutional right—"

The officer cut in as if he knew where this was going. "Ma'am, if you raise that sledgehammer over your head with ill will and intent to harm or destroy property in anger, even if you own it and no one gets hurt, I can arrest you for a DV—a domestic violence violation."

Biz tried to distract the cop. "Hey, didn't you go to Larkspur High?"

"I have a situation, here, ma'am. I'd prefer if you—"

"Got it. Sorry. Carry on, officer. It's Bruce, right?"

"Yes, ma'am. Officer Bruce Wade."

"Wait, isn't—" said Biz, but Charlie cut her off, whispering, "No. That's 'Wayne.'"

Georgia had a revelation. "Hey, Batman! I remember you!"

Foster gave Georgia the stink-eye. "Officer Wade, I'm *not* pressing charges."

"It doesn't matter. The state *is,* and she'll be arrested."

Everyone considered the options. Georgia broke the ice. "No one's getting arrested. I'm just cleaning out the garage. So thanks for stopping by, Bruce. This is our business . . . uh, vacation, and we'll handle . . . the packing ourselves. In private." Then she lowered the sledgehammer and underarm-tossed it onto the pile, hitting the computer and dislodging it from its precarious perch. The machine rolled clumsily down the hill and came to rest on Batman's foot. It only tapped him gently on the ankle but touched him nonetheless. Biz said, "Ohhhh, shiiiiiit."

Officer Wade said, "Now you've assaulted a police officer. You're under arrest."

Foster cut in, "But, officer—" as Georgia said, *"Whaaaaat?!"* with more indignation than she probably should have. Foster and Georgia moved toward the cop with separate diatribes, yet unified in their desire and intent. They looked like a real married couple. Charlie added to the cacophony by repeating, "Don't resist arrest, Georgia, don't resist arrest," like some mantra he'd been coached to say by an older fraternity brother. Biz went back to folding, unable to undo what couldn't be undone, and powerless to stop her undignified giggle fit.

Georgia did not resist arrest, Foster followed her to the station, and Biz and Charlie stayed behind to cover the pile with tarps. When they imagined Claire and Grandpa Dun receiving the news of the Thornden arrest, they laughed themselves silly, though it wasn't funny at all. Then they lay on the grass, trying to catch their breaths, like they did when they were kids.

At thirty-six, Biz was the manager at the local bakery—in the same town she grew up in and always assumed she'd leave. She was also a single mom to an eleven-year-old daughter, father unknown, an apparent mystery. All but one dream had fallen short, but her wish for a child had come true.

Around the time of Charlie's wedding, Biz was working in the city, still sewing during the day and waitressing at night. Then weeks after Charlie's wedding, she discovered she was pregnant. She was shocked, devastated, and unfathomably livid. *How could this happen again?!* There were two possible fathers: Finn, whom she'd bumped into at a street fair; and Charlie, in the stupid tree house after they went out for ice. Before that she hadn't been with anyone in many, many months, which was why she felt entitled to enjoy a soupçon of sex. And, yes, her drinking might have factored in, but it wasn't only her fault. Sometimes the guys had condoms on them and sometimes they didn't—and remembering to use her emergency condom turned out to be one thing, but replacing it in her purse was another. And, yes, her pill prescription lapsed that one time over a three-day holiday, but either guy could have pulled out. *I'm just unlucky,* Biz had always convinced herself, lost in unaccountability and the idiocy of denial.

As she grew more pregnant, the world moved forward swiftly without her. Career success, she felt the universe was saying, was for others to enjoy. So she gave up Outlandish Couture, moved home, and lay low. She couldn't imagine running her own business as a single mother. *Who in the world did that in 1990?* Keeping her baby was, in hindsight, a pointless retaliation. It didn't stop the sands of time nor Charlie's growing up and moving on. If she'd had a second abortion. . . . sure, she might live in California, be a married entrepreneur, but she wouldn't have her daughter. Ruby Chadwick was her world now, and she chose to raise her among family. So her daughter's world would be Larkspur, New Jersey.

Her small town seemed even smaller after living in New York City. There were endless questions of paternity and the compartmentalizing of what-ifs. "It wouldn't change anything" became Biz's party line. Plus she felt not discussing the father gave Ruby mystery and control. The bigger secret Biz harbored was her deep-seated desire to have Charlie be the one, to keep their connection alive. Yes, it was unconscionable, but what was more alive than a baby? It was supremely selfish but brutally honest—if only to herself. Though, she knew knowing the truth would bring misery to her family, so she abstained from DNA testing so she wouldn't have to lie. When Ruby turned six she started to ask about her father—needing the full story and demanding to know. Her insistence weakened until she gave in to her mom's refrain: "It just didn't matter" was all she ever heard. Ruby grew up to be mischievous like her mother, someone who enjoyed messing with her friends. Sometimes she confided her dad was on the lam. Sometimes he was a space alien or Nicolas Cage.

Eventually it was a nonissue; their town and friends stopped caring, and everyone moved on in the best possible way. Biz was glad she'd ridden out the storm and dug in her heels.

Throughout, her Aunt Cat was her greatest defender.

Bernadetta's was Larkspur's local family-owned bakery. It went up for sale the same year Ruby toddled off to preschool. Nana Miggs convinced her Dunny to buy the bakery for Biz to manage; then all she had to do was convince Biz. Nana Miggs felt strongly that as an unmarried woman, Biz should be where the townspeople were to increase her chances of meeting a man. "It's a well-oiled machine," Nana Miggs said, "practically runs itself." "But I don't bake," Biz said because it was true. "No one will care," which was as well.

Bernadetta's Bakery—or "Bernie's" for short—had been a staple for generations. It served as the town's hearth and made money hand over fist. The old guard were suspicious of Biz and her fatherless daughter. They speculated how she came to move back home from the city and why. But even the most salacious rumors faded when they learned she had no intention of making changes. They were thrilled Biz kept the same recipes and staff. The espresso stayed legit and the coffee cake crumb-y. Bernie's would continue to be beloved, cozy—for the older folks as well as the hip.

Biz couldn't bake—it was a running joke—but none of her employees minded. Her years of waitressing paid off; she was a natural behind the counter. Her employees liked that she was organized and communicated clearly, and those with a sense of humor appreciated hers as long as she stayed out of everyone's way. Two of them became her first close girlfriends. Anna-Maria Theresa—Annie Mae for short—age sixty-none-of-your-beeswax, was as tart as a pippin apple pie. Muriel had burned out on teaching "grubby fourth graders" by her late thirties, though she confided, actually by thirty-one. Biz delighted having these funny female compatriots. Both women were hard workers, loyal employees, and gems.

Biz leaned on the center workspace in the cramped, bright kitchen watching the icers work their magic on cookies and cakes. This morning smelled of buttercream frosting, strawberries, and rhubarb. Yesterday it was cherries, chocolate, and mint. Heavy white bowls full of pastry bags in Easter-egg shades sat next to stacks of rainbow-colored sprinkles and sanding sugars. Biz was learning how to hold the bag and twist just so with delicate motions of surefire wrists. At first, the graceful lines she meant to leave behind came out like a rabid snail. She failed repeatedly at keeping the flower petals stiff and the spokes on a bicycle straight. She joked, "I must remember not to get wasted before work," a silly notion, as her shift began at 4 A.M. But there were uncomfortable titters as they caught each other's glance; Biz occasionally gave off the tangy tinge of recent pickling.

Sometimes she went straight to work from a late night at Dickbird's, the pub downtown officially named the Cock and Crow. Dickbird's owner was smart enough to recognize they had plenty of family-friendly bistros. What it needed was a dark, child-unfriendly dive where locals could go to drink quietly and shoot pool. Ruby knew if her mom wasn't home or at work, she should use the signal she had set up with the bartenders. They would find Biz and tell her Ruby needed to chat. Dickbird's was only a few doors down.

"So where did you end up burying it?" asked Tookie, a gullible short-term hire. She wiped away a tear Annie Mae had clearly not shed for her own dead cat. "Who said anything about burying?" Annie Mae replied, bopping to the music as she iced. "Not funny, you guys," said Tookie with a furrowed brow. She was the perfect target for crusty Annie Mae. Muriel cackled as she swapped out beach-ball butter cookies for sailboats. She added, "I have a dead guinea pig in my freezer. We've been waiting for the spring thaw."

"It's June already. You waiting for the next ice age?" cracked Annie Mae.

"I keep forgetting he's in there," said Muriel with a chuckle.

"No kidding. I already have a couple of gerbils in our basement freezer. I forget about them until we decide to have ribs. Now I've got this cat, too, and the freezer's not that big."

"Well, they're not going anywhere," reasoned Biz.

"Stop!" yelped Tookie, and covered her multi-pierced ears with her tattooed hands. "You guys are horrible."

"How 'bout a dumpster?" said Annie Mae. "I could set my alarm for the dead of night."

Biz said, "I get it. The 'dead' of night." Tookie looked about to cry in earnest.

Annie Mae shifted into her soothing grandmother routine. "I'm only kidding, sweetheart. Don't cry. We'll head out to the garden with Popsicle-stick crosses and my kid will play 'Amazing Grace' on his recorder."

Biz said, "Nice touch," and Muriel mouthed "dumpster" and winked. Tookie said, "That sounds nice," to which Annie Mae replied, "You're not invited." Biz and Muriel lived for Annie Mae's tough broad act. Biz laughed with more gusto at the bakery than she did anywhere else. *I'm lucky I ended up here,* she even thought when she was alone, and wallowed in what-could-have-been far less often.

Ever since Finn, Biz's ears pricked up when she heard an Irish accent. The lilt could transport her back to her twenties and Mongey's endless nights. That autumn, she peered through the baking racks and inched around the giant mixer to get a full view of the man at the counter who had a familiar lilt. His short hair was conservative, yet vaguely reminiscent of punk. It had gone completely snow white, but his eyebrows were still bushy and dark, which made his sky-blue eyes pierce with even more devastating accuracy. It was Finn. In Bernadetta's Bakery. One of Ruby's possible dads.

Biz grabbed an empty cupcake box and walked it over to the counter so she'd have something fake to put away, then looked up—with fake surprise. In the voice of Scarlett O'Hara, she said, "Why, Finn O'Donoghue, as I live and breathe." She said it quietly and deadpan but could feel her eyes glistening and tried to will them to settle down. Finn twinkled as he sipped from a coffee to go cup. He'd aged in the maddening way the Irish age—with frustrating youth and undeniable charm.

"Elizabeth Chapman," he said in an Irish brogue as thick as the day he'd arrived.

"Chadwick," Biz corrected politely.

"Chickwick," he pronounced with a thumbs-up as if he'd nailed it this time.

"Chadwick," she repeated with a mixture of annoyance and humiliation. She thought she'd made a bigger impression the last time she'd seen him. Hadn't they had a steamy one night stand around the time Ruby was conceived? Could she have possibly remembered that incorrectly? She questioned her increasingly spotty memory. But then the corner of Finn's mouth curled to reveal his megawatt teeth, which had evidently been given a once-over by an American orthodontist. He was no longer a shy guy with a hesitant smile. "I'm just giving you crap," he said, rolling the *r* in "crap" with a smirk, his whole body gloating. "You little shit," said Biz. She leaned over and punched his arm. "You haven't changed a bit." Just then someone called from the back. "Biz, did you want me to bill the Bigelow order?"

She shouted over her shoulder, "Yes, please. It's on my desk!"

"You have a desk. Manager?"

Biz squared her shoulders. "Owner," she said, trying to curb her own gloating. She could feel her self-control leaking out of her like water through a pinhole in a cracked rubber hose. "Huh," he said, and looked around the charming bakery and coffee spot. He took in the sunny room with butter-hued walls where mismatched wooden chairs sidled up to retro aluminum-topped tables. "Really?" he said, drawing out the word until it lasted three syllables of disbelief. "I wouldn't have pegged you for the baking type. A real homemaker, are we? Would have guessed you'd a become more of a home-wrecker." Biz rolled her eyes.

The bakery's front door opened and a crusty old man with a greasy ponytail and two sets of eyeglasses boomed, "Fuck you!" He flipped dual birds toward the crowd in an effort to reach the patrons and staff with equal aplomb. Finn let a "Ha!" escape with wide-eyed wonder, then looked to Biz for her re-action. Much to his delight, the entire staff and some of the patrons—including Biz—smiled brightly at the bedraggled man. They pointed a middle finger, and responded, "Fuck you, Carl!" like the chorus in a Gilbert and Sullivan musical. Fuck You Carl strode toward the cup of coffee Biz held out to him as if he'd done it a thousand times. He grabbed it without saying thanks, then took off out the door, the tails of his trench coat lifting slightly in the air behind him. In that small gesture Finn thought he glimpsed a Biz who was now vulnerable herself and sympathetic to others' wounds. He saw a humbled interior where her youthful hubris used to reside. She caught Finn staring at her and returned to her composure. "What are *you* doing here?" she asked.

"Twenty Questions, eh? I'll give ya one answer per visit."

"Oh, brother, really?" she said. "What are we, eleven years old?"

"No, Elizabeth," he said so that only she could hear, "we are no longer eleven."

Biz felt a pang of sexual awakening the moment Finn called her Elizabeth. She'd forgotten he'd refused to call her Biz and remembered he was gorgeous naked. She cased Finn's left hand for a wedding ring—found no tan line, either. Somewhere deep in her body something was opening to possibility, and it wasn't an unwelcome feeling. It had been ages since she'd had sex. The pang took her back many, many years and how he disappeared on her the way she'd done to him—no call, no encore. She dismissed him when he finally called, not wanting to become tangled in his commit-me-not web of booze and women. She wondered what he remembered now and if he was Ruby's father. Then she reprimanded herself for wanting to know. She'd spent years instructing the world it didn't matter. But to a secret hidden part of her it did.

"Tah," Finn said. He twinkled his leprechaun eyes at her one more time and left. Biz waited for him to turn around, to wave or wink, but he didn't. He walked directly out into the glorious October morning as if he'd ordered it thusly for himself. Clearly his shyness had been replaced by the arrogance some expats accrue after living in the U.S. and gaming women. His accent hadn't remained thick by accident. Biz watched Finn's sweet ass recede from her, round and lovely in his perfectly worn Levi's. His collared shirt and Carhartt jacket were squeaky clean. Construction management? Landscape architect? *Hot damn, who cares,* she thought, and went back to work, thinking of little else.

Finn returned at closing. Biz waited until he walked all

the way to the counter before giving him a blasé stare-down, though every cell was on high alert. "Welcome, customer," Biz said. "We still have a few sundried tomato cheddar scones left and, it appears, half a pot of regular brewed sometime in the last week."

"I'll take all the scones and the rest of the coffee," he said with a straight face.

"Really," she said. It wasn't a question.

"Really," he replied, and Biz told the last two employees that they could leave. When Muriel raised an eyebrow Biz had to turn away from her quickly. *She can see my inner shit-eating grin a mile away,* Biz thought. Muriel took a detour to grab something inconsequential from under the counter so she could get another thorough look at Finn.

"'Night," Muriel sang when she reached the door.

"Yeah-yeah," Biz said, and locked it behind her.

"Still Chadwick?" Finn said to Biz. She placed the scones in a bag with tongs.

"Yup."

"What does your husband think of that?"

Biz looked at Finn. *It's now or never,* she thought and inhaled. She might have held her figure together, but it was a dog-eat-dog dating world in the suburbs and all the good ones, as the saying went, were taken. It would still be a few years before the second round of divorces began—at least that's how her mother had explained it. Biz wanted more than anything to grow old with a partner and have a consistent dad for Ruby; she ached for it. She was pretty sure Finn wasn't that guy—but for the short term, he was a known quantity. And if nothing else, a little sex was overdue.

Biz cocked a hip, lowered her chin, and smiled. "Let's cut

to the chase," said Biz. "I'm not married. Never was. I have a plucky, lovable, headstrong daughter, and, no, I don't know, nor am I preoccupied with, who the father is. Yes, I still live in the town I grew up in, but it doesn't mean that I haven't evolved. It's a safe, charming town, and I needed the help and didn't have the emotional strength to raise a child by myself. I own this bakery, though I'm a lousy baker. I like dried apricots and peonies, and any movie with Genes Kelly or Hackman. I have an irrational fear of tree stumps and a rational fear of clowns. There. That about covers it."

Finn let her languish in her monologue, squirming until she looked away. He watched her fold the top of the bag and seal it with one staple in the middle. "I love this song," he said, then sang, "I like coffee, I like tea, I like the java jive and it likes me . . ."

Biz nervously rambled, "Annie Mae's son rigged Napster to play only music from the thirties and forties. It's mostly coffee-or tea-inspired songs."

"It works. Wonders."

The Ink Spots hummed their smooth close harmony ge-nius in the dim, dusky light of the empty bakery. Finn wanted more than ever to take his dear old Elizabeth in his arms and shuffle her around the room in small steady steps—a prelude to seducing her—but he knew she would make him work for it. She always had. Finally he spoke. "Don't forget the java." Biz reddened, then circled the room turning out lights. As she reached the last switch Finn was standing there, blocking her path to the front door. For a moment she flashed to Charlie and that unforgivable dorm room episode, but this was the new millennia with new rules. It was 2002 and sensitivity training was a thing and date rape had a name. She didn't feel unsafe but thought she should probably start charging her cell phone. Ruby thought it ridiculous her mom never had it with her. But then what? Biz had said. "Walk around with it in my pocket all day? That's dumb." Who did that? No one she knew.

"Can I buy you a cosmo?" asked Finn.

"I need to finish closing up. There's still office stuff I need to—"

"How about a dance, then?" And without waiting for an answer, he put his hand on her waist and moved her across the room to Helen Forrest singing "Too Marvelous for Words." How incredible it felt to be held by someone attractive. Her whole body was alight and nearly imploded from mirth. As they danced, Finn began, "My turn. After you and I, uh, parted ways for the second time——"

"You mean you blew me off—"

"—I bartended, drove a cab, then went back to Ireland. Married Margaret, my high school sweetheart, then she left me for Mary, her best friend from high school—incidentally the last girl I dated before Margaret, which makes me the only man in all of Ireland to bed not one but two lesbians." His inflection was proud, as if he'd won a spelling bee.

"Impressive," said Biz.

"I thought so. They're now raising my daughter, and I come to the States six months out of the year to do landscaping work so that I can send money home to Margaret, some to Mom, and some to—"

"Another? Wait. Let me guess. Mary-Margaret."

"Close. Shannon, who's raising my son—our son—about twenty minutes from here in Collier Hills, though she, too, is doing so without my say-so. It appears I have yet to master the basics of, um—"

"Commitment?"

"I was going to say relationships."

"And condoms, apparently," said Biz.

Finn chuckled. "Yes. That, too, I'll admit." She waited a beat, then grinned. She was shocked that he still felt so familiar to her, that their banter was still so nimble. She was also stunned by how complicated his life had become; by comparison hers felt tame.

"So, you have two ex-wives, two kids on two continents, and a lesbian ex-in-law on a six-month rotation. Sounds like a shit-show."

"It is. A total shit-show." Finn exhaled deeply. "I spend most of my time on this side of the Hudson now, because it's where the money is."

"And the lawns, I'm guessing."

"And the lawns. Correct."

Billie Holiday cooed "It Had to Be You" while Biz took a moment to assess. Finn was a minor train wreck, which wasn't the end of the world—so was she. But she didn't care in this moment as he danced her around the room. She wasn't thinking about a future with Finn, she was imagining reaching orgasm, or trying to—it had been so long, she could hardly remember when. Could he get hard? That was her main concern. Nothing else mattered. Not even her darling daughter Ruby.

"I didn't track you down, Elizabeth. I was as surprised as you were when I saw you in this wee bakery in your wee town. I came back tonight to tell you that you're even more beautiful now than you were . . . and I like peonies enough, though they're petulant divas if you must know. I despise apricots, honestly, they're smug and there's nothing worse. But I would make out with Gene Hackman right here and now if given the chance.

And tree stumps, well, I'm a landscape designer, so I can protect you. And clowns are evil incarnate, no question, so at least we agree on—" Biz planted a wet one on him right then and there, right at the opening riff to Squeeze's "Black Coffee in Bed," which seemed awfully conspiratorial. Then Biz backed away, head woozy, and minced off to the basement office. Finn was happy to follow her down the stairs.

Their kiss turned voracious in seconds. Her hunger surprised them both—it had been ages since she'd tasted someone she truly desired. Biz moved her lower body against Finn's and found him hard. *A hard man is good to find,* she thought, and they devoured each other further. Then she grabbed Finn's ass through his jeans and felt a rush of energy, like a powerfully irresistible drug she'd all but forgotten. "Ohhh," she let escape into his ear. "I'm quite rusty."

"You'll catch on. It's just like falling off a—"

"Bicycle?" Biz cut in.

"I was going to say freight train." Finn grinned.

She whispered between heavy breaths, "You can't imagine how long . . . and who knows when I'll get the chance . . . Just fuck me, please."

"Such a romantic."

"And stop talking."

"Yes, ma'am," said Finn, chuckling.

And so the fucking commenced.

Biz pulled flattened cake boxes off a high metal shelf and let them fall, covering the cold cement ground. Then she unbuckled Finn's belt. His hand cupped her breast, and Biz responded with a wild jolt. "Mmmmm," she hummed with a grounded urgency. Then he slowly slid both hands down into her pants from either side so that his fingers met in the middle. This was new to his bag of tricks since she'd last been with him; Biz was elated by his creativity.

"Still in the same place, eh?" he whispered.

"Right where you left it." At the same moment Biz found him swollen and ready. "Ahhh," they said in unison. His brain was shutting down, and they both knew it would be a while before he returned. Finn's last clear thought was that he was glad he'd been hired by some rich Jersey divorcée named Amanda. Biz's last thought before she untied her apron was that she was glad she'd shaved her legs. Finn lifted Biz onto the desk and enjoyed giving a bit of head as she reclined, knocking the stapler onto the floor. She straddled him on her desk chair until her knees began to cramp; then they lowered onto the flattened boxes for climaxing. But the real prize was how he felt inside her—*full-filled in the literal sense,* she thought, noting the double entendre for the first time.

"I'm enjoying the fucking very much," Biz said out loud.

"Are ya, now?"

"I are," she said, then yelped, "Oooh," filling the room with sound as she plunged herself onto him again and again. The deeper she pulled, the more her tiny sparkles filled the air. She gripped the shelving so she could slam him harder. "I'm close," she said, "grab my arse," and he gamely did. She was certain her whoops and squeals would hoist her to the precipice, unaccustomed to the ecstasy that was catapulting her into space. But Biz didn't realize her crescendoing screams had reached beyond the basement walls. Finn was loud, too, his grunts winding their way around her moans. And just as they cleared the peak together, he released a deep roar, but a third shriek was heard from the door. *"Mom! Oh my God! Are you okay?!"*

Biz and Finn froze midthrust and hugged each other close.

They required a three-second delay to understand what was happening. Was there a girl in the basement? But Ruby had play rehearsal. Had Biz forgotten to lock the back door? She grabbed another flattened cake box and covered them as she shouted, *"Back away, back away!"* at her eleven-year-old daughter. "What are you *doing here*?!" Ruby was standing on the threshold, her fingers not quite covering her eyes. She bellowed, *"Mom, I'm scared! Are you okay? I'm calling the police!"*

"Wait!" was all Biz could think to shout. *"Sweetie, I'm okay!!"* But the only reply was running feet and a muffled pre-teen's cries.

"My daughter—" Biz whispered to Finn. Her head was in a fog. It was disorienting down in the office/illicit sex lair. "I got it," he panted, and sighed as they disengaged themselves. Her inner glory of fullness was now bereft. If there could have been a sound effect it would have been a clown's slide-whistle "b'woop." *Jesus, can I please catch a break?* thought Biz. *I'm thirty-six and feel wholly deserving of an uninterrupted fuck in the place I own, for chrissakes.* But Ruby sounded wounded, poor girl, and would have to be consoled. Plus there was the matter of a few unusable cake boxes, the likelihood of police arriving, and small-town public humiliation for the Thornden family—again.

Ruby, a budding clone of her mother, stood sobbing at the bakery's back door. But she was also really pissed at her mom, that deranged-sounding stranger, and the whole fucking world. Ruby let loose a deluge the second she laid eyes on her mother. *"Oh my God!! Oh my God!! Are you kidding me?!!* Are you fucking *kidding me*?! Were you having *sex*?! God, you're *so gross*!" Biz tried an empathetic hand on her shoulder, but Ruby flung it off. "Is *that* what sex sounds like? I thought you were being *murdered*!"

"Honey, why aren't you at rehearsal?" Biz noticed she'd missed one of her buttons. Finn showed up, running his fingers sheepishly through his hair.

"Miss Haarmann decided to let us go early. Who the fuck is *this guy*?"

Finn started, "I'm—" but Biz cut him off and spoke in her damage-control voice. "Ruby, please stop swearing. Even on this occasion, the F-bomb is unacceptable."

"This *occasion*?! You mean the *screwing occasion*?! Stop *swearing*?! How about *stop screwing*!"

"Honey, people have sex. Grown-ups have sex, it's what we do. It's how humans propagate the species and why we're here today. Sometimes it gets loud and sounds scary, but it's actually pretty fun when it's uninterrupted, and when you're much, much older hopefully you'll enjoy it, too. Now I need to say good-bye to Mr. O'Donoghue, and then we'll head home and have plenty of opportunity to talk—"

"Well, I don't *fucking want to talk,*" Ruby said. "I don't ever want to talk to you again as long as I live." Then she turned on a youthful heel and stormed off.

"Oh my fucking God," said Biz. Her head was spinning. *Christ,* she thought, *I don't even know where to begin.*

"You've got quite an eloquent daughter," said Finn, sensing the all-clear to speak.

"You should probably—"

"Yeah."

But just then, two cop cars pulled up—walkie-talkies crackling, flashers whirling—and a familiar face emerged from one. It was Batman.

"You're shitting me," uttered Biz.

"Good evening, folks. I'm Officer Wade."

"Hey, Batman," said Biz.

"How do you two know . . . ?" was all Finn could say. Then to Biz, "Did you just say 'Batman'?"

Biz returned home to discover Ruby wildly tossing clothes, books, and her favorite stuffed animal, Boinkers, into an NSYNC rolling suitcase. Biz hovered near the door in order to give her space. "Sweetheart, where are you going?"

"Somewhere where there's no sex."

"A nunnery? No, actually, they . . . never mind."

"I'm going to Gigi's. Aunt Georgia said I can have a guestroom."

"Aunt Georgia has sex."

"But Uncle Foster moved out."

"Doesn't mean she stopped having sex, dear. In fact—"

"Ewww!" Ruby stomped her feet. "It's so disgusting! I hate everybody!"

Biz moved gingerly across Ruby's IKEA rug and sat on the edge of her IKEA bed. "Well, everybody loves you, especially me."

"Why did you even have me if you hate me so much?"

"I don't hate you. I *had* you because I *wanted* you. Because I knew you'd be just as bright and creative and funny as you are, or can be under different circumstances. And because I knew my life would be less spectacular without you, because I'd have no one to love."

"You could have loved my dad."

"Your sperm donor was never in the picture, sweetie, you

know that." Biz reached out for Ruby's hand, and this time she let her hold it. "You can't fathom how much I love you. With every fiber of my being, I love you, a hundred thousand times more than you love Boinkers. You know we can talk about 'the Donor' anytime you want, and I'll try to answer your questions as best—"

Ruby removed her hand. "I still want to sleep at Gigi's because I still hate you for getting jiggy with that stranger."

Biz's cell phone dinged from somewhere in the apartment. "He's not a stranger to me. Hold that thought, sweetie, I should find my phone." She was worried it was the police, but when she returned she was peering at the closed top of the clamshell. "It says one text from Rah. That's dumb. Why doesn't it tell me what she says? Do you think it just means I'm supposed to call her back?"

"God. Mom, *flip* open the phone. The *name of the thing* is a *verb. Do the verb.*"

"I hate these things." Biz turned the phone in her palm, looking for the correct side of the crack to open.

"Oh. My. God, Mom. Give it to me."

"No, I can do it. It just says, 'Grandpa Dun died.' Why would it say that?"

Ruby paused and looked at her mom as if she couldn't believe they were related. "Because maybe he did?"

Biz gasped. "Oh, my dear, do you think Grandpa Dun died?" She reflexively covered her heart with her hand.

"Um, yeah," said Ruby. "Why don't you text Aunt Rah back to make sure."

"I don't know her number."

"You just hit REPLY."

"How do I do that?"

Ruby looked as though she wanted to crawl out of her skin. "Ohmy*god*, Mom."

Biz stood up in a daze. She was processing; she was also in shock. She guessed everyone would convene at Aunt Cat's. That's where Grandpa Dun and Nana Miggs had moved after they sold the big house to Foster and Georgia. Rah used her old room sometimes for visits, and Charlie and Piper had their own house with their kids, Gigi and Thorn. Cat's downstairs study had already been retrofitted for her illness, so they figured it would make for the smoothest transition for Marjorie and Dunny, and it did. At no time in the discussions did Claire offer her place, even though she lived alone now, and had for some time.

Biz said to Ruby, "You'll have to hold off on hating me until after the service, I guess. I think your Great-Grandpa Dun has died."

Grandpa Dun had been ill for a while, but the assumption was that he would carry on for years and years, languishing in a slow gray fade. No one thought he would actually die. But that night at Aunt Cat's the general mood was a surprising combination of shock and positivity. The family gathered expecting Nana Miggs to be inconsolable, but she seemed chipper and unexpectedly luminous. "Buck up, everyone," she said, wearing coral lipstick. "Resentment has little usefulness in life and death," followed by, "The dead don't mourn for us, so we shouldn't mourn for them."

"They can't," said E.J., "they're dead."

Nana Miggs left the room to wait with her Dunny to get him ready, she said, for his voyage. Rah waited until she was out of earshot before whispering, "When she says 'the dead,' she knows she's talking about her beloved husband of sixty-one years, yes?" Everyone nodded. "Does anyone else think it's weird she's taking it so well?" Foster added, "She left out, 'Don't cry for me, Argentina.'" Georgia rapped Foster, saying, "Not funny." Biz chuckled. She needed a laugh. Piper whispered to Charlie, "None of your family seems very upset." Biz said, "There's no right or wrong way to mourn." Piper glared at her. Charlie shot Biz a look, then put his hand on the small of Piper's back. He said, "That's because we're WASPs, dear. WASPs don't feel emotion, you know that." Biz felt the pang of wanting someone's hand on the small of her back. It was times like these she found it especially crushing to be alone.

Once Nana Miggs combed his hair, Grandpa Dun looked relaxed and ready for backgammon. She invited everyone into the bedroom to say good-bye, then shooed them away. She spent her remaining time with Dunny before the coroner arrived serenading him with his favorites from long ago. Her voice was quiet as if she were making it tiny on purpose, so he could fit her songs in his pocket and take them with him on his trip. The others broke open his good scotch—the bottles he'd squirreled away—and told Grandpa Dun stories around Cat's kitchen table. In the background was a lone sweet voice, thin but sure of the lyrics, singing "The Very Thought of You," and "Seems Like Old Times."

Early the next morning, Biz awoke crying in her pillow. She'd dreamed about her grandfather's manners and ludicrous bon mots. She would miss the man who taught her not to say "yeah." His death also served to amplify how short life was.

Nana Miggs's saying was said to punctuate how important it was to find a partner, but not just anyone—someone who celebrates and cherishes you for who you are. *Is Finn that guy for me?* Had she blown it with him again? She cried, utterly selfish in the face of Nana Miggs's loss. But how was it some people had the good fortune to spend their entire lives with someone they adored and others weren't so lucky, always searching, never to be found? Was Biz experiencing karmic payback for some heinous crime committed in a past life? Why was Piper more deserving than she? Nana Miggs and Grandpa Dun were a shining example of divine union. Better to have loved and lost than never to have loved at all. Then Biz splashed her face, as Nana Miggs would have instructed, and headed to work in the dim light of dawn.

Biz's plan was to tell Muriel about Finn and the cops before she heard the news. They might need to brainstorm a little spin to keep the local rumormongers at bay. Muriel opened the conversation with a hug and empathetic words of condolence, then sat down in Biz's desk chair and told Biz to sit across from her.

"You know I love you," she began with an unusually professional tone.

"I do." Biz was hesitant. Muriel had never said that.

"Have you been drinking?"

"No!" At least she hadn't been since last night. She and Ruby had gone home from Cat's early.

"I have to take you off the counter."

"*What?!*"

"Everybody knows."

"Knows what?" Biz's mind was racing; the possibilities were numerous. Muriel gave her a "duh" look, and Biz guessed the most obvious of her indiscretions. "About Finn? How does everyone know?"

"Texts."

"People spread rumors typing texts? That's the dumbest thing I've ever heard."

"That's how the teenagers do it today."

Biz got the picture. "Oh, crap. Did Ruby?"

"Yes. Everyone knows everything. Including that the cops came, and sex is supposedly fun—according to you—except that it's gross according to her."

"*Those* were her takeaways?" Biz wanted to wring Ruby's neck.

Muriel remained composed. "Look, it's just for a few days. Or weeks. Until the gossip subsides. I hardly hear anyone talking about Georgia's arrest any more."

Biz was aghast. "*Were people talking—*"

"Of course. Look. I'm doing it for the bakery, and you know it's the right thing. You can help with the cakes."

"Cakes hate me."

"You're a natural. You'll learn how to assemble! C'mon, fillings, crumb coats . . . you'll be a wiz with cake combs and offset spatulas before you know it. Why don't you spend a week learning base crumbing. You'll move up fast. You're creative. Come to the dark side."

"You know what? Fine. Maybe I'll learn to love cakes, but I hate everyone in this town."

"Now, now."

"They're all so small-minded, and conservative and, and . . . easily contained. Where are all the John Waterses and Bette Midlers? How are artists supposed to thrive once they have children, out in the suburbs? And why do Americans have to be convinced that art is important? I should be a costume couturier. I would have been incredibly valuable in prairie times. I could have quilted, and made clothes. I would have had the respect of—"

"All the prairie drag queens. I know. Listen, you're getting off track, but okay, sure." Muriel settled in for the long haul—she was used to these frenetic tirades Biz's drinking caused. She said, "You can do all those things now, and since when do you care about respect? I didn't think you gave any fucks."

"I still have a few to give."

Muriel paused, lit a cigarette, and offered one to Biz. They knew it was a no-no, but their lives had become so predictable that this little rebellion felt reasonably anarchistic. Plus the ventilation system at Bernie's had been updated and was top-notch so they indulged. Biz watched the long plume of smoke trail from her pursed lips. Muriel reached behind her without looking and grabbed a plastic to-go lid for ashing.

Biz said, "How the hell am I supposed to have sex if I can't have it in my own business?"

"Most people do that sort of thing in their bedrooms."

"I have a daughter whose bedroom is right next to mine!" Biz didn't mean to raise her voice, and Muriel knew it wasn't personal.

"So do most people. What is this really about?"

Biz jumped up and paced the room while Muriel routinely affixed Bernadetta's labels to brown paper bags. "I'll tell you. You and everyone else in this town got married right out of college, and you've all totally forgotten what it's like to be single. You have zero awareness of what it's like to always be stuck sitting at the end of a long rectangle table full of couples and an empty chair across from you. It's a literal reminder that I have no date even when I'm out with other people trying to forget I'm alone. It's like having a neon sign around your neck blinking 'unlovable.' *It's awful!*"

"I'm sorry to hear that."

"But I grin and bear it. Because people don't mean to be cruel. And no one likes a sourpuss. Then, *finally*, an attractive, STD-free, straight man walks through the door with a well-maintained hard-on and wants to put it in *my* vagina. But there's only cardboard on the floor, so we make do, but my daughter gets hysterical, and the cops come, and my employee demotes me!"

"Sucks for you. Did you use our cake boxes to—"

"It's bad enough I have to make do with flattened boxes when everyone I know has a husband and a soft bed." Tears were beginning to well. "I just wanted to have a little sex."

"I know, honey. And people are busy with their own lives, and no one's thinking about yours."

"No *shit*!"

"And maybe next time say, 'Hey, can I sit in the middle?'"

"*I do!* But sometimes I'm the last to arrive!"

"Well then, get there early. And John Waters and Bette Midler moved to big cities."

"But I *don't want to move to a big city* because I like *raising my kid in the suburbs,* and I would miss the bakery too much, and I would miss you." Biz valued Muriel dearly and bet she was a phenomenal teacher in her day.

"Are we almost finished? You've hit your tantrum quota for the month."

Biz chuckled. "Okay, fine. I'm done."

"Fabulous. Nice speech. I've got to get upstairs. Why don't you recycle those boxes—and watch your step, I hear the floor may be sticky."

"Hardy-har."

"How was Finn? We never got to him. Do you think you'll see him again?"

"Ha. Yes, I like him. He's a train wreck but great in the sack, and, oh yeah, he's on his way back to Ireland, and PS, I *almost got him arrested*. Do *you* think I'll ever see him again?"

Muriel said, "Salient point. I'm really sorry about your grandfather. Now splash your face, get some coffee, get to work, and don't go near the counter." She left Biz standing in the basement alone, angered and frustrated by so many things she'd already forgotten where to start.

The intimate wooden-shingled church was not as packed as Claire anticipated, but Grandpa Dun's old golf buddies and bridge friends arrived early and sat in the front. Rah was chosen to read something she'd written to represent the grandchildren, and Claire and Cat spoke in tandem about being raised with good manners and sense. They agreed the great-grandchildren—"the Greats," as they were lumped together—were too young for the responsibility of speaking in front of the crowd and that funerals were adult affairs, though they were allowed to attend as long as they remained quiet.

E.J. wanted to speak, but the family wouldn't allow it. A funeral was "not the time nor the place" for him to try out new material. It was bad enough he'd quit a top-tier law firm to become a stand-up comic; he would *not* be using his grandfather's funeral to do a quick set. "I promise not to work blue," he pleaded, "obviously, Jesus. Who do you think I am? It'll all be very tasteful, life affirming, what's-it-like-on-the-other-side stuff." But his mother, sister, aunt, and cousins were unified in their answer. There was no need to take a vote.

The minister deferred to Marjorie Thornden's wishes by allowing the church choir to lead the congregants in singing "What a Wonderful World," and there wasn't a dry eye in the house. The reception was at the golf club, where she'd insisted on a live jazz trio, much to Claire's chagrin. They played Thornden family favorites: Cole Porter and the Gershwin fellows, as Dunny used to say time and again. And after a stiff old fashioned, Nana Miggs demanded Charlie fox-trot her around to "Easy to Love" or be cut from the will. Claire was livid about the impropriety, but once others joined in she gave up and poured herself another chardonnay. Sissy Bickers danced with her husband, and Muriel brought the ladies from Bernadetta's, who danced with each other like in black-and-white wartime photos. "Dr. Rebekah" aka Becky from Fall Festival weekend was there. After college she became a pediatrician. She and Biz had reconnected recently and become fast friends when she relocated to Firth with her second husband, who was, at last, Jewish.

Charlie would've danced with Piper, but she no longer liked to dance. He wanted to dance with Biz but knew he shouldn't. Instead, he focused on his grandmother and how she lit up in his arms. Her cheeks still formed tiny apples when she grinned. He was proud of how she'd held up and wondered if he'd be as lucky with Piper at the end of his days. He looked for his wife in the crowd and found her glowering back at him as if she, too, were annoyed there was live music at a memorial. He wished he could please her. He usually fell short. But Piper was the mother of his children.

Biz knew she was drinking too much and didn't care. The service unexpectedly served to amplify her loneliness. All that damn soul-mate talk sent her into a funk, so she treated herself to a craft beer, two cosmos, and a chardonnay. Rebekah tried her best to distract her from the bar, Muriel even took a glass out of her hand. And Sissy pretended not to notice Biz's slurring, unaware that she was wobbling herself. Watching Charlie dance with Nana Miggs didn't help matters; Biz missed dancing with him terribly. She told the girls how when she and Charlie were little they memorized all the fast musical numbers from *Grease*. They also made up elaborate choreography to George Michael's "Faith" and an epic dance/mime odyssey to Michael Jackson's *Off the Wall*. They danced up stairs and leaped off patio furniture like Fred and Ginger—though Charlie insisted they were Fred Flintstone and Ginger from *Gilligan's Island*. Rebekah said she thought it permissible if they shared one dance, though Sissy advised against it with a shake of her head. Muriel told her that not only should they get out there and dance together but she would tell the jazz trio to play "Don't Stop 'Til You Get Enough." Biz laughed, but even drunk, she knew that was a bad idea, though to her, she and Charlie would always be a team.

Out of the corner of her eye, Biz caught the sight of Hugh Billings winding his way toward her. "You should dance with Hugh," encouraged Sissy. "You should definitely *not* dance with Hugh," said Muriel, and Rebekah laughed in agreement. Hugh was the local widower, bookstore owner, and perfect gentleman. Biz had known him and his wife, Adele, for years as the most graceful couple in town, seemingly older than their early forties. They brought calm and dignity to every committee meeting they attended and were the sort of couple one couldn't possibly imagine having sex. But Biz appreciated Hugh's breadth of intellect, good posture, and steady demeanor. So when he asked permission to kiss her at the end of their first date, she stood on tiptoe and planted a warm one on his lips. Hugh recoiled slightly, shocked by her forwardness, and set her gently back down. Biz smiled thinly, said good night, then went upstairs to pleasure herself. She politely declined a second date.

But tonight she was too desperately lonesome to turn Hugh down and wept as he shuffled her awkwardly around in a stiff two-step. He gallantly offered her a handkerchief from his breast pocket, but what she really wanted was for him to make her laugh. Meanwhile, Charlie led Nana Miggs around the club's parquet floor in elegant gliding sweeps. Biz watched them with a mix of morose envy and joy. When Charlie passed her, she silently begged him to cut in on Hugh and take her in his arms, but it was no use. She suspected Charlie could no longer read her mind. The thought fueled more tears, and her cheeks glistened.

Claire marched up to Cat, incensed. "This dancing really should end soon."

"Come on, Claire, no one cares. They're actually having fun. Grandpa would—"

"It's inappropriate and flip. It's crass and simply not done."

Cat took a large swig of her club soda and lime. Ever since breast cancer, her tolerance for petty bullshit had dwindled. She squared her shoulders and looked up at her sister. "I don't just mean no one cares what we do *today*, I mean no one cares what we do *ever*. No one cares whether we do the right thing anymore because they no longer care about us. When will you accept that? I would have thought it was painfully obvious to you based on the attendance at the church earlier. The forty-seven people in this room right now are the only ones left who give a crap about our family, and in another fifteen years it will shrink to twenty. And that's going to be fine with me because I'm tired of caring what others think, Claire, and I would think you'd be exhausted, too."

"I think you're being ridiculous," Claire said, but she didn't storm off.

"*Stop. Caring.* I mean it," said Cat, then turned to face the dance floor. "Our family is imploding bit by bit, because that's what families do. People try and fail, and hopefully they learn. Nothing gold can stay. Our children are jailbirds, comics, alcoholics, and sexual deviants, and we're going to have to be okay with that. No one family can hold on to a social hegemony forever—it goes against the law of averages—and who would want to? It's too much pressure. Families are too multifaceted to remain on a controlled trajectory indefinitely. Even the royals are a friggin' mess. Perfection is unattainable, Claire. The sooner you—"

"I never said—"

"You didn't have to. We've all felt it for years, the oppression of perfection. You got it from Dad. Stop it. He's gone, and there's no one left to impress. Worry about your inebriated daughter and your fatherless granddaughter. Give E.J. some love, for godssake, before he's so ornery and misanthropic that no one will ever love him, and let these miserable people have a moment of joy on an incredibly sad day."

Claire had never imagined her family was miserable. To this, she had no reply.

E.J. and Georgia walked up. "Hey, who's that tall old dude with the white ponytail and the Hawaiian shirt?"

"Ah, case in point," Cat said, eyeing Claire. "That's Gordon. He's Nana Miggs's watercolor-landscape instructor and special friend." There was a brief pause as E.J. and Georgia registered what Cat was insinuating. Devastation slowly bloomed on Claire's face. She hissed, *"Mom brought a date to Dad's funeral?!"*

E.J. said, "Gives new meaning to 'Doing your Thornden best,' don't ya think?"

Biz and Rah sauntered up. "What did we miss?"

Georgia said, "Nana Miggs invited her side piece to the funeral."

"What?!" they said in unison.

Cat ignored them and continued, "It would appear so. And I would advise you all to roll with it. The woman's just lost her husband, and we are in no place to judge." E.J. giggled and said, "Oh, shit." Claire pinched her son on the shoulder. E.J. said, "Ow!" then clapped once and said, "This is gonna be *great.*"

"Don't use this," Rah said to E.J. "This isn't fodder for your dumb jokes."

"Yeah, off-limits" and "Really, E.J.," layered Georgia and Biz.

"You can't tell me what I can't use. It's all material. Whatever happens to me in my life is mine. And you're not the boss of me." He was still grinning like a bastard.

Claire said, "Our personal family business has no place in your comedy routine. I forbid it."

"You know, Mom, you can't *forbid me* from anything. I'm an adult and a working comic. It's my job, so it's fair game."

"What's fair game?" said Charlie, just joining them.

"Define 'job,'" said Rah.

"Shut up, lesbitch," said E.J.

"Fuck you, you hack."

Biz blurted out a laugh and Charlie elbowed her in the ribs.

Ned spoke to the motley crew in a stern yet reasoned tone. "Your language and attitude has no place at this event. Show some grace and respect or help yourself to the door."

"Yeah, c'mon, man," said Charlie.

E.J. shot him a searing look. "Said the guy fucking his cousin for the entirety of our childhood." Everyone erupted at E.J., horrified and incensed. Charlie lunged at him. Biz seized in panic; she'd seen him that way before. Claire shouted, "*Enough!* Everyone go home and go to bed. *Now!*"

Cat said, "And stop drinking, for crying out loud, all of you, before you say something you'll regret. That goes especially for you, E.J. Move it. Charlie, take a chill pill. Let's go."

Cat had Ned run Biz and Ruby home and escort them all the way into their apartment. She told him to make sure Biz got up the long flight of stairs safely. Ruby carried her mother's purse and unlocked the door.

"Thanks, Uncle Ned," Biz slurred.

Ruby said, "Just dump her on her bed. She can sleep in her clothes, she's done it a million times."

"If you say so, champ," said Ned, and deposited her as directed. When he returned a moment later, Ruby was brushing her teeth. "You all set, young lady?"

"I gah dis," Ruby said with a mouth full of toothpaste. Ned waved good-bye over his shoulder so as not to make Ruby feel more embarrassed than she might already be and let himself out. Ruby yanked off her mother's shoes and folded her into the bedspread like a burrito. It was only 7:30 P.M.

Ned stopped off at Dickbird's to have a quiet beer. It had been a long day of Thorndens and he needed a break. As he waited for the foam to settle on his Guinness, he noticed Charlie nursing a Brooklyn Lager by himself in the back. He slid into the booth across from him and let a long silence go by. He wanted to see if Charlie had anything to get off his chest first before he set the tone for the conversation they may or might not have. Ned finally spoke. "There are so many things I'm probably supposed to say. Do you want to hear any of them?"

Charlie responded without looking up, "Not really."

"That's a relief," said Ned. He watched Charlie's face working hard to conceal his conflict. "You've been a great stepson, you know."

Charlie knew he'd been as lucky with his second dad as he'd been unlucky with Dick, his first. Ned had a kind heart that radiated patience and empathy. "And you've been a terrific stepdad. I mean it."

Ned continued with great delicacy. "If there's ever anything . . ." He trailed off and waited. He knew from what Cat had shared with him that it must be painful for Charlie to see Biz so unhappy while being only marginally content with Piper himself. And there was the notion of Ruby's paternity. Ned worked hard to remain open-minded. He was forgiving in the way someone who's been imperfect can be.

Charlie stared at the thin grooves in his beer mug. His mind was fixed on regrets and desires. He felt at fault for Biz's current situation, for attacking her in his dorm room, then bolting and leaving the country. She'd never had the opportunity to be angry with him to his face, to process her pain and rage. That couldn't have been healthy. It wasn't fair to abandon her so abruptly, leaving her with no best friend, no other friends, really, for support. She'd clearly ramped up her drinking while he'd been gone; who knows how many men she'd slept with. Then there was that one night in the tree house, right before he got married, then took off again, this time with Piper. He'd abandoned

Biz again, though he knew it was to save himself one last time. Then Biz's and Piper's daughters were born weeks apart. He'd always wondered, and though she never told him he always felt he knew. She kept saying not to worry about it and to focus on Piper—that in the long run, they were all still family.

Charlie spoke hesitantly. "There's something I want to fix very badly, because . . . I'm pretty sure I'm to blame. But I also know we're not supposed to try to fix other people . . ."

Ned considered this. "That's true." He had years of sobriety under his belt and as many in 12-step programs.

Charlie continued, "We're supposed to let people fix themselves."

"If they want to be fixed, yes. Someone's been to therapy." Ned grinned.

Charlie tried to grin back but labored. "Turns out I'm pretty broken."

"We all are to some degree. Awareness is the first step. You're well on your way."

"Jesus, I hope so."

Charlie wanted Biz to be happy, so much so it was breaking his heart. Was *he* happy? He grew quiet thinking about his own marriage. There were things he still wished for and things he was working on no longer wishing for. "Manage your expectations," Nana Miggs reminded her grandchildren over and over, "then get rid of them." So he did. He decided things between him and Piper were probably as good as they were going to get, which wasn't great but good enough after thirteen years. Theirs was an ergonomic love with stalwart systems in place. The sex was consistent and they communicated well enough, though he often felt Piper was disappointed in a thousand little ways. She'd been an unforgiving but reliable mother to their son and daughter, and understood the tapestry and expectations of his world. She was willing to take on his family and his past, which had counted for a lot at the time he married her. But now there was no spark when they looked at each other, no excitement for the future. He'd given up on that long ago—had traded it in for fidelity and a warm hearth.

Charlie said, "The rules . . . can be hard to follow."

Ned nodded and sipped his beer. "They can be."

Three and a half hours later, at 11 P.M., Biz woke up. She had to pee. She also had to take her dress off or she would go mad. She reached for the zipper behind her neck but couldn't get the correct angle. She tried swinging her elbow around and under, but that approach didn't work. Biz tried rousing Ruby, gently. "Hey, sweetie, I need your help," she coaxed in a loud whisper. "Can you wake up for a sec to unzip me?" Biz took Ruby's limp hand and tried to pinch her thumb and pointer together but realized it was folly. "Hey, wake up," she said, resorting to full voice, but Ruby was totally out solid. Biz wondered if she'd been drinking. Eleven was about the age she and Charlie had started sneaking half-empty cans of lukewarm Bud at family gatherings. And Ruby was not even stirring.

Biz grabbed the car keys and made it down the apartment stairwell, gripping the handrail.

She'd insisted on living on her own once she became pregnant and chose an apartment in the business district purposefully. She didn't want to be cloistered away in a little Victorian house at the edge of town where she'd have to get in her car for human interaction. She wanted to be forced out into the world where she'd have to face the people. Raising her little fatherless

child on the outskirts of town would send the wrong message—
that she felt shame or remorse, which she did not. Biz knew
she'd played her cards right, because before long, her baby was
no longer that wupsey-daisey but darling Ruby Chadwick, that
pistol and little ray of sunshine.

Epicenter or no epicenter, Larkspur was a small town and
this was a weeknight. The streets were usually rolled up tight
by about 11 P.M. Biz had hoped she might find someone outside
whom she could ask to quickly unzip her. She also knew she
could have called Hugh. Nope, a loiterer was preferable. But
the only life form she came across was the busboy from the pub,
having a smoke. *No way,* she thought, even in her state of desperation. Why had she chosen this tight outfit? Why had she been
compelled to show off her figure at a family funeral? To prove
she was still viable? Her family knew what she looked like.
The truth was . . . the sad truth was . . . the only man who'd
crossed her mind as she was getting ready was her damn cousin,
Charlie.

Charlie would unzip her.

Bad idea.

She should definitely not drive over to Charlie and Piper's
in her state. In any state, really. But she knew that out of all
her family members he was the only one who might be up late,
noodling away on some forgotten screenplay. His converted-
laundry-room office on the first floor was far from the master
bedroom he shared with Piper. Biz drove over telling herself
she only intended to see if the light was on. What harm and all
that. It was only an unzip. Well, that wasn't true, not even close.
She needed a lot more than that. She needed to be held, to have
sex, thank you very much. And not on cardboard boxes but in

a bed, where she could wake up the next morning wrapped in strong arms. She needed someone to help her locate the leak above her washing machine, and to say "Love you" before getting off the phone. She needed to be heard, she longed to be cherished, and for someone to ask her how her damn day was every once in a blue moon. And eventually, at the end of a long night, maybe a family funeral . . . to be unzipped.

Biz parked on the opposite side of the street and quickly turned off "Bootylicious," which might have been playing a bit too loud. She slipped off her shoes and chucked them into the backseat. Walking away from the car she thought to herself, *Charlie is family, and I know he's up, and I need a favor, and so what?* The grass was cold and wet on her feet, but she didn't care. She rounded the corner of the house; a single desk lamp lit a trapezoidal swath of their blackened backyard. Biz tapped on the sliding glass door and waited on the chilly slate patio. Widening her big eyes to appear awake and sober, she hoped they would tell her story without having to say much: So sorry, I know it's late, I wouldn't be here if I didn't have to be, etc. But the body that blocked the light wasn't Charlie's. It was undeniably, regrettably Piper's.

"What are you doing here?" Piper said.

"I know, it's so embarrassing," said Biz, looking right at Piper, hoping to convey an obvious expectation she would answer the door. In truth Biz was firing on all cylinders, immediately more sober. *Holy hell,* she thought. *Keep it together, for godsake.*

Piper remained annoyed. "Where are your shoes? Jesus, Biz, come in."

"Jesus Biz! That's funny, I thought his last name was Christ."

Biz was going for yucks, but Piper shook her head, then took off her slippers. She kicked them over to Biz as if to say, *Here, take these*. "Are you still drunk?"

"Not anymore," said Biz. "Maybe a little. It's fine. I'm the only one out there. Just me and a bunch of judgmental mailboxes." Piper didn't laugh. Biz couldn't remember the last time she'd seen Piper laugh or even her teeth. She inched her feet into the slippers and mumbled, "Thanks."

Piper retied her bathrobe. "Why are you here?"

"Oh God. It's the dumbest thing. I can't get my dress unzipped. I tried to wake Ruby, but she wouldn't budge. I went into town, but there was no one. Normally I would just sleep in my dress but it's that old taffeta that doesn't give and I could use a decent night's sleep and I figured . . ." She trailed off.

"You figured Charlie would help."

"Sure. Why not. You or Charlie, whoever was up. What are you working on so late?" She hoped she sounded casual enough. Harmless.

"Family vacation. I knew I wouldn't be able to sleep until I had the hotel squared away."

"Nice. Where ya goin'?"

"Biz," Piper said, refocusing their conversation. She paused just long enough to make Biz squirm. Biz looked away from Piper and to all the family photos, each in a sterling silver frame, depicting a calculated life—skiing, sailing, tennis—clustered on every shelf in the office, evidence Piper was living the life Biz coveted. They all looked happy. They sure seemed occupied. Why did Piper get everything she wanted? She wasn't even really that nice.

Biz could feel herself sway and planted her feet wider to

stop the movement. She hoped Piper hadn't noticed and said, "Remember when we were friends?"

"Of course," said Piper unconvincingly. "We still are."

"You think so?" said Biz. Something in her—an alcohol-fueled antagonistic streak—egged her on. "We spent a lot of time together growing up. I was thinking about it the other day. All those summers as mothers' helpers and hanging out after school in your room, listening to records and making up dances to the Carpenters—"

"I forgot we used to do that." Piper allowed for a pleasant smile.

"We probably logged hundreds of hours together, and the thing I kept recalling was . . . you weren't very nice to me." Piper's face fell. Biz said, "You were a bully and the queen bee—bossing me around, insisting I always be the backup dancer and you always the star. I remembered you forcing me to ride the roller coaster at Jenkinson's, then ditching me for another friend after I threw up." Shame kept Biz from calling her mom to come pick her up because Claire would have blamed Biz somehow and Piper would have tattled. It was such a small town. Which was why it was so odd for her—both of them, really—when Piper showed up in Paris.

"I might not have been . . . ," Piper said. There was a slight pause. "Very kind."

"You weren't. You were mean, and I cried a lot as your friend. I felt ugly and untalented and full of self-loathing when I was with you. And yet I remained your friend for years until Charlie made it end. I should have been stronger. It's my own fault. I know now that people treat us the way in which we let them. I should have found new friends. But I must have been weak enough, or just insecure enough. I was this nice kid who wanted to be your friend. What happened to you that you would treat someone that way?" Biz was poised and emotionally detached. She was simply curious to know.

"I'm really sorry for . . . You're definitely none of those things now. You never were."

"I know. And the wonderful thing about being adults is, we don't have to be friends anymore." Biz was calm as she spoke to Piper, her confidence laced with pity. "I think we do an adequate job when the family is together, but I know we're not friends. I've known it for some time."

Piper managed, "Okay."

"And I'm sorry you're unhappy."

"*I'm* not unhappy."

"And I forgive you."

Piper hardened again. "I'm not looking for *your forgiveness*. And while we're on the subject, *you're* the unhappy one—showing up here, looking for Charlie—"

"I wasn't—"

"You must see how pathetic it is."

"I just needed—" Biz stopped herself. "There you go again. Mean."

"Look, whatever happened between you and Charlie has nothing to do with me. I knew that in Paris. You were pushed together since you were little, and I guess in some weird universe it was possible you two would have eventually, well . . . let's just say it was none of my business."

"Nothing happened—"

"But it's my business now. I'm his wife and the mother of his children. This is my time with Charlie. I want to make that clear. Please look at me."

Biz set down the framed photo of Charlie, Piper, Gigi, and Thorn on a ski lift and looked Charlie's wife in the eyes. It was one of the most difficult things she remembered ever doing. How much did Piper know? How much had Charlie told her, and how much had she guessed? Or perhaps it was all conjecture. Biz had never told a soul.

Piper said, "I'm sure Charlie will always be there for you. This I've accepted. But as *my* husband. He's *my* best friend now. Am I clear?" Her jaw tightened. *"Am I clear?"* Piper restated, raising her voice a hair. Biz understood what kind of mother she must be.

"Crystal," said Biz, unintimidated. She was reminding her a lot of Claire.

Piper retied her robe again. It was time to go.

"You'll remember this conversation in the morning?" Piper asked.

"Most definitely." Biz gave two thumbs-up, then felt dopey.

"Fine," Piper said, looking somewhat dubious. "Now, turn around."

Biz turned tentatively, saying, "Are you going to shoot me?"

"No, I'm going to unzip you. This isn't *The Godfather.*"

"Oh, right. Of course."

Piper unzipped Biz. "Thanks," Biz said on her way to the door, then, reflexively, "Tell Charlie I said hi." *Ugh.* Biz wished she hadn't said it the moment it left her lips.

"I sure won't," Piper said, and shut the glass door behind her. Biz crossed the lawn, proud of herself for calling Piper out on her childhood bullying. *It's amazing how long it's taken me to say that,* she thought. *I wonder why tonight? Ye olde liquid courage?* When Biz arrived at her car she realized she was still wearing Piper's slippers. She zipped back in bare feet, dangling them in her two fingers. When she arrived at the back door again, she laid them quietly on the mat. Looking up, she saw her brother, E.J., through the glass door, fucking Piper against Charlie's desk from behind.

Biz went home, slammed a shot of tequila, then stared at the clock, wishing it would hurry the hell up and get to morning. She hoped the image of Piper and E.J. would seep out of her head, but it remained there, tenacious and sticky. She arrived at the bakery a little before 5 A.M., when she knew Muriel would be starting her shift. She put Norah Jones's "Come Away with Me" on the iPod dock, so loud it bounced off the linoleum floors. Biz had listened to it endlessly since its release and hoped it would calm her, keep her from punching a hole through a wall.

"What are you doing here?" said Muriel, putting her purse in her cubby. "You're off today." She took out a Marlboro, tapped it on the side of the box, and snickered as Biz manically hung the washed cookie cutters on the wrong hooks. "What's on your mind? Your hamster wheel is going. And you're doing a shitty job."

"I'm going to marry Hugh," declared Biz, not stopping or slowing down.

"Are ya now," said Muriel, unconvinced. She exhaled and began a well-worn circuitous path through the bakery, switching on lights and ovens, and pulling flats of eggs out of the fridge so they would warm to room temperature. Biz trailed behind her, spouting, "Life is shit and love is *really* bullshit, and everyone's a fraud, and *what the fuck*."

Muriel was unfazed. "Eloquent. Is that Shakespeare?"

"I'm serious. No one takes love seriously, or believes in it, so why should I? It's all about who fits the requirements at the time, or furthers whatever agenda they've plotted for themselves, so I'm just going to marry Hugh. He'll be a nice father man to have around the house for Ruby, he's got enviable table manners, likes books, so, there you go."

"Father man? What is that, Amish?"

"He can't dance worth shit, but who cares about dancing?"

"You do."

"Well, not anymore. Hugh's game, so he's the one."

"Literacy and table manners. That's your bar, huh? Sounds ducky. Let me know how that works out. And how do you think the sex—"

"Don't mention sex right now." Biz returned to the cookie-cutter wall and rehung them on the right hooks.

Muriel began prepping pans, coating them with butter and flour. "I thought good sex was part of your mission statement. How do you foresee Hugh satisfying that particular requirement?"

Biz whipped around. "*Fuck sex!* People have it with whoever the fuck they want to eventually anyway. Why should I play by the rules if no one else is? Fuck the rules."

"What 'people' are we referring to?" Muriel prodded.

"I can't tell you. Not yet. I don't even know . . . how to . . . maybe after the next round of divorces . . ."

"You're babbling."

Biz wished she had a blackboard and a piece of chalk. "Mom once told me the first round of divorces happen in the first four years of marriage. Those are the 'I've made a terrible mistake' people. I'm thirty-six and never been married; I skipped that round. The next is after seven to ten years. Those are the 'We never have sex anymore' people. Those are my people. Those are the divorced guys available to me, though they want younger women. Hugh isn't in that camp because he's a widower and, knowing him, probably didn't mind that he never had sex. Or lame sex . . ."

"Get back to Claire's algorithm." Muriel was listening with rapt attention. She was married, but not happily and hadn't been for a while.

"Oh, right. Then you skip to eighteen years of marriage. That's when 'Is this all there is?' sets in. I could wait for that group of dudes, but I'd rather not if I don't have to. They're all basket cases. The last round is about twenty-six or -eight years in. Those are the couples who decide early on to 'stick it out for the kids' and end up doing the most damage right up until the last one goes to college. Those guys definitely want younger women. I hope to be dead by then."

"Boy, Claire really worked it out for you, didn't she?"

"I think the shame kept her awake nights."

"You don't need a man—you've got your family and you've got me."

"Please don't mention my family right now," Biz said, rubbing her face.

"Wh—"

"Just don't."

"Fine."

Biz watched Muriel pour out ribbons of banana bread batter without spilling a drop. Mesmerized, she lit a cigarette. For a tough broad, Muriel could be an incredibly solicitous confidante. Biz said, "Okay, so, my friends are you and Rebekah. And Georgia, when she's not in jail, or kicking Foster out, or taking him back. And Sissy, I guess, though there isn't much to her, but I suppose beggars can't—"

"Do you know how many friends people need?" Muriel was pointing at her with a rubber spatula. "They've done global longitudinal research on this—real science-based stuff for child development purposes. Guess."

Biz thought. "Four? Seven. No, three. Three?"

"One," said Muriel. "People need one friend. The rest are gravy. One friend helps a child grasp sharing and compassion, trust and accountability, taking turns on the swingset and all that other shit we're supposed to learn so we grow into law-abiding citizens and well-informed voters. You've had one good friend, haven't you? Before me?" Biz nodded. Charlie had always been there. Or almost always. "So then why are your knickers in a twist? Did something happen?" Biz stared at the cigarette pack as images of her and Charlie blowing smoke rings and looking for shooting stars intermixed with Piper having sex with E.J. To think she and Charlie barely spoke anymore because it was better for *his* family. And for Piper. *What an unbelievable cunt.*

Muriel took a sip from a mug that read ESCHEW OBFUSCA-TION. "You're staring," she said. "Sorry. Yeah. I mean, yes." Biz grinned. She felt soothed by the notion of Grandpa Dun correcting her grammar.

"Truthfully, I see the way your family orbits you and is aware of your life, and is part of your life—in the best possible way—without being too invasive. I think *they're* your closest friends. It's okay if your family is your best friend. It's allowed."

Biz said, "Not all of my family is my friend, currently." She was bursting at the seams to tell Muriel but kept it inside for Charlie's benefit. Why not tell the world what she knew about E.J. fucking Piper, and Charlie possibly being Ruby's dad? She already felt relegated to the fringes of Charlie's world; how much worse could it get? Fuck everyone. Her good friends would stay her friends. Besides, she only needed one. And Ruby could handle herself—she was tougher than all of them put together.

"I've got to go," Biz said, and took off her apron. She didn't want to be having a full-blown breakdown when the others arrived.

"Fine, but tell me something . . . ," said Muriel.

"What?"

"Is Charlie sleeping with Amanda Bendridge?"

"*What?* No. Who's *she*?"

"Formerly Tindy Weldon. She went to camp with my sister forever. She grew up in—"

"I know who she is." Biz's heart started to pound. "We went to college together. She was my roommate, for chrissakes. Does she *live* here? When the hell did she move here?"

"She lives over in Shellbing. I've only heard it once or twice. Maybe I misheard it. People are idiots."

"Ha! You don't have to tell me," said Biz.

"What about *your brother*?"

"*What about* my brother?" said Biz. Her volume went up.

"Apparently E.J. was at Dickbird's, bragging about getting laid. Supposedly it's someone in town."

Biz was so mad at her brother she wanted to spit—directly in his face. "By 'no one' do you mean, 'everyone'?"

"It's not a big deal. Skip it," said Muriel. "People love secrets. Most of them are nothing, and all of them are old news before you know it."

"Like Georgia's jail time?"

Muriel snapped her fingers, yes. Biz dropped her car keys and wobbled a bit picking them up.

"You okay?"

"I'm fairly certain I'm so damaged I'm unlovable. But otherwise . . ."

"Don't let that stop you. Doesn't stop anyone else."

"I have to take Ruby to her thing," Biz said on her way out.

Muriel called after her, "Hey, have you been drinking?"

"No! A little. Bye!"

"Sober up first!" Muriel shouted, but the advice fell flat.

Charlie was up with the late Indian summer autumn sun. He went over to his mom's—this time to borrow a bag of charcoal from Ned. It still felt odd to see their old backyard so lackluster. The barbecue was rusted and tilted from a missing wheel, and the patio furniture looked grubby and worn. A mostly deflated soccer ball was wedged in where springs were missing on the trampoline, and the cobweb factor in the shed was off the charts. It still housed the Ping-Pong table, though. The right half sagged from a leak—bowing the composite wood beyond repair—but it was still playable.

Charlie was heartened to find there were still three sandpaper paddles underneath—not enough for doubles, but at least two could muster a scrappy game. He'd spent so much of his youth here that he imbued the table with the respect one might give a grandfather clock or favorite reading chair. Ping-Pong was one of the few truly friendly games—equal parts conversation, goofballery, and sweat, he always said. He set the paddles on either side—one atop a dirty white ball—so the table would be welcoming for play. The noise from Charlie poking around drew Georgia toward the shed. She'd stopped by to borrow a bicycle pump for the kids. She appeared in the doorway in a tight striped sundress. Her ample curves still dipped and turned, giving off a confident sensuality most Larkspur women couldn't pull off, and wouldn't dare to try.

"What's going on?" said Georgia.

"It's me," said Charlie, "pilfering Ned's charcoal."

"I'm here for a bicycle pump."

"Hey, can I borrow Foster's nine-iron next week?"

"Help yourself. Wrap it around a tree if you like."

Charlie found the charcoal. "I guess that answers my 'Is she still pissed at Foster?' question."

"It does and I am."

"Let's go. Twenty-one," said Charlie. He picked up the chipped sandpaper paddle.

Georgia wasn't having any of it. "C'mon, Charlie, I've got shit to do."

"We've all got shit to do. Come on, it's like you women are waging this lifelong contest to see who's busier. *I don't care that you're busy. Honestly, no one cares that you're busy.* Pick up your paddle. Twenty-one, let's go." Charlie served an easy lob, giving Georgia enough time to pick up the paddle and return the ball deftly over the sagging net.

Charlie asked, "So why are you two still together?" He wanted to pick someone's brain his age about marriage, and Georgia was the only one of his sibs or cousins who could relate. He knew hers wasn't exactly a model union but suspected they still had their fun. His and Piper's seemed to have dried up long ago.

"The sixty-four-thousand-dollar question," Georgia said as she returned the ball.

Charlie said, "Forget it. I'm sorry. It's none of my—"

"No, it's fine. You're family."

"Until I'm voted off the island."

"Huh?"

"From *Survivor,*" said Charlie. "C'mon. You know the show with the supposedly real people on the island. Aren't you watching it? Gigi's obsessed. It's a 'reality television' thing, though it seems incredibly fake to me. It's too well lit."

"Oh, yeah. I read about it in on the internet." Georgia got all her news and current affairs from a slew of pop-culture websites. Foster hadn't seemed to mind she wasn't nearly his intellectual equal until recently, when his third affair—with the head of the Contemporary American Literature Department at Princeton—was discovered and he was kicked out of the house. Again.

Charlie said, "You know, you can just say 'online' now."

"I know. I keep forgetting. Everything gets renamed so fast."

"So what's the plan with you and Foster? Poison him slowly in his sleep?"

"Is that allowed?"

"That reminds me, did Officer Jackass or whatever his name was, didn't he go to high school with us? Didn't he have a thing for you?"

"Yup."

"So why didn't you play that card the day you got arrested?"

"I wanted to embarrass Foster. And, if I'm going to be honest, the family, too."

"Huh," said Charlie. He was not expecting that answer; it got his full attention. "I get Foster, but why us?"

"Because I think we're all full of crap. Your serve."

She may have a point, he thought. They hit back and forth, keeping score in their heads. Finally Charlie said, "I think I understand."

Georgia said, "The way I see it is I've been as guilty as

anyone of perpetuating the Thornden mystique, but I'm over it, as you can see by this sausage casing that used to be loose on me." She gestured to her sundress. "I'm tired of dieting; I'm sick of Atkins. I'm over Aunt Claire's perfection-obsession. We're all basket cases on the inside, ready to implode, and I'm calling bullshit. Once the walls come crumbling down, hopefully we'll all be able to relax for the last fifty years or whatever we've got left. You'll thank me one day for paving the way."

"Will I?"

"And Foster can go jump in a lake for all I care."

"But sometimes I still see you two giggling."

"Oh, we do. But it doesn't mean he doesn't infuriate me."

"Huh," said Charlie. "Fifteen all. Your serve."

Georgia said, "Look, Foster will grow up and out of this phase, eventually, and want to come back. And I'll take him because he still puts up with me, and makes me laugh. Do you know why I agreed to marry him? Because he was smart, good at sex, and the only man I'd met who didn't have an issue with cheese. Everyone else I'd dated was allergic, or a snob about it, or some bullshit called lactose intolerant, whatever that means. No one could just order a cheeseburger, for crying out loud, but Foster could. So I married him. I blame cheese." Charlie let out a great guffaw. Georgia continued, "As I see it, I'm skipping our divorce and going straight to reconciliation. He's great with the kids, and the sex still rocks, so who cares, really, as long as he doesn't give me herpes. We're doing what works for us; in the meantime I'm not taking it personally. I've got four kids to raise. Besides, I get to sleep around, too, if I want, just like you. I'm just too busy right now."

Charlie hesitated. *What the holy hell is she talking about?* He said, "I beg your pardon?"

"Oh, come on. The whole town knows about you and Tindy. And if by some miracle it's not happening, it may as well be, because everyone thinks it is."

Charlie held on to the ball; his face lost color. He looked as if he'd discovered a tiny baby bird under a high nest, dead on the ground. "I'm not sleeping with Tindy."

"But you are sleeping with Biz."

"I am *not* sleeping with Biz," Charlie said quietly, shaking his head. Anger welled in his stomach and moved upward through his body. This time he knew to keep it in check. He breathed slowly, inhaling deeply the way Nana Miggs had taught him to do.

"You're not? Well, maybe we should sleep together finally." Georgia laughed.

"Georgie. It's not funny."

"I'm not trying to be funny. I'm serious. Piper's got whatever she's got going on with whatever arrangement you've made, and I've got nothing going on for the moment, and we're not related, so I'm just suggesting that if you ever—" Georgia missed the ball. She followed it as it bounced and rolled behind a stack of overturned clay pots. "It's convenient—"

"I will never. Jesus, Georgia, *stop*!" Charlie rested his paddle on the table, aware of his staggering hypocrisy. Then he looked over his shoulder at the array of wooden racquets on rusty nails. Bjorn Borg, Arthur Ashe, they were all there, some still in their presses. He wished they could materialize and come to his defense. He watched Georgia look for the ball. She'd lost her spark so long ago he couldn't place from where it had originally emitted. Her smile? Her eyes? He wanted to feel compassion, truly wanted her to find happiness. Charlie knew she'd had it rough and felt he probably should have been much kinder to

Georgia, more empathetic when they were all young. But she came on so damn strong, he had to push her away. *What happened to her? To all of us?*

Georgia returned to the table. "I know, I know. Sorry, I don't know why I do it. I really need therapy. And I'm sorry for throwing myself at you for all those years. I was so convinced you and Biz . . . I think I was jealous, and wanted to be a part of this stupid family so badly. I think that's what Foster and I had in common. Turns out it wasn't enough to base a marriage on, because we stopped caring about you idiots and then we were stuck with each other. And ignore what I said about Piper just now."

Charlie thought, *Wait, what did she say before?* He said, "Piper and I don't . . . what do you mean 'arrangement'?" Charlie looked pained, confused.

Georgia hadn't meant to upset him—she'd always suspected he was more fragile than he appeared. "Nothing. I just had a feeling. I think once you marry someone who cheats, you think everyone cheats. It's like having paranoia as a Spidey sense."

"Georgie, what the hell have you heard?" Charlie worked hard to manage his volume level, his rising rage. *Deep breaths, dammit.* His head swirled. Sometimes he got a feeling he couldn't place when Piper came to bed at night distracted. But he'd always assumed she was just teeming with checklists, the administrative detritus that clogs the mind of a modern woman. Maybe he'd been right to be suspicious. Perhaps she wanted things he couldn't give her. But doesn't everyone want more? He couldn't fault her for being like himself. He'd always assumed he'd been enough, was giving her enough. Was that the Thornden arrogance Georgia was talking about? *But Piper would have come to me, demanded more,* he thought. He couldn't think about it now. He'd bury it, along with his longing for Biz. And what did Georgia mean by "going on at the moment"? Had Georgia cheated on Foster? Was that why she didn't end the marriage?

Georgia could see Charlie was struggling with the truth. She backtracked, "It's just my imagination, I promise. Sorry. Forget it." She was pretty sure Piper was fucking around. E.J. was one of her theories. Sometimes Piper ignored him a little too much when he was telling some crass story. If it was about women, she left and did the dishes. It wasn't overt, and there was no tell in their body language, but Georgia picked up a vibe one day when they were all at the pool—it was about the way he watched her climb up the aluminum ladder in her wet bikini. She gave him an admonishing glance reserved for an intimate, not on the roster of looks one gives a cousin-in-law. It was followed by a quick survey to see who might have caught it.

Georgia had.

"Gotta go," said Charlie.

"But it's game point," Georgia said, forcing a smile that weakened at the corners.

"You win," said Charlie. He tried to smile but couldn't think of anything to merit one, so he walked out of the shed, forgetting the bag of charcoal.

On her way home from the bakery, Biz felt menaced, her mind spiraling and infested. She was in a full swivet trying to deny Muriel's recent revelations while trying to shake the lewd image of Piper and E.J. *Gross!* Biz knew she had to snap out of it in time for Ruby's doctor's appointment, so she had a tiny nip of vodka and cleaned the whole apartment. *What could it hurt?*

Steady the nerves. Good way to project a relaxed mother: house straightened! Biz licked a gob of peanut butter off the end of a butter knife. She reaffirmed her mantra, *I am doing my Thornden best.* Her perceptive friend Rebekah would be impressed. A second voice in her head wisecracked that perhaps she wasn't trying that hard—*if we're really going to be honest, you're totally phoning it in. More like doing your Thornden half-assed.*

She woke Ruby with some toasted frozen waffles and grabbed a banana to eat in the car. A knock on the examining-room door took Biz's attention from *People*'s Sexiest Man Alive, year 2000 edition. *That Brad Pitt can do no wrong,* she was thinking when Dr. Rebekah—formerly Becky—walked in.

"How's everyone today?" she chirped in her doctor-y voice.

"Next question, please," muttered Ruby from atop the examining table.

Biz said, "You stole my material."

Rebekah addressed Ruby. "Your great-grandfather's service was lovely."

"Thanks," she said. "How did you two meet again?"

Her mother and doctor said, "College," in unison and shared a conspiratorial smile. Rebekah was still a short, compact woman with dark brown hair, but now curly streaks of gray wound through her tight spirals. She wore glasses in tiny black rectangular frames and a wedding ring lousy with diamonds. *Smart* and *successful,* Biz thought to herself, *and probably married to a great guy who loves her sense of humor, chutzpah, and razor-sharp mind.*

"So, vaginal itching and burning?" said Rebekah.

Ruby nodded.

"And your chart tells me you've just started menstruating."

Ruby deadpanned, "The bastard child has become a bastard woman." Ruby loved to introduce herself to grown-ups as such. She would extend a hand and lean in with a smile, declaring, "I'm the bastard child you've heard so much about." It caught people off guard, much to Ruby's delight. "Ignore her," Biz would add with a grin. They made a good comedy duo.

"Glad to see you're enjoying womanhood," said Rebekah.

"Woop-dee-doo," said Ruby.

Biz said, "Okay, enough with the sarcasm. Hand me your Britney Spears article, please. Dr. Rebekah is a health care professional who will be an important figure in your life when you have questions about avoiding unwanted pregnancy."

"Where was she twelve years ago?" Ruby quipped like a Borscht Belt comic.

"You have never *not* been wanted, my precious pumpkin."

Rebekah refocused. "Let's get started. Ruby, how often would you say you're in a wet bathing suit?"

"I live in one."

"Then it's probably a yeast infection. Anyone can get one at any age. Make sure you change into dry clothes."

"Is that an STD?"

"No, dear," said Rebekah. Biz perked up.

"What?" said Ruby defensively. "They've been talking about STDs in health class."

Rebekah said, "And what have you learned, young lady?"

Biz kept her mouth shut tight as she listened to their STD chat. She hoped her daughter would be better informed on the subject than she'd been and wouldn't take the unbelievably stupid and unnecessary risks she had.

Rebekah said, "Ruby, I'm going to ask your mom to step out of the room."

"Go for it, but you don't have to. I have no secrets." She looked askance at her mom. "Yet." Biz grinned and stayed put.

Rebekah asked Ruby, "Are you sexually active?"

"*I* am not. But *everyone else* in my family is. My mom is screwing some Irish dude she barely knows, Nana Miggs is screwing that old weird dude from the funeral reception, and Grand Cat supposedly once *screwed my principal*—"

"Whoa. *What?!*" said Biz. "Honey, you don't know what you're saying."

"It gets better. Gigi thinks Uncle E.J. is *screwing Aunt Piper,* and Uncle Charlie is screwing some divorced lady. Oh, and Aunt Georgia and Uncle Foster are screwing other people but not each other and it's gross and I hate it. Plus I hate everybody. But no, I'm not having sex."

Rebekah raised her eyebrows at Biz, who downshifted into her calm voice. "Ruby, dear heart, where did you hear all this?"

Ruby said, "I hate when people ask that. Like it matters."

Rebekah cut in. "Okay, you two. Break it up. I am not Sally Jessy Raphael and this is not a talk show. I have patients waiting."

Biz said to Ruby, "We will discuss this later, missy."

Rebekah wrote out a script to treat Ruby's candida while Biz's head quietly spun off its axis. Her eyes watered and stomach seized as the full force of what she'd heard tightened its grip on her brain and her gut. Her shame was replaced by the rage of disquieting incredulity. How could *everyone? How could Charlie?!* Then Rebekah asked Ruby to wait outside, so she stuck out her palm at her mom. Biz handed over the Britney article, and her daughter left, leaving the two adults alone.

Rebekah reported, "She's doing fine," but Biz gave no reaction. She was staring. Rebekah tried again. "Irish guy, eh?"

Biz shook it off. "Unfortunately, yes," she said. "They lure you in with their pointy green shoes . . ."

"Run away."

"Uh-huh," she murmured.

"Ruby seems fine. You're doing a good job."

"Am I?" mumbled Biz. Her eyes darted, looking for something to cling to. She wanted Rebekah to hug her but didn't dare reach out.

Rebekah said, "You can have the room for as long as you want." At the door she stopped. "You okay?"

Biz squeaked, "No," then decided to take a chance. She was exhausted from keeping the secret that had been chipping away for twelve years. Biz thought she was strong, but who was she kidding—she was fraying at the goddamn edges. And now that Charlie was . . . and E.J . . . and what was that about Aunt Cat? She no longer felt fortified by her privilege. Her fragile ground was undeniably giving way.

Biz took a deep breath. "Ruby might be, is probably Charlie's daughter. No one knows, including Ruby. And even I'm not one hundred percent. How would I go about . . . ?"

Rebekah didn't flinch. She spoke professionally—and mercifully—without judgment. "A simple paternity test, cheek scrape or hair follicle. Takes a few months to get the results. We have genetic advisers on staff, or I can do it."

"You can?" Biz whispered. A seismic whoosh swept over her, and she started to cry—great heaving, silent sobs, her face raining tears. Bound by the Hippocratic Oath, Rebekah could be trusted implicitly to hold this info tight and share its weight so Biz didn't have to balance it on her psyche alone. Her secret had been tyrannical, its toll devious and incremental. She saw the breadth of this now as she held her head in her shaking hands.

Rebekah maintained a professional air but exuded empathy as she spoke. "You know, Biz, first cousins have children together all over the world in many, many cultures. In certain countries twenty to sixty percent of all marriages are between close relatives. It's unreasonably cautioned against in this country because of genetic misunderstanding, but those risks are seven percent at the very most. And we have prenatal tests now. It's not nearly as serious as people think it is. It's just our lingering puritanical dogma out to do more shaming."

"Really?" Biz hiccupped between attempts at steady breaths.

"Both Einstein and Darwin married their first cousin. Darwin had ten kids—all of them healthy. How's Ruby's health? Her mental acuity?"

"She's amazing. I mean, besides being eleven, and sometimes awful, she's wonderful. Healthy and . . . perfect." Biz started to gasp again. She was overwhelmingly grateful and relieved.

"Then you're in the majority. You should also know it's legal in half the states in the U.S., including New Jersey. We do genetic counseling for this kind of thing all the time. Nowadays, our governing bodies instruct medical personnel not to shame newly arrived immigrants with cultural norms outside our own seeking treatment. Seen through a larger lens, there's nothing wrong culturally, scientifically, or legally with this choice. The reaction of your family and community is the only hurdle. It may be viewed as unorthodox, yes, but many paths we choose are. It's what you make of it and decide to stand behind. For you and your daughter and her father."

"You won't tell anyone the results, will you?"

"I can't and I wouldn't," Rebekah said with genuine affection. Biz wiped off the tiny creek of snot running alongside the corner of her mouth, then inadvertently smoothed it into her hair while tucking it behind her ear. She peeled herself off the Naugahyde seat, leaving Brad Pitt's understanding and supportive face beside her on the chair. "Thank you," she said. The words were not enough.

Ruby was called back into the room. She was tall for her age and striking. "Come here, sweetie," Biz said, "Your hair is in your beautiful face." She reached out and fingered through Ruby's lush brown locks.

Ruby recoiled. "Stop it. What are you doing? Have you been *crying*? Are you drunk?"

"Ruby!" said Biz. Rebekah was taken aback.

Ruby said, "What? That's one of the ways I know you're drunk. What's the big deal?" Then she looked at Rebekah. "You're her friend. I thought everyone knew that."

"Young lady, turn and look at me," said Biz sternly. Ruby only half faced her mother. "Being eleven does *not* give you license to be impudent."

"Foshizzle, Mom. Sorry, whatever," said Ruby, and shuffled out of the room.

Biz looked to deflect. Was it guilt or embarrassment? Probably both. "Preteens. Can't live with 'em. Can't shoot 'em." She mustered a thin grin.

Rebekah told Biz to open her mouth. Biz did and Rebekah sniffed. With detached coldness, she said, "I'm having the front desk call you a cab."

"I'm fine," said Biz.

"You're lucky I don't call Child Services. I would if I didn't know you."

Biz half muttered, half sang the hit single, "If, you, don't, know, me, by nowww—"

"Knock it off. I'm really pissed at you."

Biz looked down at her hand and a single strand of her daughter's hair was there, caught in her ring. Her eyes locked with Rebekah's as she gingerly handed it over. Rebekah took it and said, "I do *not* like being taken advantage of, and Thorndens be damned, you are *not* impervious to the law. Go home and go to bed. I'm really pissed off." And with that Dr. Rebekah Gustafson-Rosenfeld walked out of the room, closing the door a little harder than she would have only a minute before.

A block away, Biz asked the taxi driver to pull over and handed Ruby a ten. "I have to run a quick errand, sweetie, I'll meet you at home," she said, and hopped out of the running taxi. Ruby said, "Whatever," and returned to her phone. Biz walked back a block to her car. It was starting to rain and she had no umbrella, but she needed to talk to Charlie. He would typically be at the theater now.

He found her in the main lobby soaked through to the bone, eyes ablaze, hair dripping onto the rug. Forgoing niceties, Biz said, "Can we use your office?" Charlie knew his employees would have seen her arrive. He was also aware Biz was transmitting at an uneven frequency and wanted to talk to her out of sight, but . . . He rubbed his face with both hands. "I don't think—"

"For talking, Charlie. If I don't talk to you my head will literally explode, sticky brain matter all over your nice, new carpet, people stepping in it to buy popcorn—"

"Fine. I need to talk to you, too."

"Fine."

Charlie's office was a hodgepodge of movie equipment and

memorabilia. Posters of *She's Gotta Have It, Repo Man, Diva,* and *The Adventures of Buckaroo Bonzai* were fastened to the walls with brass thumbtacks. Shelves were piled haphazardly with old metal film reels, Super 8 and 16 mm projectors, and a Bolex. On a large aluminum desk sat a framed movie still from the infamous scare scene in *Jaws,* and a candid shot of John Cassavetes and Gena Rowlands laughing, plus a posed photo of Charlie's family. Two beanbag chairs flanked an aging velvet couch, but Biz chose not to sit. She felt nauseous and wondered if she was becoming ill, or if it was a reaction to her life imploding around her. She stood near the wastepaper basket in case she had to vomit. Better safe, she thought, than sorry.

"I have five things and I need to go first," Biz opened. She'd planned her speech in the car.

"Five things, that's an entire hand's worth. I've got work to—"

"This is important. Okay, we know that Nana Miggs is sleeping with Weird Hippie Gordon. And possibly started sleeping with him while Grandpa Dun was alive, but that seemed to be their arrangement, so what are ya gonna do. Moving on."

"What does this have to do with—"

"Just hear me out. We are agreed so far, yes?"

"Yes."

Biz counted the second finger on her hand. She was fired up. *This might take a while,* Charlie thought. Biz carried on while he sat. "Okay, what was the next one? Oh, yeah. Has your mom ever slept with Principal Romanelli?"

"I beg your pardon?" Charlie found the notion ludicrous. "Mom is sleeping with Ned."

"I know, I mean before she met him."

"Fuck, no."

"Okay. Don't get testy. That's two down."

"Where are you hearing—"

"Ruby."

"Oh my God. Do you think Gigi thinks—"

"Who knows. But he's the principal, and kids love to mess with—"

"But why Mom? That is the most bizarre thing I've ever heard. *Mom is fifty-seven.*"

"Not now, when she was younger. And so? I'm going to be fifty-seven one day."

Charlie said, "I didn't mean that."

"Hang on, there's more." Biz tried to remember; she wished she'd written them down. Third finger. "Is Rah gay?"

Charlie said, "I beg your pardon?"

"Ruby started speaking in tongues this morning. I think she's still pissed about walking in on me and Finn at the bakery."

"Jesus, *get it together*!" Charlie raised his voice, then reined it in. After all these years the notion of Biz being held by another man still stung. He'd grown comfortable with the idea she'd stay single forever—possibly waiting for him, though he would admit that to no one. He took a deep breath.

Biz objected. "*Me get it together?!* First of all, Ruby wasn't supposed to be finished with rehearsal for another *three hours.* And second of all, *fuck you,* married guy. You get to have sex *whenever the hell you want* and I *never do anymore*! With your wife *and,* apparently, *Tindy Weldon.* Oh, excuse me, *Ah-man-da Bendridge.*" She thrust a fourth finger at him.

Charlie cocked his head and furrowed his brow like a confused dog. "Where did—"

Biz kept at him. "People always ask that as if it matters. It doesn't. It's her long legs, right? And probably a boob job by now. And she works out, I bet. Where did you bump into her, the *gym*? Was she wearing a little spandex thing with a matching whatever? I can't believe you're sleeping with *her,* of all people. It's so fucking cliché. *You* get it together."

"I'm *not* sleeping with Tindy. Christ, who started this rumor? You're the second—I want to fucking kill them."

Biz looked at Charlie. "Are you being honest with me?"

"I swear. Georgia said the same thing."

"Are you sleeping with *Georgia*?!"

"*What the hell?*" Charlie freaked.

"Did you ever sleep with Georgia?!" Biz was off task but had wanted to ask him for at least fifteen years. It was a small relief to finally say it out loud, but now she dreaded the answer.

"No. Godammit. You were the only—" Here, Charlie cut himself off. He melted from righteous indignation into melancholy, his voice becoming small, pleading like a child offering the only thing he has access to, the truth. "It was only ever you. I know I married Piper, but . . . honestly, there's no one like you." He said it with heavy resignation, as if finally giving up a race he'd been running his whole life.

Biz melted. "Do you really believe that?" Her eyes locked onto his.

"Sometimes. Yes. Do you?"

"When I let myself think it. Yes." Biz wanted to go to him. She wanted so badly to envelop him in her arms and kiss him. She could summon his taste, the smell of his skin. Her voice, too, was wavering. She took a small step forward, then stopped herself. *Bad idea. Do the right thing for once.* Charlie shifted to behind a tall wing chair. He wanted a physical barrier between them, so he gripped it and held on as if to a buoy below darkening skies. He'd made questionable choices his whole life:

not fighting for Biz; marrying Piper; and not demanding a paternity test for Ruby. He honestly thought doing the right thing was the same as doing what was right. Now he wasn't so sure. He tried to convince himself he had no other options at the time—though that was a lie. *We always have options.* They could have fled to California or Canada, but once Piper became pregnant . . . If only he were a different man born into a different family. Or if he were simply . . . a man.

Biz said, "I've got one more." She was holding her pinky between her thumb and forefinger.

Charlie cut in. "Wait. I've been meaning to apologize again for—"

Biz waved him off. "You already have. It's in the past."

Charlie looked toward Biz without meeting her eye. "I know, but I still feel . . . I didn't realize it at the time, but I pushed you down, I held you . . . You must have been terrified."

"I was. That's why I hit you so hard."

"I'm glad you did. I deserved it."

"Hell, yes, you did."

"I almost . . . um . . . raped you. I see that now. It was attempted rape, an assault, and I'm deeply sorry—"

"I know. I was there. I get it. You're forgiven."

"Why? I mean, are you sure?"

"I said forgiven. I haven't forgotten."

"Okay, that's fair. Do you think it did . . . um . . . irreparable harm?"

"Do you mean am I still single because I have intimacy issues stemming from . . . Did it fuck me up permanently? I don't know. Maybe. I don't think so, but it could be part of it."

"I am and will always be deeply sorry. If there's anything I can do—"

"You can stop bringing it up. I've let it go. Or I'm trying to, but you keep talking about it. Honestly, the rest is between you and you. You've got to forgive yourself."

Charlie looked up and saw the same luminous beauty in Biz he'd always seen. Before he could stop himself, he uttered the only phrase he'd never second-guessed. "I love you."

This wrecked Biz. Her head buzzed and her eyes ignited from within. "I know you do, my friend," she said. "I love you, too. So much." She said it as if it were the most natural thing in the world. She felt her body awaken and her urges swell. She didn't trust herself alone with Charlie, so refocused the course of the conversation. Now more than ever, she wanted to tell him about Piper. She would fight for a second chance with him.

Charlie was rattled. Whatever he wanted with Biz couldn't happen tonight or ever. He wouldn't. He was a principled man, dammit. He'd made mistakes, poor choices. But he was committed to his family. He'd change the subject and shut it down. Charlie said, "You asked if I knew if Rah was gay. All I can say is who knows and who cares."

"You don't care if your sister is happy?"

"Of course I do. But it doesn't matter if she's gay."

"Don't you want to support her if she wants to come out?"

"I can support her by not making a big deal over it or treating her any differently than I would any other smug, pain-in-the-ass sister."

"Okay. So what do we do?"

"Nothing. We let her live her life. It's 2002. If she's gay, she's gay. If she wants to tell us she will."

"That's enlightened of you."

"Piper and the kids and I love *Will and Grace*."

And just like that, the image of the four of them snuggled

on a couch together—under a throw blanket, the little ones in pajamas—slapped her in the face. It was his marriage, his family, and his life. *I have no business . . .*

"Okay, then." Biz paused and tucked the E.J.-and-Piper pinky away. "That's all of them," she said convincingly, or so she thought.

"I thought you said there were five things."

"I got confused." Biz pointed at a movie still from *The Piano.* "Jane Campion is a genius. You could take any frame out of that movie and hang it in the Met. What did *you* want to talk to *me* about?" She hoped Charlie would never find out about Piper. She understood implicitly that Piper did *not* have her back and would *never* return the favor if the roles were reversed—it was Charlie she was saving from the pain of discovery. Meanwhile, she hoped E.J. would get hit by a bus and end up in traction for being such a colossal dick. And that right now a phone call, meteor, or some mangy, rabid animal would materialize and interrupt their conversation. "I should get going."

"Wait." Charlie looked down. He mumbled, "Have you heard anything about Piper having an affair?" It hadn't been easy to say out loud. He was hoping for a perfunctory answer.

Biz said, "No, not a thing," a little too quickly. She could *not* be the one he heard it from, she decided; in fact, she was the *worst person* he could hear it from. She muttered, "Why, what have you heard? Not that it matters. Do you think she is? I mean, *I don't,* but it's your . . ."

Charlie rubbed his thumbs against his temples. "Georgia said something about Piper and me having an arrangement. I can't even begin . . ."

Biz knew that if anyone was going to tell him it should be Piper. "Why don't you talk to Piper about it?"

Charlie said, "Because I think it's true."

Biz froze. She said nothing.

He continued, "I've always had this tiny suspicion she feels the way I do—that we're going through the motions. That maybe we're passionate people who never had passion for each other. We just . . . we made *sense* together at the time and still do, I guess. But we never . . . I've always wondered, that's all."

"Who would she be having an affair with?" This was insidious of her to ask, Biz was well aware. *Back away,* she thought. *Tread lightly.*

"That's the part I can't figure out. There aren't many single guys in town."

"No joke." Biz rolled her eyes.

"So he must be married. But I can't imagine who—"

"Wait, we're getting ahead of ourselves. Talk to Piper. Do it and tell me what she says and we'll take it from there. There's no point . . . there's just no point in—"

"I know. You're right." Charlie stood up. "Ahhh, all right, I've got to get back to work. Are you going to E.J.'s thing in a few weeks?"

Biz was taken aback. "What thing?"

"He's got some comedy gig in the city, and supposedly there are scouts coming. Mom said we should surprise him and be there to support him and laugh heartily. If you would get a smartphone we could all be on a group text chat together. It's really useful."

"Or you could call me. Because that seemed to have sufficed for a hundred years."

"I'll send a pigeon."

"Perfect."

Charlie walked Biz to his office door. He leaned in to peck

her cheek. She had to stop herself from swooning. "Have you been drinking?"

"Nah," she said, and took the stairs.

Biz left Charlie's in a state. Some things had been resolved, but certainly not all. In trying to tie up loose ends Biz worried she created more fray. She put a Cake CD into the car player and turned up "I Will Survive" mind-blowingly loud so she wouldn't have to hear herself cry, or sing. Then she examined all the ways in which her life was a mess, and how there was a very real possibility it wasn't "all going to work out" as Nana Miggs and her Aunt Cat had always promised.

Rounding the sharp turn on Winding Hill Road, Biz accelerated at the anthem's chorus and swerved to miss a chipmunk darting across the road. In jerking the car she hit a patch of gravel in just the wrong way. Her car slid off the road and into the ditch along the edge of the woods near a driveway, knocking over a mailbox before coming to a jolting rest at a large oak tree. The whole thing took about four seconds to unfold but felt terrifyingly interminable. She was alive, but banged up; the car, however, was totaled.

Her instinct was to put her shaking hands up to her face. She noticed blood and glass on her trembling fingertips. Biz tried to make a sound but only emitted a squeak. Glistening shards of glass fell from her hair and rested on her arm, but there was her seat belt, intact. She checked her face in the rearview mirror. A wide red gash cut across the bridge of her nose. She looked over at the passenger seat to where her beautiful, petulant daughter would have been sitting, and an oak tree loomed instead. This was an older-model car, bought before air bags were mandatory. If Ruby had been sitting there . . . if Ruby had been sitting there . . . She panicked and began to hyperventilate. Not since the news of Biz's second pregnancy had she felt this much disequilibrium. A wave of nausea revisited her like an unsympathetic friend, and she unceremoniously threw up in her lap. Unaware of what to do next, she repeated "Um, um, um," until she remembered Ruby had made her start carrying her cell phone. *I just need one friend,* she remembered. *One friend is all I need.* She called Charlie. "I'm so sorry," she said over and over, repeating it like a scratched record, hiccupping gasps of air. It was the only shred of concrete truth that felt real to her in that moment. The rest felt utterly surreal.

When Charlie arrived on the scene he threw his car into park and ran to her, leaving his own motor running. Biz was so relieved to see him she burst into fresh tears. "Shh," he said, "it's okay. I've got you." Gingerly opening the driver's side door, he knelt on the dirt and held her cheek gently in his hand. The blood made it look worse than it was, but still, she was in rough shape. He resisted the desire to hold her because there was too much broken glass, so he said sweetly, "Hey, pal, what's new?" as he picked the shards out of her hair. Biz attempted a fragile grin. "You know," she answered, "same old, same old." Charlie nodded, smiling, as Biz's eyes shone bright. She was so grateful to see her very best friend.

A few weeks later the Thornden clan finally got some table service at a dank comedy club on the Lower East Side.

"And for you, miss? Let me guess, a cosmo?" the waitress asked.

"No, thank you," Biz mumbled, "I'll have a seltzer with lime." Her accident had left her with sixty-four hundred dollars in car damage, insurance and medical bills, three cracked ribs, and seven stitches. It also left her deeply humbled and in no position to haggle with Aunt Cat over going to AA meetings. It was time Biz—and everyone around her—finally admitted that she was depressed, spiraling, and powerless over alcohol. It was also time she embraced her longing for Charlie with grace and gratitude. She was tired of trying and getting nowhere. She was ready to accept what was.

E.J.'s comedy show was Biz's first outing to an establishment that served booze since first going to meetings after the accident. Initially she tried to beg off with a phony illness at the last minute, but then Ruby told Gigi, who told Charlie, that she was faking. She couldn't imagine anything more brutally awkward than watching Piper watch E.J. and have to pretend. If ever there was a time to want a drink it was going to be tonight. But her sponsor felt this would be the right event for reentry. With so much family surrounding her and Aunt Cat at her side, she would presumably feel safe, secure, and supported. Unable to think of a viable excuse on the spot, Biz climbed into the back of Charlie's car with Aunt Cat and Uncle Ned—Piper in the front, of course—and off they went. The sound of Piper's voice made Biz cringe and she'd forgotten to bring her last Percocet; otherwise, she would have swallowed it without water.

They met up with the rest of the immediate family at the venue: Nana Miggs and Gordon; Georgia and Foster; Claire; Rah and her roommate, Susan. It was like a mini reunion, a cause for celebration. Biz was on the mend, and E.J. had a real shot at success. The mood was buoyant; things were looking up for the fam. Seated elbow to elbow around the table in the far back corner, they planned to clap heartily, laugh loudly, and show their pain-in-the-ass E.J. that they loved and supported him in spite of himself. Then they'd surprise him after the show.

His family didn't know much about E.J.'s style of comedy because he'd always forbidden them from attending. Apparently it was more like storytelling than "set up the joke, punch line, and laugh." Charlie explained to the family—from conversations with E.J. at holidays—that E.J. didn't think he deserved to even be there. He continually doubted his decision to give up his law career for a "questionable dalliance with the humor arts," as was Grandpa Dun's refrain.

E.J. was going up in ten minutes, and the lights would be so bright it wouldn't matter where the scouts were sitting— from the stage E.J. wouldn't be able to see. Rah warned Nana Miggs and Gordon that it wasn't too late for them to duck out and have a nice aperitif in a hotel bar somewhere—she was concerned the show would be too blue for their delicate ears. Nana Miggs assured her that she'd heard it all before and told her thoughtful granddaughter to stop fussing. "There's very little I can't handle, children. When are you going to figure that out?" "We're starting to," said Foster, and winked. Most were cautiously hopeful E.J. would do well and not embarrass the family, except for Biz, who had a sinking feeling, and Piper, who had a pit in her stomach the size of Rhode Island.

E.J. took the mic and a swill of his beer, then leaned toward the audience with a menacing threat and growled, "I don't do jokes, I'm telling you right now, but I do tell the truth."

"Oh, brother," Rah stage-whispered to the table, and Georgia rapped her on the shoulder. Susan placed a calming hand on

Rah's arm. E.J. couldn't hear them and plowed right through as if monologuing at the dinner table, except that onstage, there was no family member to stop him.

"You know how everyone's always telling you to 'write what you know'? Writers hear it, comics hear it. *As if we had a choice!* Makes me want to kick 'em in the shins. How can you write what you don't know? It's cognitively impossible for us to access and retrieve information that simply isn't in storage. I mean, we can feasibly assess we don't know something because we're always going to know enough about it to know we don't know it. I could try to write what I don't know—otherwise known as 'making shit up'—or, for you liberal-arts educated, fiction—but it's still coming from the great wellspring of inane pablum we keep handy for most occasions needing sober thought, for instance: holidays and other forced family functions, blind dates, and dinners with the person-we're-fucking's parents. They're all ripe occasions to unload our made-up bullshit into someone else's psyche, in order to make more room for new bullshit. It's a very tidy closed circle, not unlike the water cycle we learned in science class, right, nerds?"

E.J. had the audience's attention. They liked that he spoke intelligently and at a brisk clip. And because he was unwilling to talk down to them they felt smart, and E.J. knew audiences liked to feel smart. Foster said to his tablemates, "So far, so good," to which Claire whispered, "Hush up," and Nana Miggs let out a small "Mm." Both Biz and Charlie remained riveted to the stage, while E.J., the apparent comedian, continued.

"So here's another one for you, one you don't hear ad nauseam. I like to call it 'Fuck what you know.' Turns out there's science on why we're attracted to people who are sickeningly like our mothers or brothers and why we end up fucking them."

The audience laughed with mirthful discomfort and knowing recognition. Biz's eyes bugged as Charlie choked on a sliver
of ice. Georgia leaned forward to ask if he was okay, but didn't
pat his back.

"That's some Sophocles Oedipal shit, right there. We read
this pulp in *Maxim* between yanks, and in *Cosmo* when we're
getting our nails done, right, ladies? And though adequately
forewarned, we still end up attracted to men with hairy backs
or women with bad breath, because that's what we grew up
with—that's our norm. So what's the problem? Well, it turns
out that too much inbreeding isn't stellar for the gene pool.
Thanks to addled monarchies, for instance, Hawaii or Great
Britain, we learned that brothers fucking sisters begat weird
twips of near-humans, not quite ready for prime time. Missing
some of their spines and most of their marbles, these children
of the damned weren't fit for day labor, much less ruling a kingdom, so cousins were summoned.

"Now we're talking. Cousins. Close enough but not too
far—you in the Ozarks know what I'm talking about, am I
right? This is our range of fuckage, people. Our close range,
you might say. How many of you have ever been attracted to
one of your cousins?"

E.J. was daring the audience to buckle in and take a ride with
him, and the majority of them nodded and raised an embarrassed
hand. Charlie jiggled the ice a little too loudly in his glass, then
began jiggling his knee before he caught it and stopped. Cat and
Claire sat stone-faced, and Biz was bolt upright and frozen, like
in a fierce game of high-stakes freeze tag. Piper wanted to be
vaporized from space.

"Yes, uh-huh, I thought so. Turns out a lot of us have. I
know, because I've asked. And a lot of us have done something

about it, haven't we? I see that shit-eating grin in the second row. Look at her blushing."

E.J. pointed his beer bottle at a blonde holding hands with her meathead boyfriend.

"Cousins are everywhere you go, aren't they, doll? Only way to avoid them is to not have any. And if you're Catholic, hyper-Christian, or a super-Jew, forget it—you're swatting cousins out of the way like gnats. They're at weddings and funerals, in church pews, and at picnics. Always somewhere when you have to be recently showered and smelling nice. You don't find them at the laundromat or the DMV. Oh, sure, there are other people's cousins at the DMV, but they don't smell as pleasing to you, do they? No, they don't. That's Darwin. We'll get to him later."

A few people chuckled, knowing he was getting at the fact that Darwin married his first cousin.

"Sometimes your cousin is in her bikini at the pool, and you know what that's like for a fourteen-year-old boy? 'Hey, see that girl over there with the pert little breasts, round ass, and dewy skin? Yeah, you can't fuck her.' 'Why not?' 'Because she's your cousin.' 'So?' 'So it's not right.' 'Why?' 'Because the Bible says so.' 'No it doesn't.' 'Oh. How do you know?' 'My friend looked it up.' 'Well, just don't.' 'But why?' And that's where I have no answer for you and your raging hormones. Except to say that it's more puritanical hooey, the kind that no one buys across either ocean where the rest of the world is fucking their cousins because there's a chemical comfort level there that no one can dismiss or dispute. Visual coloring, smell, timbre of the voice, c'mon, it's all there. And so convenient. Because basically, we're lazy pieces of shit, aren't we?"

This was the moment Piper grew nervous. Something in E.J.'s posturing told her that he was going to lay it all out, that he was going to sacrifice his family for the almighty "big break." He wanted the scouts to see him kill, and he would spare nothing and no one to get those sidesplitting laughs and a sterling career. Which was what? Piper wondered. Love from the unwashed massed? Respect from his curmudgeonly peers? Why was there such a gaping hole in his heart, and why, of all people, did she choose him to fuck? Was it laziness? He was eager in bed, but he was so unhappy. Piper had to admit, she was, too.

E.J.'s diatribe reached a fervid pitch, and the audience was dying—covering their open mouths in mock horror and swatting their friends in recognition. He was outrageous and engaging, and very sexy, Piper thought—maddeningly so.

E.J. went on.

"Then, to make things worse, your cousins grow up and marry attractive people, and we're told that they're our relatives now, and we can't fuck them, too. But they're not related to us! They're random strangers who married our relatives, because they reminded them of their relatives. They're just fucking—or not fucking once they've been married—the people we were told we can't fuck. So now no one's fucking who they should, but everyone wants to fuck who they're told they can't."

Piper thanked God Charlie couldn't see her face; she was certain she'd appear ashen if the house lights suddenly went on. Cat and Claire glanced at each other and knew they were thinking exactly the same thing. *Too close to home. How do we get Nana Miggs out of here?* Nana Miggs listened intently with curiosity.

"And they're around us all the time now: birthday parties and bat mitzvahs, Jesus, we can't escape them. Reaching across our chests for sweet potatoes at family dinners, rubbing shoulders with us on TV-room couches watching Sunday football.

Now I know we're not supposed to fuck them, but if one of us married them they must smell like us and get our jokes, so why not keep it in the family? And that's where things get complicated."

Claire brought her fists down on the table, and Cat snapped at her with a severe "No." Georgia let out a "Ha!" and Foster asked the waitress for a fast check. Ned gathered up Cat's things, sensing they might need to make a hasty exit. And E.J. was on fire; the audience was eating it up.

"Men used to head off to war all the time and never come back, so the widow married his brother. Why not? Or the wife dies in childbirth in a covered wagon crossing Nebraska. Husband says, 'She got a sister? She does? Is she a size six? Seven-and-a-half shoe? Perfect. Her husband ate a bad carrot and now he's dead? Helluva shame. Which tent is hers? That's okay, I'll find it myself.' Then there are stepsiblings, perfect strangers moving into the bedroom across the hall because Mummy and Daddy couldn't keep it in their pants. Now you've got blended families. That's some Brady Bunch hide-the-sausage shit right there."

Georgia let out a whoop, then covered her mouth right away. She was finding the whole thing darkly funny. The crowd hooted and hollered, clapping at the most audacious parts, and E.J.'s eyes were lit up. He'd hit a nerve—a taboo one, the very best kind. Through Piper's haze of vitriol, a thought wedged its way into her anxious mind—one she'd never had before: *E.J. looks radiant, glowing, happy.* Followed by: *I can't believe I've been sleeping with that asshole for so long.*

"How many of you wanted Greg and Marcia to get it on? Uh-huh, that's right. They were super-groovy dressers for big fuckin' teases. I mean, they weren't real brothers and sisters, so why the hell not? You wanted that episode to happen, you know you did, because deep down you want to fuck your brother or your cousin or your step-whatever. You're compelled to get that person into your bed, because your Darwinist cravings are firing on all cylinders, because these are the people that know us the most deeply and thoroughly. And we confuse knowing with love, don't we? It's either these people or cheap stand-ins for our family members masquerading as 'other people,' so why not go for the original model. Man, you should see *my* family. Everybody's fucking everyone, but no one's supposed to know. It's total Bacchanalian debauchery . . ."

That was when Piper gasped an inhale of breath so loud and so sharp that not only did everyone hear her—including Charlie—but people at the tables around them turned. Hers was an unusual reaction for a comedy club, which made it stand out in the extreme. It was unfortunate. And that was the moment that Charlie finally knew. When Piper exhaled, the secret of her affair left her body and reentered Charlie's as the truth. In a jolt he saw clearly that his wife was fucking his cousin, and probably had been for some time. He looked at Biz, who was already staring at him with painstaking empathy, then he stood up and stormed out of the room.

Outside Charlie tried to catch a cab. He thought briefly about going to Brighton Beach, chugging vodka with Soviet prostitutes, then walking into the ocean—fully clothed—fistfuls of rocks in his pockets. Biz caught up and put a hand on his shoulder. He jerked it off. *"Did you know?!"*

"I didn't think it should be me who—"

"I thought you were my *best friend*!"

"No, *Piper* is your best friend. And I was the last person who should have told—"

They were interrupted by Foster, Georgia, and Rah, who asked if Charlie wanted to ride home with them. He said, "No, I don't fucking want a ride." Then Piper came out of the club, followed by Cat, Ned, and Claire, and he started walking away, but then turned back and made a brisk beeline for his wife.

Charlie raged, *"Are you fucking kidding me?!"* He loomed large in her face.

"Charlie," Piper said, but he cut her off with a punctuated shove. *"No!"* He said it with such force no one dared interject. *"No fucking way!"* he shouted, and this time gripped her shoulders tightly. Biz calmly said, "Charlie, don't. Take a step back." Piper wheeled her arms around, sending his hands flying off her and hissed, "Don't you fucking dare." Then to Biz she said, "Maybe *you* should step the fuck back."

Biz recoiled. "I didn't—"

Piper went after Biz, leaning close to her face and poking her chest as she spoke, her own rage teetering on the edge. "You *damn well did* and you *know it,* you *drunken whore.*"

Ned intervened, placing his open hand gently but firmly at the center of Piper's chest and moving her backward out of Biz's personal space. "Piper, enough. I think maybe we should all head home and reconvene—"

"Don't *you* dare," Charlie erupted at Piper. "You have *no* right. You *disgust me.*"

"Well, that makes two of us, then. Mutual disgust," said Piper. There was ire in her eyes, not seen before by her in-laws. Even Biz had never witnessed that kind of anger emanate from Piper in all the years she'd known her. It was as if a pent-up wellspring were finally being released—a tide of years-old vengeful acrimony.

Claire said, "We are *not* going to do this now on a public street like hoodlums."

Foster said, under his breath, "It's New York City, Claire, I hardly think it matters—"

Claire said, "Shut up, Foster."

Georgia smirked at Foster and said, "Ooooo." Rah grabbed Charlie at the elbow without looking at him and said, "Let's go." She was small but scrappy and tried to get him moving in the right direction, which was out of this shit storm and back to New Jersey. Charlie whipped his arm out of her hand and said, "Leave me the fuck alone." His elbow caught Ned square in the face, which started a chain of events that no Larkspur family would be likely to admit to.

Cat snapped, "Calm down," at Charlie, who lurched toward the club door to rip E.J. from the stage. Rah and Susan went to block him, but the bouncer got roped in when Charlie tried to shove his way past him, which was not feasible due to the simple physics involving the bouncer's height and weight and the dimensions of the doorframe. Foster explained the scene to the bouncer, who listened patiently with Charlie in his grip like a marionette. Ned's nose was bleeding profusely, so Georgia gave him her pink pashmina, which he used to soak up the blood. Charlie called Piper a low-rent whore, which got her swinging at him, thus once again involving the bouncer, who was using his clipboard as a shield as if he were a paid performer at a regional stage combat demonstration. All this was underscored by Claire, who was screaming manically about civility like someone whose purse had been stolen in 1979. Add to that the Technicolor flair of Cat holding up an increasingly crimson pashmina to Ned's swollen, leaking nose.

During the mayhem, Georgia and Foster caught each other's eye and shared surreptitious delight with Nana Miggs. Then as an aside to her during the dramatic bottoming out of her progeny, Foster said, "Doing our Thornden least." It was a tour de force of public déclassé behavior—Charlie Chaplin meets Jerry Springer. All that was missing was a wheelbarrow of whipped-cream pies. Even the junkies and homeless were chuckling.

It was at this moment that E.J. came outside to have a victory smoke after his triumphant set and chat with scouts. Shocked at the sight of bedraggled members of his family, standing before him in various states of civil disobedience and duress, he froze, his forefinger on the matchbook's strike path, his cigarette wavering at his lips. "What the hell are you all doing here?" E.J. said with an air of disgust. He was annoyed to see them, his usual default to being in their company. But then it dawned on him with a cartoon flick to the brain that they must have been there for him. He was momentarily overcome that all these idiots had made the pain-in-the-ass trip in, which meant he had more paying customers than he thought filling seats. A tiny voice in his head wanted to say, "Really?! *For me?!* Gee, thanks!" but that would have been too much gratitude, incongruous with his normal "asshole" schtick. Instead, he said, softening, "I mean, what the fuck? You came?" They looked at E.J. with the wrath of a family publicly undone by one of their own—heartbroken, upended, and betrayed. A group, collectively, in a very bad mood. Then the third wave of realization finally hit E.J.—they had heard his set. *Oh, shit. This is not good.*

"Fuck you" came back at him in crisp layers from familiar voices; even his Aunt Claire chose to join in. So many fuck-yous, he felt, more than there were people on the sidewalk. Did some say it twice? Had the bouncer joined in the chorus? It was a rough-hewn combination of exhausted and stunned fuck-yous, but no less heartfelt by all in attendance. Nana Miggs saw E.J. gear up to refute.

"Now hush up, all of you, and listen to me!" Nana Miggs commanded as if stepping on a soapbox. She looked at E.J. "Especially you. You cretins think you invented everything—sex, infidelity, screwing around with your cousins—but I have news for you, you didn't. It's all as old as the hills. The only thing new is your generation, who are too repressed to let people do what they're going to do anyway and not worry about it. If you didn't draw so many damn lines in the sand and take everything so personally, you all wouldn't be so miserable. Stop behaving like little children who didn't get everything you wanted. You're all a bunch of damn toddlers with small minds to match. Wake up! The world is not black and white. That's a child's perspective, and it's caused you nothing but grief. I urge you to embrace the gray. It's a helluva lot more interesting than the standards you all hold yourselves to. What on earth are you trying to prove, anyway? You think you're going to get a little trophy when you get to heaven, do you? Why don't you idiots try talking to each other and asking for what you want? What a bunch of puritans you all are. I'm bored to tears with your silly judgments. Although, I must say, this evening's been highly entertaining."

Nana Miggs's eyes twinkled as the blast of a fire engine's siren punctuated her dramatic conclusion. Charlie caught the bouncer saying, "Your grandma's fierce."

Nana Miggs piped up, "That's right, young man, I am fierce."

Foster added, "Huzzah," and got another sharp elbow from

Georgia. He knocked into Biz, who winced in pain. Charlie went to her, asking, "Are you okay?" Piper said to Charlie, "Why am I not surprised. Why should anyone be surprised? You will *never* love anyone more than you love her. Not your kids, not your—"

Biz did everything in her power not to cry, but warm tears welled in her eyes, and sliced her cheeks as she gritted through the residual pain of her throbbing healing ribs.

Rah commanded, "Shut up, Piper. Talk to the motherfuckin' hand."

Cat said, "I need to get Ned home." Foster added, "His nose bleedeth over." Charlie offered, "Ned, let me give you a ride." It was a caring voice, full of kindness and love. It was the voice Charlie's family was used to hearing—the voice of a bighearted man. Charlie turned and said to Biz, "Get in. Ride with us." Then he placed his hand on the small of her back. "I'll get you there safely." She nodded and climbed in because she knew in her heart he would.

Claire's worn, out-of-date, sparse kitchen,
Larkspur, New Jersey

The sun cast slivers of morning light through Claire's kitchen blinds and lit her short white hair from behind like a broken halo. Stacks of bubble wrap and yellowing copies of the *New York Times* littered the counters; cardboard boxes stood in for chairs. Claire was adamant she wouldn't be entrusting "those rough-and-tumble punks" from moving companies to wrap her stuff, so Biz offered to help her mother finally move out.

Now that she was past seventy, Claire's ego had finally succumbed and she let the grays consume her gorgeous coiffure. Passersby were bewitched by the striking juxtaposition of her cobalt blue eyes with dark eyebrows and silver hair. Biz was nearing fifty and sober for many years now. She'd finally healed from the accident and embraced being single. Those who knew her remarked how beautiful she'd become with middle age. Charlie still found her absolutely stunning.

Wrapping a melon baller in newspaper, Biz asked, "Did you ever in your life use one of these? Be honest." Then she realized it didn't need to be wrapped and chucked it in a box.

"There were dishes in the sixties that called for it."

"I bet. Hey, Mom, why did you always tell me everything would work out?"

"Because that's what my mother always told me." Claire still wore cranberry lipstick in the never-ending attempt to hold on to her quietly ebbing beauty. Though she was slightly kinder now since she'd been forced to let go of the control she thought she had for so many years. "In fact, your Nana Miggs told me everything would work out just the other day."

Biz thought about the visual comedy inherent in a ninety-some-odd-year-old telling a seventy-something-year-old that everything's still going to work out. Biz asked, "So now, with heaps of perspective, do you think it's useful or harmful in the long run? Does that mind-set encourage a sort of blithe optimism or set the bar for disappointment?"

"Why do you ask?"

"Just curious. I was thinking the other night that everything hasn't worked out. Not in the conventional sense. I'm forty-eight and single—"

"That's a blessing. Men are overrated."

"Mom. Please. I'm living in the same town I grew up in—"

"Nothing wrong with Larkspur," said the lifelong resident with pride.

"True," Biz nodded in agreement. She'd loosened her grip on the dream of moving west once Ruby graduated, instead choosing to remain close by in case she was needed. "I'm an alcoholic—"

"Recovering," Claire said, also with pride.

Biz kneaded the pain in her upper arm, which occasionally seized as if in an unrelenting vise. "I have frozen shoulder syndrome."

"Oh, I've had that. Mind over matter."

"Did a male doctor tell you that, Mom? It's not hysteria. It's a real thing."

Claire ignored her. "What else have you got on that gripe list of yours?"

"I never became what I always dreamed of. Etsy didn't exist before I gave up—"

"But you design those beautiful cakes that bring joy to so many."

"Thank you, Mom. Please stop interrupting. And I live alone."

"You can always move in with me, Cat, and Ned. We could use a fourth musketeer."

Biz rolled her eyes at the thought. "Mom, I appreciate the offer, but I can't play Little Edie to your Big Edie, I just can't do it." She was hoping it wouldn't come to that but knew it wasn't out of the range of possibility—little else had gone the way she planned. "Why did you marry Dad? He's gay, you know."

Claire thought about this briefly. "Probably."

"No, Mom, he is, and everyone knows it. That wasn't an isolated event. Gerard is his boyfriend, not his business partner or his roommate." Twelve years earlier, a few months after E.J.'s public family bloodletting, Les had been caught canoodling with a local's husband. He was summarily drop-kicked out of the closet and officially booted from the Thornden family, to his immediate and gratifying relief. Most were empathetic enough at the time to realize how much turmoil he must have been in and how he must have suffered for so long; Claire was not one of them. She blamed him for the family's further social decline—though the rest of them had long stopped caring—and conveniently remained in denial until this day. Biz felt a huge wave of relief knowing she wasn't to blame for his unhappiness and supported him fully as he emerged from chronic depression.

Claire didn't look surprised. "I know, I know, okay, he's gay. Don't rub it in."

"Don't take it personally," Biz said, "He's not gay *at* you. So why did you marry him? No wonder the poor guy was miserable. He felt emotionally, physically, and socially trapped and he was an alcoholic and chemically depressed."

"Everyone's a little depressed."

"Mom. Dad was clinically depressed and should have received proper help."

Biz waited for her mother's reply. Claire took her time responding, mulling over how much truth to dispense and then decided on all of it. "Your Aunt Cat was the pretty one and got married first, and I thought I should be married, too, since I was older. I felt entitled to marriage, which as it turns out isn't an entitlement. It's meant to be earned. And not everyone is capable. I do feel poorly in hindsight, and I should probably be nicer to him."

"You definitely should. But I thought *you* were the pretty one."

"I had the looks, but Cat had the spark. It was the wrong reason to marry Les, and it would be the wrong reason for you to marry Hugh."

"Mom, I'm not going to—"

"I see you sizing him up as you get older, making trade-offs in your head. But you shouldn't settle. You should wait until you find someone who 'gets you.' Nana Miggs is right about that. Surround yourself with people who light up when you walk in the room. I didn't wait, and I should have—marriage is not a contest. Though I'm thankful I have you and E.J."

"The bane of your existence."

"You are not the bane of my existence-"

"No, I meant E.J."

"You are both the light of my life. I was just never very adept at showing it."

"At all," said Biz with an impish grin. She paused in the middle of wrapping a stack of Archie-comics juice glasses and four egg cups. Biz wanted what she said next to sink in, so she spoke slowly, with grace and assurance. "Mom, I don't think there's anyone out there for me. I don't think I'm one of the lucky ones, and I've made peace with that, and I hope you can, too."

"What happened to that Irishman from the bakery who was arrested?"

"He wasn't arrested. And we dated when he came back from Ireland, remember? It didn't work out. Now he's with Muriel, and they're a better fit for each other." Biz and Finn had been on a few dates after he returned from Ireland and she was recovered from the accident and going to meetings. But it only took two dinners and a movie for her to admit she didn't love him enough to jump into his three-ring circus. He was fun and without a doubt funny, but there were too many places where they didn't connect. So she slept with him casually on and off for a few months, knowing it wouldn't last. And it didn't. Then Muriel's marriage unraveled. Finn asked Biz if he could ask her out. Biz gave them both her blessing, and they all remained friends.

"I thought Muriel was married."

"She was and now she's not. People trade partners, Mother. It happens all the time. Life's a big square dance and we're all allemande-lefting each other every few years, trying to find the best fit. Some are happy to stay with the one who brung 'em, but many switcheroo. Sometimes more than once."

"It's 'brought,' and it sounds exhausting."

"I know, Mom, and it *is*. Square dancing is *exhausting*." Biz labeled the box she'd taped shut KITCHEN CRAP MOM DOESN'T NEED with a black Sharpie. "My mission is to keep in mind that I have a handful of close friends, a thriving business, and a terrific kid, wherever she is. Prague, I think, this week. She emails me where they're sending her, but I get her clients confused. All I'm saying is, I feel very lucky. I have a lot going for me."

"Well, you certainly have an excellent attitude."

Biz said, "Ha! You bought that load of crap? I'm faking it, but good to know it works." Claire smiled, glad her daughter still had her sense of humor, though to her it had always been a mystery where it came from.

Biz continued to work during Claire's smoking break, emptying the entire contents of one drawer into a box. Grapefruit spoons and corn-cob holders, a pizza cutter and egg poacher, she wondered where this trove of obsolescence would ever end up.

"Mom, what the hell is that brick on the counter covered in tin foil? Are you seriously moving it over to Aunt Cat's?"

"Yes, and don't ask unless you're willing to hear the entire tutorial."

"Fine. I'll take a pass."

Smoker's lines crisscrossed Claire's face like roads on a folding map. And though it made her lips appear permanently pursed she refused to give up her beloved cigarettes. Her Liz Taylor–esque beauty had taken a backseat to a life spent finding fault with others, yet her eyes were still as piercing and she continued to speak with the air of a queen. Claire looked directly at Biz for a moment, exhaled, but said nothing.

"What?" said Biz.

"You're a wonderful mother."

Biz was shocked. "I *am*?"

"Why do you look so taken aback?"

"Because you've never told me that."

"That's because I'm a terrible mother," Claire said matter-of-factly, then went back to nesting Pyrex mixing bowls into a larger box. Their moment of intimacy was over; Biz didn't move. She allowed for a long, momentous pause to savor her mother's comment. She wanted the statement to ring out in the air, unchallenged by even her own breath for as long as possible.

Finally, Biz said softly, "You can be," and Claire said, shockingly and unexpectedly, nothing.

It had taken many years for wounds to heal and E.J. to be forgiven. The Thornden dynasty had inelegantly imploded after that fateful night in New York. It was a rare treat now when they were all together, and this Easter would be one of those times. An early dinner seemed to be best for everyone's schedules, and it would be held at Nana Miggs's old house, as per her wishes. It hadn't felt like Nana Miggs's home for years, now. Georgia and Foster had remodeled the kitchen, blowing out walls and updating all the major appliances. The cozy kitchen nook was gone, replaced by an island so big that if a tangerine came to a rolling stop in the middle, one would have to climb on all fours up on the table to retrieve it. Not exactly intimate, but it still felt appropriate for Easter dinner—especially since Claire was in the midst of moving in with Cat next door and getting her house ready to put on the market. The long table was gone, and there weren't enough stools at the island to accommodate everyone. Some stood or leaned, and some piled cookbooks on chairs to be level with the crowd. The single bulb had been replaced by high-watt pendant lamps that were attractive but not on a dimmer, so the overhead lights glared, instructing as opposed to coaxing them to relax.

At 7 P.M., the older adults were wrapping up their meal, and the children—now in their early twenties—were already done. They had pitched in to do the dishes and were happily ensconced in the den watching *Close Encounters of the Third Kind*, which they were referring to as a "film classic."

Georgia said to Biz, "So, how's the move coming along? I can put in some hours this week."

"Thanks, that would be great. Slowly but surely—"

E.J. and Charlie said in unison, "Don't call me Shirley."

Biz said, "Oh, that reminds me, I found our Farrah and Jaclyn wigs."

Charlie said, "Nice. Let's wear them to Rah's wedding."

Rah said, "Very funny."

"Wait, wasn't there a gay Charlie's Angel?"

"Don't even go there," cautioned Rah. Then, addressing Biz, she lowered her head and looked over her shoulder at Claire, who was slowly returning from the restroom. "How's it really going? Do you want to kill her?"

Biz said in singsong through gritted smile, "Each and every day."

E.J. said, "Why do you think I'm not helping," and took another swig of whisky.

"It never occurred to any of us you would," Biz said, and E.J. shot her a look.

Claire said to her son, "Why, I'd love your help, dear. Thank you for offering."

E.J. responded with sarcasm. "I can think of nothing I'd rather do more, Mother. Oh, wait, yes I can—pretty much everything."

Rah said, "You're a regular riot tonight. Working on a new set?"

"I haven't gone up in years and you know it. Retirement's my gift to the world."

"Actually, the proper usage is 'present.' Grandpa Dun taught us gifts come from God."

Foster whispered to Rah, "Ix-nay on the omedy-kay, ease-play."

Biz added to the E.J. pile-on. "Dude, what's with the booze?"

"And the shitty disposition?" added Rah.

Claire admonished all the cousins, "Don't start."

"Too late," said Charlie. Claire's comment, as usual, was wishful thinking.

Nana Miggs piped up, "That reminds me, while we're all together, I have presents for you kids." She spoke slowly now, and a shade more softly, but not labored. At ninety-six her mind was as clear and sharp as a tack; her knees were another story. Still, she felt doted on by "My Gordon," as she called him, and her sparkle hadn't faded. Gordon painted gorgeous landscapes with red barns in the middle distance and occasionally impressionist nudes of Nana Miggs with titles like *Marjorie in Repose*. Claire insisted the canvases stay confined to their bedroom. Nevertheless, the Greats were occasionally discovered crowded around them, staring. "Great-Grandma Miggs, is that you?" "You *bet* it's me, honey-bun. In *all my glory*! Isn't My Gordon a talent?" Claire would try to deflect, but Nana Miggs always shot straight from the hip. There was nothing anyone could do at this point about any of it.

She asked Her Gordon to fetch a Bonwit Teller shoebox

covered in the distinctive violet nosegays of a bygone era. Setting the box on the counter before her, she removed the faded lid, and opened the folds of haggard tissue with delight. Then Nana Miggs closed her papery lids and released a slow path of air as if she were exhaling a ribbon of smoke from long ago.

"Dunny and I both wanted to give each of you something. We made a list, and here we all are. So, before something happens to me . . ."

Charlie said, "Is there something you're not telling us?"

"*Mom,*" Cat said, "nothing's going to happen to you."

To which E.J. said, "Famous last words."

"Ignore him," said Claire, glaring at her son with weary disdain.

"Never," said Nana Miggs, and smirked, her eyes tired but still twinkling. "I'm going to start with the men—"

Rah interrupted, speaking to Susan, "Because our family is ensconced in a fifties patriarchal hierarchy as old as basement linoleum."

Charlie said, "Easy, Rah."

Nana Miggs went on, "Bloodline was important to Dunny . . ."

"So Ned, Gordon, Susan, and I will get the dregs. I get it," Foster said with a grin. "Would you like us to take a walk around the block?"

"Don't be ridiculous."

"It's totally fine, Marjorie, we understand. Please continue," said Ned.

Nana Miggs winked at Ned and went on. "Charles, I'd like you to have your grandfather's pocket watch."

Charlie was blown away. A tear sprang immediately to his

eye. "Thank you, Nana." He got up out of his chair and kissed her sweetly on the cheek.

"Oh, don't get up," she said, relishing the kiss. "You can all kiss me at the end. To E.J. I'm bequeathing his wallet." She handed her grandson a dark brown leather billfold. Its corners were worn from use, and the edges were shiny from years of handling. It curved like the final sliver of a waning moon. It was a precious thing for any man.

"It smells like his butt," E.J. said with ersatz wonderment.

"*E.J.!*" the women cried in unison.

"And to think he's never found a wife," said Foster.

"Fuck you. You should talk," E.J. growled. "I love it, Nana Miggs. Thank you."

"You're welcome, dear," she said with her endlessly forgiving smile.

He got up out of his chair even though he'd been instructed not to and went over to her, swaying a bit. Putting his arm around her narrow back, he deposited a kiss with delicate finesse, though clearly quite drunk. "You're the best. Stay alive, will ya?"

"I'll try," she said.

Claire was given his sterling money clip, and Cat, his wrist-watch. Ned received cuff links; Georgia, his Irish wool cabbie hat; and Biz was given his walking stick. That got a chuckle from the crowd. "Okay!" she said, enthusiastically making the best of an odd choice, and did a little time-step tap dance, à la Ginger Rogers. Foster was given Dunny's shiny U-shaped briarwood pipe, which he reflexively rubbed on the side of his nose, working the oils into the wood as he'd seen Grandpa Dun do hundreds of times. And Rah lit up when she was presented with his leather belt, its buckle engraved with the monogram "DBT." When her fiancée, Susan, was given Grandpa Dun's

288   V. C. Chickering

favorite hunter-green Yahtzee dice cup, Rah gasped in appreciation, then beamed at her entire family through watery eyes.

Once everyone had their special item, Cat and Claire returned from the butler's pantry with a bottle of reserve champagne and a stack of juice glasses. It was fitting they weren't using champagne flutes. That way of behavior had been laid to rest long ago with Grandpa Dun, and life decidedly was more relaxed now, less prescribed. It had been Dunsfield Thornden who insisted on tradition not as a choice but as a familial mandate. As comforting as it was, it might have also been stifling. Biz and Charlie felt this blind adherence to tradition fostered a subsurface fear of forward thinking, risk-taking, and tiptoeing outside the box, but they kept their opinion to themselves.

Charlie gave a lovely toast to Grandpa Dun, squeezing Nana Miggs's hand at the end for punctuation. Then they all sipped the good stuff, remembering the man who seemingly brought them together from disparate places, as if handpicked from thousands of eager applicants. A moment later, E.J. went through the folds of his deceased grandfather's empty wallet, tilting it toward the light to catch all the crevices. He pulled out a thin piece of leather-stained paper that had been hiding under a flap and unfolded it carefully, trying not to tear it across its well-worn creases. Rah noticed and said, "Um, guys?" to the room. Then to E.J., "What does it say?"

E.J. looked at Nana Miggs, eyes full of contrition.

Nana Miggs waved him off. "Oh, I know. It's okay, dear. Read it. The old bird's dead. No harm done."

"But, Nana . . . ," was all E.J. could say before the interruptions began.

"Read it! What does it say?" asked the family in layers of curiosity.

"Go on," said Nana Miggs. She seemed perfectly content to hear what was on that nearly translucent slip of paper and took another sip of champagne—her signature pinkberry lipstick scalloping the edge of her glass.

E.J. spoke with disbelief. "Dunsfield, Dearest, A part of us will always belong to each other and no one else—and you know which part. Love, E."

Claire said, *"Who's E?!"* with indignation on behalf of everyone.

"Edith. Or Evelyn, or Beth Anne. She was an Elizabeth. I lost count. Didn't matter."

Rah said, "I don't . . . understand." Of all of the grandchildren, she seemed to be unraveling the most. Cat was also piecing it together in real time. "Does this mean what we all think it means?"

"It means I didn't take it personally, and you shouldn't either." Nana Miggs's eyes calmly and confidently scanned the room, landing on each member of her family. "We had an arrangement. Suited us just fine."

Everyone was too stunned to speak, their minds a whir. Only Biz spoke. "What about you, Nana? Did you enjoy *your side* of the arrangement?"

"Of course. It's how we stayed married all those years. You kids are doing it all wrong."

Biz chuckled, and E.J. laughed out loud. Georgia looked at Foster, who checked his cell phone. Neither of them found this very funny. The other women were even less amused.

E.J. giggled. "We assumed you were . . . um . . ."

"Careful, E.J.," Biz warned.

"Conservative," he finished tactfully.

Nana Miggs grinned and said, "On the outside," with a wink.

Cat said, "Why didn't you *tell* us?"

"You wouldn't have wanted to know."

Claire cut in. "Mother, *are you saying—*"

"I'm saying no more. Case closed."

The Thornden clan was silent; they had so many questions. Instead, they looked across the kitchen island from face to face—all eyes were wide, all mouths agape. Finally Foster said, "Nana Miggs, have you been a secret Buddhist all this time?"

Nana Miggs glanced at Gordon and said, "Maybe."

Ruby, Gigi, and their boyfriends, Miguel and Oliver, came into the kitchen, pushing through the swinging door, one of the last vestiges of the original kitchen.

"What's the ruckus?" said Ruby. "Is Uncle E.J. pissing everyone off again?" She had the dark beauty and chutzpah of Biz at that age with a big, unwieldy heart and surefire sense of humor. But years ago, she courted mischief more than her mother had in high school and could be unreasonably stubborn and combative. Biz worried Ruby was heading down a questionable path with the wrong kids, so she dragged her to evening AA meetings, claiming she couldn't find a sitter. She knew in her soul it was saving both their lives, which Ruby would one day figure out.

"Hey, Dad," Gigi said to Charlie. She was tall like Ruby but fairer, with a mop of strawberry hair the color and thickness of Piper's. Her hazel eyes were like summer moss and the almond shape of Charlie's. Her dimple made her and Ruby look like sisters, and they were often mistaken for such. Gigi was an avowed observer and tended to follow Ruby's lead, but their friendship had an equanimity and rhythm that mirrored Biz and Charlie's. "Hey, kiddo," said Charlie to Gigi, and reached out for her hand. She let him take it. She liked her dad. "Are you sleeping at my place or your mom's tonight?"

"Mom's. And Steve's." Gigi rolled her eyes, and Charlie grinned patiently. "Mom's awesome new boyfriend," Gigi added, dripping with sarcasm. The family nodded and exchanged looks of acceptance and support. A few glanced at E.J. to gauge his response. There was an awkward pause; E.J. squirmed and downed his fourth drink. He was still bitter and embarrassed after being dumped by Piper, though everyone felt it was well deserved. It hadn't been easy to forgive him for the fiasco back in 2002, and for the affair and the end of the marriage. Especially after all that selfishness amounted to nothing once he cheated on Piper and lost her for good. She moved nearby to Stonemere to have joint custody of the kids, but eschewed most Thornden family gatherings. In all honesty, they were relieved. Piper and Charlie were partners in parenting, but no longer soul mates or friends.

"So, what were you guys all shouting about?" asked Ruby.

"None of your beeswax. Go away," slurred E.J.

Ruby was part of a new generation who stood up to bullies, with no time for dismissive rhetoric or misogyny. She was also twenty-four now and didn't stand for being publicly admonished by an ornery alcoholic. Miguel was a new boyfriend, and she wanted to make a good impression. She turned to the guys and said, "This is our Uncle E.J. He once tried to be a stand-up comic, but he sucked, so now he drinks all day. It's pretty cliché. Hey, Uncle E.J., what can you tell us about Aunt Piper's new boyfriend, Steve? I hear you two were in the same class in high school." She meant it as a jab; she was asserting her power. She was tired of everyone excusing his behavior. E.J. prickled at the comment. A former jock, Steve had a firm grasp on Piper and her sweet ass. E.J. was in no mood for Ruby's defiance. Plus they were out of Maker's

Mark. He taunted his niece, "I don't know, Ruby. Why don't you ask your *dad*."

Biz straightened. "Knock it off, you two, seriously."

Ruby said, "You know darn well I was born of the Virgin Biz."

Claire commanded, "E.J., Ruby, that's enough."

E.J. went after his niece without mercy. "I just realized, Ruby is a *perfect* name for you. Do you know what 'rube' means?"

Charlie said, "E.J., what is *wrong* with you?"

"It means someone too dumb to see what's right in front of her face."

Biz said, "You're an asshole." Charlie got off his stool. But Ruby forcefully cut in. "No, no, hold on, everybody, I can handle this myself. Uncle E.J., why are you so mean? Did my mom grab your toys when you were a kid? Is it because Uncle Charlie ended up with your childhood crush? Or are you pissed Aunt Piper left you for someone funnier than you?" Gasps were heard, but Ruby continued, addressing Miguel and Oliver. "There are those who think my Uncle Charlie is also my father. Gigi and I have known this for years and don't care." Ruby looked directly at her boyfriend, Miguel. "Do you care if my uncle is also my sperm donor?" The young man shook his head no. Ruby said to Gigi, "Do you care if we're half sisters?"

Gigi barely looked up from texting. "Oh my God, that would be so chill."

Ruby said, "I know, right?" then looked around the room in full command of the conversation. "Does anyone in this room care who my biological father is? I honestly do not. And if I don't, I don't know why you all should. Hasn't it ever occurred to you that our heads may be nestled too comfortably up our own asses?"

Biz said, "Ruby, watch your language."

"Look, I'm guilty, too! But at least I'm trying to be more self-aware. There are events of dire consequence impacting us beyond the Larkspur bubble! There're the school shootings and the marathon bombing. Global warming is totally nuts. Syria is using chemical weapons against its *own people*, and Trayvon—have you guys even *heard* of Black Lives Matter?" Only Susan, Rah, and Nana Miggs nodded in awareness. "Because exactly *none* of our small-town bullshit matters."

Claire said, "I beg your pardon, young lady."

"Nana Miggs knows it's true," Ruby said, looking at her great-grandmother, who was possibly the wokest person among them. They exchanged a look of compassion before Ruby continued, "Uncle Charlie, I love you. Like a father, or uncle, whatever, you decide. And if I'm your daughter, that's totally dope. Mom, I love you, you've done a great job keeping me off the pole. Not sure why you weren't using birth control at the time, but—"

Biz shook her head. "Oh my God, I was so irresponsible. Please don't be like me."

"No joke, Mom, you were totally insane. And I'm not perfect, but I'm working on it, right, Gigi?"

Gigi snickered. "Whatevs."

Ruby resumed. "Can we all agree that I turned out awesome?" The room nodded. Biz was tearing up. Ruby said, "Uncle E.J., I love you, too, even though you're always angry. I have a few ideas why, but I wish it bothered you as much as it does the people trying to love you. I may be the only one, so you should be nicer to me and maybe, just maybe, I'll change your diapers and wipe your sorry ass when you're a grizzly old bastard—even more than you are now—because no one else I know will. Until then, you're welcome to join me at AA—'cause you, my friend, are a hot mess. And you can find a new victim to torture from now on, because I truly don't care."

Everyone looked astonished. Claire was bristling. Ruby said to Biz, "We're taking off, Mom. There's a band playing in the city." To Gigi she said, "Are we taking your car?" Gigi muttered, "Yeah." Every Thornden family member, save Gordon and the boyfriends, reflexively corrected her, saying, "Yes." Then they all shared the laughter and relief of life's small triumphs. Biz was in watery tears; Claire and Cat were choked up. "Inside joke," Ruby said to her beau. "C'mon, let's roll. We're off like a prom dress. No offense, Mom."

Biz cracked a smile and tugged Ruby's sleeve. "You still love me?"

"Obvi," Ruby said with a peck to her mom's cheek. Then added, "Except when you blast that old crapass music through-out the apartment."

Biz put her hand to her heart. "K.C. and the Sunshine Band will forever rock my world."

"Nobody says that anymore, Mom. You're dating yourself. Bye, all!"

"Bye!" echoed the room.

Ruby pushed the swinging door open, and Gigi and the guys followed.

"Watch the alcohol consumption!" Cat called after them.

Ruby shouted, "I'm the designated driver! More Ruby awesomeness!"

"Good work, pal!" They all turned to Biz, who was burst-ing with unforeseen pride. For as much as she'd fucked up, she'd still managed to raise a funny, take-no-shit young woman with personality to spare. It was hard to fathom, and she was grateful as hell. Charlie reached across the island and gave her hand a squeeze—he, too, had become emotional. It was the first public display of affection he'd made toward Biz in twenty-five years—in front of the family who'd kept them apart, the very people who were evidently caving. "And good work to you, too, Mom," said Charlie. The room nodded in agreement.

"Thanks," said Biz with a fragile squeak. "It was no trouble at all."

.   .   .

The kitchen had cleared out for the night; only the sisters were left. Cat collected linen napkins off the table and threw them down the laundry chute. Claire turned on the faucet and rolled up the sleeves of her cream-colored silk Talbots blouse. *"What the fuck?"* she spat with twenty years of unleashed rage.

"Claire!" Cat admonished. "Mom is right upstairs." She'd never heard the F-word cross her sister's lips in her entire life. She found it kind of funny to hear it now.

"I don't care! Jesus Christ." Claire scrubbed a pot as if her life depended on it.

Cat chuckled, "Wow, our lord and savior, too? Are you practicing to become a Hell's Angel? Nothing would surprise me at this point."

Claire ignored her sister. "Is that *all* that's taken you by surprise tonight?"

"Are you upset by Mom, Dad, Charlie, Ruby, or E.J.?"

"At *all of them*! What the *fuck has happened to this family*?!"

"Wow, there you go again. I'm not used to you swearing. You'll have to give me time to adjust."

"Well, screw you, too, then. Screw everyone. I've had it," said Claire. She was washing each plate and glass thoroughly by hand before loading them into the dishwasher. Cat subtly removed and dried them, then quietly put them away without Claire noticing. "I just can't believe that Dad was . . . and Mom knew . . . and didn't care . . . I'm just. It's not right."

"And Mom apparently enjoyed herself, too."

"Cat, please. How did we not know this was going on?"

"We were kids? Enmeshed in our own worlds? Unless we walked in on one of them, how would we have ever . . ."

Claire froze, staring, the sponge poised in midair. A shade shorter but still lithe, not a hair out of place, she looked like a vitamin ad for seniors.

"What?" said Cat. "What do you remember?"

"Nothing." Claire resumed scrubbing.

"It's *not* nothing. Tell me. I can read your mind."

Claire turned to Cat with a quizzical look. "Is it possible that when Mr. Powers was working on the plumbing in the master bathroom . . ."

Cat said, "Nooooooo," and froze, too, her mind fluttering a catalogue of images through her brain.

Claire spoke slowly. "They would go into her bedroom together, we would hear the shower run, then they would come out twenty minutes later."

"He always said, 'Allllllll fixed,' and Mom would giggle, remember?" Cat cracked up.

"It's not funny," said Claire.

Cat's eyes came alive. "I came home early from a dance once and there was Mr. Appleton in the living room. It never occurred to me that Mom probably wasn't getting a lesson from our piano teacher at nine at night."

"And where was Dad?"

"At the club."

They both looked at each other with eyes alight and exclaimed, *"At the club!"*

"Jesus Christ," said Cat. "I thought he was playing cards or watching sports in the downstairs bar."

"Well, now we know," said Claire. "Unbelievable."

"He still might have been doing those things, he just might have *also* been living it up with E. Or one of the many E's, according to Mom. Holy hell." Cat couldn't suppress a mischievous grin.

"Holy hell is right." Claire was not smiling. They resumed the kitchen work, but now Claire handed the cleaned dishes directly to Cat to dry. "Wait. Do we even know that the E was a woman?"

Claire said, "Stop it. I can't even. Just stop it right there." They both paused and stared at the steady stream of water running purposefully and without hesitation from the faucet. Cat uttered, "Could be. I supposed anything's possible." Claire broke in, "I thought I knew them. It's so weird. These people are *our parents.*"

"We *did* know them," said Cat empathetically. She could tell her sister was feeling personally hurt. "We knew as much as we were supposed to know at the time. They weren't under contract to tell us everything. We were their kids, not their peers."

"They didn't have to tell *us,* but I think they should have told *each other.*"

"I have a feeling they *did.* I think their agreement worked for them."

"I think secrets cause cancer," said Claire, and began to sponge off the counter.

Cat paused to push her own secret out of her mind. She spoke carefully. "I think there's more to it than that. I think people can have privacies, there's a difference. As long as no one gets hurt." Cat reflected on what she had just said. Had she caused her Charlie harm? She wondered how many of Biz's unfortunate challenges had come from her own choices and how things might have been different if Charlie—if everyone— had known his truth all along. Charlie felt immense guilt for his behavior; Biz felt terrible, too. They had all suffered because of the lie. Hell, Cat had battled cancer. Was her secret the cause? She knew how much Charlie loved Biz and that he would still do anything for her. She was right to keep the secret, wasn't she? *Would anyone care in this day and age?*

Claire returned the sponge to its cradle and surveyed the pristine kitchen. It was as if no intimate family gathering had taken place. Untying her apron she said, "Aren't you disgusted by your son?"

"By my son? *No.*" Cat was taken aback. "Are you disgusted by your daughter?"

Claire lit a cigarette. "It's been established that Charlie used force with Biz in the past. It's quite possible that Biz was—"

"Don't you dare." Cat glowered at her sister.

Claire said, "Fine. Let's say they were both willing participants. Biz was single at the time, but Charlie was engaged to be married. Maybe if you had led by example and instilled in your son the importance of fidelity when making a commitment, they wouldn't have ended up together the week of his wedding."

Cat couldn't believe what she was hearing. All goodwill and forgiveness toward her sister vanished. "I think we should stop this conversation right now. We're throwing a wedding together and will have a much easier time of it if we're still speaking." She started for the door.

"You know I'm right," Claire said after her.

Cat spun around. "I know that you're mean and combative

when you've been drinking. And your children are fucked up and you refuse to take any accountability for it. I know that people who feel safe and loved don't become alcoholics like Biz, and that E.J. is always the angriest person in the room. There's an excellent chance they'll probably both wind up alone, and you'll never acknowledge the part you played in their outcome because you were too busy going to garden club meetings. It may be too late for them, but it's not too late for Ruby. But that means you have to participate in her life and stop giving a shit about how she came into it."

Not one to not have the last word, Claire followed Cat to the front door, listing all the ways in which her children were fucked up: Georgia the jailbird, married to an adulterer; Charlie's failed marriage and unplanned fatherhood; and Rah too afraid to come out for all those years. At this last comment, Cat stopped with her hand on the knob. The suddenness had the effect of halting the swirling air around them.

"You're incredibly sad," said Cat with genuine regret—deep, despairing, and permanent. "I wish you felt loved and safe." She added, "We'd have all been much happier if you did. I'm exhausted and am going home to sleep in my own bed. I'll be back in the morning to help with breakfast. Happy Easter."

Over the course of the next few days, both Cat and Claire independently imagined how challenging it might be to host a wedding for Rah and Susan while living together and not killing each other. So, for the purposes of the upcoming June wedding, the sisters called an unspoken truce, effective immediately. It was excruciatingly hard, but guilt took a backseat and blame got a much-deserved rain check. For two and a half months,

Cat worked hard to let go of trying to enlighten her sister, who was unlikely to change. And Claire found consolation in the fact that most of her friends' kids hadn't turned out perfectly, either. Thank God, at least, for everyone's health—even Les's, whom she was finally beginning to accept. *Enough bothering about what could have been,* thought Claire. *It's time to buckle down and throw a gay wedding.*

"Weddings aren't gay, Aunt Claire, people are," said Rah. She had to gently remind her family of that point often during the weeks ramping up to their big day. Thankfully she was bolstered by Susan's patience and strength, and in too good a mood to take it personally.

Rah came out to her family in 2010, and no one was the least surprised. Forty was late, but, she and Susan reasoned, it was no one's business but her own. Even when Ellen DeGeneres came out on national TV in '97 and was featured on the cover of *Time*, it took Rah another thirteen years to be relaxed enough to tell Grandpa Dun and her family. She worried the news would provoke E.J. and Aunt Claire, and possibly hurt Grandpa Dun in some way. But one night Rah and Susan were helping bundle Nana Miggs into the back of a car after a party. As they leaned in to tuck a blanket over her lap, she said, "You two don't have to pretend for me. Love is a magical beautiful thing. Let us celebrate with you. We're your family." Rah teared up, unable to respond. Susan conveyed warmth speaking for them. "Someday, Nana Miggs. Thank you very much." That was enough for the time being. After that, Susan looked much more at ease at family gatherings. She always made sure Nana Miggs had a refill at cocktail time and a hand to steady her at the stairs.

The couple held a commitment ceremony for close friends at Susan's summer place on Lake Winnipesaukee. It was a small, casual affair held in a rustic A-frame—with lots of happy tears, laughter, and dancing. Though disappointed they hadn't been invited, their families were congratulatory when told the next morning. Then when same-sex marriage became legal in New Jersey, Rah proposed again and Susan agreed. Thus began the planning of their legally sanctioned, family-approved, New Jersey, Thornden-masterminded gay-not-gay wedding.

While running down the laundry list of RSVP admin, Rah thought, *this is clearly a self-selecting affair*. She said, "Nothing like a gay wedding to find out who your real friends are." Susan corrected, "It's a wedding, not a gay wedding, remember, dear?" The responses from Larkspur and Firth families dribbled in, which suited Rah and Susan just fine. Fifty was the perfect number of guests as far as they were concerned. Rah only wanted folks who mattered to her and not an overwhelming home court advantage. Except for Claire, who thought there should be more in attendance, and that the reception should be held at the club. However, while reeling from Biz's drunk-driving accident, and Piper and E.J.'s affair, the family had stopped going as often. Membership outreach had been paltry. Old-timers who still remembered the Thornden family pretended not to notice their absence, and newer members who saw no social advantage to befriending them continued not to care. Regardless, the cousins convinced Cat and Claire that their grand backyard would be perfect. Or at least the half of it they would still own when the wedding rolled around. The house was going on the market, and buyers were sure to circle. So, Ned led the charge to revitalize the landscaping, and Rah solicited estimates on a fence, nice and tall.

With four weekends until the big day, any family members around were put to work. There were detailed instructions to

ready both neglected homes with much-needed TLC. Garden
beds had overgrown, the shed needed desperate painting, the
hedges needed trimming, the pool needed scrubbing—the list
was very long. And then it was discovered Claire's real estate
agent would be holding the open house on their wedding day.
No one could believe the timing, but they concurred with shaking heads that neither were they very surprised.

The last Saturday before the wedding was a gorgeous May
evening with no humidity and low expectations. Pizzas were
delivered because everyone was exhausted and no one wanted
to cook. As various yard projects were wrapping up, before
they started on indoor tasks, Ruby asked who was interested in
getting some fresh air, a quick walk around the block. Biz and
Charlie were the only takers, so they headed off together, just
the three odd musketeers—alone for the first time ever.

"Look at us," said Ruby, "just a mom, her kid, and her uncle-
slash-possibly-father out for an innocent stroll."

Biz shot Ruby a look as if to say, *No way, not here, not now.*
She could feel a hot flash starting to swell. Ruby read her mother's mind and decided to ignore her. "Hey, why don't you two
tell me the story of how I might have been conceived." Charlie
let loose a chortle, then gave Biz a look. "C'mon, you two.
Everyone's been fed. Grandma Claire and Great-Aunt Cat have
everyone dusting framed photographs and polishing silverware.
Let's do this. Now's the time. Tell me everything."

Biz looked over at Charlie. "She's never asked until now."

"Fine with me," he said affably. He'd longed for this conversation forever.

"Okay, fine," said Biz, fanning her open collar. "You know
the Roundsavilles' tree house?"

"No," said Ruby, her face a blank. The ladder rungs had

rotted off by the time Ruby would have been old enough to climb. "Was I conceived in a *frickin' tree house?! Oh. My. God. That's so lit!*" Ruby scanned all the nearby trees and took out her phone to text her friends.

"Hold on, young lady," Biz commanded sternly. "If you text one word of this—"

"I agree with whatever she's about to threaten you with," said Charlie.

"You'll get no story."

"And no inheritance," added Charlie, joking. It was common knowledge there was very little left.

Ruby looked at them and put her phone away. "Big deal. You guys spent it all."

Biz took her grown daughter's hand and spoke to her plainly and with respect. "I'm not going to tell you that what we did was right, I'm just going to tell you what happened. Decent people can make poor choices." Charlie agreed from a few paces behind.

"Mom. I get it. You're not a bad person. You did a bad thing. Just tell me the story, God."

"I prefer dumb thing, not bad. But okay. We were at Charlie's engagement party—"

"You guys had sex at your *engagement party*?! To *Aunt Piper*?!"

Biz stopped short in her tracks. Biz said, "If you're going to freak out or judge us, we're not—"

"Okay, okay. Sorry. Go on."

Biz looked to Charlie. "Hey, pal, feel free to jump in anytime."

"You're doing just fine," he said, smirking.

"This is why I've avoided—"

Ruby tugged on her mom's arm. "I know, I'm sorry. Keep going."

Biz winced. "Okay, but you can't tug on my arm that way. I have some bullshit called frozen shoulder." Biz rubbed and squeezed her arm up and down from her upper arm to her wrist. "It happens to women-of-a-certain-age. And it's boring, trust me, but hurts like hell."

"Oh, sorry," said Ruby. She meant it.

"Your Grandma Claire and Great-Aunt Cat were hard at work throwing one of the last parties they would host for a very long time. It was a huge Thornden shindig, loads of people at the house—two hundred at least. Charlie had been traveling with only short visits back home every so often, and we hadn't had much time together. We'd been best friends growing up, and now he was getting married."

Charlie said, "And we'd been, um, experimenting with each other incrementally over the years."

"No shit. And sex was your last hurrah."

Biz said, "Are you going to let me tell this story or not?"

Ruby demurred. "Sorry, I'll stop."

"Jeeze."

"Jeeze," Ruby said, mimicking her mom. "Didn't you guys talk at all? Weren't there phones back in the eighties and nineties?"

"Yes, there were phones. But it was different. There wasn't texting. There was email, but it felt too business-y for a lot of us for a very long time. You have to remember, my generation grew up writing letters. And when you traveled you used pay phones, when you could find one that worked. And if the person didn't pick up, you left a message on an answering machine. But if you had roommates, it couldn't be private. It's hard to explain . . ."

Charlie said, "It was tricky to coordinate, so people didn't talk as much. There were postcards, but . . ."

Biz added, "But we had a big falling-out before he left, so—"

Ruby said, "Over what?"

Biz looked at Charlie and said, "That will remain private."
Charlie nodded in agreement.

"Roger," said Ruby with a little salute.

"So, I digress. Where was I? I'm so old I can never remember
what I was—"

"The engagement party. And you're not old, Mom, you're
only forty-eight. Forty-eight's the new thirty."

"Ha. Thanks, kid. Here's five dollars. So, all the guests had
arrived and there were a million cars in the driveway, and I was
supposed to get more ice. And your Uncle Foster was blocking
everyone in, so I went back to get his keys from him, but I
didn't drive a stick."

"A stick? Was that a Hogwarts broom thing?" asked Ruby.
She honestly didn't know.

"A manual shift car. I'll teach you someday. So your Uncle
Charlie intercepted me and asked where I was going, and I told
him about the ice, and he said he would drive me because he
needed a break."

Ruby turned to Charlie. "You wanted to leave your own
party?"

"People take breaks from parties all the time. We're doing
it now."

"Oh, true. Okay, then what?"

Biz continued, "So we went to get ice and started talking and
on the way back got into deep conversation very quickly . . ." Biz
trailed off, her attention caught by what was left of the tree house
high in a towering maple. Her throat tightened as she thought
about that night. She found it difficult to look directly at Ruby.

Charlie noticed her eyes misting a little and jumped in. "So we were talking, and that led to, um, not talking, and I got out of the car and climbed up the ladder."

Biz pointed to a partial platform with a dangling, rotted railing. Ruby craned her neck. "*That thing?* You two were *whack*."

Charlie said, "We were a little drunk—"

"I was a lot drunk," said Biz, "and I was wearing a dress with the biggest shoulder pads you've ever seen in your life."

"Like a linebacker," Charlie added.

"But I was game," continued Biz. "And the tree house was awesome back then. It was like a cozy fort up in the air, with double-hung windows, and curtains . . ."

"And a bed?" Ruby asked.

"A futon couch," Charlie said, glazing over. The room was coming back into focus. "Covered in pollen, as I recall."

Ruby said, "Ah. Ye olde futon couch. They factored largely into your generation, didn't they? All my friends' parents had them in their basements growing up."

Biz said, "How would you . . . You know what? Don't tell me." They all stood wordless for a moment, drinking in the last vestiges of where Ruby might have been conceived as if they were looking at the detritus of a shipwreck.

"And the ice?" Ruby asked after a reasonable pause.

"Soaked the back of Foster's car. But we salvaged some of it. We weren't, um, long."

"So, a quickie? I was possibly conceived *in a quickie?*"

"It was slightly more romantic than that," said Charlie.

"Only slightly," Biz said, and Ruby laughed. Biz felt a deeply profound sense of relief to be telling her story to Ruby, as if the shell around her heart were finally breaking open, letting in sunlight, allowing it to beat freely. "It was a . . . decidedly poor choice."

"You and your 'Make good choices.' What a killjoy," said Ruby. "And what a hypocrite!"

"If you want me to be brutally honest, I think I was worried I was on the verge of losing my best friend. In my day, wives didn't let their new husbands keep contact with their former female friends. Once a guy got married, that was it, finito. Those friendships ended."

"Why?"

"There was no Facebook. No texting or Insta, no way to keep in touch, and phone calls and letters seemed too intimate."

Charlie added, "Because they *were* intimate."

Biz continued, "The wives felt threatened—sad but true—so I panicked, plain and simple. I felt this was the end of us and I think I just wanted a souvenir piece of him for myself."

Charlie smirked, "So to speak."

Ruby said, "Ew, that's gross."

Biz rolled her eyes, then elbowed him in the ribs.

"So what you're saying is, I'm like a key chain?" Ruby joked.

Biz said, "You're more than a souvenir."

Charlie added, "Only slightly. But to be serious, I want to add, I felt the same way for the same reasons. I think I thought this would keep us connected to each other even if our lives became separate. I knew it was wrong, obviously, but . . ." Here Charlie paused, then looked away. "I'd always felt the rules didn't apply to us."

Ruby snickered. "God, you guys sure did lead a life of privilege. I've wondered if you were ever self-aware enough to notice. All of you in your tiny white world, forging ahead as if nothing else existed. Well, I exist, so thanks for conceiving me. I'm hella glad to be out in the actual world. Let's hope I'm more self-aware than you two. Kidding, not kidding. You guys are great." Ruby got off her high horse and looked at her mother and her Uncle Charlie. "And how do you both feel about each other now?"

Neither of them said a word, so they all just turned and headed back. It was a topic for which neither of them had prepared.

.   .   .

By Tuesday, Claire was fully moved out, and painters were scraping flocked wallpaper, and painting every room a dismal—yet inexplicably popular—shade of putty gray. She was doing her level best to keep from feeling any sense of regret. A final walk through the formerly vibrant and colorful house offered only echoes and scuff marks to remind her of the past. The stagers had brought in their own "fresh and updated" furnishings, which had offended Claire to no end. To keep things cheery, Rah gathered all the women on Cat's backyard patio. It was time to write out table-number cards and tie rainbow ribbons around Almond Joys. Looking to spark a lively debate, Rah asked the group, "To what do you think we owe the Thornden downfall?" Cat scoffed, but Biz hit the table with her palm and said, "Ding! My drunken car accident, hands down." Ruby also hit a pretend buzzer and offered, "I would have said your bastard child takes the cake." Biz said, "I get it. Cake. I'm a baker. Hardy-har." Cat said, "My affair with Ned definitely got the ball rolling." Georgia hit the table and opined, "E.J.'s comedy set was the straw, for sure." Ruby said, "What comedy set?" and they all colluded in pretending not to hear her. Rah suggested it was Georgia's arrest that did them in. Georgia grinned and said, "Or what about the whole Charlie-might-be-Ruby's-dad thing?"

Ruby jumped in. "That gets my vote."

"Piper's affair," reminded Biz.

"Foster's affair," Georgia added, then, "My affair!" and they all laughed.

Nana Miggs said quietly, "My affair," and their eyes grew as wide as their smiles.

"I don't like this game," said Claire.

"Well, I'm playing the bride card," said Rah, and pointed to Susan, who hit the table and then threw all vest-wearing lesbians under the bus. Cat guffawed, so Rah rebutted by throwing all divorcées under there with them. Ruby reminded everyone of her mother's scandal with Finn at the bakery, which Biz pointed out wouldn't have been a scandal if she hadn't called 911, then texted all her friends. Nana Miggs winked at Ruby and said, "Nice going, kid." Ruby chuckled, embarrassed, then added, "Or was it Aunt Cat and the principal?"

"Oh, yes!" said Biz, turning to Aunt Cat. "I've always meant to ask—"

"*Mom!*" gasped Rah. Her face was shocked; she'd never heard. Aunt Cat collected her thoughts, then spoke sheepishly. "There might have been ten minutes in there between your father and Ned . . ." Howls overtook the room as Susan slung her arm around Rah, who hung her head in her hands for comic effect. Biz and Georgia fanned themselves—hot flashes taking over—and Rah said to Susan, "Are you sure you want to marry into this cockamamie family of dysfunction? You could get up from the table now and run as fast as you can . . ."

"I couldn't be more sure," said Susan, and planted a sweet kiss on Rah's lips.

Cat said, "Well, I think we're damn lucky to have you."

"Thanks. I think you are, too," cracked Susan. The room broke up. "Notice I'm waiting until *after* we're legally married before I let you all *really* get to know *my* family." More chuckling as each woman was warmed by Susan's love for their caring Rah. Susan continued, "Honestly, I couldn't be more impressed that you're all still speaking to one another. In my family . . . forget it."

Biz said, "Sometimes I think life is just one long painful repeat exercise in forgiving everyone."

Georgia added, "And ourselves."

"Yes. Boy, oh, boy. *Especially* ourselves."

Claire rolled her eyes as she lit a cigarette. Cat noticed her derision and said, "Still think this family's reputation is salvageable?" Claire looked around the table at all the bright, expectant smiles. Everyone seemed to be trying to find their way. They'd all made poor choices, and she had, too. In that moment Claire chose to accept the reality that none of their children had turned out the way she'd planned. And that was okay. It would have to be. They had done their Thornden best.

Biz said, "Well, Mom? What's the verdict?"

Claire exhaled a thin plume of smoke. "I give up. I've decided to no longer care."

The women looked agape at one another, then erupted into raucous cheers.

The day before the wedding, the bakery was humming. Muriel pulled the cake layers out of the freezer ahead of time, and Biz came in early to do the filling and crumb coating. Georgia joined them in the back after assembly and frosting were complete so they could all decorate it together. Rah's directions to them had been "Knock yourselves out," so they planned to do just that. Huddled around a chocolate cake holding pastry bags in different shades of green Swiss meringue icing, they wore BER-NADETTA'S aprons and sipped coffee while they worked. Except for Biz, who was taking a brief dance break to sing along to "Put Your Records On" beneath the framed NO SMOKING, BIZ! sign. Muriel had hung it with mockery years ago, and though the laws had become more strict and Biz had long since quit, they left it up for comic relief.

Muriel hadn't changed save for an additional fifteen "happy" pounds she'd put on since she and Finn got together. They made her hourglass figure look even more lush, and she radiated the energy of a woman cherished by the right man. Muriel was extremely generous with Biz and bestowed upon her an oeuvre of cake-decorating expertise. Biz blossomed once she made peace with her default career and began to respect the discipline and finesse inherent in the cakely arts. She fully embraced gum-paste sculpture as the means of indulging her creative whimsy; her cakes impressed the hell out of patrons and bakers alike. It took time and effort, but the practice was worth it—Biz felt a creative resurgence. Her new bliss was wild cake embellishment and she thanked the universe every night.

Biz inched the tall fondant-covered cake around slowly on a raised rotating iron stand while applying diagonal stripes of buttercream frosting in shades of chartreuse and parakeet green. It was meant to suggest the forest where Rah and Susan met on a college birding trip. Georgia and Muriel, in charge of gum-paste birds and wildflowers, were succeeding and failing with various degrees of charm. There was also an attempt at matching sleeping bags and pajamas. And two statuettes of lady birders, with oversized binoculars trained on each other, were awaiting placement on center top.

Finn walked upstairs from his shared basement office, where Muriel was helping him learn a new bookkeeping program for his business. He laughed as soon as he saw the cake. Biz said,

"Excellent! That's the reaction we're going for. We hope to make the bride and bride giggle." With wide open arms he boomed, "Hello, darlings! Give us some kisses." Finn was genuinely pleased to see Biz and Georgia there. He walked around the table, giving them both pecks on the cheek, then landed a juicy one on Muriel with a warm embrace.

"Thanks for the sugar, sugar," she said, and returned his randy smirk. "Hey, do us a favor, will ya? Load these into the car. Cookies first, then come back for the cake."

A lithe, tanned blond woman in a linen sundress and boho sandals peeked around a tall rack of baking sheets. "I'm sorry to interrupt. I was told the bathroom was through the kitchen."

Finn said, "Oh, hey, Amanda. Right through here."

Biz spat, "*Tindy?!* Wow. Finn?" It was Tindy-friggin'-Weldon.

Finn said, "I've been working for Amanda off and on for years. How do you two—"

"We roomed together in college." Biz forced a thin grin as she introduced Tindy to Georgia and Muriel, whose names she promptly forgot. Once recovered, Biz said by way of welcome, "How are you, Tindy? I mean, Amanda. What brings you into Bernadetta's bakery?"

"I'm picking up a strawberry rhubarb pie." Tindy's smile was nervous, genuine, and shy. Biz's smile was frozen and totally unnatural. "Yum," she managed to add. Then Finn broke the awkwardness. "Well, it was nice running into you." Everyone nodded like idiots in agreement.

"Yes. Me, too. Oh, and I guess I'll see you tomorrow night at your cousin's wedding."

"You *will*?" Biz was thrown, yet again. Tindy continued tentatively. "Um, I have plans I can't cancel, but Charlie told me it was casual and that I should stop by afterwards for dancing."

Georgia blurted out, "*Charlie* Charlie?" then felt like a total dork.

Muriel glossed over her remark. "How lovely. Like as his date?"

Tindy shook her head. "Um, no. Or, I don't think so. I'm single. Divorced, so maybe. But . . . I'm not sure. I just bumped into him at The Wonder at a birthday party for my son."

In a gesture of supreme generosity, Biz rescued the moment. "It doesn't matter. Come as you are. We'd love to have you. It'll be nice to catch up and for Charlie to have a dance partner. He loves to dance."

Tindy lit up. "Oh, so do I!"

"Okay, then," said Muriel, with slightly less generosity.

"Okay. I'll use the restroom," said Tindy, and ducked behind the door.

Georgia whispered, "Is anyone going to ask her if she had an affair with Charlie while—"

Biz elbowed Georgia, "No, shh," then added, "She seems nice." Finn offered, "She is. Lovely woman. Pleasure working with her. Always pays on time, mannerly."

Biz said in a hushed tone, "Of course she is. And she looks fucking fabulous. I know you're all thinking it. I am. Why couldn't she be a bitch? Or have leprosy or a hump?" Biz felt a hot flash begin to well inside and take over her sweaty body's useless, broken temperature gauge. She unbuttoned her blouse as low as decorum would civilly allow, grabbed a flattened cupcake box, and fanned herself like a maniac. "Of course I'm flashing, adding insult to injury. She probably doesn't even get them."

Georgia said, "Why are you getting so uppity? I thought you'd be happy for him—"

Muriel startled in her chair a little. "Oh, crap."

Biz said, "What?" so she wouldn't have to address Georgia's remark.

"Is now the time to tell you that Hugh finally eloped with that dental hygienist?"

Finn said, "The one with the big boobs?"

Biz asked, "Once a fallback, always a fallback. There goes my chance."

"Bullshit. You had your chance for nine years!"

Biz said, "People can simmer on your back burner for a very long time. What made you think of that, Muriel—does she have leprosy?"

"No," said Muriel sheepishly, "she's gorgeous. And young."

"Nope," Biz said, still fanning herself, processing the information, turning it over in her head. "Not a good time," she said, and tried not to cry.

"I didn't think so," said Muriel, and grabbed a flattened box to help fan. "Definitely not a good time."

On the big day, the reimagining of the Thorndens as a family embracing diversity and acceptance was in full view for all guests to witness and appreciate. The house and yard had cleaned up nicely. The trampoline was disassembled, and they'd lost the pool to Claire's side but, thank heavens, kept the Ping-Pong shed. There were strings of white Christmas lights wrapped loosely around shrubs and trees, and locally sourced daffodils, tulips, and hyacinth in mason jars dotted card tables with vintage tablecloths and candles. A sign on a wicker basket suggested that guests leave their cell phones and pick up a bottle of bubble stuff with a small wand to keep their thumbs occupied. An iPod with a nineties playlist stood in beautifully for a live band, and deviled eggs were, of course, omnipresent.

Rah and Susan looked amazing, though both would have scoffed at the thought that somehow their outfits bore mentioning over the importance of legalized gay marriage in their state. Nevertheless, Rah looked very sharp in a white collared shirt with crisp oatmeal linen pants, and Susan wore a long-sleeved white dress with a slight scoop neck and zero appliqué. They each sported a crown of white roses, daisies, and hydrangea—and held hands all day, teary and beaming. The entire family was in attendance, minus Piper, who said she had a work trip. E.J. arrived late with his new girlfriend and missed cocktail hour, much to everyone's relief. Les came with his business and life partner, Gerard, whom Biz was thrilled to see. She introduced them to everyone at the whole wedding, saying, "This is my dad and his partner-partner." And Dick slid into the back row for just the abbreviated outdoor service, then made a hasty departure with his trophy wife and their sullen fourteen-year-old son.

The fence Rah had put in did a great job of ensuring their privacy, but the white balloons confused more than a few prospective buyers looking for Claire's open house. So for five hours, friendly young couples—dressed smartly and wanting to make the right impression—wandered into the wrong house and had to be sweetly turned away. By the middle of Susan and Rah's vows it became something of a running joke. And by late afternoon, a chorus of drunken revelers could be heard shouting jovially, "Next door!" then pointing at the other side of the fence in hilarity. Biz occupied herself by doing everything in her power to not drink in order to obliterate the thought of Tindy as Charlie's date. To this end she reverted to her inner waitress and cleared all the dishes, swooping in within nanoseconds of unsuspecting guests' last bite. Charlie kept an eye on his film-student videographers, giving them tips on lighting and composition, while Ned bartended alongside Ruby's and Gigi's boyfriends, Miguel and Oliver.

Gordon's full-time job was to tend to Nana Miggs, who still cut a modest but legitimate rug. When Charlie rolled the piano out to the patio, she insisted Gordon dance with her. They requested "Make Someone Happy" and together with Susan and Rah were first on the floor. Foster asked Georgia to dance, which shocked more than a few. She made a fuss at first for comedy's sake, but by the third song he had her laughing. Others joined in and held someone tight: Finn and Muriel; Ned and Cat; Rebekah and her husband; and even E.J. and his new girlfriend. The Greats danced with either their dates or each other, and the rest of the floor filled in with friends of the newlyweds from various chapters of their lives. It was easy to tell their Austin friends from their chemical-engineering and bird-nerd friends. Someone projected a slide show against a white sheet held between two trees. Charlie's live playing added an old-timey sweetness to the slowly moving, cross-faded images of Susan and Rah falling in fabulous love. When the slide show was over, the tissues were gone and Charlie kept going. He played jazzy lounge versions of "Harvest Moon," "Brass in Pocket," and "Valerie," and everyone danced.

With the exception of the cynical mother/daughter team of Claire and Biz. Perennially too prickly to invite offers, Claire looked perfectly contented picking up empty glasses and dirty plates, just as Biz had done earlier. Horrified to see herself in her mother, Biz shuddered, then vowed her mother's plight would *not* be her own. Though she had no one to dance with, Biz swayed on the outskirts with defiant optimism, enjoying the movement of synchronistic feet and watching Charlie play. Later, Gordon's grandson, DJ Davy-Dave, took over and played an awesome mix of seventies and eighties pop. Charlie sidled up to Biz and asked if she wanted to dance. "C'mon. It's 'Got to Get You into My Life.' You can't not dance to Earth, Wind, and Fire. It's the law."

"Isn't Tindy showing up soon?" she said without looking in his direction.

"Biz," he started, then stopped. "I bumped into her, and—"

"You don't have to explain."

"Right," he said. "She's just an old friend. And she's not coming until later. So dance with me now. Everyone else is out there. Our whole family is—"

"No, thank you."

"Why not?"

She snapped at Charlie, "You know why. *Because we can't.* We're . . . *not everybody.*"

"That's just it, I think we are." They watched their family and the true friends they'd amassed, with Susan and Rah at the center of it all, completely at ease and full of joy. Cat and Ned danced over, saying, "Come on, you two, get out here!" but Biz waved them off with a fake smile.

"See? It's okay now," Charlie implored.

"Well, I think we should wait."

"For what?" He faced her. She had no choice but to look at him. "The second coming? The zombie apocalypse?" He said it with a slight laugh, hoping that if he made light of the situation she would relent.

"Yes, the zombie apocalypse. Or when everyone we know is vaporized from space. Or we're shipwrecked. Or sent to colonize Mars. Though they probably wouldn't choose us. Plus I would hate the weather. Though if Matt Damon were there . . ."

"I'm serious, Biz."

"So am I," she said, and her throat choked up. Her eyes began to water. Biz turned away from him, refusing to wipe anything away with so many people watching. Damn her hormones. Menopause was turning every conversation she had into a Lifetime movie, and it sucked. "I think we missed our chance," she said, resigned to giving up.

Charlie continued his plea. "The kids don't need us anymore. They're all basically good—no one's in jail, no unplanned pregnancies. That we know of." Biz elicited a "Ha" along with one raised eyebrow. Charlie felt a familiar rush; if he could still make her laugh, he had a chance. "In the scheme of things," he said, "none of it matters anymore."

Finn careened by with champagne flutes full to the brim. "Elizabeth and Charles! Glad to see you two finally together." He winked, then hustled by.

"We're not!" Biz called after him, but he was gone. Through gritted teeth and a fake smile she said, "Please don't make me have this conversation here. I'm too hormonal and frankly, I'm forty-eight. *We're almost fifty.* That ship has sailed. The horse has left the station or the barn after the door or something. I can't remember anything anymore. This fucking menopause. I'm losing my mind."

Charlie gently placed his hands on her shoulders and very seriously said, "So am I." He was through pretending. He wanted to spend the rest of his life with her starting tonight. Sooner than tonight—*beginning with the next song.* He hoped it was something romantic. Biz panicked. She felt hardened and convinced she'd lost her chance at love and was destined to wither away. But now this guy—her damn first cousin—was looking at her with those stupid eyelashes and that damn dimple, still caring for her, interested, and wanting to make her laugh. *This,* she thought, *is everything and terrifying.*

Out of the corner of her eye Biz caught a leggy blonde moving toward them. Relieved and annoyed all at once, she said, "Perfect timing."

"Shit," Charlie said under his breath as Biz waved Tindy over.

Soon after their greeting Tindy began to explain why she was late. Biz ignored her, nodded, and gave them a shove toward the dance floor. "Later, gators. Get dancing, you crazy kids. No time to waste."

Charlie and Tindy danced awkwardly to "I Confess," her long legs stepping out of time to the English Beat's fast ska. Her toned shoulders glistened under the twinkling fairy lights. *Michelle Obama's arms have ruined it for the rest of us,* Biz thought as she watched Charlie and Tindy for as long as she could withstand the torture. Biz's Irish ankles and frozen shoulder would never be able to compete with Tindy's arms, even if she . . . *Oh, forget it. It's never going to happen.* So, she watched, complacent in the knowledge that so many members of her family were inching toward whatever happiness they would allow themselves. And that at least Tindy would always be a lousy dancer.

Sissy Bickers walked up with Hugh and Mrs. Hugh trailing. Biz wanted more than ever to commit seppuku. Sissy introduced them, then bubbled with inane pablum about their elopement and how adorable the whole thing was. "Oh, my gosh, wouldn't it be fun if they bought the house next door?" Sissy gushed, and Biz echoed, "Fun!" with manic game-show glee. But she was gracious with her congratulations and managed not to slug Sissy—even when she leaned in after Hugh and Mrs. Hugh left and whispered, "Missed your chance." Muriel saw what was brewing from across the yard and swooped in to save her friend. Thankfully there was a diversion: Fuck You Carl. Frail and skittish at best, he was waiting on the sidewalk in front of the house. He had come to pay his respects to the brides. Biz offered Fuck You Carl her arm and led him around back to see Susan and Rah. As he offered a quiet "Fuck you," locals watched reverently as if a visiting dignitary were on the premises. Folks on the dance floor called out, "Fuck you, Carl!" with a hearty welcoming wave once they recognized him, and a few went over to say hello. The gleam in his eyes told folks that though the script was the same, his words belied a worn-out, softened heart. After a few sips of coffee Biz packed him off with a piece of wedding cake, some leftovers, and as much of a hug as the old man could handle.

"That was sweet of you," Ruby said to her mother, and nudged her in the shoulder. "I think everyone got a kick out of it. And he looked as happy as I've ever seen him. I think he'd even combed his hair."

"I'm a pushover," said Biz, but she meant idiot. She was watching Charlie dance with Tindy to "Cheek to Cheek" in great galumphing stomps, arms practically flailing. Even Ruby could see they were mismatched. "Is that woman having a seizure of some kind?"

"Be nice" was all Biz said. She wished desperately she could cut in on them. She wanted to show Ruby how it looked when two people are in total sync and gliding through the air in each other's arms as if the universe were leading. "I'm a very good dancer," Biz said, then whipped around to her daughter and gasped, "Oh my God, you've never seen me dance, have you?"

"No," said Ruby. Biz almost burst into tears. *My own daughter has never seen me truly happy,* she thought. *I can't take it. This wedding is killing me.*

Rebekah joined the mother-daughter team. "What's going on? I noticed you look a little off. Are you okay?"

"I'm fine. Couldn't be happier for the lucky couple."

"Be that as it may . . ."

Biz fought off tears. "People know what torture weddings are for single people, right?"

"No, dear, most of them don't. They're only thinking about themselves."

"Right! I keep forgetting. I need to have that tattooed on my forehead."

"Or not," Rebekah said, and put her arm around Biz.

Ruby asked, "Hey, Dr. Rebekah, don't you think Mom and Uncle-Cousin-Maybe-Daddy would make a nice couple?"

"It's not up to me," said Rebekah. Biz shook her head no. She was working incredibly hard not to cry and thought it best not to speak. Then Ruby lit up. "Do you know anything about genetic testing?"

"I do," said Rebekah, "as a matter of fact."

"Can you do me?" gasped Ruby. Biz gave Rebekah a highly suspect look.

"Sure, I just need a cheek scrape. Open your mouth and say, 'Ahh.'" Ruby did as she was told, and Rebekah wrapped a clean cocktail napkin around the tip of her finger and scraped the inside of Ruby's mouth. Then she inspected it closely and held it up as if checking for wind direction. Biz rolled her eyes.

"Yup, he's your father," said Rebekah.

Ruby cracked up. "Very scientific."

Rebekah smiled and said, "What do you care? Do you want him to be your dad?"

Biz snuck a peek at Ruby, who answered, "Heck, yeah! That would be so fun!"

"Okay, then, poof—he's your dad."

"You're amazing. I'm going to go tell Gigi we're half sisters."

Ruby took off. Biz looked askance and said, "Really?"

"Remember that day you brought Ruby in? The day of your accident? You handed me a hair follicle. I ran the test, but you never brought it up, so I didn't, either."

"And? What did it say?" Biz said.

"What do you want it to say?"

"Cut the shit, Becky."

Rebekah patted her friend on the back and said, "She's Charlie's."

Biz's heart exploded. She felt a seismic shift somewhere deep within as if her soul had begun a great waltz and didn't know whether to laugh or cry so did both. Rebekah was whisked away by her husband, but thankfully Muriel noticed Biz, looking schizophrenic. Hooking Biz's arm in hers she said, "You're laughing by yourself, and you look insane."

"I'm fine," said Biz.

"Like hell you are. And you're not dancing, even though everyone knows you should be. And even though you and Charlie are relatively smart, you're both too stupid to admit you want to be together."

"*He's* not too stupid. He told me earlier."

"And what did *you* say?"

"That it was too late and I'd never have tits like Tindy's or arms like Michelle Obama's."

"You said *that*? Then you're a dipshit. Why don't you get

over yourself? According to my yoga instructor, you're not supposed to care what other people think." Muriel waited for a pithy comeback, but Biz only said, "You're taking yoga?"

Nana Miggs shuffled up on Gordon's arm and spoke admonishingly. "Look at them. Pathetic. No chemistry." They knew damn well she was referring to Charlie and Tindy. "You two should be out there. These are *your* friends. And Rah's lesbians. *We all love you. We want to see you happy.*" Biz wanted to be happy so badly—so badly she was afraid to want it. She ached to want it.

Muriel said, "Nana Miggs, you seem mad."

"I am mad. *I'm livid!*"

Muriel said, "I agree with your grandmother. This motley crew has made dumb mistakes, too, ya know, and if they haven't yet, they will. No one is throwing stones in this crowd, except maybe Tindy, but she's too dumb to understand the metaphor." They all looked at Tindy dancing totally out of step to "Take on Me"—knees up in the air on the offbeat, Charlie looking pained.

Nana Miggs commanded Biz, "Go dance with Charlie and tell the world I said to buzz off."

Muriel said, "Yeah, you've got tits. *Good tits.* Show us how it's done, cowgirl."

"But I've got frozen shoulder and I'm hot-flashing like once an hour. I'm a mess, and she looks like a Rockette."

Nana Miggs said, "We don't care and neither does he."

"But he's . . ." Biz broke down and finally began to sob. "He's my cousin and . . . and . . ." How could she tell them the truth about Ruby? How would they take it? What would Larkspur think? *How would her mother react?!* Biz's shoulders began to shake.

Nana Miggs said, "I've had enough. Muriel, go find my daughter Catherine and tell her to meet me on the patio immediately." Muriel did as she was told while Nana Miggs and Gordon shepherded Biz over to a quiet couch in the corner of the far patio.

"You rang?" said Cat, then, "Biz, sweetie, what's wro—"

"Sit," said Nana Miggs, and her daughter sat next to Biz.

"What's going—"

Nana Miggs said, "Look at me, young lady." Cat looked squarely at her mother. "When you and Dick returned from your year in London, whose baby did you return with?"

Cat was thrown. So far, in her long life, she didn't have a good answer to that question because no one had ever posed it. "Uh, um," she stuttered, "what a crazy thing to—"

"It's not crazy and you know it. Was it Dick's mistress's? His mother's?" Now Biz was thrown. "*What?!*" she said. "Are you talking about Charlie's Grandmother Agnes?"

"Who were you protecting, young lady?" Nana Miggs continued fiercely. "Answer me, Cat. Your son's very happiness depends on it."

Cat knew her mother was right. Times had changed, and there was no longer a legitimate reason to protect anyone from the truth. *This was 2014!* Dick, Claire, hell, the entire town would have to deal with it. Her son deserved happiness and was only going to find it with Biz.

Cat sighed. "He was Peggy's."

Nana Miggs said, "I assumed as much. That baby was too big for his age."

Biz said, "Who's Peggy?" She'd stopped crying, but her head was pounding.

Cat was shocked. "Mom, *you knew* and didn't say anything?"

"It was only a hunch. What was I going to say? You'd made a grown-up decision and a very brave choice, and I didn't want to put you in a position of having to lie to me. If I was wrong, then it was moot. Either way, Dunny and I were thrilled you finally had a baby of your own. And at the end of the day it didn't matter to us where our Choo came from."

Cat went on, "Except to Dick. Agnes didn't account for her son's hardened heart."

Nana Miggs asked sharply, "Did she threaten you two?"

"Not exactly. But she pulled strings at the bank to get us sent over there when she found out about Peggy. I think she might have been someone powerful's mistress. Dick was promoted and given a raise, which meant everything to him, and I didn't mind not having to go through the whole adoption rigmarole. Plus she set up a trust for him. It's where the theater money came from. It's his money."

"*Who's Peggy!?*" demanded Biz, feeling invisible.

Nana Miggs said, "Cat, tell her."

Cat pivoted to Biz. "Charlie's father, Dick, had a sister, Peggy. She lived in London and became unwittingly pregnant at the same time Dick and I were trying to conceive. She was unmarried, and her reputation would have suffered irreparable damage. So the baby was offered to us—"

"Thrust upon you," interrupted Nana Miggs.

"But I didn't feel that way. He felt like mine from the moment I laid eyes on him. I bonded with him immediately. His father, however . . ."

Nana Miggs was irate. "Dick was a prick, and you were lucky to be rid of him. I'm not surprised he didn't have the generosity of heart to raise another man's child as his own."

Biz was still confused. "But why didn't you tell Charlie?"

Cat said, "We didn't want him to feel unwanted. Or to be treated like a bastard child by anyone else, or especially himself. That was a real thing in my day, and we didn't want it to affect his self-worth. We were naïve. We thought we were doing the right thing."

Biz asked, "But wasn't it worse that people thought we were related?"

Cat said, "I always thought you two would find other people, so I was willing to wait and see. He found Piper, so I never had to tell him. But now I realize you were the one all along. I hope you'll forgive me."

"So that means . . ."

Nana Miggs said, "It means it doesn't matter what we think and it never did."

Cat added, "It means you and Charlie are not first cousins. You're not even blood relatives. Now go tell Charlie and tomorrow I'll tell your mother."

Muriel told the DJ what to play while Biz excitedly cut in on Tindy, explaining she would need to borrow Charlie for an unplanned, two-person nuptial flash mob. Tindy was gracious and Charlie perplexed, but not half as surprised as the hot, perspiring crowd when the funk juggernaut "Brick House" switched gears mid-song. Some let out an "Aww" of disappointment, but at the familiar opening bass line the Thornden clan let out a huge whoop. Michael Jackson's "Don't Stop 'Til You Get Enough" was about to blast off. They hoped the infectious beat meant Charlie and Biz would be doing one of their terribly choreographed routines from childhood. Foster had heard tell of the lore. And when Charlie and Biz moved to the center of the dance floor and froze in a tableau like Olympic ice skaters, E.J., Georgia, Foster, and Cat knew their dreams had come true. Rah signaled Susan to come watch, Gordon moved Nana Miggs closer, and Claire good-naturedly resigned any opposition and sat.

What followed was possibly the worst dance spectacle set to a Michael Jackson hit ever choreographed by preteens and performed by forty-eight-year-olds. Charlie had forgotten most of the steps, and Biz could only use one arm because of her frozen shoulder, but they boogied and twirled just as poorly and robustly as ever. Even after Charlie pushed up his sleeves and Biz kicked off her shoes, they still danced like Fred and Ginger's lesser-talented relatives. Grapevining and moonwalking themselves into an unattractive flop sweat, they giggled as the jitterbug and a bit of bus stop were triumphantly remembered. There were moves borrowed from *Flashdance, Grease, Dirty Dancing,* and *Saturday Night Fever* that were so bad they were unrecognizable to all but family.

Some onlookers laughed so hard they wept. The pair were dazzling in their commitment and ineptitude. When one of the New Hampshire guests asked Ruby and Gigi who was dancing, their response was earnest and simultaneous. Gigi said, "My dad and Aunt Cousin," and Ruby said, "My mom and Uncle Dad." The guest looked confounded but unruffled. At the historic conclusion, Biz and Charlie lay collapsed on the dance floor and the audience cheered like crazy. It was without a doubt one of Susan and Rah's favorite wedding presents and sealed Biz and Charlie's fate, publicly and forever.

While Charlie and Biz were still on their backs, catching their breath, Susan and Rah and a few others stopped by to compliment their abysmal choreography. They gave all credit to dancing school, then the music cranked up again and everyone's shoes were kicked off into the grass. Still panting in a pool of their own sweat and lost dignity, she said to him, "You're not going to believe what I'm about to tell you." "What?" he said, feeling the joy of exhaustive fun for the first time in years—until Tindy's voice interrupted them. "Great job, guys!" she cheered, making her way over. "Are you two professionals?" She wasn't kidding; she spoke without irony. Biz quickly said to Charlie, "Stop by tomorrow morning. I'm going to blow your mind," then kissed him on the lips, directly and purposefully, in front of Tindy and a reception full of loved ones no longer paying attention.

Charlie stopped by Biz's first thing. He'd been awakened early by his mother, who called to ask if he'd had fun at the wedding, and to remind him he should live the life he wants to. This was his second chance, Cat said—*don't waste it*. He thanked her before hanging up, though he hadn't realized his mother liked Tindy so much or had even had the chance to know her. It felt like an odd chat for eight on a Sunday morning.

His head buzzed with anticipation as he knocked on Biz's door, and he realized he was incredibly excited to see her. It took her a while to answer. "Hi," she said, opening the door in her pajamas. She looked a wreck and sounded like Louis Armstrong.

"Is Ruby mine?" he asked, unable to feign detachment one second longer.

"Even better. But easy, cowboy, come in." Biz's hair stuck up funny in the back, and her eyes were pink and puffy.

"You're sick," said Charlie.

She waved him off. "Probably just coming down with a cold. Did you bring me soup?"

"I didn't know you were sick, but I'm happy to go get you some."

The cell phone in her hand buzzed. "Hold on a sec," she said then looked at her phone. "Match.com." Into the phone she said, "Oh, hey! That sounds super fun, but I can't. I've got prior plans." Then she reached outside the doorjamb and felt for the doorbell. She pressed it, and it went ding-dong just like in a cartoon. Into the phone she said, "That's my ride, gotta fly. Talk to you soon," and hung up. She looked blankly at Charlie. He looked back at her, incredulous.

"Is that to make men think you're popular?" said Charlie. The idea of Biz dating other men was not sitting well, never did. He thought the two of them, after last night with their dance and that kiss . . . but maybe he thought wrong. *What the heck's going on?*

Biz said, "Whatever it takes, my friend. Muriel taught me that one. Works like a charm."

"On *whom*?"

"On *everybody*. Or at least everyone online. It's a gullible demo out there, and at my age I've got to play every card trick I've got. How's Tindy?"

"She's, uh . . . she had a blast last night," said Charlie.

It wasn't what Biz had hoped to hear; her confidence started to slip. "You know what? Don't tell me," she muttered, and yanked last night's clothes off the floor one piece at a time with her toes. "I have exciting news for you. Maybe you should sit down. You want breakfast?"

"You sit down. I'll make it." Charlie opened the fridge. "How about eggs and toast?"

"Perfect," she said, sitting, light-headed but happy to be alone with him.

Biz watched Charlie cook, forcing herself to wish him and Tindy well. They'd lost Grandpa Dun, Dick, and Piper along the way, but they'd gained Gordon and Rebekah, Finn and Muriel, Gerard—and now Tindy. She thought about the circularity of her life and wondered if everyone's worked that way—people reemerging from the past to play totally new and unexpected roles in the present. She wondered how many more randoms from her past were still likely to pepper her future. There was that old adage in show business about being nice to the people you meet on the way up because you're going to see them again on the way down. Biz rewrote it in her head: "Be nice to the people you meet on the way up because you're going to end up fucking some of them, and rooming with others, and they're going to end up marrying your friends, and maybe moving in next door, and possibly ending up as your child's pediatrician, or your cousin's husband, so watch your step, pal, and be kind and forgiving to everyone." Had a nice ring to it. Would make a good bumper sticker.

"So what's the news?" asked Charlie. He was dying, trying to be casual.

"I'll wait until we eat."

"Tell me now. I can cook and listen at the same time."

But it turned out Charlie could not. Biz told him about his birth mom, Aunt Peggy; his Grandmother Agnes; his sculptor dad; and the wily web that was woven. The butter burned while he took in the news, so Biz turned off the stovetop. "I don't understand," Charlie said over and over. Biz sat him down and answered his questions, summoning reserves of love and empathy for him she never knew existed.

"So then, you and I . . ." he said, stunned.

"Are not related by blood."

"And Ruby . . ."

"Is your daughter by blood."

"And you . . ."

Biz paused. "I'm your best friend."

"Is that all?"

"I guess so. What about Tindy?"

"Didn't work out."

"Ya think?" Biz laughed. Charlie wanted to but was in shock. He wanted to jump and yell and high-five the sky, but instead he hugged Biz. It was a long grappling bear hug, and he buried his head into her neck as he cried tears of anger, joy, blame, and regret, wondering which one would trump the rest. Into her tear-moistened ear he said, "There's an entire universe I'm feeling and things I want to ask my mother—and my conversation this morning with her is now making a lot more sense. But one thing that's very clear is I love you, I have always loved you, and I think we should be together forever, starting right now."

"*Really?*" asked Biz. Still, she worried. She knew Charlie was in shock and might not feel this way next week when all the news had a chance to sink in. "What if I'm too old?" she said. "Remember how broken I am? And I think I've forgotten how to have sex. I'm fairly certain my hymen has regrown itself."

Charlie laughed loudly. "What if *I've* forgotten? I'm not who I once was . . ."

"Promise?" said Biz with a slight grin. She was tingling.

Charlie shook his head. "Back in the tree house I was nervous and didn't, um, tend to you as well as I should have. I'd like the chance to try again," he said kindly, and drank her in.

She was pale with greasy hair and residual mascara under one eye, but he adored her with every fiber of his being. Charlie reached for his iPhone, pulled up a song, and set the phone into her dock. The dreamlike reverie of the Stones' strumming guitar on "Waiting on a Friend" filled the apartment, and Biz swooned. "Will you dance with me? For real and not jokey this time?" said Charlie, holding out his hand. The morning sunlight brightened the celery walls of Biz's little kitchen as Mick Jagger whistled his friendly, beckoning tune. Biz took Charlie's hand without reservation, held it as tightly as she could, and let him lift her into his arms to dance.

The playlist transitioned and they glided effortlessly into the living room during the Talking Heads' "Naïve Melody," and Keb Mo's "Life Is Beautiful." Biz felt like a breeze in Charlie's arms, taken care of, safe and calm. They slow-danced circles around the coffee table and couch, then into Biz's bedroom, until she was light-headed and had to sit. Charlie leaned her back in his lap and scratched her head and squeezed her neck, then rubbed her shoulders, down to her arms and wrists and fingers. Biz began to tear up—again. She hadn't known a true love; his kindness was overwhelming, and she felt cherished.

Damn, these hormones are relentless, she thought. "Why are you being so nice to me?" she asked, dabbing her eyes with her pajama sleeve.

"Because I can be, now. And I want to take care of you. Because life is short."

"And long, according to Nana Miggs."

"It's that, too," Charlie said, then leaned her back up and turned to face her. "What if I asked to kiss you, not to practice for other people, or because I'm drunk, or horny, or scared of wanting you or losing you, but because I like you. And love you."

Biz answered by closing her eyes. Charlie lifted the hair off her neck and kissed her just at the nape, behind the ear, until she weakened and jolted awake. He moved in to kiss her deeply, desiring to rediscover every part of her. He couldn't believe he was here again with her—this person who had occupied so much space in his mind and body over the years. She'd never completely left him. And now he could devour her in small mouthfuls. Biz wanted to kiss him but didn't have the energy, so she pulled him down onto her, wanting to feel his skin, and the full burden of his weight. She wanted this to happen, the scrape of his beard, the sound of his breath. She wanted the touch of his hands to soothe her, his mouth to take her in. She craved the fullness she had forgotten until now, but didn't want to rush it. So she let Charlie do the slow work of unbuttoning every button on her pajamas. "You could help me, you know," he smirked.

"I could," she said, lying back down. With one precise touch from Charlie, Biz's body flushed and her breath quickened. After the dips and swirls of his fingers, he used his tongue and she writhed with joy. Then he built her up slowly and shot her into space, hovering. When she knew she was close, Biz stopped and beckoned him to her. She wanted to make him writhe, too. She wanted him inside.

They realigned their bodies, her hands grabbing at him in fistfuls. She said, "I may not want to stop doing this anytime soon."

"We can order takeout."

"For the rest of our lives?"

It was the last thing either would say for a while.

He took his time with her topography, drinking in every wrinkle and mole, then made love to her slowly, giving Biz plenty of time to reach the sky. She muffled her screams and squeals while up there, waking no one in the building. Sparks of energy filled her head as if she'd been plugged in and switched on. She delighted at his climax, taking his weight once he finished, trembling under his embrace with aftershocks and quakes. With nowhere to rush to, they rolled off of each other and lay mooning in satisfaction's shiny veneer. The air around them swirled like chalk dust fading in a classroom. They fell asleep in each other's arms, and Charlie snored in peaceful slumber.

Biz grinned as she contemplated her long-awaited prize. She hoped she'd remember every minute thing that had just transpired. She'd already started to plan when it would happen again. To her, Charlie smelled and tasted like home. And to Charlie, Biz was his home.

Then Biz awoke giggling and madly kicked off the covers. She was flashing, her body's core raging like an inferno. Charlie grabbed a magazine from the nightstand and fanned her until it subsided. *This man's a keeper,* she thought. Then they rolled back toward each other and breathed each other's exhales—compelled as new lovers, slightly worried it wasn't real.

Charlie said, "You know, we could do this against the Ping-Pong table in the shed."

Biz chuckled. "Oo, that's an option. What about your projection room at the theater?"

"Ha. *Really?*" said Charlie. "There are so many possibilities . . ." and then he paused. He was overcome with the curious beauty of timing. They could finally stop running and stroll.

Cousin or stranger, Biz was his partner, and he would never let her go again. And in Charlie, Biz saw the man she'd always loved and had quite possibly held out for—her former first cousin and partner for good. She rolled onto her side and looked into his eyes; they were moistening. "What, Charlie?" she said sweetly. "What's going on?"

"I can't believe how much time we've lost. I feel like an ass. I never should have married Piper. I should have waited until you forgave me—"

"Don't say that. You wouldn't have your kids. And maybe I wouldn't have mine."

"But why did we wait so long after my divorce? Why on earth did we keep caring what their friends would say or the people in this stupid town? We've been pathetic little children in grown-up disguises, trying to endlessly make our parents happy. We're *so dumb*. Why did we give them so much power over our lives? We should have done what was right *for us*, not *the right thing*."

"Who says the right thing for us *isn't* the right thing?"

"Society," Charlie said, and shook his head. "We shouldn't have listened."

"We were weak."

"We were wimps."

"Not anymore," said Biz with bravado.

Charlie pounded a fist to his chest and said, "Strong like bull!" Then he brightened and whispered, "The linen closet."

"Ha!" Biz shouted, hearty and strong. "Yes! The linen closet!" She propped herself up on an elbow. "How about this," she said, "I'll make a deal with you."

"Anything," said Charlie.

"I will love you forever and have sex with you anywhere."

"I will take that deal," he said, and kissed Biz sweetly on the mouth, without regard for the world and with permission from absolutely no one. Charlie thought for a moment, then said slowly with a Nana Miggs twinkle, "You know, 'anywhere' is *a lot* of places."

They resumed making breakfast, feeling whole, these two, for the first time in ages, in a simple and obvious way. There were no lightning bolts, merely a knowing and calm, which took neither by surprise as they set the table. Biz felt like a better version of her former self, and Charlie felt like a man. A man wearing his best friend's kimono and a dark brunette wig. Biz, of course, was wearing the Farrah.

A key turned the front door lock, and Ruby walked in. She was startled at the sight of a man's back. She was also not expecting her mother to be wearing a blond shoulder-length wig with her pajamas. And, oh, her Uncle Charlie wearing one, too.

"Hey, honey!" said Biz awkwardly, reminding herself to be casual.

Ruby said, "Hi, uh . . . I guess I'll start knocking first," with a chuckle.

Biz said, "Always wise."

"We found our old *Charlie's Angels* wigs during your grandmother's move."

"I see that," said Ruby.

"We can take them off, if you'd rather—"

"No, no. They look fetching."

Everyone did their best to be relaxed as Ruby explained she was swinging by to pick up a few things before heading back to the city. Biz poured Ruby a glass of orange juice and asked her to join them for a minute. "Thanks, Mom," Ruby said, and sat. Then Charlie placed a plate of scrambled eggs in front of

her, and she paused and said, "Thanks, Uncle Cousin Dad." To
which Charlie said, "Needs tweaking." Biz said, "Speaking of
which . . . ," and together they brought Ruby up to speed. She
kept shaking her head as she listened, repeating, "Ohmygod,
ohmygod, ohmygod." At the end of the story, Biz leaned over
and kissed Ruby on the cheek, then Charlie lightly on the lips.

"*That's* going to take some getting used to," said Ruby.

Biz said, "Sorry, honey."

"No, it's okay. It's good. It'll be fine. I'm happy for you both."

"And I think this means you can call him Dad."

"Is that chill with you?" Ruby asked Charlie.

"Sir Dad, if you don't mind."

"Oh, I mind," she said with a chuckle.

Ruby moved on to explain how she and Miguel had spent
the night in an Airbub refurbished tree house. "Clever idea,"
said Charlie. "Wonder where that came from." She described
how magical it was waking up high among the trees, but there
were spiders, and mosquitoes, and the birds' songs woke them
insanely early. "So most of the time it was pretty uncomfortable, but in the end, we decided it was worth it."

Charlie caught Biz's eye and said, "That about sums up life,
kid." "More than you'll ever know," added Biz. Then they
grinned as they took in their beautiful child—so full of typical,
everyday promise, rough edges, and exquisite imperfections.

"Here's to my former niece and new daughter," gushed
Charlie, raising his glass.

"Here's to my not-so-secret dad," Ruby said and raised hers.

Biz said, "And here's to the family I always wanted and sort
of had all along. And, yes, we're a little unconventional. And
we'll probably keep screwing things up, but we're doing the
best we can—which is to say, not *the* best, but our Thornden

best. And, so, cheers." Biz started to raise her glass, then re-membered her frozen shoulder. She winced in pain, started to flash, and laughed. "I give up." Charlie pulled off her wig and fanned her with it. Ruby grabbed her napkin and fanned her, too. Biz managed to clink glasses as Charlie beamed. "There is definitely no one like you."

ABOUT THE AUTHOR

V. C. Chickering has written for Comedy Central, MTV, Lifetime, TLC, Discovery, NickMom, and Oxygen television networks as well as for *BUST, Cosmo,* and *The Washington Post* magazines. She's written screenplays, has a local newspaper column entitled "Pith Monger," and writes a blog. She lives with her family in New Jersey, where she also writes and performs witty, original songs for the alt-bluegrass/indie-jazz band Tori Erstwhile & the Montys. *Twisted Family Values* is her second novel.